DEATHBORN

Sovereigns of Bright and Shadow Book One

C. E. Page

First Published 2020 in Australia by Enchanted Castle Press

PAPERBACK ISBN: **978-0-9925548-4-2**

EPUB ISBN: **978-0-9925548-5-9**

A catalogue record for this work is available from the National Library of Australia

Cover by: Joolz & Jarling – Julie Nicholls & Uwe Jarling
Map by: Fictive Designs
Formatting by: Enchanted Castle Press
Edited by: Creating Ink –Anna Bishop

Author website: www.cepageauthor.com

All text and images in this book were created by a human with no assistance from any kind of content generating program or generative artificial intelligence.

DEATHBORN

SOVEREIGNS OF BRIGHT & SHADOW

BOOK ONE

C. E. PAGE

ENCHANTED CASTLE
— PRESS —

HARTSWOOD
DEL HAROL
LITTLE·BROOK
MERSTON
WARREN'S GROTTO
DUNHOLD
FORT BRAEMAR
THE FENLANDS
HILLSIDE
KILTON
SWINTON
LONE OAK
FENGATE
LOCH·BASTIEN
NEW BRENNA
THE CROSSROADS
KALHANNA
BELDAREN

To Evan, Seth and Royce, for being patient all those times I said: "I just need to finish this sentence."

CHAPTER ONE

MARGOT

Margot wasn't sure what had woken her. The warehouse was quiet save for the sounds of her sleeping companions, but she could feel a small pull of dread deep in her stomach. And when she closed her eyes, Nea's deep violet gaze flashed across the inky blackness. With a long sigh she sat up and the woman beside her opened one cornflower blue eye to stare blurrily at her.

"It's alright, Mol. Go back to sleep."

Molly gave a sleepy murmur in response before rolling over and taking the blanket with her.

No one had seen Nea in the three years since the purge at Kalhanna. No one who actually knew her anyway. There had been rumours from time to time about a wandering necromancer fitting Nea's description and that was enough for Margot to keep alive the hope that she was alright. But she would have given anything to see her again.

Pressing a palm to her chest to still the thundering ache that thoughts of Nea had dredged up, she slid delicately from the bed, trying not to disturb Molly again. Then, noting the pool of orange light that shone beneath the door, she pulled a faded blue shawl around her shoulders and tiptoed across the room. She carefully opened the door wide enough to slip out, then closed it quietly behind her before turning to take in the main room of the warehouse they were using as a base of operations.

Declan was sitting at the large table in the room's centre. The light of several candles cast a golden sheen on his black hair and illuminated the steaming teacup balanced precariously on one of the piles of books and scrolls that cluttered the scarred surface before him. As though he'd sensed her watching him, he looked up, his bright green eyes appearing almost yellow in the candlelight, and she bit back a grin as she noted the smear of ink on his cheek.

"Seems like it's the night for insomniacs." He gave her a wide, roguish smile.

"Something like that. Mind if I join you?"

"Not at all. Your company is always delightful, my dear Margot." He took a sip of his tea.

Margot sat across from him and examined some of the pages strewn across the table. Diagrams of plants and notes on their properties were mixed with patient reports and complex calculations. She picked up a drawing of a star-shaped leaf; there were several words crossed out in the smudged notes underneath it, and small water stains made the rest indecipherable.

"Still messing around with mage bane and Mother's balm?"

"No. I have given up on that avenue." Declan snatched the page from her and studied it. "I was so close ... but no matter. What is it that has you wandering about in the middle of the night?"

Margot rubbed her arms. "Bad dreams mostly. Did you know that tonight is exactly three years since Kalhanna was purged?"

Declan's eyebrows rose. "Three years?" He looked at his notes then back at Margot. "You were dreaming about Nea?"

"No ... I don't know. Maybe. It's just not like her to disappear like this. Three years is a long time for her to be ..." She pressed her palm to her chest. "I miss her."

Declan sipped his tea again. "You don't believe she was capable of—"

"Of course not!" There was a murmur from the other room and Margot lowered her voice. "Nea may have worked for the king but things between them had become strained, and she would never have condoned what was done at Kalhanna. If anything, she would have forcefully tried to stop it. You saw the aftermath, the way those bodies were laid out. Those mages were her friends. And as for the rumours that she corrupted the entire college and turned it against the king ..." She chewed her thumbnail. "Everyone knows that corruption doesn't work that way."

"When you say *strained* what exactly do you mean? I heard a rumour recently that she attacked Evard before running off to Kalhanna."

Nea *had* attacked Evard. Margot didn't know all the details surrounding the incident, but she knew enough. "Evard has always had a fascination with mages, but necromancers in particular pique his curiosity more than others. And Nea ... Nea was something of an obsession for him. She's not like other necromancers. Her relationship to the source is *different*."

His dark brows lifted slightly, and he leant forward. "Different?"

"You've heard the rumours about what she did at Kalhanna. Let's just say some of them have a kernel of truth."

"Really?" He shuffled his notes. "I would love to meet her."

Margot gave him an appraising stare. Declan and Nea were rather similar in that they both shared curious minds that were ever-searching for answers to seemingly impossible questions. A laugh built low in her stomach at the thought of them in the same room. "I think the pair of you would get along rather well." She tapped her chin and added, "Perhaps a little too well."

"Oh?"

"In a purely academic sense. Your minds work in similar ways." She drummed her fingers on the tabletop and sighed. "I just wish I knew why she disappeared, where she went ... It's ... it doesn't make sense."

His mouth twisted as he regarded her, before he reached across the table to cover her hand with his and still her tapping. "Are we still talking about Nea?"

She started to nod but then shook her head. "She's part of it. The whole mess with Kalhanna and corruption and ... I don't know. She warned me something was going to happen, that Evard had become unhinged."

"Evard has always been *mercurial* though. Do you think things would have been different if you'd been at Kalhanna instead of Loch Bastien back then?"

"Maybe. Maybe, I could have prevented it ... tried to reason with Francesca or ... I don't know. Wishing things were different won't change the past, but there had to be a better way, didn't there?"

He downed the last of his tea and sat back, cradling the empty cup. "I admire that you always approach problems from a logical standpoint but have you considered that sometimes there is no logic to be found?"

"That right there is something Nea would say." She scoffed.

"It's a hard truth that rational types like you and Garret always have trouble grasping. Take what happened at Kalhanna for instance. I think if you had been there, things would have still ended exactly the same, only it is highly likely you would also be among the dead." He placed the cup on the table and shrugged. "Nothing about the purge made sense. We were told that the mages had become corrupted. Nearly an entire college, which is ridiculous. You and I, and pretty much anyone with keen-sense, know that corruption doesn't work that way. But let's assume it does. You would expect that if an entire college became corrupted, there would be some sign of it other than a vague rumour. None of the reports from survivors mentioned anything about corruption and we saw no signs of it on any of the bodies." He shuffled some of his papers. "I find it more likely that Evard chose to use Kalhanna as an example of what he *could* do to mages who were vocal in their dissent of his desire to take the reins of the order. It is no secret that both High Mage Francesca and Warden Commander Adam had been open about their objections to Evard's plans."

"And why wouldn't they object? As soon as the wardens came under the agency of the king, he essentially had control of all mages as well," Margot said as she played with her shawl pin, a delicate circle of ivy. The deep green enamel had chipped off in places from wear.

"Which is why I have always thought the purge was a political move. The corruption story seemed a little too convenient. Then a rogue necromancer gets thrown into the mix? A perfect scapegoat. Anyone who knows the basics about corruption knows it comes from the Between. And which school of magic is tied irrevocably to the Between and what lies beyond?" He sat back, a satisfied smirk quirking the corner of his mouth. "Kill two dissenting birds with one well-thrown stone as it were."

"But the people would never stand by while he ordered the slaughter of the entire college of healers for the sake of a handful of vocal mages." Although they might have if he'd spun the details the right way. In his younger days, Evard had earned a reputation for being very charismatic.

"Exactly. And that explains the corruption story but not why he thought the entire college needed to be purged. There is something else in play that we are not aware of. Or maybe he finds the Bright Order easier to manipulate and wishes to give them a leg up over mages."

Margot rolled her eyes. "Those temple charlatans? Offering a *new way*. Giving blessings for the sick and prayers for the dead." She scowled. "Blessings will not mend bones or cure plagues. Which is abundantly clear now the population of healers has been decimated."

The door flew open, slamming against the wall. A chilly gust of late winter air charged into the room sending Declan's papers flying. A shadow loomed in the doorway for a moment before a man stepped across the threshold, his hand pressed to the bloody stain on his shirt. Margot's chair rocked as she leapt to her feet and hurried over to close the door before helping the man to a seat.

"Warden Commander Garret said I'd find a healer here." His words were thick and slurred.

"I'm a healer." She drew a mage light to life as she spoke. The small orb of pale green light hovered in the air between them as she gently rolled his eyelid open to check his pupils. Then she lifted his shirt to assess the angry slice in his side. As the light bobbed over his skin illuminating the dark spiderwebs of corruption ringing the cut, she recoiled. "Where did you get this wound?"

The man's head lolled to the side. He grunted and gripped his ears. "Too loud. Too loud. Too hot."

Declan sucked a breath through his teeth as he bent to inspect the black marks on the man's side. "Is that corruption? Margot ... he's not a mage."

Margot frowned and brushed her magic over the man. His essence felt strange, like sound underwater or a touch through cloth. So different to the prickling brightness that was Declan standing beside her, or the soothing warmth of her own magic. "He's a *warden*."

Declan nodded. "Why do those marks around his wound look like corruption? Corruption is a mages' disease."

The man lashed out, grabbing Margot's arm hard. "Make them stop. They want me to ... to ..." He squeezed tighter and Margot gasped.

"Let her go," Declan growled, and the static prickle of his keen built in the air.

The man's grip tightened and he began to twist Margot's arm. Her teeth gritted against the pain and she started to gather the source, ready to defend herself.

Wardens, on instinct, usually suppressed the connection between mages and the source when they felt threatened, but this man did not. There was a hollow look in his eyes that suggested whatever bit of his sanity was untainted by the corruption was hiding deep.

Margot pushed out the source she had collected, focusing on the fingers around her arm. They twisted backwards with an audible snap and the man yowled in pain. He fell forward out of the chair and Margot jumped out of the way.

A thud sounded in the other room, and then Emil and Molly came barrelling through the door. Emil had his sword drawn, his long black hair rumpled from sleep and his amber eyes scanning for danger. Close behind him, Molly had her crossbow raised. Her creamy-blonde braid rested over the bare shoulder visible through the skewed neck of her nightgown.

Margot turned back to the man, who was now kneeling on the floor whimpering and supporting his broken fingers. "Now, you need to listen carefully. I can fix your fingers and the wound in your side, but I cannot fix the corruption. The voices you are hearing are tied to that. I've never seen corruption on anyone who is not a mage, so I cannot tell you what is going to happen. But my friend, Declan, here might be able to help you. You just need to remain calm. Okay?"

The man nodded.

"Alright. I am sorry, but this is going to hurt." Margot pulled a thin thread of source and focused it on the man's fingers. The coil of pale green smoke drifted over his skin and with a loud *pop,* his fingers wrenched themselves back into place.

He yelled in pain and recoiled. Then relief crossed his features and he slowly tested his fingers by opening and closing his fist.

Margot shifted her attention to the wound in his side. His movements had caused blood to flow again but she could fix it quickly enough. She brushed her magic over the cut, using it to draw the edges closed and knit the flesh back together. The man grunted and tensed as the thin green smoke danced lightly over his skin. The black marks of corruption shifted, growing bigger and seeming to consume the thread of Margot's magic. She pulled back and examined the thick pink scar in the centre of a massive whirl of black that spread like fibrous roots across his stomach and up to his armpit. Margot met the man's eyes and recoiled as black spiderwebbing consumed his sclera. He started to shake, and she backed away farther.

His weight shifted and he lunged.

"Margot, get down!" Molly yelled.

Margot dove forward. Her arms shielded her head as her stomach slammed against the floor. The man's footsteps slapped the hard surface, followed by the *whoosh-thud* of Molly's bolt finding home. There was a meaty thump as the floor beside her vibrated. She scuttled away from the still-twitching fingers as Molly skidded into her vision.

"Are you alright?" Molly's blue eyes were full of concern and her hands took a light hold on Margot's shoulders.

Margot nodded. "I'm okay."

Relief crossed Molly's face before she engulfed Margot in a hug and pressed a kiss to the top of her head.

Declan clicked his tongue and prodded the corruption marks with his index finger as he crouched beside the body. "How ..." he muttered under his breath and looked at Emil. "I really would have liked to study him. I've never seen corruption in a non-mage before. To think, a warden can be corrupted."

Emil's mouth pulled into a tight line. "His name was Peter. I'll make sure his wife is notified." He moved to the table and took a blank piece of parchment and Declan's quill.

"Margot?" Declan enquired.

She untwined herself from Molly's arms. "Yes?"

"Have you ever heard of corruption starting in a wound?"

Margot started to shake her head then stopped and turned to Emil, who was watching them, the quill poised above the parchment. He mouthed a word and Margot frowned before looking back at Declan. "You've heard of Amelia?"

Declan's eyebrows nearly disappeared into his hairline. "You don't think she's responsible for ... *this*?" He thrust a hand at the body.

"I heard she bit one of the mages who was tasked with imprisoning her and he went mad. He wounded two mages and a warden before they were able to bring him under control," Emil said.

"Bring him under control? What happened to him?" Declan asked.

"They killed him. They had no choice," Margot responded.

"So, Amelia's *bite* corrupted the mage? Does Garret know about this?" Declan asked Emil.

"Most likely. But the mage may have already been in the early stages of corruption, and accessing the source to bind Amelia would have accelerated its growth, causing the madness to take over." Emil tapped the end of the quill against his chin. "It is highly unlikely that Amelia biting him had anything to do with it."

"High Mage Niall wouldn't have risked taking a mage along for Amelia's capture who had any signs of corruption though, and even in its early stages, corruption is nearly impossible to hide. Especially from a mind mage as powerful as Niall." Margot had gotten to her feet and was collecting the papers that had been strewn around the room.

"Can I ask something?" They all turned to face Molly as she spoke. "If Amelia can give others corruption, wouldn't that require her to be corrupted as well?"

Margot shook her head. "Not necessarily. Corruption doesn't work like other diseases that can be passed from person to person.

It is more of a ... *blight* that occurs if a mage channels too much of the source or messes around with something they shouldn't. It's a crude explanation but you could call it a type of possession."

"Is that why you can't heal it? Could a mind mage heal it? Or, if it's a type of possession, a necromancer?"

"No. Corruption feeds on magic. Not just the magic of its host but any magic used on it," Declan answered. "Which this little altercation has made abundantly clear."

Molly frowned. "So how did a warden get it? Wardens are the complete opposite of mages, aren't they? There is no connection to the source, no magic for the corruption to feed on."

"Wardens suppress the source but we're not the opposite of mages. In fact, Father often says that wardens are just another type of mage, but we get singled out because we don't do anything flashy like knit flesh back together or toss around lightning bolts," Emil said with a wry grin in Declan's direction.

"But Declan said wardens can't get corruption. That—"

"Bind-shackles!" Margot exclaimed. "Bind-shackles prevent corruption from spreading because they cut off a mage's connection to the source. Even if suppression is a type of magic, the corruption can't get a foothold because the source is not being actively channelled. But if you could somehow seed corruption in the body of a warden, it could overwrite the instinct to suppress." She glanced at Declan, who shrugged then nodded.

"It's plausible."

"Peter didn't try to prevent me using my magic when I broke his fingers. He would have felt my keen building and he did nothing to stop it."

"But why give wardens corruption?" Molly asked.

Margot and Declan looked at each other, but it was Emil who answered. "Control."

"Control?"

He placed the quill down delicately. "Evard might be in the process of absorbing the order into the king's guard, but there are many wardens, mages, and even keen-less who are still against it. And at the end of the day, the warden commanders still have final say on all matters pertaining to both the order and mages. Evard wants full governance, and if people find out that wardens are just as susceptible to corruption as their charges, that resistance he is coming up against will erode entirely."

"Wait. If you can ... how did you put it, Margot? Seed?" Molly looked at Margot, who nodded. "If you can seed corruption in wardens, then can the same be done to keen-less?" There was an edge of fear in her voice.

They shared a look but no one answered her question.

"We need to talk to Garret as soon as we can. He sent Peter here but I need to know if he was aware of the corruption," Declan said, moving to the table and gathering his things. "Emil, you should go to Del Harol and see what you can find out about Amelia. High Mage Niall trusts you and if he won't talk to you, your father may know something that can help."

With a nod, Emil disappeared to get his things.

"What do you want us to do, Declan?" Margot asked.

"Molly can check in with the gossip chain to see if there have been any other cases of corruption reported. Or any strange illnesses. Margot, you need to—"

"Keep a low profile. I know." She sighed and moved to grab a blanket to cover the body.

Declan watched her with a frown. "You can come with me to see Garret if you want. I'm meeting him at The Rowdy Badger in Fengate. Molly can handle things here, can't you?"

Molly nodded but there was a despondent look on her face. "I guess ... Ryan and Jasper are due back tomorrow, and Haley the day after. What do you want me to do with him though?" She pointed to the body as Margot laid the blanket over it.

"Load him in the wagon. I'll take him out of the city and see he's taken care of." Emil came back from the other room, tightening the buckle that secured his scabbard. He tested drawing the sword, then gave a nod of satisfaction.

"So, Margot, what do you want to do?" Declan stood with his stack of books and notes.

"I'll come with you to Fengate." She turned to Molly, who was watching her with a twitch of worry at the corner of her mouth. "I'll be safe, I promise." She reached out and took hold of the other woman's hand before giving it a small squeeze.

Molly smiled and tugged Margot's hand, drawing her into a hug. "I know. Declan will make sure of it." She drew back and brushed her lips gently against Margot's.

Margot chuckled against Molly's mouth. "You do realise this is Declan we are talking about? More likely I'll be the one pulling his backside out of trouble."

"Hey, now!" Declan mocked a look of hurt, but then smiled and left the room.

Molly pressed her lips against Margot's again, this time deepening the kiss. One hand lifted to cup the back of Margot's neck as the other drifted down her spine and across the small of her back, pulling their bodies against each other. Margot let out a small moan and Emil cleared his throat.

Molly pulled away, resting her forehead against Margot's, and smiled before quickly pressing one last chaste kiss to her mouth. "You'd better go get ready. Declan probably wants to leave before dawn and that can't be too far away now."

CHAPTER TWO

GARRET

The man across the table shook his head and rubbed a hand over the scruff on his jaw. "Seems we are at an impasse, Commander." He leant forward and rested his chin on his tented fingers. His deep blue eyes were watery and red-rimmed.

Garret chewed the inside of his cheek. It wasn't that he didn't like working with Marcus, but the old mage always had a way of making the transactions feel, for lack of a better word, dirty. "You want to know what's in it for you? I told you—"

"You promised me the usual payment. Yes. But you're not the only one looking for this particular mage."

Garret took a sip of his ale. "Do I need to remind you who helped with the Remy incident?"

"Course not." Marcus ran a finger along his lower lip and sat back, crossing his arms over his chest. "But then again, you neglected to tell me the bastard had corruption before you sent me after him."

Garret shrugged. "I didn't know at the time. And I made it up to you afterwards." He pulled out a heavy purse and slid it across the table. "Double the usual. Do we have a deal?" He kept his hand over the purse while he waited for Marcus to answer.

Marcus made a show of picking at his teeth. "She's got a reputation."

"I am aware of the rumours."

"And they say the king himself would like a *word* with her." He eyed Garret. "They also say you're pretty cosy with him these days, and I'm not in the business of selling my kind out to the likes of Evard. Regardless of their *reputation*."

"If you don't want the job, Marcus ..." Garret started to draw the purse back across the table, but Marcus's hand closed over his.

"Tell me one thing." He glanced around then leant forward, his voice lowering to a whisper. "You going to hand her over to Evard?"

"I haven't decided yet."

Marcus sat back. "Make sure you think long and hard about that decision." His fingers twitched, and Garret removed his hand from the purse. Marcus snatched it and tested the weight before nodding. "You got anything that belongs to her?"

"No, but she probably does." He pointed to the door where a slender woman with soft golden ringlets was standing, her whiskey-coloured eyes scanning the room.

A tall man with tussled black hair entered behind her and placed a hand on her shoulder before pointing towards the table where Garret and Marcus were sitting. The woman nodded and crossed the room to join them.

"Hello, Garret. I hope you don't mind me tagging along with Declan." Margot smiled as she slid into the chair next to him. Her gaze fell on Marcus and she gave him a curt nod.

"Not at all. It worked out well actually. We need—"

"Marcus the Mutt, is that you under all that hair?" Declan clapped the mage on the shoulder before dropping into the last empty seat.

"Declan, I'd say it's good to see you, but I still haven't forgotten that lass in Red Meadow and the run around the pair of you gave me," Marcus said before his attention moved to Margot.

Garret could feel the thick pressure of Marcus's keen as he investigated her. "Margot, may I introduce Marcus. He's—"

"A finder," she said as the warm throb of her keen swelled in response to Marcus's.

"You one of the ones who survived Kalhanna?"

Margot tensed. "I wasn't at the college during the purge." She looked back to Garret. "You were saying you needed something?"

Garret nodded. "I've just hired Marcus to find Nea."

Margot's eyes widened. "Why do you want to find her?"

"Evard wants her found." He noted a man a few tables away had his head tilted slightly towards them and chose his next words with care. "I'm just doing my job as warden commander. I know she was your friend, Margot, but—"

"She won't be easy to find, even for the likes of him." She jutted her chin towards Marcus. "If Nea doesn't want to be found, I doubt even the Bright Mother could find her."

Declan laid a hand on Margot's arm. "Easy now." He scanned the crowd. "No need to draw too much attention to ourselves."

Margot sat back in her chair. "What does he need? I can't tell him where to start looking; no one has seen Nea in three years."

"Something that belonged to her. I can find her without it, but it's easier with an anchor."

Margot dug into the pouch tied to her belt and pulled out a delicate bracelet made of oblong bone beads and roses carved from amethyst. Marcus reached for it and she swiftly withdrew it as she regarded his weathered fingers with a frown.

"I'll not damage it." He held his hand out.

Margot gingerly laid the bracelet across his open palm and he flicked his fingers closed before bringing it to his nose and inhaling sharply.

The source stirred and the thick pressure of Marcus's keen rose once more in the air around him.

Marcus's fingers stroked the bracelet as a lurid smile tugged the corners of his mouth. After a while, he opened his eyes and examined the bracelet before switching his focus to Margot. "Well now. She's something else, isn't she?" He stroked the bracelet again then held it out to Margot, who snatched it from him before cradling it to her chest.

"You found her?" Garret asked.

Marcus ran his tongue over his teeth and nodded. "More or less. She felt me searching and fled into the Between. Never known a mage who could throw me off the scent like that. It was exhilarating." He grinned.

"Is it because she's a necromancer?" Declan leant forward.

Marcus shook his head. "I've had to find necromancers before; they're no different to any other mage when it comes to tracking. She's different though. Right down to the way her keen feels." He sat back and crossed his arms over his chest. "You've got your work cut out for you." He directed the line at Garret.

"How so?"

"The lass is right." He indicated Margot. "She doesn't want to be found."

"You—"

"No. I'm not going with you to track her. It wouldn't work anyway. She has a feel for me now."

Garret's mouth pulled into a tight line.

"Give me the bracelet back for a minute." Marcus snapped his fingers at Margot and held his hand out.

She looked at Garret, who nodded, and then she placed the bracelet in Marcus's palm again.

He closed his eyes and ran his fingers over it. His keen thickened the air and then seemed to pull into the bracelet. It vibrated on his palm and glowed red for a moment before it was still again. "There you go. That should lead you to her." He held the bracelet out to Garret.

Garret gave Margot a small smile and took the bracelet. "I'll take good care of it. I promise." He slipped it into his pocket.

"Well I don't know about the rest of you, but I need a drink." Declan stood and headed to the bar.

After Marcus had left, Garret took Margot and Declan to his private room. Margot sat on the bed while Declan leant against the desk. His arms were folded over his chest and he had that look in his eyes, like he wasn't sure whether he wanted to hit Garret on the side of the head or congratulate him.

"Something on your mind, Declan?"

Declan opened his mouth, but Margot cut him off. "Did you know Peter had corruption?"

Garret stiffened but then schooled his features. "Peter? Had corruption? He's a warden, Margot. Last time I checked, we were immune to corruption."

"*Was* a warden." Declan was playing with something on the desk and didn't look up.

"Was?"

"Molly had to kill him. I've never seen corruption progress that quickly." Margot levelled her eyes on him. "You weren't aware he was corrupted though were you? Do you know how he got that wound?"

"What wound? Neither of you are making sense. I haven't seen Peter since first frost."

They shared a look. "Garret, Peter said you told him he would find a healer at the safe house. You didn't send him?"

"I most certainly did not." Garret ran his hands through his hair.

"Then who—"

Garret raised a hand and cut Declan off. "Tell me about this corruption. You're certain that's what it was?"

"Yes. At first, I wasn't sure because, well, Peter was a warden and the corruption seemed to originate in the wound in his side. But then we deduced"—Declan indicated Margot and himself—"that someone had somehow seeded corruption in the wound to counteract the warden's natural instincts to suppress the source."

Garret shook his head. "You can't give a person corruption. It doesn't work like a common disease."

"That's what we thought. However ..." Margot cracked her knuckles. "Have you heard of Amelia?"

He gave one curt nod. "I'm aware of her. I've heard the rumours."

"*All* the rumours?"

He nodded again. "You mean the one about her supposedly biting one of the mages who imprisoned her and giving him corruption?"

"We think there might be some truth to that one," Margot replied.

"Was Peter's wound a bite?"

"No, a slice most likely made by a short-bladed knife. What if somehow his attacker had treated the blade? If the corruption could be delivered straight into the bloodstream like—"

"But corruption is—"

"I am well aware how corruption works, Garret," Margot snapped, but then her features softened again. "Look, if I hadn't seen it myself, I would be questioning it too. But there was no mistaking it. Peter had corruption."

Garret leant against the doorframe and sighed.

"I've sent Emil to Del Harol to see if he can find out anything about Amelia. Where she might be and if the rumours about her are true," Declan said.

"Fort Braemar."

"Sorry?"

"Amelia is at Fort Braemar."

"You knew already? Of course you did." Declan crossed his arms once more.

Garret shrugged.

"Then that is where you should go next." Both men looked at Margot as she spoke. "If Amelia is linked to corruption, you might find some answers there. And, Garret, the east side safe house needs to be vacated. Until we find out who sent Peter there, we have to consider that it has been compromised and is no longer safe." She turned her full attention to Garret, a shrewd look in her brown eyes. "Now, are you going to tell me why you really want to find Nea?"

Garret's jaw tightened. "I told you, Evard wants her."

Declan scowled. "You can't be seriously considering handing her over to him. Especially given the rumours about her."

"I don't know what I am going to do yet." Garret pushed off the wall and paced across to the window on the other side of the small room. "Evard is starting to get suspicious. If I can allay his concerns by giving him Nea ..."

"Please, Garret." Margot's voice was barely above a whisper. "Please don't give her to Evard."

"I have to find her before I can make any decision on the matter," Garret said softly. "For now, let's just focus on getting to Fort Braemar and seeing what we can learn about Amelia and corruption. Are you any closer to finding a cure for it?" He directed the question at Declan, who shook his head.

"I managed to create a short-term treatment."

"That's a start. If it can be treated—"

"It only lasted half a day and relies heavily on mage bane which, of course, prevents the subject from accessing the source. And long-term use of mage bane comes with its own host of problems, the least of which is insanity." Declan ran his hand through his dark hair. "We'd be better off just slapping a pair of bind-shackles around the wrists of every mage who develops corruption."

"That's highly impractical."

"It was a joke."

Garret's eyebrows rose and he crossed his arms.

"I didn't say it was a *good* joke."

Margot chuckled from her perch on the bed before she sobered again. "I won't be accompanying you to Braemar. I'm going back to the clinic."

"I don't think that's a good idea. Evard has been asking questions about you, and he's had his guard watching everyone who comes and goes there."

"I know but you need eyes and ears in the city, Garret, and the people need a healer."

"What about coming with me to find Nea?"

Margot chewed her thumbnail. "You might spend the next year searching for her. Even with that bracelet charmed by Marcus. She doesn't *want* to be found, Garret. It's highly likely she is in Osmar or beyond. It would be better for me to stay in the city and you can send word when ... *if* you find her."

There was a sharp rap on the door, and they all looked up. Declan crossed and opened it to reveal a short boy with a grey cap pushed down on a head of unruly red curls. He lifted his freckled face to look Declan in the eye and shifted the weight of the messenger bird that was pinned under his arm. "You're not the warden." He wiped his free arm across his pink-tipped nose.

"I am." Garret stepped next to Declan and placed his hand on the mage's shoulder. Declan moved out of the way and joined Margot on the bed.

The boy looked Garret up and down, then held out his palm.

"Message first," Garret said as his gaze switched from the boy's fingers to his face.

"It wounds me to think that you don't trust me, sir."

Garret cleared his throat.

"Fine." The boy dropped his hand and dug in the pouch at his side to retrieve a coil of parchment. He held it out and Garret took it before handing over payment. "Thank you."

Securing his hold on the bird, the boy gave a stiff nod before he took off down the hallway and out of sight.

Garret closed the door and unrolled the parchment. It was blank but magic stirred in gentle ripples across it. He handed it to Declan, who whistled softly as he inspected it.

"Now that's a handy little trick. I've never felt that magic signature before though. Any idea who it might be from?"

Garret shook his head.

"High Mage Niall," Margot said.

They both looked at her.

"I'd hazard a guess and say it is actually from Emil but Niall enchanted it so it couldn't be read."

"How do we read it then?" Garret took the parchment from Declan and focused on suppressing the magic that shielded it. Nothing happened.

Declan snatched it back from him and smoothed it out on the bed. "You can't bludgeon this type of enchantment. It's like picking a lock." He cracked his knuckles and held a hand out over the parchment.

Garret shifted as the static sensation that was Declan's keen set the hairs on his arms on end.

Declan's tongue was between his teeth in concentration and his brow began to furrow. After a while, he gave up with a frown.

Margot shook her head with a wry smile and took the parchment. "Maybe Niall just wanted you to think it was complicated." She moved to one of the candles on the mantle and tilted the corner of the paper until it touched the flame. The whole thing went up in a *whoosh* and she dropped it to the floor where it curled into a pile of black ash.

The all stared at the pile for several heartbeats.

"Margot that—" Declan stopped talking as the ash reformed into a fresh sheet of parchment, this time with words in Emil's careful handwriting across the surface. "Well, there you go."

Margot picked the letter up and held it out to Garret.

Emil's correspondence was always concise. This letter was no different. It quickly outlined what he had learned from High Mage Niall and that he was on his way to Fort Braemar. It also mentioned several cases of corruption and missing mages, mostly relating to those living outside the colleges.

"Well?" Declan was sitting forward in anticipation.

Garret read back over the letter one more time before speaking. "Emil is going to Braemar and suggests we meet him there. He mentions that High Mage Niall and several of his brethren have become concerned about the growing number of cases of corruption in mages living outside the colleges. Lastly, he discovered a rumour about a journal that reportedly belonged to a necromancer by the name of Samson. The journal apparently documents his studies into corruption."

Declan's eyes lit up. "Tell me he is bringing the journal to Braemar?"

Garret shook his head. "He said it is currently missing but there might be clues to how to find it in Little Brook, of all places."

Margot made a soft sound of recognition at the mention of Little Brook and they both looked at her. "What?" she asked, suddenly defensive.

"You made a sound when Garret said Little Brook."

Margot rubbed her neck. "No, I didn't."

"You did. What is at Little Brook?"

"Nothing of consequence. It's a decent-sized village on the foot of the Spine. Close enough to Hartswood that the villagers have a certain rapport with the necromancers." She adjusted her shawl around her shoulders. "It was also one of Nea's favourite places outside of Hartswood itself."

Garret pinned her with a look. "You didn't think that was worth mentioning before?"

"No, because it's likely to be one of the last places she would go. Too many people there know her." She placed her hands on her hips. "It also happens to be only about a two day ride from Fort Braemar."

"That settles it then." Declan clapped his hands together. "We'll go to Braemar and then, after I've had a chance to study Amelia, I'll continue on to Little Brook and look for this journal."

"I'd best send a letter to Lord Alric letting him know to expect us. You're certain you won't come with us, Margot?"

She nodded. "One last thing, Garret. You heard what Marcus said about Nea's keen, how it's different. Well her relationship with the Between is also different. She might prove our best hope of figuring out a cure. Especially once Samson's journal is found." She chewed her thumb.

Garret bit down on the back of his cheek. "Margot—"

"I'm not saying it to cloud your judgement or because I would say just about anything to protect her. Nea really could help us and she doesn't deserve whatever torture Evard has planned for her, regardless of what her involvement in Kalhanna was." She swallowed and closed her eyes. "Just promise me you'll weigh up *all* the options."

He rubbed his hands over his face. Nea was like a sister to Margot but he also knew Margot was not one for twisting the truth to suit her whims. "I already told you I need to find her before I can make any decision on the matter ... but I promise when the time comes the decision won't be made in haste." That was all he could give her. Evard wanted Nea and he suspected Garret's loyalties were divided. Tasking Garret with her capture was a test, one he wasn't sure he was ready to fail.

CHAPTER THREE

MARGOT

Margot was sitting at her desk in a patch of weak sunlight, sipping her tea and writing a quick note to Garret. Over the past week, the rumours about corruption had been growing. The most recent suspected case was a seer just outside of Fengate; he was the first *reported* victim that wasn't an actual mage. Seers were closely related to mages in the way all keen-folk were, but they could not draw or manipulate the source.

It had Margot curious as to whether it was a genuine case of corruption or another like Peter, who had been given corruption on purpose. And if someone was deliberately infecting people, who was it and how?

She smiled. As awful as the thought was that someone could be going out of their way to give others corruption, Declan would be in his element. He loved having a problem to solve. Garret, on the other hand, had probably ground his back teeth right down to the gums by now.

She signed her letter then sat back, pressing her hands to the small of her back as she stretched. Her spine gave a satisfying crack and she sat forward again to fold her letter.

A small part of her might have regretted not going with Garret on his hunt for Nea. He was good warden, one of the best, but the game he was playing with Evard was going to get him killed sooner rather than later. That was a fact Garret himself knew and he had been right that delivering Nea to Evard would appease him. But at what cost? And how long would it be until Evard decided Garret had outlived his usefulness?

She shook her head and got up to tidy the clinic. Thankfully, she hadn't had much time to dwell on the what ifs. With winter giving way to spring, the warmer days and cooler nights had set off an increase in seasonal illnesses. Not to mention, she had seen more broken bones in the last week than she had all month, and delivered the baker's wife's twins. There was something oddly satisfying about the dull ache in her body after long hours helping the sick and injured.

The door opened and a woman in the robe of a temple sister entered. Her dark hair was pulled into a tight braid that made Margot's temples twinge just looking at it. Her thin mouth drew into a tight line when her dark eyes found Margot. "Are you the healer?"

"Yes. I am Margot." She held out her hand. "What can I help you with?"

The woman studied the hand, licking her lips and rocking back on her foot as though she wanted to flee. "It's not for me."

"Oh?" Margot withdrew her hand and indicated the padded chair by the hearth. "Sit. I'll make you a brew."

The woman looked at the chair and shook her head. "I won't be here that long."

Margot gave her a practiced smile. "Please, you look like you could use a break. I'm sorry I didn't catch your name?" She turned to make the tea.

"Uh ... Cara."

When Margot turned back with two cups of chamomile and peppermint tea, Cara was sitting in the chair, her fingers wringing the fabric in her lap. She took the offered cup with a small smile.

Margot sat in the identical chair across from her and blew on her tea while she waited.

Cara shifted in her seat and took a sip before placing the cup aside, her dark eyes wide as she settled them on Margot. "If someone wanted to get rid of an unwanted pregnancy, how would they do it? Is there something I could give her? A tonic?"

Margot chewed her thumbnail. She'd thought as much. Over the years she had seen enough young women in the same state that she didn't even need her magic to confirm it these days. Still, she let her keen stir brushing it lightly over Cara, who shifted as though she could feel it. She wasn't a mage or a warden, keen-touched in some other way perhaps? A seer? *Focus, Margot.* As her keen smoothed over the other woman, she felt the steady throb of her heart and the rapid tattoo coming from deep in her womb. She gave her a tight smile. "I could give you a tonic, but the process is painful and best overseen by a healer. Or I can use my magic."

"No. No magic," Cara said quickly.

Margot placed her cup aside and crossed her arms. "It is safer to do it with magic, less painful, though not without its own risks. And once we're done, I will give you a recipe for a tea that you can make so this doesn't happen again."

Cara chewed her lip and stared into her cup like it held all the answers. With a deep breath, she lifted her gaze to meet Margot's once more. "Alright."

Margot was just finishing up with Cara when the door banged open, causing them both to jump.

"Margot of Kalhanna." The voice that spoke was gruff.

Margot turned to face its owner, a man bearing the green tabard of the king's guard. "Yes?"

"His Majesty requires your presence at the palace. I am to escort you." He took a step towards her and she noted that his fingers twitched to the hilt of his sword.

"A show of force is not necessary. I will come quietly. As soon as I am done with my patient." She lifted a hand to indicate Cara.

The man blinked. "We were told—"

"That I am an unreasonable wretch who would fight tooth and nail to avoid the summons?" Margot gave him a patronising smile.

He pulled out a pair of bind-shackles. "Then you won't mind me putting these on you."

Margot eyed the thin bands of rose-gold metal. "You don't need to shackle me."

"His Majesty insisted." The soldier took a step forward.

"Are you sure that is necessary?" Cara said in a crisp voice. "Margot is being compliant."

The guard studied Cara, his gaze lingering on the eight-pointed star stitched on the front of her priestess robe. His mouth twisted as he was though fighting some internal battle. "It's the king's *orders*, your grace."

"Cara, it's alright." Margot didn't like the idea of facing Evard without her magic, but she had a feeling that one way or another, that was how she would be leaving the clinic. She held her arms out, shaking the long sleeves of her linen shirt back to expose her wrists.

The soldier took another step forward and clipped the first shackle around her left wrist. The metal was so cold that for a moment it felt like it was burning. Then the seam where the two pieces joined shone and vanished, cutting her connection to the source to a dull thrum. When the second shackle closed, a moment of vertigo washed over her as her connection was cut off entirely.

She was examining the delicate bands which now hugged her wrists as Molly came through the door.

"What's going on here?" Molly's cornflower gaze snapped from the soldier to Cara and then to Margot.

"Molly, stay there." Margot lifted a hand to stop her.

"Why are you wearing bind-shackles?" Molly moved to step between the soldier and Margot.

The soldier gripped the hilt of his sword before drawing the blade several inches.

"It's okay, Molly. I'll be alright. The king just wants an audience." She flicked her eyes to the letter on the table. "Can you let *Uncle Gerald* know I may be late for dinner?"

Molly eyed the soldier. "Alright." She approached Margot and pressed a chaste kiss to her lips. The soldier tensed but made no move to separate them.

"I'll be okay," Margot whispered.

Molly gave her a hug, then cupped her face before giving her another kiss. She stepped back next to Cara and watched the soldier with a scowl but made no move to stop him as he guided Margot out onto the street.

"You, priestess, tell me everything that just happened," was the last thing that Margot heard before the door banged shut.

As the soldier led her through Dust Town, Margot walked beside him with a light step and her head held high as though nothing were out of the ordinary. People still paused and watched them pass. Some with curious heads tilted, whispering mouths hidden behind hands while others frowned chores forgotten as they shared anxious looks.

The palpable tension in the air didn't lift until they left Dust Town and started through the wide, cobbled streets of the upper market. The thin thread of the temple sisters singing their choir reached them as they neared the castle gate. Margot spared the temple a glance, shielding her eyes from the afternoon sunlight that glinted off the white spire.

Several heads turned as they crossed the main courtyard to the massive doors that led into the castle. The slabs of stone beneath their feet echoed the sound of their footsteps across the grand entryway.

The chamberlain came to greet them. He smoothed the front of his green overshirt and looked down his hooked nose at Margot—which was quite a feat, considering he was a good inch or two shorter than her.

"His Majesty is expecting you." He snapped his fingers and turned on his heel.

The soldier gave Margot's shoulder a nudge and she followed after the chamberlain's quick steps.

It had been quite some time since she had last stepped foot into the grand throne room, but it had not changed. The heavy green drapery, the too-hot fire in the impressive hearth, the courtiers who existed merely to kiss Evard's arse, and Evard himself, sitting like a glorified vulture on his mahogany throne.

The king, like his throne room, was the same as he had always been. His chin rested on the bony fingers of his left hand while his cold grey eyes scanned the room—bored. Though when his gaze fell on Margot, his posture changed remarkably. Pale lips pulling back to reveal his teeth in a mockery of a pleasant smile, he leapt to his feet and stepped down from the dais to greet her.

"Margot." He rolled her name over his tongue like he was seducing a lover, and Margot repressed a shudder.

"Your Majesty." She dipped into a curtsey, her eyes raising to glance at the scar that ran through his left eyebrow and down his cheek. Nea's handiwork.

"Rise and let me look at you." He reached out and cupped her chin before tilting her head and letting his fingers caress her neck.

She swallowed and took a step back.

"As lovely as ever. Though still a pale comparison to your precious *sister*." His smile was dangerous. "Do you know why I summoned you?"

"I cannot even begin to guess."

"You are far too intelligent for that. But I will humour your attempt at naivety." He returned to the dais and took his seat on the throne. "There have been rumours of late about a necromancer who bears a striking resemblance to *our* dear Nea." He purred Nea's name but there was something in his eyes that made Margot's stomach drop.

"And? There are always rumours, and they always lead to dead ends."

Evard studied her. "Indeed, that has been the case. But I have something now that I did not have before."

Margot swallowed. She didn't need to ask but she found herself doing it anyway. "And what is that?"

"Bait." As Evard said the word, the soldier grabbed hold of Margot.

"She won't come for me." She knew that wasn't true. If Nea learned that Evard had Margot in his possession, she wouldn't hesitate to turn herself in.

"Oh, Margot, my dear, you know that is a lie." There was a hint of humour in his tone. "I wondered, when word of your return reached me, how long it would take Nea to surface. But still, she's eluded me. I assumed this was because you were not in any foreseeable danger. I had mentioned to Warden Commander Garret that your arrest would bring her out of the woodwork, but he thought it unnecessary, instead choosing to waste his time chasing shadows and rumours. But she is close now; I can feel it. And you, my darling little healer, will bring her straight to my door." He turned his attention to the soldier. "Please escort our guest to her *room.* Then return to the clinic and burn it to the ground. If her little blonde lover is there, kill her."

Margot snapped her arm out of the soldier's grip and tilted her chin. "I hope this trap of yours does bring Nea here. Even if you manage to shackle her, she won't need her powers to finish what she started." She drew a finger down her left cheek.

Evard leapt down from the dais and the back of his bony hand struck her cheek with a resounding slap.

Margot met his glare. "You're terrified of her. That's why you want to control her, isn't it?"

Evard grabbed her by the throat and pulled her forward so her face was only an inch from his. "One more word and I will snap your pretty neck." He shoved her away.

She coughed, lifting a hand to rub her throat. "You won't. You need me alive. Nea will never cooperate if you kill me and you know it."

"Take her away," Evard growled as he took his seat on the throne once more. "No need to be gentle."

As the soldier dragged her away, the last thing she saw was Evard's cold smile.

CHAPTER FOUR

GARRET

Garret brought his axe down with a loud *thwack*, splitting the log in two. He huffed as the pieces fell from the block before lining up another hunk of wood and swinging the axe again.

He felt Declan approach before he heard him. The static prickle of Declan's keen flitting up his spine made him roll his shoulders and set the axe aside.

"Word from the capital?" Declan eyed the decent-sized pile of split logs.

Garret shook his head. "None. What do you make of Leon?"

"Leon?" Declan shrugged. "Arse-kisser if I ever met one. Perhaps a little too interested in Amelia." He rubbed his chin. "Any reason you're asking?"

Garret frowned and took up the axe again, hefting its weight before splitting another log.

"This mood you're in, honestly, is it about Leon or something else? A woman perhaps? One who is proving extremely difficult to pin down?" Declan lifted his hands in surrender when Garret glared at him.

"Marcus has never failed me before." He tilted the axe to examine the head before looking up again. "And Emil is no more help than

Margot was. He just keeps telling me she doesn't want to be found and as long as that is the case, I'll never find her. Enchanted bracelet or not." He pulled the bracelet out of his pocket and squeezed it in his fist. "I'm starting to think she's more of a ghost than an actual person."

"Mind if I look at that?" Declan held his hand out for the bracelet and Garret gave it to him with an exasperated sigh. "Curious." Declan rolled the bracelet around in his fingers. "It's like a heartbeat. If I just ..." The static prickle became white-hot as Declan channelled the source and then the bracelet shone for a few moments. "Interesting. What if—"

"Give me that back." Garret snatched the bracelet from him and considered it. The energy was different now. Cold. But not in a way that was unpleasant, and he felt a tug at the back of his mind to the east. "What did you do?"

"I'm not a hundred percent sure."

"What if you disrupted Marcus's enchantment?"

Declan shrugged. "I don't *think* I did."

Garret was about to speak when he noticed a soldier coming towards them. He recognised the neatly trimmed head of mousey hair and the clipped gait. *Leon.* He drew a breath and tilted his head in Leon's direction.

Declan turned to look and let out a groan. "I'll be in my room. Come find me when you're done with Captain Kiss-Arse." He took off in the direction of the fort, giving Leon a curt nod as he passed him.

Garret slipped the bracelet into his pocket as Leon reached him. "You have news, I take it?"

Leon stood tall with his arms behind his back, the sun hitting the saffron stitching on his green tabard. "A necromancer was seen outside Carroc. Though no one seems to have gotten a good look at her, she apparently bore some resemblance to the mage the king is searching for. We should move on this before the trail goes cold."

"Carroc?" Garret glanced to the east.

"Yes. Much closer than I would expect, given the reports of her *elusiveness.*" Leon brushed something invisible from the shoulder of his uniform. "If we leave this afternoon, we can be in Carroc and on her trail in three days, maybe two, if we don't spare our horses."

"If news of her is only reaching us now, it is likely the trail has gone cold already. Did you find any other information? Where she was heading? If she's travelling alone?"

Leon shook his head, a strange glint in his eye. "You're just going to let this chance slide like you did with that lead in Kilton."

"The sighting in Kilton wasn't her though; it wasn't even a mage." Garret crossed his arms over his chest. "I do think we should investigate this lead, Leon. I just don't want to go riding off half-prepared. And I'd like to take Emil with us, but I don't know if he'll be back in time to leave today." Even if he was, Garret wouldn't be leaving right away. The weekly update from Margot was late and he wanted to give it another day before he sent someone to check on her and Molly.

Leon's cool façade slipped, the corner of his mouth curling into a sneer at the mention of Emil. "Do we really need another warden? Especially one who has emotional ties to this particular mage?"

"Those ties are exactly why we should take him. *We* might not be able to get close, but maybe someone she knows can."

"And what if she needs to be eliminated? Emil will hardly stand by and let his *friend* be put to the sword."

Garret's jaw tightened. "Emil is one of the best wardens I know. If it comes down to it, he will not let his feelings get in the way of what needs to be done. And regardless of that fact, the king wants Nea alive, so until that order changes, *no one* will be putting her to the sword." The bracelet in his pocket vibrated and the cold feeling coming from it intensified. He glanced to the east once more; could Nea really be that close? "We will leave for Carroc as soon as Emil returns."

That strange glint had returned to Leon's eyes. "As you wish, *Commander*." He turned on his heel and strode in the direction of the fort.

Garret fished the bracelet out of his pocket and studied it. It was still again, the gentle throb against his skin the only indication that Marcus's enchantment was still in place. Remembering Declan's request, he rested the axe against the chopping block and followed after Leon.

When Garret arrived at Declan's room, the mage was pacing and muttering excitedly to himself. He stopped, looked at the clutter on his desk, and snatched up a piece of parchment. He glared at it for several heartbeats then shook his head and thrust it back onto the pile. Then he started pacing again, his long fingers curling through his hair.

Garret watched him for a minute before he cleared his throat and said, "You wanted to see me."

Declan paused in front of his desk again and shuffled through the parchment. "It won't work ... will it?" His attention was firmly on his notes. He picked up a book and flipped through a few pages with a scowl. "Of course, if I were to—"

"Declan!"

He looked up, his green eyes narrowing at the interruption. "Garret? How long have you been standing there?"

"Long enough." Garret leant against the doorframe and crossed his arms. "You wanted to see me."

Declan tilted his head. "Yes, of course I did. I'm leaving for Little Brook in the morning. I need to speak with a seer by the name of Emma. Apparently she's a descendant of Samson and may know the best place to start looking for the journal." He straightened some of his papers. "She is said to be related to Nea also."

"So that would make Nea a descendant of this Samson as well?"

Declan shrugged. "It would be safe to assume this rumour about your elusive quarry is indeed true. Necromancers are very particular about their bloodlines, and given that it is one of the few types of magic that can only be inherited by blood and not appear spontaneously, it stands to—"

"Short version."

Declan rolled his eyes. "Yes, Nea and Samson are related in some fashion."

"Does that mean she is tied to corruption? Or her bloodline is?"

Declan shook his head. "Without the journal, I couldn't tell you the link between Samson and corruption, but I can tell you that you can count on one hand the number of necromancers with *confirmed* cases of corruption."

"But corruption comes from the Between, doesn't it? I would think that necromancers would be at a higher risk than other mages." Garret rubbed the scar above his lip. It would make sense that necromancers and corruption were tied in some way, even Margot had implied as much.

Declan tapped his fingers on his chin and referred to his notes. "The theories about that are conflicting. But I did find one interesting detail." He unearthed a thin tome from the pile on his desk. "This is a study done by Yolanda of Kalhanna. She was a contemporary of Samson and she talks about his study and a mage by the name of Johanna who was allegedly a deathborn."

"Deathborn are a myth though."

"Yolanda didn't seem to think so and the way she describes Johanna, I'd say she was very similar to our Amelia."

Garret shook his head. "Amelia is a reanimation, not a deathborn."

"You're splitting hairs." Declan gave him a lopsided smile.

"Or you're jumping to conclusions based on the opinions of a bunch of long-dead historians." Garret smiled back.

"Scientists, Garret. I don't bother too much with accounts of shipping manifestos and what Her Majesty Hildegard the Fourth ate for lunch."

Garret shook his head with a laugh. "Right then. So, you called me up here to tell me you are leaving. Was that all?"

"And the thing about Nea being related to Samson, yes."

A knock on the door announced the arrival of Charles, the head of staff at Fort Braemar. "Forgive the interruption, Commander, but master Emil has returned. He is awaiting your presence in the south training yard."

That was sooner than Garret had expected. "I'll be right down."

Charles dipped his head and backed out of the room.

Garret turned to Declan, but the mage had already returned to his notes, his brow furrowing as he muttered under his breath. With a smile and a shake of his head, Garret left the room to go and find Emil.

The next morning, Declan left just after dawn and Leon, who had convinced Garret to let him ride ahead to Carroc, not long after. He studied Leon's back as he rode away, still not convinced letting him go off on his own was the right thing to do. But regardless of that reservation, a small part of him was happy to have Leon out of his hair, at least for a short while.

He turned to find Emil watching him and started over when the sound of hoofbeats echoed through the gate.

A dark horse charged into the yard. Its rider pulled it up hard enough that it skidded, its hindquarters dropping slightly in an effort to stop before it trampled Garret, who leapt nimbly out of the way. He took hold of the bridle, eyeing the flecks of foam that covered the animal's velveteen muzzle.

Drawing a slow breath, he gently murmured to the horse, who was looking around wild-eyed and prancing to the side despite his hold on the reins. "Easy now. That's a good lad." He lifted his curled fingers and let the animal sniff them before gently stroking its cheek.

The rider leapt down, startling the horse again, and her hood fell back revealing a long blonde braid and blue eyes that had dark circles beneath them.

"Garret! Thank the Bright Mother you're still here." She collapsed against him, a ragged shudder following her words. "You have to return to the capital right now."

Emil appeared and took the reins of the horse before leading it towards the stables as Garret placed a hand on each of Molly's shoulders and held her at arm's length. "Calm down, Molly. Tell me what happened."

"There's no time. He took Margot."

Garret drew a careful breath. "Who took Margot?"

"Evard. And then he had the clinic burned to the ground." She was shaking, though Garret thought it was mostly from lack of sleep.

"It's okay, Molly." He kept his voice level and looked over her head to see Emil returning. "Margot will be fine."

"How can you say that? Evard has her. What if he kills her?"

He gave Molly's shoulders a gentle squeeze. "He won't kill her."

"You can't possibly know that." She shook free of his grasp. "He'll torture her. You know what he does to people who don't give him what he wants."

Garret took another breath and, as gently as he could manage, said, "It is highly likely that he *will* torture her." Evard was rather fond of torture, and Garret didn't really want to think about the things he would do to Margot. "But she's strong, Molly, and I promise he won't kill her. At least not until he has Nea."

"What has Nea got to do with it?" She spat the words out.

"Evard is trying to draw her out," Emil said.

"You honestly think that will work?" Molly whirled around to face him.

"Yes. There are very few people in this world who Nea would sacrifice herself for and Margot is at the top of that list."

Molly shook her head. "I call bullshit. If Nea actually cares about any of you, where has she been the last three years?" Emil opened his mouth, but Molly prodded the centre of his chest with her finger. "You and Margot talk about Nea like she's some hero from a children's story. You're so wrapped up in the idea of the person she *used* to be that you are both blind to the reality of it. If she actually is the person you claim her to be, why is she hiding away like some coward while the rest of us are risking our lives to stop the world from going to shit?"

"*Molly.*" Garret touched her shoulder but she shook him off.

"Don't you dare *Molly* me, Garret." There was fire in her eyes as she spun to face him again.

"Getting worked up about this isn't going to change things," he said. "I can't go running to rescue Margot. If I did, I might as well lay my head on the block at Evard's feet."

Molly sniffed and folded her arms across her chest.

"Look, Molly." Emil drew her attention back to him. "I understand you're worried about Margot. We all are." He glanced over her head at Garret. "But up until now, Margot has been safe and Nea would have been staying away because she thought that was the best course of action." He drew a deep breath. "Nea is many things, but she's not a coward. The second she hears that Evard has Margot, she will march herself right into his throne room."

Molly scoffed but said nothing.

Emil turned to Garret. "If you were considering keeping Nea away from Evard, I suggest you try and find her before she learns that he has Margot."

Garret nodded. "Go ready the horses." As Emil headed to the stables, Garret said to Molly, "We'll rescue Margot, I promise. But we need to do it right, and we can't until we have Nea." And until he'd had a chance to decide if handing her over to Evard was the right thing to do. "Come on," he directed her towards the fort. "I'll introduce you to Lord Alric and the others before I leave."

CHAPTER FIVE

NEA

Nea ran a hand over her hair. The thick storm-grey curls had been restrained in a neat braid, but several tendrils had escaped under her ministrations. She chewed the inside of her cheek and crouched to inspect the body.

The man's face was obscured by the muck from the roadside trench. In fact, if it hadn't been for the tacky stain of blood on his neck and shoulder, she would have thought he was just some drunk who had stumbled into the furrow and drowned in the ditch water. It wouldn't be the first time she'd witnessed such a death.

Without glancing his way, she waved to the gangly youth who had been tasked with showing her the body. "Rhett, I need you to help me roll him over. I want to check his throat."

He hurried over and crouched beside her. "Are you sure you need to? I don't think it will be pretty."

Nea schooled her expression. She often forgot that not everyone was as used to seeing death, no matter how gruesome, as her. "Of course it won't be pretty. I suspect his throat's either been cut or torn out. Now stop stalling and grab hold of his hip."

Rhett jumped at her tone and latched onto the dead man's hip as instructed.

"Good. Now, on three." Nea took hold of the shoulder and a good chunk of shirt, then planted her heels. "Three."

They both heaved, and though the mud made a wet, sucking sound as the seal between it and the man's chest was broken, the body tilted but didn't roll.

"Come on, Rhett, you've got the light end. Put your back into it!" Nea ground out through her teeth.

They heaved again. This time, the body shifted. It wobbled on its side and then made a wet *smack* as it slammed into the mud.

Lifeless green eyes stared skyward and little bits of mud and debris from the ditch were stuck to the man's sallow cheeks. Nea sighed as she grabbed his chin and tilted his face to inspect it before checking inside his mouth and finding nothing out of the ordinary save a slightly swollen tongue. Next she turned her attention to the neck; it was a clean slice. *Sharp blade.* She probed the wound with her fingers and Rhett groaned before dashing into the bushes beside the road to relieve himself of his breakfast.

Finally, she checked the dead man's pockets. Nothing. Was it as simple as a roadside robbery ending in murder? She stood and, wiping her fingers on the hem of her dark blue tunic, moved to the centre of the road where the footprints had been mostly scuffed away. But she didn't need footprints to work out what had happened. She closed her eyes and focused on the pull of magic building behind her navel. It bloomed in a cool rush, thin filaments charged her hair with static, and images played across the back of her eyelids.

Dark shapes ran down the road towards her. Two. One pursuing the other. They collided several feet in front of her, one knocking the other to the ground. She inhaled as the scents of dust and blood clouded her senses. The figures leapt apart and one scrambled away, passing straight through Nea's still form. He staggered towards the tree line on the other side of the ditch. His attacker leapt for him, pushing him back to the ground. There was a small splash as they rolled into the ditch and both gained their feet. A blade flashed in the moonlight and one man dropped to his knees, a dark line across his throat, before he keeled into the mud. The smell of blood was stronger now as the attacker started to frantically search the dying man's pockets. He rolled him over and checked under his shirt before throwing his arms up and pacing to where Nea stood. Clenching his fist, he turned in a small circle and kicked the ground—

Nea stumbled and fell to her knees as she was pushed from the road, her spell broken along with her concentration. Rhett was panting beside her, still looking pale and shaky. "Forgive me, Nea, but you weren't responding and, well ..." He lifted a shaking hand towards the dark horse who, under his rider's command, was wheeling around to charge back towards her.

"What in the name of the Bright Mother were you doing, woman?" The rider, wearing a tabard emblazoned with the hunter green and gold colours of the king's guard, leapt from his saddle and stormed towards her. "You were almost trampled!"

Nea got slowly to her feet and smoothed her hands over her body to brush the dust from her clothes. "I could ask you what you were doing, riding like the hunt was on your tail this close to the village." She indicated the smoke plumes over the hill that betrayed the location of Little Brook.

The soldier puffed out his chest as he studied her, a nasty twist working across his mouth. "Your name, necromancer." The words were not a request.

She folded her arms. "Who is asking?"

The soldier's mouth pulled into a tight line, and there was a look in his eyes that made Nea feel the urge to take a step backwards. She didn't though. Instead, she planted her feet firmly and stared him down.

"Your. Name. *Necromancer.* I will not ask you a third time." He shifted his weight, as though he were about to grab her, as two more riders came down the road, wearing the simple dark leathers of wardens.

"Leon, you were to go ahead to the village. What are you—Nea?" The younger of the men slid from his mount.

She glanced up and caught his amber eyes watching her. His long dark hair was tied back today but she knew it shone like a raven's wing when free. "Emil?" She rocked back on her foot and swallowed.

"Nea." Leon's mouth curled, and he glanced at the second warden, a stoic-looking man with a head of dark auburn hair. "Of Hartswood?"

She fought the urge to roll her eyes but she couldn't manage to keep the snark from her voice. "No, of Dunbrolga."

Emil bit back a smile, and the third man tilted his head as though sizing her up. The steady pressure of his keen-sense rolled down her spine, the chill of her own keen stirring in response. Leon, however, scowled and stepped forward until his nose was almost touching hers.

"Leon, was it? I suggest you take a step back. I don't appreciate intimidation tactics from self-important soldiers."

He grabbed her arm, his grip vice-tight. "How dare you."

Nea pulled gently on the source and focused on Leon, pressing the weight of the Between down on him, opening the door separating the worlds just wide enough to give him a glimpse of what was on the other side. The air grew cold and he got a wild look in his eyes, his breath coming out in white puffs.

"*Nea,*" Emil said delicately, and he lifted a hand to stop the other warden as he moved to dismount.

She felt the creeping numbness of Emil suppressing her power and gave him a rueful look before releasing her hold on the source. "You know if I really wanted to ..."

"I know." Emil glanced to Leon, who was rubbing his arms, his lips edged in blue. "What *did* you do to him?"

"Nothing really. Just gave him a taste of the other side." She glanced at the other warden. "Now, if you have business with me it will have to wait until my previous engagement is complete. Rhett, bring the wagon." She said the last over her shoulder to the boy, who was watching the exchange, white-faced. Between the dead stranger and the arrival of three agents of the king, this was the most excitement Little Brook had seen in years. "Rhett!"

He blinked at her and she pointed to the wagon. "Right away, Nea."

"You're just going to let her get away with this insolence?" Leon glared at the still-mounted warden. Nea followed his gaze and noted the red bars of the rank stitched to the sleeve of the man's jacket. He almost looked too young to be a commander.

Emil caught Nea's attention and tilted his head in the direction of the pair of legs sticking out of the ditch, a silent question on his lips. Nea shrugged.

"She's the one the king wants and you're just sitting there doing nothing."

She bristled at the mention of Evard. Since the purge at Kalhanna, his treatment of anyone who refused to dance to his tune had been brutal.

Aware of the commander's gaze on her, she flicked her eyes up to meet his. They were unreadable—a cool deep grey, and almost familiar.

"Look, I don't have the grace of payment from the royal coffers whether I am standing in the middle of the road chatting or doing actual work. So, while you two have this little battle of wills, I'm going to get back to it." She moved to the waiting Rhett and patted his sleepy ox on the forehead. "Right, you get his feet."

"What's this?" Leon turned his attention from the commander back to Nea.

She had bent and grabbed the dead man's shoulders. With a huff, she dropped the body back into the mud and settled her hands on her hips. "My job. What did you think mages of my sort do?"

"Who is that man?" Leon asked.

"Your guess is as good as mine."

The commander pinned Rhett with a calculating look. "Do you know, boy?"

Rhett cringed under the scrutiny. "He was staying at the village, only yesterday on dark, he just took off, leaving most of his things behind. Gran saw his ... well ... she ..." Rhett wrung his hands. "That is, she asked me to fetch a necromancer. She said something wasn't right about the way he ... he... died."

"Your gran saw his death?" The commander leant forward in his saddle.

"It's alright, Rhett." Nea lifted her gaze to meet that of the grey-eyed commander again. "Perhaps you can ask her yourself once you reach the town. Her house is the one with the big garden at the edge of the field."

His mouth formed a tight line as he regarded her, the movement highlighting the small scar that marred one side of his upper lip.

Emil dismounted again. "I'll help you get him into the wagon. I assume you're taking him back to perform the rite."

"Leon, you help too," the commander said as his horse pranced, bored with standing in the road.

Grumbling, Leon moved over and elbowed Rhett out of the way. Nea stepped back to allow Emil to get hold of the dead man's torso. The two men heaved the body up and deposited it in the wagon. Leon walked to his horse, but Emil was looking from the dead man's face to Nea.

"What is it, Emil?" the commander asked.

"It's Declan."

"Declan?" The tone of his voice cut through Nea, and he held her attention as he dismounted and was by the cart in a moment. He stared at the dead man, the colour draining from his face and his fingers twitching into fists. He rounded on Nea. "Tell me everything you know." His voice had taken on a dangerous edge.

She licked her lips. "I know very little. He was chased from Little Brook by another man. There was a scuffle here." She walked to the middle of the road. "He managed to wound his attacker and flee but was caught. There." She indicated the ditch. "The rest you can probably gather from the gaping hole in his neck."

"Was he carrying anything?"

"His pockets were empty and he has no satchel on him."

"The other man, did he take anything?" The commander closed the distance between them.

"I don't know."

"This is nonsense. How can she know all these things?" Leon asked.

"Did he—"

"That is all I know."

The commander was uncomfortably close but she didn't take a step back.

"Leon nearly trampled me with his horse and broke my connection. The re-enactment only works once."

The commander turned to Leon, a dark look stealing across his features.

"I believe this Declan was staying in town, was he not, Rhett?" Nea asked.

"Yes." Rhett tore his eyes away from the dead man's face long enough to answer, but looked away again when the commander levelled his stormy gaze on him.

"Where was he staying?"

"The ... The ... Leaping Cow."

The corner of Nea's mouth twitched. "There you have it. I suggest you investigate his room at The Leaping Cow." She lifted the thin blanket they had brought to shroud the body and passed it to Rhett. "Now if you'll excuse me, I would like to get the rite performed while we still have some daylight."

"Thank you for your cooperation." The commander moved back to his horse, who had dropped her head to pick at the grass growing along the roadside.

"You're just going to let her go?" Leon was incredulous.

"Now is not the time, Leon." The commander's voice had an edge to it that made the hairs on Nea's neck prickle. "Get on your horse and head for town."

Leon opened his mouth.

"It was not a request." The commander cut him off, his fists clenched and the muscles across the back of his shoulders straining under the leather of his jacket.

Leon glared at Nea but followed the order.

"Ready, Nea?"

She had been watching the men ride away towards town, but Rhett's words brought her attention back to the moment. She nodded in answer and Rhett took the lead attached to the ox's halter. With a click of his tongue, he pulled on the rope. The ox heaved, and the wheels rolled steadily forward. Once they had moved several feet, the wagon started to roll more smoothly and the old ox didn't strain anymore.

Rhett's father and several other men from the village had seen to digging the grave. Emma, Rhett's grandmother, had arranged small bouquets of herbs and tied them with coloured string: one red, one white, and one black. She had also arranged a proper shroud to wrap the body and was waiting by the grave when Nea and Rhett arrived with the wagon and their gruesome cargo.

They didn't speak as they stripped Declan's body and then carefully wrapped him in the cloth, tucking the herbs and various charms in the neat folds. Once they were finished, Nea had Rhett and his father lower the body carefully into the hole.

Breathing deeply, Nea held her hands palm down over the grave and someone cleared their throat. She half-turned to see the commander and Emil standing a short distance away, but Leon was nowhere to be seen. For that, she was thankful—there was a malice deep in his eyes that reminded her of Evard.

She returned her attention to the task at hand and centred herself again before reciting the rite. "From the source we come, to the source we return. Rest now, child of the Bright Mother, and may you find salvation in the forest of ancestors." The phrasing of the words really didn't matter. She'd learned long ago that it was for the comfort of the living. It was the subtle push of magic that opened the gateway for the soul to return to the source that was the most important part of the rite.

A breeze ruffled the loose tendrils of Nea's hair as the gate between worlds shifted in response to her magic. A massive hedge of pale pink roses erupted before her. No one else gave any indication that they could see it.

The branches of the hedge stretched towards her and she lifted a hand. A silent suggestion and gentle flick of her fingers sent them collapsing back on themselves. Beyond the now open barrier, the rolling landscape of the Between opened out, a twisted representation of the village. She could feel things lurking just out of sight, but none approached.

The thing she found most strange was the lack of the dead man's soul. Occasionally, the deceased did accept their death and move on without her aid. But that was not usually the case with brutal or sudden deaths, like murder.

She let her keen-sense wash over the body but could feel no attachment. Drawing a breath, she allowed the hedge to roll back into place and the branches to knit together again, sealing the gate. Then she gave a nod. The commander took the shovel from Rhett and silently started filling the grave. Rhett's father and Emil joined him.

At a light touch on her elbow, Nea turned. Emma gave her a small smile before beckoning her away from the graveyard and towards the house. Nea glanced at the men around the grave but none were paying her any heed, so she followed the old woman with a sigh.

The main room of the cottage was small, so small Nea couldn't imagine how both Rhett and his father could fit comfortably in the space. Herbs and charms hung from the pitched rafters alongside pots, pans, and various other implements. The fresh scent of the bunch of mint in the basket on the little worn table mingling with comforting aromas of stew and fresh bread made her mouth water.

"Sit down, my girl, and I'll make us a brew." Emma gestured towards one of the chairs by the hearth.

Nea sat obediently as the old woman pottered about preparing the tea. It felt so familiar, like she was back at Hartswood with Nonna. She almost expected Warden Commander Godfrey to walk through the door with that booming laugh of his, telling Angus not to bother with his boots or his coat; he could handle them himself. A younger Emil would have been hot on his heels, complaining about his empty stomach or sore backside from the hours in the saddle riding from Del Harol to the homestead.

The gentle pressure of Emma's fingers on her shoulder brought her attention back to the room and the steaming cup of tea being offered to her. The aroma of her favourite peppermint and camomile mix made her sigh. She met Emma's eyes—so dark a blue, they were almost indigo. Nonna's eyes were lighter, closer to the deep violet of Nea's own. But it was clear that the seer and Nonna were related by the line of their jaws, the dimple in their left cheeks, and their strange ability to know exactly what type of tea would sooth a person's soul.

"Thank you." Nea took the cup and inhaled the fragrant steam.

Emma sat in the chair opposite and waved away Nea's thanks as she stretched her feet towards the glowing coals in the hearth. "I'm glad you were close by; I'd heard there was a necromancer in Walliston but I never imagined it would be you." She gave Nea a calculating look.

A small boy with an unruly head of smoky curls came padding in from the other room with Rhett's older sister, Noelle, chasing after him. "Come back here, you little wretch!"

Noelle caught the boy just as he reached Nea. His little hands grabbed at Nea's knee as Noelle hauled him into her arms, her dark blue eyes widening as they settled on Nea. "N—Nea?" She blinked, her grip on the child tightening as she took several steps backward.

Nea stiffened as she studied the child. "Is that?"

"Henry, yes. He's grown since you last saw him, as wee ones tend to do." Emma chuckled.

"He's ... why haven't you sent him to Hartswood?" She glanced from Emma to Noelle.

"I'll just ... Come on, Henry," Noelle said. Henry's large grey eyes watched Nea over Noelle's shoulder as he was dragged from the room.

Emma shrugged. "He's barely old enough to dress himself and you want him sent off for training?"

"He'll need to go there eventually."

"And he will. Soon, I promise. Or, if it concerns you so much, you could take him there." Emma studied her over the rim of her cup.

Nea focused on her own tea, blowing it gently to cool it. "Rhett said you'd seen the man, Declan's, death."

"You can't avoid Hartswood forever, Nea. But I'll let you change the subject this time." She took a sip of tea. "I saw the death, in a sense. The visions do not always play out in full detail." She gave Nea a pointed look. "Nor do they come when bidden, as you well know."

"Point taken." Nea swirled the tea in her cup. "Yesterday, before Declan left, did anything unusual happen, or did you see his attacker?"

"The man was hooded; that's all I know." Emma took a long sip from her cup. "But best you not get tangled up in it. You've had your fair share of being involved in the events of gods and kings."

"The events of gods and kings? I doubt—" Someone pounded at the door and Nea jumped to her feet. Tea splashed her boots and pooled on the floor, filling the air with the scent of peppermint. "I'm sorry." She grabbed a cloth and bent to clean the mess as the pounding started again.

Emma frowned and opened the door. The commander came rushing into the room, his gaze zeroing in on Nea. "You're coming with me."

"I'm sorry?" Nea straightened, placing the rag and empty cup on the table. "That didn't sound like a request."

"Because it wasn't. I'll put you in bind-shackles if necessary."

Emma hummed to herself and moved to the hearth to check the slowly bubbling pot she had hanging near it.

Nea glared at the commander. "Let's pretend for a moment that you didn't barge in here and threaten to arrest me." The fact that he hadn't attempted to shackle her yet made her wonder if he had any intention of doing so. Regardless of his intention, he had her curiosity piqued. "Why would you think that I would go calmly with you, given that one of your number has already suggested handing me over to the king today?"

His jaw clenched and Nea was sure she could hear the grating of his back teeth. "Listen, mage."

"Nea," she said calmly.

"I'm sorry?" Confusion crossed his features.

"Nea, my name is Nea. Now, perhaps we can start over and, despite the fact that your feathers are obviously ruffled, you can display some common decency." She schooled her features into a non-threatening smile and held out her hand.

He stared at it a long time before giving it the briefest of shakes. "Garret."

"That wasn't hard, was it? What can I do for you?"

"I need you to come and inspect the room where Declan was staying."

"Why?"

"He was a mage, and I believe he may have hidden something there. Something that only another mage can find."

"Or a warden. I am sure both yourself and Emil are more than capable of finding items that have been shrouded by magic." She crossed her arms.

Garret made a noise low in his throat and ran his fingers through his auburn hair, causing it to stand on end. The thick waves caught the light of the fire and shone copper a moment before they settled once more. "Are you always this ..." He huffed and threw his hands in the air, knocking one of the pots and sending the others trembling. "We can't find it. We've been over every inch of that room and there is nothing there."

"Then did it occur to you that perhaps there is nothing there to find?"

"I ..." He frowned and let out a reserved sigh. "Please. Will you please just take a look at the room?"

She was taken aback momentarily by the exhaustion in his tone. No, it wasn't really exhaustion—soul weariness, Nonna would call it. "He meant a lot to you, this Declan?"

Garret looked at Emma, who had been silently busying herself with the meal in the pot. "He was a friend. But he was here looking for something important and I believe he found it ... Will you come and look for me?"

"What makes you so sure there is something there?"

He pulled a crumpled piece of paper from his pocket and held it out to her. When she took it, she felt a prickle of magic dance through her fingers and zing down her spine. There were words on the paper in an elegant hand: *Found it. Bring a necromancer.*

She sighed and ran her hand over her hair, causing one languid curl to fall across her face. She brushed it behind her ear. "Are you going to arrest me the moment I find whatever it is you are looking for?"

What could have been a frustrated smile ghosted across his lips as he crossed his arms over his chest. "My orders say I should."

"And?"

He studied her for so long she wasn't sure he was actually going to reply. In a soft voice, he said, "I don't know."

"You don't know?" She felt the corner of her mouth curl. "You'd consider ignoring a direct order from the king for a mage you don't even know?"

He gave a minute shake of his head. "Not usually."

Nea glanced at Emma, who gave a tiny nod. "Okay, I'll see if I can find anything in the room. Lead the way."

The Leaping Cow was quiet, and given the time of day, it wasn't overly surprising. Leon and Emil were the only patrons and they sat at one of the rickety old tables in the corner.

Emil's bright gaze met Nea's as she entered the room, and she thought a flash of relief touched his features. Maybe Garret's threat about the shackles had indeed been real.

Both men moved to stand as Garret walked over to them. Nea stayed where she was and surveyed the room.

Gerda was in the kitchen, banging away and shouting orders at her husband, Bertram. Though she hadn't been to the tavern in at least four years, it was nice to see some things never changed; even the reedy black cat by the fire and scent of spiced apple tart were the same.

Nea walked over to the bar and cleared her throat just as the thickset tavern owner came through the door from the kitchen.

His flushed cheeks shone with a thin sheen of sweat and his arms were loaded with wood for the hearth. But when he spotted her, a wide grin crossed his face. "By the Bright Mother! Is that you, Nea?" He bustled to the hearth and dropped his load of logs onto the pile in the wood box. "Come here, girl, and let me get a good look at you." He waved her over, careless of the looks from his three customers.

"It's good to see you, Bertram. Business is well, I take it?"

He waved her attempt at polite conversation away and looked at the men in the corner. "Business is business. It ebbs and flows like the tide. You're not here to discuss business though, are you, lass?"

She shook her head and he glanced at the ceiling. "He was in the room at the end of the hall on the right. But that can wait—"

"I'm afraid it can't." Garret had moved over to them and was standing by Nea's elbow.

Bertram scowled. "Right you are, Commander." The scowl was gone completely when he turned back to Nea and took hold of her hands before giving them a good squeeze. "You come and see Gerda when you're done. She'll want to feed you before you go."

"Alright." She turned to Garret. "After you."

Declan's room was meticulously tidy. None of the items laid carefully on the bed gave off even a hint of magic, but the air in the room held an eerie feeling, like the stillness before a storm. Nea slipped her satchel off and placed it on the chair under the window before walking to the bed. She picked up a well-worn journal and opened it. A crimson leaf pressed within the pages fell out. Nothing. Not even the slightest coil of magic.

"What type of mage was he?"

Garret sighed behind her. "Is that important?"

"Yes. Tracing magic will be much easier to do if I know what his proficiencies were. What college was he from? I know he wasn't from Del Harol or Hartswood or ..." She slid the leaf back into the journal and returned it to the bed. "Kalhanna." Very few of the mages from Kalhanna had survived. Nea could still smell the blood, taste the smoke, hear the screams—

"Loch Bastien. He was a storm mage." Garret's voice snapped her back to the room.

"That explains the latent energy." She rolled her shoulders and Garret made a noise that could have almost been the start of a laugh. When she turned to him, though, his stoic expression was firmly in place.

Nea frowned back at the room. "What makes you think there is something hidden here, aside from the note? There is nothing here. No signatures, nothing to trace ..."

"I thought you could do a re-enactment, and the note did specify to bring a necromancer." He looked at the crumpled piece of paper in his hand.

"May I?" She held her hand out and he passed the note to her. She could feel the magic that saturated the paper. It was bright and churning, and almost coaxed a smile to her lips. "Maybe."

"Maybe?"

"It is highly unlikely to work without the body nearby, but there may be enough residual energy in the room." She traced the words on the paper with her finger. "Bring a necromancer. Why?" She remembered the strangeness when she had tried to send Declan earlier. "That would be impossible, surely." The paper seemed to grow hot between her fingers.

"I'm sorry. You've lost me."

Startled, she glanced at Garret. "I'm going to try something. Stand there and don't move." She sat on the edge of the bed and closed her eyes. As her magic built at her core, the static in the room shifted in response, sending a wash of prickles down her spine. She rolled her shoulders again to shift the feeling as she let her keen out in a cool wave, still focusing on the paper in her hand.

It shone lilac for a moment and then there was a flash of white light and she could see Declan pacing, tearing at his dark hair. His movements were frantic as he shuffled his things again and again. Suddenly, he stopped and looked at his reflection in the window. He spoke to himself then clapped his hands together—

"Ha! It worked! So, who are you then?"

Nea jumped as the bed beside her depressed under the weight of the man whose body she had just finished burying. "Nea ... I'm sorry, what worked?" She glanced to Garret, who leant against the doorframe, frozen. Not even his chest stirred with breath.

"Nea of Hartswood?" Declan let out a wry bark of laughter, the corners of his green eyes crinkling. "When I said to find a necromancer, I didn't think it would be *you*."

"I'm sorry?"

"A lot of people have been looking for you. For a while actually, and here you are, sitting on my bed. You're different to what I imagined."

She flicked her gaze to Garret's immobile form.

"Oh, never mind old Garret. He can't see or hear me. I'm in here." He tapped her temple lightly and she flinched.

"This isn't a re-enactment." She twisted to look at the room. An hourglass she hadn't noticed before was sitting on the bedside table, the sand slowly floating from bottom to top.

"Just catching on now, are you? It's a spell—my spell—and it won't last much longer." He sighed wistfully. "When I realised Harold was sniffing around, I figured I'd need to leave a message for Garret, but one that would be nearly impossible to find. I'll admit, I was thinking about something Marcus said about *you* when I came up with this spell."

"Marcus?"

"When he was tracking you, he said you slipped into the Between to evade him."

She rubbed the back of her neck. "The finder."

Declan nodded. "I thought, what if I could create a kind of pocket between worlds and set a magical trap that would spring the second a necromancer did that little re-enactment trick. Very clever on my part, but absolutely untested and thus totally unpredictable—"

"Impossible." She shook her head. "You're dead, you know? I just laid you to rest."

"Yes. I am aware." He frowned. "It's alright though. I'll go completely once this spell has broken. Which reminds me." He looked at the hourglass. "We're almost out of time."

"Garret seems to think you hid something here."

"Because I did. This spell and that." He pointed to a board just under the side of the bed. "Garret will have to knock on the board, like the one in the library. Tell him not to fret, not that it will help. But this"—he indicated himself— "it wasn't his fault. Tell him it was Harold and to make sure he twists the knife good and hard." He started to fade. "I need you to send me."

"Oh." Nea lifted her hands and gave a gentle push of energy, her brow furrowing as she met a resistance before the hedge between worlds appeared. The branches groaned as she pressed her magic against them. She focused and pushed harder, causing some of the pink roses to burst into flames, leaving dull grey blooms in their place. Then, slowly, the branches gave way, rolling back and finally snapping open.

Declan smiled as the twisting ever-changing landscape of the Between rolled out before them. "Thank you."

Then he was gone and Nea found herself flat on the bed, the hard edge of Declan's journal digging into her hip. "What in the ...?"

Garret was suddenly looming above her. "What happened? What did you see?"

"Give me some space please." She pushed him away and sat up. There was a throbbing ache between her temples, like she'd drunk her way through half of Bertram's cellar. She shielded her eyes from the light and drew a few breaths.

Emil skidded into the room with Leon hot on his heels. "I felt strange magic. Are you both okay?"

Too many bodies crammed into the small space. Nea's skin crawled and she tried to stand but fell back on the bed. "Out! All of you. I need some space for a minute."

"Nea, I don't think—" Emil started.

"I said, out!"

Three pairs of eyes blinked at her.

"Best do as she wishes, lads, or you'll have to answer to Gerda, and I doubt you'll want that. Come on now. Dinner is ready." Bertram's voice rumbled from the hall.

Leon backed out of the room, followed by Emil, who gave her a concerned look. Garret, however, didn't budge. The look in his grey eyes was unreadable.

"Come on, Commander. Let the lass gather her wits. She'll join us presently, I am sure." Bertram appeared in the doorway.

"It's alright, Bertram. He can stay. We'll be down shortly." She offered him a wan smile.

With a concerned twist of his mouth, Bertram nodded and then followed after Emil and Leon.

The air grew thick and uncomfortable as neither of them spoke. Garret moved to the window, rubbing his finger over the scar above his lip and drawing a heavy breath.

"It's not your fault." The effort to form words made her tongue feel thick and the room seemed to dim. She sat up straighter and leant her head against the wall, forcing her eyes to stay open.

"Not my fault?" He stared at her reflection in the window.

"Declan said that it wasn't your fault. I think he meant his death, but I can't be sure."

Garret's jaw clenched and then he sighed. "He would say that. Anything else?"

She lifted her hand to stifle a yawn. "There's something under the bed for you. Apparently you have to *knock*." Her eyes refused to stay open and the room seemed to tilt. She slid down the wall and her head hit the pillow. Someone was speaking but the words were too far away for her to hear.

CHAPTER SIX

GARRET

The next morning, Garret returned to Declan's room to check on Nea. He stood in the doorway and watched the thin slants of light from the shuttered window play over the loose curls that were fanned over the pillow. Like all necromancers, she had grey hair, but he'd never seen such a stormy shade of grey. It matched her personality, or what he'd seen of it thus far. He frowned, noting the shallowness of her breath and the deathly pale shade of her skin.

Sensing Emil behind him, he turned.

"Is she?" The concern in his tone was palpable.

"Still breathing."

"Should we try to wake her again?"

Garret shook his head. "Gerda is right; we just need to let her sleep and hope whatever this is runs its course."

Emil studied him. "What about you? You don't look like you slept at all last night. Are you alright? Declan ..."

"I'll be fine." He swallowed the lump that rose in his throat. "When she wakes, it's probably best you don't mention Margot. At least not yet."

Emil glanced at Nea. "You should trust her. She didn't have to help with Declan, and she did anyway, knowing full and well that you have orders to arrest her and take her to Evard." He started to walk away.

"What do you think I should do ... honestly?"

Emil turned back to face him. "I'm not the best person to ask, Garret. I'm too biased. It would be like asking you what to do if it was Declan Evard had wanted." He clapped Garret lightly on the shoulder. "Whatever you decide though, I won't stand in your way." His footsteps were light on the stairs as he left.

Garret sat against the wall outside the room. He rested his head back but didn't close his eyes. Instead, he pulled the small journal he'd uncovered under Declan's bed from inside his jacket and glared at it.

He opened the cover and the faded script was penned in a hand that reminded him of Declan's: long and elegant but getting progressively messier until you could almost feel the fervour leaping off the page. He didn't read any of the entries, just flipped through it, each new page increasing the heavy ache in his chest. He snapped the journal shut and shook his head.

With a huff, he got to his feet and took another glance at Nea before gently closing the door and heading downstairs. He found Emil and Leon outside.

"Where's the mage?" Leon looked up as Garret approached.

"Still sleeping."

"Maybe you should get the shackles on her now." There was fear in Leon's eyes. Whatever Nea had done to him yesterday still haunted him.

Garret remembered the chilled despair that had thickened the air when she'd used her magic on the soldier. It had been different to the comforting coolness of her magic during the re-enactment. That had felt more like soothing fingers pressed to feverish skin. It was the same feeling he got periodically from the bracelet.

"That's what I would do. Tie the pretty little bitch up and take her straight to the king." Leon was still talking.

"We're all aware of what you would do, Leon, but the king didn't put you in charge." Emil's tone was tight. "It's your call, Commander."

Garret rubbed his chin. "We'll wait until she wakes."

"You're making a mistake. If she—"

"Enough. I've made my decision. If you need something to keep you occupied while we wait, I suggest you hunt down some supplies and an extra horse." He tossed a coin pouch to Emil.

Leon grumbled but followed Emil down the street.

Garret looked back at the inn. He knew he should wait here in case Nea woke up and decided to run, but he needed to clear his head. He dropped his hand into his pocket and gave the bracelet a squeeze before he started down the street in the opposite direction to Emil and Leon.

He soon found himself in front of the seer's door and when he knocked, he heard voices and the laugh of a small child on the other side. He ran a hand through his hair and drew a breath as the door was pulled open to reveal the seer herself. Her dark blue eyes shone as she seemed to stare through him and he noted they were the same shape as Nea's, though Nea's irises were an other-worldly shade of deep violet.

"Here with news about my niece, Commander?" One grey brow rose and for a moment, Garret felt he was being stared down by his own grandmother.

He actually didn't know why he was here but that seemed like a good enough excuse. "She's fine, as far as I can tell. She collapsed—"

There was a shout from inside and a pair of large grey eyes on a dirty face peeked around the seer's leg. The child was whisked away with a squeal but not before Garret saw a tangled patch of grey curls.

"She collapsed?" The woman's voice drew his attention back to her face.

"Ah ... yes. We're not exactly sure why but Gerda suggested she be left to sleep."

The seer nodded. "There isn't much that Gerda thinks can't be healed by a good nap or a bowl of soup. What ails Nea isn't that simple ... Mostly demons of her own making." She pinned him with another of those soul-scraping stares. "Though, you're no stranger to those kinds of demons either."

Garret rubbed the back of his neck. "I was just wondering if she left any of her things here."

"And what are your intentions with her? Going to hand her over to that lunatic of a man who calls himself king?" There was a murmur of alarm from inside and she called over her shoulder. "Leave me be, girl. I'm old enough to have earned the right to my opinion." She turned her attention to Garret again. "She didn't leave anything here. Her entire world exists in that satchel of hers, but wait there."

She disappeared, and Garret got another glimpse of the strange child, who was wriggling in the arms of a curvy woman with mousey brown hair and deep blue eyes. He stopped moving when he saw Garret and then Garret felt a familiar cool sensation seeping into his spine. The boy's head tilted and the woman holding him said something inaudible through her gritted teeth.

The seer returned, and the sensation of the boy's keen stopped. "Give this to Nea please." She handed him a neatly folded shawl.

"The boy—"

"Is none of your concern, Commander." She started to close the door. "You just worry about what you're going to do with that niece of mine."

The door clicked shut and Garret was left staring at the bundle in his hands.

When he entered The Leaping Cow again, Nea was sitting at a table near the bar. Gerda sat across from her, the surface between them littered with ledgers and the remnants of a meal. Neither of them had noticed him yet and as Nea let out a short, clear laugh, he felt like he was intruding on something private.

He cleared his throat and she stiffened, half-turning to stare at him with those strange violet eyes.

"You're awake," he said stepping forward. "Do you know what happened? We tried to wake you but couldn't."

She ran a hand over her hair. "I was just exhausted; it was a long day yesterday."

"That's wasn't just exhaustion—"

"I'm fine." She didn't look fine; she looked pale, and the dark circles under her eyes told him she could have done with more sleep.

"You—"

"Don't you dare start fussing, Commander. That's my job." Gerda closed the ledger in front of her with a snap.

"I'm guessing you found what you were looking for." Nea pushed the empty bowl in front of her aside.

"Yes. Thank you for your assistance."

Her mouth twitched upwards at the corners, though he wouldn't call it a smile. "You're welcome. What would you like done with Declan's things?" She indicated the pile on the chair next to her. "Does he have family they can be sent to?"

Garret ran his fingertips along his lip and stared at the pile. "His mother, at Loch Bastien."

"I can see to that." Gerda rose from her seat and scooped up her ledgers. "It's a shame. I really liked that boy." She sighed wistfully and heaped Declan's things onto the pile.

Garret didn't stop her. He'd written a letter to Aveline last night when he couldn't sleep. It had been the hardest thing he'd ever had to write. He fished it out of his pocket and held it out. "It's for his mother. To, ah … let her know."

Gerda took it and added it to her pile, then left them alone.

When Garret turned back to Nea, he found her watching him, her head tilted as though he was a puzzle she was trying to solve. A lock of hair had escaped her braid, obscuring one of her eyes. She brushed it behind her ear and straightened in her seat. "So, Commander."

Garret licked his lips. "So."

One of her iron-grey brows lifted slightly.

"Ah, this is for you." He held out the shawl from the seer. "The seer wanted me to give it to you."

"Thank you." She took it and laid it over her satchel. "What do you intend to do now?"

Garret knew she meant 'Are you going to arrest me?' He was surprised she had sat calmly and had a meal with Gerda, knowing that Garret had orders to seize her and take her to Evard. Most mages in her situation would have taken the chance to run.

"What do you think I should do?" He settled in the chair Gerda had vacated.

"You're asking me? Most wardens wouldn't hesitate to complete the job. Especially now the order is under the thumb of the king."

He shifted in his seat. Those who had been vocal about the order being absorbed into the king's guard had ended up like the mages at Kalhanna. And, now that Evard held the reins, those who refused to comply would have their families tortured or killed.

"In fact, were I sitting here with your friend Leon, I would already be in shackles and on my way to the capital. What makes you different?"

Garret rubbed the back of his neck. He thought of Elenora and what he would do if she were in Nea's place. He could never let Evard have her, just because of what she had been born. But he also couldn't imagine Elenora being as dangerous as Nea supposedly was. She hadn't hesitated to use her magic on Leon yesterday, though that was more his fault than hers ...

"You're being awfully quiet, Commander."

He didn't like the way her mouth curled over his title like she was goading him into abusing his position, testing him. "You can just call me Garret."

"I-okay, Garret. Are we going to keep dancing around this subject?"

"Why didn't you leave?"

She gave a little twitch and shifted in her seat before her eyes met his. Something fragile swam in those violet depths as she studied him. The corner of her mouth twisted as she worried the inside of her cheek, then finally, in a voice so quiet he almost had to lean forward to hear it, she said, "I can't keep running."

From what? He didn't actually ask. "What if I didn't turn you over to Evard?"

Her eyes narrowed. "You'd be dead the minute he realised you had betrayed him. If you were lucky, he would put you to the axe before he made you watch whatever family you have burn."

She was right. The fact that Evard would go after his family was the only thing that made him even consider handing her over. Not that Evard knew anything about his family—Declan had been the only one who knew about them. "Is that why you've been hiding? To protect your family?"

"Would it sway your decision to know the truth?"

He shook his head. "Probably not."

"Look, as nice as this little getting-to-know-you chat is, I—"

He pulled the bracelet from his pocket and held it up. Her eyes widened and she leapt to her feet, the movement causing her chair to scrape backwards and teeter on its back legs.

"Wh-where did you get that?" There was a wild fear in her eyes and he felt the coolness of her keen as she pulled the source to her.

"Easy now. A mutual friend gave it to me."

She ran her tongue along her lips, and her fingers twitched as though she wanted to snatch the bracelet from his hand. "Where ... where is this mutual friend now?"

Garret rubbed his scar, as he contemplated telling her the truth. "She's—"

"Garret, we're ready when—Nea! You're awake." Emil came into the room. His eyes fell on the bracelet in Garret's hand and he stopped in his tracks. He swallowed and his gaze flicked between Nea and Garret.

"Where's Margot?" Nea asked Emil. Her voice had a cold edge that made Garret glad it was Emil getting the brunt of it.

"*Nea—*"

"Don't *Nea* me." She paced towards him. "Where. Is. Margot. And, why does *he* have my bracelet?" She thrust a finger in Garret's direction.

"She's ..." Emil looked at Garret around Nea's shoulder. "Nea, maybe you should calm down first."

"I am *calm*." She didn't look it. "Tell me the truth. Or are you going to sit on your hands and play dumb like you did when Evard threw down the order to purge an entire college?"

Emil went white. "Nea, I didn't—"

"Exactly. You did nothing when he slaughtered every mage and warden who refused to skip to his tune. You weren't there when Tobias lay drowning in his own blood. When I sat in the mud and ash, cradling what was left of Francesca so she didn't have to die alone." She was shaking; the source quivered in icy spikes, responding to her mood. Garret had never felt it react to a mage that way before.

Several things crossed Emil's face and he clenched his fists. "That was three years ago, Nea. Maybe if you hadn't been hiding from everyone who cared about you, Margot wouldn't have been taken by Evard." The moment the words left his lips, he clapped his hand over his mouth and Garret groaned.

Nea rocked back on her heel and Garret thought he heard her gasp. He got slowly to his feet as she turned, her pale hand pressed over her mouth. He was sure the look in her eyes was the same one he'd had when he realised it was Declan on the back of that cart.

"Evard has her." The words were soft, as though the realisation had winded her, and she squeezed her eyes shut.

Garret wasn't sure what to do. Cold fury was easy enough to deal with but this shattered despair was something else entirely. He took several slow steps towards her. "Yes. Evard has her. But if you come with us, we can get her back." He kept his voice level, as though he was facing a frightened animal who could lunge at any moment.

She shook her head and opened her eyes. Tears shone along her lower lashes. "No, you can't. Evard won't give her up; he needs her to control me."

"Nea, I'm sorry. I didn't mean to tell you like that."

Garret glared at Emil over the top of Nea's head. She wasn't supposed to find out at all. Now he had to figure out how to stop her running off and doing something stupid.

"If you weren't going to take me to Evard, where were you taking me?" She took a step back.

"Fort Braemar," Garret replied.

She smoothed a shaking hand over her hair. "Fort Braemar? Why there?"

"I can't disclose many of the details here." He glanced at the kitchen door. "The risk is too great."

"If I refuse to go with you, will you arrest me?" Despite the waver in her voice, it still held a hint of humour.

Garret rubbed the back of his neck. "I'd rather it didn't come to that." She crossed her arms, and he added, "But no. It is entirely up to you whether you come or not. If you do, I promise we will figure out how to get Margot away from Evard."

She started to shake her head again but then stood taller. "Okay."

"Okay?"

She nodded. "I'll come with you to Fort Braemar."

CHAPTER SEVEN

NEA

As the turreted towers, which rose like thick fingers from the grey stone walls of Fort Braemar, came into view, the horses' gaits changed from the steady roll they had been to a clipped pace. Nea held her mount back as she looked up at the gate of the fort; once she rode through that stone arch, there was really no turning back. She twisted in the saddle. The road behind them was open, beckoning her, and she wondered how quickly Garret would catch her if she bolted now. But Evard had Margot. Fear slid down her spine and she turned back to face the fort. Garret was a short distance away watching her. His grey eyes were as unreadable as the stoic set of his mouth. It was a look she'd gotten used to over the past couple of days.

She touched her horse's sides with her heels and it started forward again. Was that relief that fleeted across Garret's face?

"You were worried I would run?"

He tilted his head as though he was about to shake it. "If you were going to run, you've had better openings than just now." He reached out and took hold of her horse's reins as she drew level with him, tugging them to halt the animal. "Before we go in ..." He looked at the ground and his shoulders dipped almost imperceptibly.

"Is it about Declan?"

His head snapped up and the look in his grey eyes reminded her of the last time she'd seen—no, she couldn't go there, couldn't think of that time before Kalhanna.

"You need to tell them but you're dreading the moment because it means admitting that he's actually gone." People often danced around the announcement, like saying the words out loud snatched away the rickety bridge over their chasm of grief. Like it made the truth real and inescapable.

"That is a surprisingly accurate assumption."

"In case you hadn't noticed, I am a necromancer. Death and grief are kind of my bread and butter."

That got her a smile. A small one, but also a real one. Not the hollow representation she'd seen him give Emil when he'd been trying to cheer him up.

"I'd tell you it gets easier, but I am fairly certain you already know that and don't actually want to hear it right now." She ran a hand through her hair. "Don't overanalyse it too much. Just get it out and done and then move on." She realised how that sounded and added, "As callous as that sounds, it is the best way. It is always going to be a shock and no amount of pretty words and delicate phrasing is going to make it better."

He stared at her.

"What? You wanted my opinion and I gave it. Did you not actually want my opinion?"

"I appreciate your insight and yes, I did want your opinion. I just didn't realise it would be so ..."

"Blunt?"

He rubbed the scar that marked his top lip. "That's one way to put it."

"Nonna often says I have as much tact as a hammer."

He chuckled and nudged his horse forward. "We probably shouldn't keep the others waiting any longer."

She guided her horse to follow his and they rode under the arch and into the courtyard of the fort. Leon and Emil were nowhere to be seen but there were two men waiting. Well, a man and boy, who looked a similar age to Rhett. The man had a leather apron over his blue shirt, and he stepped forward to take the reins of Garret's horse as he dismounted.

As Nea slid from her mount's back, her knees wobbled and she had to grab the saddle for support. The gelding turned his head and nudged her thigh as she pressed her forehead against the saddle and drew a deep breath.

"I can take him for you."

She nearly jumped out of her skin.

The boy stepped up beside her. "Sorry, I didn't mean to startle you," he said.

"It's alright. It's been a long ride, and I didn't realise how tired I was."

"I'm Thomas, by the way, if you can't find Harry." He indicated the man talking to Garret.

"Ah, thank you."

He nodded and took the reins of her horse before leading him away towards the stable.

Garret finished talking to Harry and as the stable master led his bay mare away, he waved Nea over and then guided her into the fort.

Nea sat in the parlour, waiting for Garret, who was in the library talking with the lord of the fort, Alric. Alric was a bear of a man with red cheeks and watery blue eyes, who had given Nea a curious once-over before ushering Garret away to talk business. What business, Nea had no idea.

As far as rooms went, the parlour was grand, with polished floors and lead glass windows. Firelight danced across the coloured glass and reflected onto the heavy tapestries that hung in every available space. Nea stood and wandered over to examine one of the tapestries.

The Bright Mother smiled serenely down at her, her silver hair cascading in a shining sheet over her outstretched arms and bare breasts. A stream of golden water flowed from the palm of her right hand, twisting around the small group of humans below. From her left hand, a red ribbon of blood dripped onto a lone figure with ash-grey hair and shadowed features. Nea knew this scene; legend had it that the Bright Mother bestowed gifts on the brightest of her followers, creating the first mages. But light could not exist without dark, and so she took her most beloved follower and gave them seven drops of her own blood, bestowing the knowledge of death and darkness, trusting them to wield the gift without becoming corrupted.

Nea lifted her hand to touch the expertly woven cloth when the door opened and a small-framed blonde woman came barrelling in. She skidded to a halt when she spotted Nea, her mouth forming a small 'O' of shock before her cornflower blue eyes narrowed and a dark look flicked through them. "So, you do exist."

"I'm sorry?" Nea glanced towards the door Garret and Alric had gone through.

"I was expecting—actually, I have no idea what I was expecting. What are you doing here? Everyone seemed to think you'd go running off to save Margot from Evard."

This must be the Molly Emil had mentioned. "I ..."

Emil came through the same door Molly had and stopped when he saw them both. "Oh, so you've met then."

They both turned to him and Nea said, "Not officially."

"Ah." Emil rubbed the back of his neck. "Molly, Nea. Nea, Molly."

Molly drew a breath. "Do you know if Garret has had any word from the capital? Or Declan?"

Emil stiffened. "No. No word from the capital, as far as I know. And Declan ... Molly, Declan ..."

"What?"

Emil gave Nea a pained look.

"He's dead," she said, not unkindly.

"Declan's ... dead?" Molly's knees buckled, and Emil reached out to comfort her, but she shook him off and rounded on Nea. "This is all your fault!"

Nea blinked. "Excuse me?"

She thrust her finger out, prodding Nea in the chest and forcing her to take a step back. "If Garret didn't have to go traipsing across the countryside looking for *you* then none of this would have happened. Margot wouldn't have gotten taken, and Declan would be—he'd be—"

"Molly, that's enough." Garret's tone was stern. They all turned to him, and Molly stepped back from Nea.

"I am sorry, Molly. I know Declan meant a lot to everyone." She met Garret's eyes before switching her gaze to the other woman. "But his death was not my fault."

"And what about Margot?" Molly asked.

Nea flinched.

"Molly." Garret's voice was almost a growl.

Molly huffed and put her hands on her hips. "I'm not going to apologise. She is the reason Evard has Margot, and she has yet to prove she is worth the trouble it was to find her."

"We're not discussing this now."

"Right you are, Garret." Alric emerged from the doorway behind Garret. "I imagine Maurice has the meal all but ready. Why don't we have our guest seen to her room so she can freshen up? I'll send for Charles." He clapped his hands together.

"That is not necessary. Molly can take her."

"What?!" Molly and Nea said together.

"Garret, I don't think that's the best idea right now," Emil said carefully. "I can show Nea to her room."

Garret folded his arms over his chest and said, "Blue room, second floor." He glanced at Alric, who nodded to confirm.

"No problem. Come on, Nea," Emil said as he touched the small of her back to guide her from the room. They were barely out the door when they heard Molly and Garret's raised voices.

Emil led her slowly through the fort. As they passed a darkened hallway, Emil quickened his steps and kept his eyes straight ahead. Nea paused. Something was moving in the dark. It slithered around a doorframe and she felt the hairs on her neck rise.

"Nea, don't go down there."

She blinked at the darkness closing in around her and turned to find Emil—the hallway stretched between them. When had that happened? What had compelled her to wander so far into the dark? She shook her head to distil the torpor that had coiled into her thoughts and rejoined Emil.

He placed a hand lightly on her shoulder and guided her away from the hall. "The south wing is off limits."

"Why? What's down there?"

"Amelia."

Why was that name familiar? "Who is Amelia?"

Emil pressed a finger to his lips and took a long breath before responding. "Garret can explain about Amelia later. Just don't go into the south wing. In fact, stay as far away as possible." He continued down the hallway and Nea followed after him, but not before throwing another glance at the darkened wing.

Nea was so focused on trying to remember where she had heard the name Amelia before that she didn't realise they had arrived at her room until she collided with Emil. "Sorry." She took a step back.

"This is the room." He indicated the door through which a maid was exiting, carrying a basket of linen. "Garret is there." He pointed at the door across from Nea's room. "Molly and I are at the other end of this hall."

"Is this the necromancer?"

Emil stiffened before he turned to face the woman, who was now standing behind them.

Both she and the maid standing beside her looked close to Nea in age, though there were thin lines at the corners of the lady's amber eyes. The yellow gown she was wearing matched the thick ribbon which secured her brown hair in an elegant roll at the nape of her long neck. Curiosity glinted in her eyes as she watched Nea, one hand resting on the gentle swell of her pregnancy, the other playing idly with the Bright Mother's eight-pointed star pendant that hung around her neck.

"Lady Vera," Emil said before swallowing. "Yes, this is Nea."

"A pleasure to meet you, Lady Vera." Nea held her hand out but Vera ignored it.

"You'll want to clean yourself up before dinner. Do you have anything else to wear?" Her eyes scanned Nea's tunic.

"I have another tunic."

Vera did not look impressed. "I'll have my maids fetch you something more appropriate and a basin to wash in." She tilted her head at the maid beside her, who dipped into a curtsey and dashed away. "I look forward to getting to know you at dinner." She nodded and left, leaving Emil and Nea alone again.

Emil shifted his weight from one foot to another. "Look, Nea ..." He rubbed the back of his neck. "I am really sorry about snapping at you in the Cow. You didn't deserve to be told about Margot like that."

She frowned. "It's fine, Emil. I'm not sure Garret would have told me the truth if you hadn't."

He continued to rub his neck, glancing at the door to Garret's room. "It's hard to tell with Garret. He's a good commander, but ..."

"But?"

"Nothing. I should let you get settled." He ushered her into the room, then turned on his heel and started away down the hall.

Nea stepped through the doorway and crossed to the bed. She dropped her satchel onto it before turning to examine the room. It was a modest space with a desk in the corner, covered in books and rolls of parchment. A series of vials on the bookshelf above the desk contained a rainbow of liquids, small floating pieces of plant matter, and—was that a finger?

She shook her head and dug in her satchel for her second tunic. She frowned as she unfolded it and held it up, it was in no better state than the threadbare one she was wearing. The holes and runs scattered across the cloth suggested it was better suited to polishing furniture than clothing a body. And the blue fabric was stained with murky patches where she had scrubbed until her fingers ached, trying to get the blood out. She really needed to stop using her hemline to clean her hands. Her pants were not much better; they too bore the stains of wiped-on grime. The dead never complained about the state of her clothes though.

A gentle knock announced the return of the maids. One placed a basin of water on the stand in the corner and the other deposited a pile of clothes on the bed before they both smiled and backed out of the room.

One paused to say, "If you need anything, pull the bell." She indicated the wide embroidered ribbon hanging beside the bed. "I'll leave you to get dressed." Then she dipped her head and shut the door.

Nea stripped to her slip and drawers and moved to the basin. She tested the temperature of the water before splashing it on her face and sighing as the grime from the road melted away.

"Well then, this is a surprise."

Nea jumped, splashing water onto the floor as a voice sounded behind her.

"Can't say I mind the view though."

Nea turned to find Declan appraising her from his perch on the bed. "What are *you* doing here?"

"Your guess is as good as mine. Could be something to do with the communication spell. I did tell you it was untested." He leant back on his elbows. "You are developing a habit of sleeping in my bed."

"Your bed?"

"This was my room."

Nea opened then closed her mouth. "I ..." She sighed. "Any ideas how I can get rid of you?"

His look of hurt was ruined by his lopsided grin. "You're the necromancer; restless souls are your department."

Nea crossed her arms. "During the—what did you call it—communication spell? You were corporeal. Are you now?"

"You tell me." He threw his arms wide with a suggestive smile.

Nea rolled her eyes.

"Can't blame me for trying. I can see why Garret is so torn about sending you off to Evard; useful and easy on the eyes. I always did have a thing for you grey-hairs." He stood and moved over to where she was standing. "Well?" He spread his arms again.

Nea huffed and lifted her hands to give his chest a shove but they went right through him, a cold tingle running over her skin where it made contact with his form.

He frowned. "Can't win them all I guess. You could try sending me again." He watched her as she moved to the bed and snatched up the shawl from Emma. She wrapped the soft green fabric around her shoulders and crossed her arms over her chest.

"I honestly don't think it will work. Each time I've tried there has been this resistance." She rolled her lip between her teeth. "I think somehow you've managed to jam yourself right between the worlds." She glanced at his desk. "It is almost like the effect created by a spirit-glass. Though it appears a lot more long-term. And, well, you don't exactly have a corporeal body to return to, so ..."

Declan was watching her with a sly smile.

"What?"

"Nothing, just enjoying watching you think. You do this thing with your mouth. It's almost endearing."

She tightened the shawl and gestured at the desk. "What were you doing here?"

He frowned and moved to the desk, resting his hands along the edge of it. "Curing corruption, or trying to, at least. Mostly I was just coming up against a whole lot of dead ends."

"Curing corruption? That's a rather ambitious goal."

He glanced at her out of the corner of his eye, a sad smile touching his mouth. "Someone had to try. Would you mind doing me a favour? Since you can actually manipulate the physical world and all."

"Depends on the favour."

He chuckled. "I just want you to give something to Garret for me." He pointed to the top drawer. "There's a letter for him in there. I wrote it before I left ... just in case."

Nea moved over and opened the drawer. She picked up the neatly folded packet of parchment. It felt heavy like it contained something more than a letter.

"Goodness, I would have thought you'd be dressed already. The others are waiting."

Startled, Nea turned to face the maid who had just entered the room. She glanced around for Declan, but he was gone.

"Sorry. I must have gotten side-tracked."

"I told them to fix this mess." The maid bustled over and reached for the clutter on the desk.

"No, leave it please." It felt wrong for the maid to disturb Declan's things. "I can fix it later."

The maid settled her hands on her hips and eyed the letter in Nea's hand. "Would you like me to have that sent out for you?"

"No." Nea held the letter to her chest. "How about you just help me get dressed for dinner and show me to the dining room? I'm not sure where it is."

✲

Sometime in the middle of the night, Nea was woken by someone calling her name. She rose slowly and listened but there was nothing stirring in the darkness. Sliding from the bed, she pulled Emma's shawl around her shoulders and moved to the door. She leant out into the hallway and listened again. Nothing.

There was a gentle pool of light coming from under Garret's door but no sounds, and certainly no one in sight. With a shiver, Nea turned to go back to bed but heard it again: a sing-song whisper and the subtle tug of magic at the back of her mind.

She tiptoed down the hall, following the thin string of channelled source, the rush of her own blood in her ears drowning out everything else like she had her head underwater.

When she reached the hall that led to the south wing, she stopped. She drew a slow breath as she watched the shadows, waiting. Then she heard it: the tiniest whispered "Nea ..." and a soft whimper like that of a child. She lifted her foot to step forward, but something closed around her arm and dragged her backwards.

"What are you doing?" Garret put himself between her and the dark hallway. His hair was standing on end, like he'd been running his fingers through it, and his shirt was rumpled, as though he had pulled it on in a hurry.

"I couldn't sleep." She tried to edge around him, but he put his arm out to block her path.

"Emil assured me he had warned you about the south wing." He glanced over his shoulder at the pooling darkness.

"He did, bu—"

"But what? You thought you'd go poking around in there regardless?" He took a step, closing the space between them and forcing Nea backwards.

Nea lifted her hands in defeat. "I heard something, saw something. What's down there?"

A muscle in Garret's neck twitched as his jaw tensed. "Nothing of consequence."

"Really? Because—"

"Neeee-aa." A sing-song voice drifted from the darkness and Garret turned, pulling Nea behind him and out of sight.

"You're no fun, Garret. Let the little mage come and play. She smells ever so sweet."

"Back to your room, Nea." He took another step backwards, pushing Nea farther away from the wing.

As they moved, she caught sight of the waifish shape of a girl pacing the end of the hallway. Where her bare toes met the wooden floor, a line of rune marks shone in the moonlight. The magic signature was one she knew all too well; it was her father's. She lifted her gaze and met the ice-blue eyes of the girl. *Amelia.* A darting pink tongue chased a wicked smile over pallid lips before they drew back to show sharp, impossibly white teeth. The neckline of her nightgown was askew, revealing one very pale shoulder and a small flower-shaped purple birthmark marring the flesh just below the corner of her collarbone. She lifted her hand and curled one finger in Nea's direction, causing the lank ribbons of her black hair to move over that exposed shoulder like snakes.

Nea felt the hooks of magic digging into her mind and some deep part of her called out in caution. But it was too late. The sticky fingers of the Amelia's keen were past her defences. She twisted around Garret, ducking under his arm and lashing out with her magic when he made another grab for her. He froze as she pressed down against his soul, pinning him in place.

Amelia's wicked smile widened, the sleeves of her filthy nightgown fluttering as she beckoned Nea forward in earnest.

"Nea? Is that you?" A voice from the dark, bright and unmistakable. *Margot.* Pain sliced Nea's chest and she stepped forward.

"Wouldn't you like to know how to save her? Or how to bring them all back? The ones from Kalhanna? Dhen, Francesca, Tobias? I could show you. After all, we're *sisters,* you and I." Amelia leant forward, the rune marks the only thing holding her at bay.

"Where are you, Nea?" Margot's voice sounded again from the darkness.

Nea moved forward. Her eyes locked with Amelia's cold gaze. A triumphant "yes" hissed from the girl's lips as she closed the trap, ensnaring Nea.

"Nea, stop!" Declan appeared in front of her and Amelia hissed, but Nea stepped right through him and across the rune marks on the floor.

"That's it. Come to me."

Bone-numbing cold raced along Nea's arm as Amelia's fingers closed around her wrist.

"I've been waiting for someone like you for ever so long." She pulled Nea farther past the rune marks.

The cold fanned out across Nea's chest, icy fingers coiling around her heart. She inhaled deeply, her breath stirring the air in a white cloud, her eyes suddenly heavy-lidded.

A searing heat erupted around her waist, bringing her crashing back to reality. Amelia shrieked and tightened her grasp as Nea was dragged away.

"No! She's mine!" She dug her heels into the floor, savagely tearing at Nea's arm.

"Nea, let go!" Garret's voice growled in her ear. His chest heaved against her back, little sparks of fire bursting along her skin where their bodies met.

Nea looked at her hand, then at the sunken eyes of the other girl, realising through the thick fog of her mind what had happened. What she had been about to do. She flicked her wrist, wrenching it from the cold-fingered grasp. Amelia's long nails tore through her flesh as Garret stumbled backwards, taking her over the rune marks.

Garret's arms were tight around her waist as the weight of his suppression pressed on her, blocking her connection to the source and dulling her own keen. Amelia hissed and shrieked behind the rune marks but made no further attempts to lure Nea back across the barrier.

After a few moments, Garret released both his grip and the pressure of his suppression. "What did you think you were doing? I honestly didn't think you'd be that stupid!" he ground out between clenched teeth as he got to his feet, then held out a hand to help her up.

"Maybe you should have given me a proper warning instead of having Emil do it." She thrust her arms in the air and started towards her room.

He made a disgruntled noise and fell in step beside her.

Once they reached her room, he said, "I trust you won't go near the south wing without an escort again."

She didn't respond, just stepped through the door and closed it.

"Stupid ... stupid," she whispered as she sat with her back against the door. She closed her eyes and let her head fall heavily against the wood.

The floor outside her room creaked and there was a soft thump on the other side of the door as Garret let his breath out in a huff. So he didn't actually trust her not to go wandering again then? She shook her head and conjured a mage light into existence. The lilac ball of light hovered beside her, allowing her to inspect the long scratches on her wrist. They stung but there appeared to be no lasting damage. Cradling the wrist to her chest, she leant her head against the wood again. "I know you're there."

He let out another huff.

"That was Amelia, wasn't it? Who was she?"

He was quiet for so long that Nea had started to get up to go back to bed when he said, "Alric's sister."

"She's dead."

"I know." He cleared his throat and Nea stood to open the door.

As the door shifted, Garret turned and frowned up at her.

"How did she die?"

He got slowly to his feet. "You really want to know? You want to sit here in the middle of the night and talk about Amelia?"

"Yes." Nea moved and sat on the bed but Garret still hovered in the doorway.

"Why?"

"Because I want to know why she's still here and why my father bound her to that hallway."

"Your father?"

"Niall of Del Harol. His magic is all over the south wing. It must have been some time ago though. As far as I am aware, he hasn't left the college in over a decade"

Recognition shone in his eyes for a moment. "I don't know all the details. But I do know that Amelia was the eldest and only surviving child from Alric's father's second wife who was apparently a necromancer."

Nea's eyebrows lifted. "I don't remember anyone from Hartswood marrying a lord?"

Garret shrugged. "It was some time ago."

"So, I am guessing Amelia died and her mother reanimated her."

He nodded. "They say her grief all but destroyed her and she resorted to the unthinkable."

"Even in grief, most necromancers wouldn't choose reanimation. It's forbidden for a reason." She rolled her lip between her teeth. "Wait, if Amelia's mother was a necromancer, was Amelia one as well?"

The muscle in his jaw tightened. "Not that anyone was aware of. When it was clear that whatever her mother had done had twisted Amelia into what you saw, they called Niall to come and destroy her. But it didn't prove that easy. So he imprisoned her instead." He had moved to Declan's desk as he spoke and was staring at the clutter.

"She couldn't be destroyed?" Nea tapped her chin. "What happened to Amelia's mother?"

Garret bit the inside of his cheek and turned to face her. "She was corrupted."

Nea frowned. "It is very rare for a necromancer to become corrupted."

He shifted his attention to her arm. "Is that arm okay?"

"Just a few scratches. It will be fine." She rubbed her fingers together to dispel the cold that had worked into her bones.

"There was a rumour that Amelia gave another mage corruption."

"That's not how corruption works." She looked at her arm again but the skin around the scratches was smooth and pale.

"So we all thought, but De ..." He scratched the stubble along his jaw. "Just keep an eye on it." He cleared his throat. "I have some business to attend to tomorrow morning but if you find me later in the afternoon, we can discuss what to do about Margot." There was a finality to his tone and he started to leave the room.

"Com—Garret, wait." Nea retrieved Declan's letter and held it out. "I found this in the desk drawer earlier."

Garret stared at the letter and ran his hand through his hair before taking it. "Thank you." He then exited the room, pausing to say, "Good night, Nea," before closing the door gently.

She shook her head as she heard him take up position on the other side of the door again. So, he *still* wasn't going to trust her not to leave the room. Not that she had any mind to. Amelia had caught her off guard and managed to dig her hooks into old wounds. She wouldn't let it happen again.

Nea settled back on the bed and extinguished the mage light. Then she lay there in the dark, her thoughts churning.

The sun was already high when Nea awoke. She rubbed a hand over her face and groaned. Last night had not been one of her brightest moments. Amelia had played on her emotions and there was something about the magic she had used, something familiar.

She lifted her wrist to inspect the damage; angry purple scratches marked her skin. Angry purple scratches from the edges of which radiated thin veins of black, like lacey spiderwebs. She bit her lip. *Amelia gave another mage corruption.* It certainly looked like corruption, but Nea had never seen it start with a wound. Corruption usually came up as a fan of black veins on the back of a mage's hands and, as she had told Garret last night, necromancers were mostly immune. Or so she had always been told.

She shivered and moved to her satchel, digging until she found the cure-all ointment Margot had made for her. She opened the jar and frowned at the scant amount left.

After taking a small layer of the ointment on her fingers, she rubbed it over her scratches and sucked a breath through her teeth as her skin burned. A thin stream of black smoke rose from the welts as they slowly coloured from purple to pink and then vanished completely. The skin of her wrist was smooth once more. She wiggled her fingers.

"Good as new." *It couldn't have been corruption, could it?*

Blocking out the hum of fear that had risen in the back of her mind, she sorted through the pile of borrowed clothes and picked out a grey woollen dress. She pulled it on then, wrapping the shawl from Emma around her shoulders, she left in search of something to quell the rising growl in her stomach.

Taking the long way around to avoid the hallway that led to the south wing, she made her way to the kitchen and peeked her head in the door. The cook, who had been introduced after dinner last night, was the only one there, his lean arms bare to the elbows as he kneaded a large ball of dough. He lifted a flour-dusted face to give her a smile as she entered.

"Hello, it's Maurice, isn't it? I'm Nea. I missed breakfast and was hoping there might be something to tide me over until later."

"There are some fresh rolls over there. Careful, they're still a bit hot. Cheese is there and if you look in the back of that shelf, you'll find some rosehip jam. It's Lady Vera's favourite." He pointed to each item in turn while his other hand kept the dough moving. "They told me the commander had found you. I'm a bit curious that he didn't have you taken straight to the king."

Nea fumbled the roll she had been holding but managed to catch it before it hit the ground. She blinked at Maurice, who was studying her with calm indifference. "Do you know why Evard wants me?" She placed the roll down and moved to get the jam.

"I'm but a humble cook. I could never guess the motive of a king."

Nea's eyes narrowed slightly. "Indeed." She smeared some of the jam on her bread and took a bite.

"There are rumours, of course. You two have a history and it's not necessarily a friendly one. After all, *rumour* has it you're the one who caused him to burn a college to the ground in a fit of rage."

Nea's hunger suddenly fled and she stared at Maurice.

"Can't believe everything you hear though, can you?" He was focused on the dough again, no malice in his demeanour despite his words.

Bile rose in Nea's throat as she was dragged back to Kalhanna. *Tobias was emerging from the main gate, his arms wide to greet her when an arrow thudded into his chest, stopping him in his tracks. Red bloomed on the front of his yellow tunic. Nea rushed forward and tried to help him back inside the college, but before they had reached the gate, another two arrows found his back and he fell from her grasp. Bells sounded, and the trees lining the road that led to the college erupted into flames as the mages roused themselves to the fight. Men and horses screamed, running from the trees, bodies aflame. The acrid scent of burning hair and flesh filled the air. Nea ran into the courtyard rubbing Tobias's blood on the hem of her tunic and almost tripping over her own feet.*

Francesca stood at the top of the stairs, yelling orders at the mages as they scurried like ants from the various outbuildings. She spotted Nea and waved her towards the great staircase with a shout. Then came the trebuchet. Balls of burning peat and stone rained down on the college, setting the buildings alight and crushing those unlucky enough to be hit directly. Dhen rushed to save the horses still in the stables as a group of green-clothed knights came into the yard—

The dough thudded onto the bench and Nea gave a startled flinch as she was snapped back to the Braemar kitchens.

"Yes, nasty business that. All those lives. Mostly healers, weren't they?" There was a coldness in his eyes that made Nea take a step back.

Her lips felt numb and she looked at the piece of bread still in her hand, the deep pink jam shining benignly in the light. She threw it on the bench before taking another step backwards. Her eyes were losing focus and her tongue felt thick. On instinct, she tried to channel the source but it barely responded, like it was too far away and floating farther with each passing minute.

She took another step back, shaking her head to try and clear the fog when she came up against a hard chest. Tight hands closed around her arms and she thrust her head back, the movement causing a wave of nausea to run through her. The man growled as her skull connected with his face and then something cold snapped around her wrist. She blinked at the band of pinkish-gold metal and another wave of nausea washed over her. The constant thrum of the source that was like the beating of her own heart was suddenly muffled. It died completely as the second shackle closed and she was whirled around to face her attacker.

Leon gloated through the blood oozing from his nose.

If her tongue didn't feel so thick she could call out, scream, anything to draw attention; as though sensing her thoughts, Leon scowled. "That wouldn't be advisable." He nodded to Maurice, who held a cup of sweet-smelling liquid. "You know what an overdose of mage bane does to the body, I take it? Make a sound and I will force it down your throat."

Nea bit her lip and eyed the cup. "What do you want?" The words slurred over her tongue and her knees gave way.

"You have a meeting with the king. One that is long overdue." He brought his fist hard against the side of her head. Her vision doubled for a moment then went completely black.

CHAPTER EIGHT

GARRET

Garret wasn't really listening to Emil as they guided their horses along the forest path. His finger stroked the edge of the letter in his pocket. He hadn't opened it yet and wasn't sure he wanted to. Somehow reading Declan's last letter would make it all the more real. Which was ridiculous. Declan was ... dead. He'd seen it himself and yet there was this knot deep inside him that refused to accept it. It kept telling him that Declan would come swanning through the door with some exciting revelation he just had to discuss at any moment.

"Garret?"

He looked up as Emil said his name and rubbed the back of his neck. He'd fallen asleep in the hallway, making sure Nea didn't go wandering and confront Amelia again, and he was paying for it. "I'm sorry, Emil. Can you repeat that?"

Emil's mouth quirked at the corner. "It's not really important. Are you sure you're up to this today? You look kind of like something my old cat would have spat out."

Garret nodded. "Yes, let's get this done. I told Nea we would start working out a plan to rescue Margot later this afternoon."

"So, you've decided you trust her?"

"I don't know that I would say I trust her, but I am getting the sense that it is better to work with, rather than against her." He rolled his shoulders as he remembered the press of her keen. It had been like she had hold of his very soul and he was nothing more than a puppet.

Emil chuckled. "That sounds about right." He sobered, his amber eyes appraising Garret. "You know if you'd like to head back to the fort, I can do this alone. It's just an information exchange, right?"

Garret let out an exasperated sigh. "You fuss more than a mother hen at times, Emil. Yes, I am tired. But I need to be moving right now. I have to return to Evard soon and I want to make sure everything here is organised." Just in case this was the time Evard grew tired of his excuses and decided Garret was expendable after all. If he took Nea with him, most of Evard's doubts about him would be absolved. But she had come to the fort with him in good faith, trusting him to help her free Margot. If he broke that promise, what sort of person did that make him? Of all the things he had done for Evard, handing Nea over seemed like the point of no return.

"Garret!"

"Sorry."

"Your head really isn't on straight today, is it?"

Garret rubbed his forehead before dropping his hand to his pocket and touching the letter again. "It—" His fingers brushed Nea's bracelet. Its energy felt erratic, fluttering out in icy spikes that stabbed his fingertips and closed around his throat.

"What's wrong?"

He drew the bracelet out and stared at it. The energy spiked again, the bracelet vibrating against his palm, and then it went still. A stone formed in the pit of his stomach as the amethyst roses glinted softly in the dappled light. There was nothing coming from it. No comforting coolness, no gentle, throbbing heartbeat. Nothing.

"Garret?" Emil reached across the distance between them and shook Garret's knee. "Talk to me. What's going on?"

As Garret wheeled his horse around to face the path that led to the fort, a flock of starlings took flight. "Go on ahead. I just need to check on something." He prodded his horse's sides and she surged forward, darting through the trees with ease as Garret let her have her head.

Emil shouted something behind him but it was lost to the wind.

Garret slowed his horse just inside the gate and the young stable hand's head snapped up. He dropped the piece of tack he was oiling and tucked his rag into the pocket of his apron before moving to grab the reins of Garret's horse.

"Thank you, Thomas." Garret glanced around the courtyard and seeing nothing out of the ordinary, headed towards the fort.

Molly came down the steps, stopping short when she saw him. "You're not due back yet. Has something happened? Where's Emil?"

"Have you seen Nea?"

She tilted her head. "A while ago. She looked like she was heading to the kitchens. Why?"

Garret nodded and stepped around her to head up the steps into the fort.

"Garret, what is going on?" Molly leapt into his path and placed her palm in the centre of his chest. "What happened?"

"Nothing."

She put her hands on her hips and her blue eyes darkened as she stared him down.

"This is acting strange." He pulled the bracelet out and held it up for her to see. "And I have a bad feeling."

Molly's mouth twisted. "The enchantment is probably just wearing off. And, Garret, since when do *you* listen to bad feelings over common sense?"

He tucked the bracelet back into his pocket. He couldn't explain the feeling he got before the enchantment on the bracelet went dead—it was almost like raw panic.

Molly was right though. He let his breath out in a huff. Since Declan's death, he hadn't felt right. He needed to stop dwelling on that and get his head straight.

Still, it couldn't hurt to check on Nea. What if she'd decided not to wait and had taken off for the capital to get Margot?

"Look, if it makes you feel better, I'll go ask Maurice about Nea."

He shook his head. "I can do that but maybe you can check her room."

Molly sighed but nodded. "Okay."

Garret continued to the kitchens.

When he arrived, Maurice was taking a break, his feet up on a barrel as he rocked back on his chair. He had a cup in his hands and, knowing Maurice, it most likely contained rum. He lifted it by way of greeting when Garret came into the room but didn't make any move to get up. "Can I help you, Commander?"

"Molly said she saw Nea come in here earlier."

Maurice looked into his cup then downed whatever was left in one go. "The necromancer? Yeah, she came in looking for a bite to eat. I fixed her up and she went on her way again."

"How did she seem to you?"

Maurice shrugged, took his feet off the barrel, and let his chair drop forward so it was on all four legs again. "Normal, I guess. It was the first time I'd met her, so I can't really say though."

"Did she happen to mention where she was going?"

Maurice pushed himself to his feet. "No, she didn't, and I didn't ask. It's not my job to keep track of random mages, Commander. It's yours. Now, if you don't mind, there are an awful lot of mouths to keep fed these days." He lifted his hand to indicate the door, but Garret didn't move. "Something else you need?"

Garret shook his head and they both turned to Molly as she entered.

"She wasn't in her room, but her things are still there."

"See, Commander? She can't have gone far."

"Thank you for your help, Maurice." Garret left the kitchen and Molly followed him.

"Maurice is right; she can't have gone far. Maybe Leon has seen her."

Leon. Garret rocked back on his heel. "Do you know where he is now?"

She shook her head. "He was in the library earlier. I have no idea why—he doesn't really seem the reading type."

Garret hurried to the library but there was no one there. He rubbed the back of his neck. If Leon had taken Nea then he would have had to get her out the gate past Thomas and Harry. He turned to head for the stables, nearly running into Molly, who was still on his heels.

"Where are you going now?"

"The stables."

"You think Leon took her? Why would he do that—never mind. He would definitely do that." She paled. "Wait. If Leon plans to hand Nea over to Evard, what does that mean for Margot? Shit. Garret, we have to find her." Molly spun around and ran ahead of him to the stables.

"Thomas!" Molly yelled as they got closer. "Have you seen Leon?"

"Not today, Molly." Thomas smiled brightly at her. "His horse is in the second pasture. He told me yesterday he wouldn't be needing it."

"Thank you." She turned to face Garret again. "So, if he did take Nea and he didn't use this gate, how did he get her out? Maybe we're panicking for no reason." He gave her a look and her face fell. "Okay, maybe not."

"We didn't expect you back so soon, Commander."

Garret hid his shock and turned to face Leon as he approached.

Molly gave Garret a confused look before saying, "I'll go and check the house for Nea again. Maybe she got lost in one of the wings."

"You've misplaced the necromancer?" Smug was the only way to describe the look on Leon's face. "This wouldn't have happened if you'd listened to my advice and taken her straight to the king. Oh, my. What will he say when he learns you had her in your grasp only to lose her again?"

Garret's jaw tightened. One of these days, he was going to enjoy punching that look off Leon's face. "You haven't seen her, have you?"

"Briefly this morning." He straightened the cuffs of his shirt. "You did warn her about the south wing, didn't you? Hopefully she hasn't found herself lost down there."

"Yes, she was warned about the south wing." She wouldn't have gone back after last night surely. Still, it wouldn't hurt to check. He turned away from Leon.

"I do hope you find her unharmed, Commander. After all, I would hate to have to explain to the king why she died in your custody when he was so *adamant* she be brought in alive."

Garret ignored the taunt and walked away with Leon's goading gaze burning his back. Once inside and well away from Leon, he picked up his pace until he rounded the corner into the hallway that led to the south wing.

He stared into the darkness. "Amelia."

She appeared, her long limbs ghostly white in the gloom. Her head tilted as she regarded him and her tongue traced the seam of her lips. "Garret," she purred his name. "You came to see me again. And alone this time. No sharp-tongued storm mage or doe-eyed necromancer." She leant as far forward as she could before the rune marks on the floor flared to life. "I will admit though, *she* was delightful." She ran her tongue along her fingertips.

"She—"

"Is why you're here?" Amelia pouted. "I wish I could say I had seen her, but after you so cruelly snatched her away from me, she has been much more careful about keeping that delightfully broken mind of hers closed. Do you know how much wickedness dwells behind that pretty face? How much potential for darkness?" She ran her hands down the front of her nightgown, pushing the fabric between her thighs, her lips pulling into a gleeful smile. "A perfect vessel for the Master's will, shame she's so morally obstinate. That will change though … She just needs the right *incentive*."

"So you haven't seen her." He started to leave. He didn't have time for Amelia's twisted ramblings.

"No, I haven't seen her, but I *felt* her."

"You *felt* her?" He turned to face her again.

"You did too." Her gaze rolled over the pocket where he kept the bracelet. "Something terrible must have occurred for her keen to spike so savagely."

"This is pointless." He shook his head and left, Amelia's stare burning his shoulders until he turned the corner.

Wind howled and lightning flashed behind the shuttered windows as the spring storm that had hampered their efforts to search for Nea raged outside. When Emil returned, they had searched the entire fort again, but it was as if Nea had simply vanished. There had been no trace of her keen to be found anywhere, then the storm had blown up and tracking her with Alric's hounds had proven nearly impossible. So they had retreated inside to wait the storm out and reconsider their options.

Alric sat at the head of the table, one hand resting on his stomach, the other lifted as he picked the remnants of the meal from his teeth.

Garret had barely touched his food, his churning thoughts chasing away any hunger.

"I don't think Nea would have run off." Emil had said it that many times it was almost like he was trying to convince himself. "I mean, she left all her things here. Surely—"

"A ruse. So we would waste time searching the fort for her and give her a chance to get away." Leon swirled the wine in his cup and sniffed it before taking a sip. "If everyone had just listened to me when we found her in Little Brook, we would not be in this predicament now."

"I hate to say it, but I agree with Leon." Molly scrunched her nose up. "I don't know why you trusted her not to run, Garret, given what we know about her."

Garret rubbed the middle of his forehead. It didn't make sense that Nea would leave her things behind if she really was running again. *Her entire world exists in that satchel of hers.* That was what the seer had said. If it was so important to her, why would she leave it?

"Well, all of this talking in circles isn't going to solve the problem. Perhaps it is time we all went to bed. I can send Harry out with the hounds again in the morning. Hopefully the storm hasn't washed away all traces of her. And Charles can go make enquiries in the village." Alric stood, leaning heavily on the table, his eyes drooping more than usual.

The others looked as tired as Alric; they all murmured goodnight and slowly filed out, leaving Garret alone with his thoughts. He dug the letter from Declan out of his pocket and opened it.

Something fell out and he caught it before it hit the table. A gentle coil of magic clung to the item like oil on water, and as he rolled it over in his fingers, he let out a tired chuckle.

It was a smooth grey stone with a neat hole in the centre. He remembered the day he had found it on the beach below the tower at Loch Bastien. Declan had been convinced it was some relic from a bygone era and had offered to do Garret's chores for a whole week in trade for it. Garret would have given it to him anyway but watching Declan oil down Warden Commander Fergus's ceremonial armour had been entertaining. He rubbed the smooth surface of the stone as he read the letter.

Garret,

If you are reading this, I am no longer with you. Bright Mother's tits, that is a stupid way to start a letter.

Let me try that again. I am sorry to say that I have died. Valiantly, I hope.

Several more attempts were scratched out and Garret felt a warm smile tugging at the corners of his mouth.

Right, well, this has been a shit attempt at a last goodbye. Don't blame yourself for whatever happened. We both knew my smart mouth would get me killed before my time. Please tell Margot she can have my collection of specimen jars, but not the finger. That one probably needs to be burned. Molly can have my illustrated copy of Lady Danella's History of Seduction *and Capernibald's* Bestiary.

I'll see you on the other side; you're not getting rid of me that easily.
Declan

P.S. Tell Emil I am sorry about his cat. I am sure the fur will grow back eventually.

Garret folded the letter and shook his head before heading up to his room. He paused in the doorway to the room across the hall. It was silent and dark but the moonlight coming in the window highlighted Nea's belongings where they sat in a neat pile on the chair by the window. They seemed out of place amongst the lingering chaos of Declan's things. A stone disrupting the flow of a stream. Anger-laced-guilt twisted in the pit of his stomach and he rubbed a hand over his face. Nea couldn't have run. If that had been her intention, she'd had plenty of chances before today.

He entered his own room and placed the letter on the desk, then he took a thin piece of leather thong from his armour repair kit. He looped it through the hole in the stone before he shed his jacket and boots and collapsed on the bed.

It felt like Garret's head had just hit the pillow when someone was shaking him awake. He opened his eyes to see Molly standing over him and Emil behind her in the doorway. The light in the room suggested it was well past dawn. He sat upright, suddenly wide awake. "What's going on?"

"Leon is gone," they both said together.

Garret felt the sudden urge to punch something and clenched his fists. "How long ago?"

They looked at each other and Molly said, "We're not sure. We think he drugged everyone."

Garret had been about to grab his boots, but he paused. "What time is it?"

"Almost noon," Emil said.

"That fucking bastard!" Garret slammed his fist against the wall.

"Garret!" Molly yelped.

He gave her an apologetic look and rubbed his fingers through his hair. "Get the horses. We need to catch Leon before he reaches the capital."

CHAPTER NINE

NEA

The room swayed savagely, setting Nea's stomach churning and bile rising in the back of her throat. Seagulls called in mournful shrieks. *Seagulls?*

She opened her eyes and sat up. Too fast. Her head swam; someone crouched in front of her and it took her blurry vision a minute to focus on their face. Recognising Declan's green eyes, she smiled. "I'm having the strangest dream. My ears feel fluffy. Are your ears fluffy?" She reached out and her hands went right through him.

"I bet you're really fun when you're drunk." A smile quirked the corner of his mouth. "But, Nea, listen to me—"

"Can you make it stop doing that?" she asked as the room shifted again. "Wait, this is my dream. I can make it stop." She tried to focus on her connection to the source but there was nothing there, just the silent numbness of an empty void. "Where are my magic hands?" She lifted her fingers and scowled at them.

Declan started to chuckle but then drew a deep breath and pinched the bridge of his nose. "Nea, look at me. This is serious. You are in the back of a carriage on the way to the king—"

"For a ball? I don't have a thing to wear."

He groaned. "Focus, Nea. You are in danger. Leon—"

"Leon? I remember. Self-important and scowly. He ..." She glanced at her hands again and noticed the shackles. "He arrested me!"

Declan sat back and rubbed a hand over his forehead. "I really need sober Nea right now."

"Am I drunk?"

"No, you're drugged. Only I don't know what he's given you. You've been in and out of consciousness for three and a half days."

"If I was going to drug someone and didn't want them to die right away ... Wait, a necromancer is pretty pointless without dead things to order around so I am not sure why I'd do that ... But *if* I did want them to ... not die, I would probably use mage bane laced with feverwort."

"Mage bane laced with feverwort?"

"Yep. They'd be like a sleepy little blob of clay and not even close to dead." She looked at him through her lashes. "Do you think I could get rid of these shackles if I cut my hands off?"

"I don't think—"

The carriage jolted and Nea fell forward straight through Declan's torso.

"Well, that was embarrassing. Good thing you're dead and this is a dream because that could have been really awkward if I'd landed in your lap. Not that I'd really mind being in your lap." She grinned. "You have really pretty eyes. So green and forest-y, like those things that grow on trees."

Declan pinched the bridge of his nose. "Is there something to counteract the mage bane and feverwort?"

"Nope. You just have to wait until it passes out of the victim's system. Why? Are you thinking about drugging someone?"

"How long does that generally take? Because I really need to talk to the normal Nea."

"I am the normal Nea. Or I will be when I wake up." She chewed her lip. "Maybe I need to go back to sleep so I can wake up again." She curled up on the floor of the carriage and closed her eyes.

&

"Mother's grief, what is wrong with my head?" Nea sat slowly and blinked the grit from her eyes. "Where in the realms ...?"

"Nea?"

She turned, or rather her neck turned. Her head just kind of listed to the side and pain darted across the front of her skull. "Declan?"

"How are you feeling?"

"Like something small and furry crawled in my mouth and died. Where are we?" She pressed the backs of her hands to her eyes and then lowered them and glared at the thin bands of pink-gold metal around her wrists "Why am I wearing bind-shackles?"

"Leon is taking you to Evard. Actually, we've already arrived at the palace but he had to wait for you to sober up before he could *present* you."

"Sober up?" She rubbed her forehead.

"Yeah, you've been pretty delirious for the last few days. You mentioned something about mage bane and feverwort during one of your more lucid moments."

She nodded slowly. "That would make sense. It causes a sort of hallucinatory dream state where victims pass in and out of consciousness, never knowing exactly what is real and what is not."

Declan chuckled. "Now I know for sure it's worn off."

"I don't follow." She frowned.

"Drugged Nea was very ... interesting. We'll just leave it at that." A smile tugged at the corner of his mouth.

A hot flush crept up the back of Nea's neck. She was about to speak when the door of the carriage opened and Leon sneered at her.

"It's time." He reached in and grabbed her by the arm then hauled her out into the light.

She blinked and lifted her hands to try and shield her eyes but Leon gripped the short rope that tied her wrists together and pulled her along behind him.

Grey walls flashed by and her stiff legs protested as she nearly had to jog to keep up with him. He dragged her deeper into the castle and then suddenly spun her into a cold room which contained a barrel of water and a small stool.

"You'll want to clean yourself up before your audience with the king." He indicated the barrel, then leant against the wall.

Nea stepped forward and peered into the murky water. "I am not washing in that."

"You'll wash in that yourself or I will make you. Even if I have to half-drown you to do it." He pushed off the wall and took a step towards her.

Nea bit down on her retort. She couldn't do much while she was shackled and even if she managed to overpower him, they were in the bowels of Evard's palace.

She dipped her hands into the barrel, trying not to wince at the icy water, and splashed it on her face before stepping back.

"You'll need to do better than that."

"And how exactly do you expect me to do that with this." She lifted her hands and tugged the rope between them tight.

"You'll make do." He crossed his arms. "Now strip and wash properly."

Nea planted her feet. "No."

Leon crossed to her in an instant and snatched hold of her hair. He twisted it tightly and tugged her forward so his nose was level with hers. "Do not defy me again." He pinned her to the side of the barrel and turned her face until it was an inch above the water.

The barrel rocked and sploshed water onto the floor as she struggled and kicked her heel against his shin. He growled in pain but didn't release his grip. "Not so tough with your powers bound, are you?" His breath hissed beside her ear as his free hand found the lacing that secured her dress. He ripped at it, tearing the neckline.

Nea twisted in his grasp again and thrust her elbow back, catching him in the lip. He dropped her and she crawled between his legs. She started to get to her feet to make a dash for the door but he pounced, capturing her again. As he hauled her up, she grabbed one of the legs of the stool and dragged it with her, swinging it at his head. But the angle he held her at made the blow glance harmlessly off his shoulder. He snatched the stool out of her hand and threw it across the room, then pressed her against the wall; his forearm was tight across her chest, pinning her in place.

"That was very unwise." He wiped the thin trickle of blood off his lip with his free hand and looked down at the red on his fingertips as Nea struggled. "You've made me bleed twice now. Perhaps I should return the favour." He drew his hand back and slapped her across the face.

Her teeth clacked together as the force of his blow made her head reel back into the wall. Tears of pain welled but she would not give him the satisfaction of seeing them fall.

"Strip and wash. Unlike Garret, I am not squeamish when it comes to breaking disobedient bitches." He shoved her towards the barrel again.

She stumbled and caught the edge of it, causing it to wobble and more of the murky water to splash out.

"What's going on in here?" The door banged open and a guard appeared.

"I'm just getting the necromancer presentable for the king." Leon straightened his tabard and lightly touched the split in his lip. "She's proving ... difficult."

The guard's gaze shifted over Nea, lingering on her dishevelled hair, torn dress, and the burning skin of her cheek. "I doubt His Majesty will appreciate damaged goods." He crossed his arms.

Leon's top lip curled. "As long as she's still breathing he'll be happy."

The guard caught Nea's eye. There was something in his gaze that she couldn't quite place. Indifference? No, pity perhaps.

"Sure. I just hope I'm in the room to see his reaction when you tell him that." He turned to leave. "I wouldn't waste too much more time in here with her though. The warden commander is due to arrive soon."

Leon snarled and grabbed hold of Nea again. "You'll have to do. I need to get you to the king before Garret gets here." He dragged her from the room, past the guard, who stood back to let them through.

Leon didn't slow until they reached the door to the throne room. Nea held her head high as they stepped into the warm bright space. She let her gaze wander over the heavy green heraldry that hung on the grey stone walls. It felt like an age since she had last been here, and yet at the same time, it was as though only a moment had passed.

As Leon propelled her across the room, she took in the faces of the courtiers present; some she knew, others she did not. When they reached the base of the dais on which Evard's throne sat, she lifted her eyes to meet his, her gaze briefly flicking to the scar on the left side of his face.

Evard stood slowly, his cold grey gaze taking in every inch of her. His tongue slowly followed the seam of his lips before he stepped down and came too close for comfort. On instinct, Nea rocked back but Leon's grip on her arm tightened.

"You may release her." Evard didn't look at Leon as he spoke.

Leon hesitated but then loosened his grip and backed away, bowing to the king as he did so.

Evard walked in a slow circle around Nea, his pale lips pulling back to reveal his teeth. As he came to the front of her again, he lifted a hand to cup her chin. "I am terribly sorry to see you in such a state, my dear." His eyes flicked to Leon and a darkness shifted in their depths. "Though I know just how *argumentative* you can be." His free hand touched his scar. "So perhaps Leon merely gave you what you were *asking* for."

Nea glanced sideways at Leon, who shifted his weight and cleared his throat. "She did prove unduly defiant."

Evard's mouth quirked into the cold shadow of a smile. "I can imagine." He released Nea's chin and walked in a slow circle around her again as he addressed Leon. "When they said you had brought me something from Braemar, I thought you'd finally figured out how to extract the girl from the south wing. Then they informed me that Nea had surfaced and you had managed to capture her. And that, my boy, impressed me. No one who actually knew her reputation would dare attempt such a feat without a warden. So, tell me, was this feat solely yours or did Warden Commander Garret have a hand in it as well?"

"The commander—"

"Starting without me are you, Leon?"

Nea flinched as Garret's voice sounded behind her.

He stepped in front of her and gave the king a short bow. "My lord."

Evard gave Garret a look of admiration that made Nea's stomach churn. When Garret stepped back next to her, she caught the livid glance he served Leon and swallowed.

"Now, Nea." Her attention returned to Evard as he spoke. "You have evaded me for some time, my lovely. Tell me, were I to make my offer again, what would your answer be?" He leant forward as he spoke and she felt the urge to headbutt him, but he wasn't close enough for that.

"My answer will never change."

"See, I knew you would say that. You were always so noble, so predictable. But then again, I never had the right ... *incentive*." He snapped his fingers and a door to the left opened.

A guard came through, dragging a tall woman.

Nea knew Evard had Margot but seeing it made her knees weaken and her lip quiver. Her golden curls had been shorn close to her scalp. Her soft brown gaze lifted, and the moment she caught Nea's eye, Margot gasped.

"Margot!" Nea lurched forward but Garret's hand closed around her arm and pulled her gently back. She glared at Evard. "You lay so much as a finger on her and I'll—"

"Ah, ah, ah." Evard wagged his finger and the guard pressed a knife to Margot's throat. "Now. Nea, I am going to ask you again. Are you willing to cooperate with me?"

Nea sucked a breath over her teeth.

"If you need a reminder of my brutality, just think of Kalhanna."

She looked away from Evard's twisted grin.

"Bring me the girl," Evard said.

Another guard entered through the same door Margot had. He was dragging a young girl who couldn't have been any older than sixteen.

"This girl was caught stealing from the palace kitchens. I thought about taking one of her hands. But they are such pretty hands. Then they told me Leon had brought you here for me. I'm glad I waited because now you can prove your willingness to cooperate and give those present a little taste of what I will do to anyone who displeases me."

Nea looked at the girl. "I will not—"

Evard snapped his fingers and the guard holding the girl slit her throat. She made a gargled sound of shock as she dropped to her knees, her dark eyes staring accusingly at Nea. Garret's grip grew uncomfortably tight and she glanced at him out of the corner of her eye. His face was pale and judging by the set of his jaw, he was doing everything in his power to maintain his composed façade.

The king clapped his hands together. "Such a waste. She was rather good at her job and so willing to *please*." His gaze shifted as he addressed Leon. "Untie her and remove the shackles."

"My lord?"

"The commander will make sure she doesn't do anything stupid, not that she will while her precious Margot is at my mercy. Isn't that right, Nea?" A signal from Evard and the guard holding Margot tensed, a thin line of blood appearing at the edge of his knife.

Nea gave the briefest of nods.

"Don't let him bully—" Margot's words were cut off as the guard holding her tightened his grip and growled something in her ear.

Nea tore her gaze away from Margot as Leon approached her. He leant close and gave her a nasty smile as he roughly untied the rope before taking the key for the shackles from around his neck. As the key touched the first band of metal it shone then sprung open. When the second metal band fell away, her connection with the source was reignited and her keen came roaring back into her body, causing her knees to buckle slightly. Garret's grip on her arm held her steady as magic prickled over her skin and rushed along every vein before it settled as a cool weight in the pit of her stomach.

"Now put her back together." Evard indicated the dead girl at their feet.

Nea started to object but Evard lifted a finger. "Let's all keep our heads, shall we?" He tilted his fingertip in Margot's direction, an unnecessary reminder of what was at stake.

Nea shook herself free of Garret's grasp. "Alright." She stepped around the girl's body and looked up again, catching Leon's hungry stare before her gaze darted to Garret with his tight jaw and unreadable eyes.

The courtiers were all so silent they might as well have not been there, but Nea could feel their excited anticipation, as though none of them were perturbed in the slightest about the brutal murder they had just witnessed. Evard had returned to his throne and sat leaning forward to watch as Nea let the chill pool in her stomach and the air in the room grew cold in response. She crouched down, careful not to the disturb the pool of blood, and focused on the barrier between the worlds. The rose hedge appeared before her, several blooms still baring charred petals from her last attempt to send Declan, and there were now deep grey flowers that hadn't been there before scattered through the pink. The leaves fluttered gently despite the lack of breeze, and as she lifted her hand, the branches rolled back smoothly. She drew a deep breath and with practised ease, stepped out of her body and through the gate in the hedge into the Between.

The landscape here was a perversion of the throne room; chairs floated at different heights, and some hung upside from patches of broken ceiling. A green fire flickered in a massive fireplace that looked like the gaping maw of some monster made of blackened iron. As Nea wandered forward, the twisted trees that lined the sides of the room arched closer. Dark shapes lurked between them. Some wore familiar faces, but they did not fool her. She kept walking forward, following the path of broken stones, and then she spotted the girl sitting in the rickety chair that had taken the place of Evard's mahogany throne.

"This is your fault. Everything is your fault." She crossed her arms and tilted her face away from Nea as she approached.

"Yes, it is. And I'm sorry for what I am about to do." That was all the conversation Nea would entertain before she grabbed hold of the girl's soul and dragged her back through the gate in the hedge to the land of the living.

Nea ignored the wave of disorientation that came with re-entering her physical form and focused on pressing the girl's soul back into the body it had just left. The corpse began to writhe and twitch in an effort to reject the soul. The fit was wrong now, too tight and too loose all at once. Nea persevered, a thin layer of sweat forming on her forehead. She bit her lip and gave a final shove of power, snapping the soul into place, and the girl sat up slowly. She looked around, the slice across her neck gaping with each twist of her head, then her eyes found Nea and she lunged.

Nea held her hand up, channelling the source into a thin thread of compulsion. A coil of lilac smoke twisted momentarily around her fingers and the girl stopped, as though rooted to the floor. She snarled and stretched her arms towards Nea but couldn't move her feet.

"You can make her do anything you want?" Evard was leaning so far forward it was a surprise he was still in his seat.

Nea gave a curt nod.

Evard licked his lips and stared at the girl. "Make her climb into the fire." He indicated the oversized fireplace at the far end of the room.

Nea hesitated.

"Do it," he growled.

She swallowed and turned her focus back to the girl, taking hold of the soul now wedged into the dead flesh. A blank look stole across the girl's face as she stopped struggling and her head tilted, causing the sliver across her neck to gape as she waited for Nea's order. Nea closed her eyes swallowed again then nudged the girl with her magic.

Without hesitation, she turned on her heel and walked to the massive fireplace. She stopped and stared at the flames but Nea gave her another nudge with her magic and she climbed in and sat within the flames. After a moment, her clothes caught alight and the fire rose in hungry orange tongues that licked her skin and consumed her hair. She shrieked and writhed, causing logs to roll from the grate, but she did not try to escape.

Nea looked away as the smell of burning flesh reached her and caused bile to rise in her throat. She shuddered and closed her eyes as memories of Kalhanna pressed against the edges of her mind.

"Enough!" she yelled, her fists clenched at her sides.

The girl rolled out of the fire and collapsed onto the hearthstones, her limbs twitching. Nea drew a hiccupping breath and severed the links holding the soul to the body. It shook under the force of her compulsion, a shimmer of lilac shrouding it momentarily before it grew still. As she pushed the soul through the gate between worlds, she fell forward onto her knees, her face pressed into her hands.

CHAPTER TEN

MARGOT

Margot stared at the charred body of the girl as Evard slowly clapped. No one else was moving. The courtiers were all leaning forward, hungry dogs waiting for their master's signal. She caught Garret's eye and noted a fleeting look of horror before his carefully choreographed calm snapped back into place. It was one thing to know what a mage was capable of in theory, but to see it actually play out was another thing entirely.

Evard stood and approached Nea. "Leon, the shackles." He held his hand out and Leon placed the bind-shackles in it. He crouched and snapped the shackles around Nea's wrists before he stroked her cheek. He whispered something to her that Margot couldn't hear, but the look Nea gave him as he stood and walked towards his throne told her enough.

As he passed Garret, he paused and ran his fingers across his chest, picking an invisible bit of lint off his armour and rubbing it between his thumb and index finger. He didn't see the look of loathing in Garret's eyes as he moved off again. "Many of you know that when the Kalhanna mages revolted, some of my men chose to defy my direct orders. Unfortunately, I had to put those men to the axe." He tutted and shook his head. "Such a waste of resources. Had

I possessed the services of a necromancer like Nea, I could have simply forced those men to comply. Puppets, you see, don't have free will and thus cannot be swayed by their own emotions or a sense of misguided morality." His eyes flicked to Garret as he spoke. "Let this be a warning to those who harbour ideas of discontent. I will repurpose the body of every traitor; there will be no more waste."

With each word, his voice grew louder until it was reverberating around the inside of Margot's skull.

Evard snapped his fingers and pointed to one of his guards. "Take her to Victor." He indicated Nea, who was still hunched on the ground, white-lipped as she stared at the body of the girl. The guard moved forward and Garret stepped in front of him.

"My lord, perhaps it would be better for a warden to escort her."

Evard appraised him, one bony finger tapping his chin. "I don't believe that will be necessary in her current state."

"As you wish." Garret stood out of the guard's way and watched as Nea was hauled to her feet and led from the room. "If you have no further need of me, I should check in with the rest of the order."

"Dismissed. But I expect you in my study after dinner." Evard waved Garret away and then glanced to Margot as he relaxed into his throne again. "Take her back to her room."

As the guard locked the door to her tower room Margot turned and scowled at the four walls she had come to hate over the past month and a half. She paced to the bed and flopped on it with a sigh.

The shock of seeing Nea had been quickly replaced with concern, and not just for their shared predicament. Nea did not look well. There was something in her eyes that had never been there before and she looked tired. No, not just tired—exhausted. Soul weary,

Nonna would call it. What had Garret been thinking, handing Nea over to Evard? If she ever got out of this room, she would shoot him in the knee with Molly's crossbow. A cold lump of melancholy rose in her throat at the thought of Molly and she crossed her arms over her head. *Mother damn Evard.* If Margot was given the chance she'd ... well, not kill him. She didn't think she could stomach something like that. She wasn't Nea. But she'd definitely make him suffer.

The *click* of the lock roused Margot from sleep. She sat slowly as someone entered the room, closing the door behind them. If she had her powers, she would call a mage light into existence, but instead she had to rely on the watery moonlight that came in the window.

The intruder was large and moved with quiet footsteps. When he reached the side of the bed, Margot lunged, knocking him off balance with the suddenness of her attack. They both fell to the floor and Margot drew her fist back to punch.

"Margot, it's Garret," he hissed and caught her fist as it glanced off the edge of his jaw.

She snatched her hand back and slapped him hard across the face before letting him up. "Bright Mother's tits, Garret, what were you thinking?"

"I needed to talk to you." He rubbed his cheek.

"I don't mean right now. I'm talking about Nea." She sat on the edge of the bed.

Garret rubbed the back of his neck. "I actually had nothing to do with that."

"You—wait, what?"

"I found her in Little Brook, of all places. And I had decided not to hand her over to Evard but Leon took matters into his own hands."

"Wait, so you had no intentions of turning her in?"

He shook his head. "It felt like the one thing I could never come back from. Not that it matters now; my hand has been forced."

"So, you're just going to let Evard keep her?"

"Yes ... no ... I don't know. It's not like I have choice now. It's going to take time to come up with a plan to get you both out. Not to mention, it's treason. So we need to be prepared for the ramifications."

She rubbed her chin as she watched him. There was something flat about the set of his shoulders. The tightness in his jaw wasn't unusual but the dark circles under his eyes worried her. In the few years she had known him, she didn't think she'd ever seen him so run-down. "Are you alright?"

He ran a hand through his hair. "I've been better, but I'm still breathing. So that's something, right?"

She patted the bed next to her. "Is it just this thing with Nea? Being outplayed by Leon, of all people, or is it something else? Are the others okay? Is Molly? Evard threatened to have her killed."

"Molly is fine."

Relief stole her breath for a moment.

"Emil too." He sat next to her.

"And Declan? Has he cracked the cure yet?"

The looked that crossed his face made her heart flop.

"Declan's ... gone."

"Gone ...? Oh." A lump caught in her throat and she felt the hot sting of tears. "Oh, Garret, I am so sorry." She bit her lip and rested her shoulder against his.

"I'm sorry to tell you like this ... on top of everything else."

"I would rather know." Her voice wobbled over the words.

He looped his arm around her shoulders, giving her a lopsided hug. She drew a shaky breath that morphed into a sob and suddenly she couldn't hold back the tears. She turned her head, burying her face in his side. It was as though the news about Declan had opened the gate on everything that she had been bottling inside since Evard had taken her into custody.

As she sobbed Garret rubbed small circles on her back and eventually her sobs died to watery sniffles.

"I'm sorry." She sat back, shrugging his arm off her shoulders and wiping the remaining tears from her cheeks.

"There's no need to apologise." He folded his hands in his lap. "Are you alright? Aside from just now? Have they ..."

"I'm still breathing ... That counts, right?".

He gave a hollow chuckle.

"Evard didn't torture me, if that's what you are asking—at least, not physically."

His gaze lifted to her hair and she ran her hand over the shortened curls.

"He taunted me, had his men rough me up a bit, cut my hair, but that was really the worst of it. He wanted to leave the actual torture until he could do it in front of Nea. He said it would sweeten the act if she was watching."

They were both silent for a while.

"So, what happens now?" she asked.

"I wish I knew. I can't leave you here. If I can get you out, then Evard won't have his leverage for Nea."

Margot stiffened. "You can't rescue me and leave Nea behind."

"But—"

"You saw what reanimating that girl did to her. If you let Evard keep her, it will destroy her."

Garret looked at his hands.

Margot crossed her arms and sniffed.

"Don't look at me like that. Getting you out is going to be a challenge. Getting Nea out is going to be practically impossible."

"What would Declan do?" It was a low blow and she felt bad, but not bad enough that she wished she hadn't said it.

Garret sucked his breath through his teeth and his fingers curled into fists then released. "Declan would ... he would tell me to pull my head out of my arse and go with my gut."

"Okay, Garret." She stood with her hands on her hips. "Pull your head out of your arse and think about this for a minute. What does your gut say? Mine says if you don't rescue Nea, you are leaving a weapon in the hands of a maniac." She lowered her voice to mimic Declan's and managed a surprisingly accurate tone. "And, regardless, I am always down for saving a pretty girl." She mimicked his wolfish grin.

Garret rubbed his finger over his scar and gave her a small smile. "Uncanny. Though his grin would have been a bit more lopsided."

Margot sighed and sat again. "I know you'll figure it out." She patted his knee. "I mean, if you don't ... you'll have to answer to Molly so ..."

"Mother preserve me, anything but that." He let out a laugh and Margot felt a smile building in response.

Two days later, Margot was taken to the throne room. A low stage had been constructed in front of Evard's dais and the walls were ringed with more nobles and soldiers than Margot had ever seen in attendance at the court. On the stage stood a man in chains, a man she vaguely recognised though wasn't sure why. The guard escorting her nudged her towards the throne and into place at Evard's left side.

"We are in for quite the treat today, my dear." Evard spoke without looking at her.

Margot stared straight ahead and didn't respond.

"You're not curious about what I have planned?"

"Not in the slightest." She gave him a tight smile. Of course she was curious ... and apprehensive. But she certainly didn't want to give him any excuse to gloat—not that he needed one.

"Tell me, are you aware of Nea's particular talent? The one that sets her apart from the rest of her kind?"

It made sense. After the display with the girl and his speech about control, she had wondered why Evard had to have Nea, and not just any necromancer, or a mind mage for that matter. It would be just as efficient, and surely there were mages who would be willing to work for him or, at the very least, who were far easier to control than Nea. She assumed his insistence on it being Nea had been simply to do with their history: his obsession, her defiance, and the spark that had resulted in Kalhanna being purged. Now she knew that whilst all of those details were factors, it was actually about something more. It was about controlling those that stood against him, about *preserving resources,* as he put it. But ultimately it was about fear.

Plain and simple fear.

CHAPTER ELEVEN

NEA

Nea could roughly tell time by the rhythm of the day. Keys jangled, doors slammed, a plate was pushed through the slot at the base of the door and the previous one taken, its contents barely touched. She'd moved from the centre of the cell to the far wall, away from the dark grate that smelled of death and decay.

The keys jangled again, coming closer. Footsteps sounded just outside her door. Another plate? No. The scrape of a key in the lock. She peered through her messy tangle of dark grey hair and her gaze met Garret's.

"Leave us." Garret turned his attention to the guard.

"Sir—"

"Leave us. Lock me in if it makes you more comfortable. I'll call for you when I'm ready to leave."

The guard grunted an affirmative and pulled the door shut after Garret had stepped through.

Garret stared at her, his arms crossed and his jaw tight. She couldn't hear his teeth grinding but she was almost certain they would be. He opened his mouth to speak then closed it again. Glancing over his shoulder, he moved closer and crouched in front of her.

"Is Margot okay?" Her lips were dry and her tongue felt thick.

He nodded. "She's fine. Evard likes having leverage. He won't do anything to her while you cooperate." He rocked back on his heels. "Look, Nea ... I'm sorry. I'd get you out of here if I could but if Evard suspects ..." He sighed and looked at his hands.

"I'm fine ... really."

"No, you're not." He stood and paced the width of the cell. "I shouldn't have gone with Emil that day. I was waiting for Leon to show his hand, but I thought he was after Amelia. That he wouldn't be brazen enough to try and go after you. I didn't think." He stopped and stared at the wall. "I was so caught up in what had happened to Declan, I wasn't thinking. I'm an idiot."

"You're not an idiot, Garret."

"No, that's a fair call. He can be a real idiot at times." Declan appeared beside her and she jumped.

Garret turned to face her. "Evard wants you upstairs. He has something planned for the court, though after that little display with Sally I can't imagine what." He swallowed.

"Sally?" Nea frowned. "Oh ..." *The girl.* She chewed her lip. "You know as long as he has Margot I'll do anything he asks?"

"I know."

"Which is why you need to get her out of here. Don't go back to Braemar. Get Margot and take her to Bright Harbour in Prahma. Ask for a boat master by the name of Heidi and give her my name. She'll take you as far as Mother's Deep, then you can—"

"And what then? He'll find some other way to make you do what he wants. I can't ferret away every person he might use to control you." He crossed his arms again.

"I'm agreeing with Garret on this one." Declan took a seat next to her.

"You won't need to. Just get Margot to safety, then I'll do my part." She stood.

"Your part? That sounds like you're about to do something reckless. You aren't ..." He stopped talking as the guard returned.

"The king wants her cleaned up before you take her to the throne room."

The guard led Nea and Garret to a small room behind the head jailor's desk. A barrel of water was waiting along with a clean change of clothes. Nea stood in the doorway and stared at the barrel.

"This is Janey. She'll help you get presentable for the king." The guard indicated a maid standing just inside the door, who Nea hadn't noticed before.

Janey's head tilted as she studied Nea, drawing Nea's attention to the jagged scar across her throat, and her hands flashed a few rapid signs at Garret, who nodded and replied with a few signs of his own. She then turned her attention to Nea, smiled, and said very slowly and deliberately, "Come. The king does not like to wait."

As she moved to close the door, the guard stopped her. "I don't think that's a good idea, Janey. Leon had trouble with her the other day."

Nea lifted her hand and rubbed the back of her head where Leon had grabbed hold of her by the hair.

Janey frowned and shook her head as she rapidly signed something to Garret.

The guard frowned at Janey's hands. "I think the commander will agree with me."

Garret studied Nea. "She'll behave, I am sure."

Nea nodded.

"I don't like this—"

"What do you want to do—sit in there and watch? Or are you hoping to get hands-on like Leon?" Nea asked and wrapped her arms across her chest.

"Of course not. It's just ... Commander?" He cast a look at Garret, who was rubbing the scar above his top lip.

Nea might have felt sorry for the guard were she not currently a prisoner. He was just trying to do his job and if she was in his place, she wouldn't trust herself either. She did have a track record of *wilful disobedience,* after all.

"I have not found Nea to be unreasonable when she's treated with a modicum of respect." Garret shrugged. "And I have no desire to rob her of her dignity any more than has already been done so."

"I won't object to the door being left open," she said, glancing at Janey, who shrugged.

"There, does that make you feel better?" Garret moved and sat on a chair in the guard's office. The guard followed him and took up the seat behind the jailor's desk as Janey ushered Nea into the room with the barrel.

Janey was silent as she helped Nea strip before she dipped her hands into the clear water in the barrel and a gentle steam began to rise from it.

"You're a mage?" Nea asked.

She nodded in response, then helped Nea scrub her skin with a soap that smelt like chamomile and lavender, until it was pink. She turned her attention to Nea's hair, gently working a comb through the wet curls to free the worst of the tangles. Once satisfied, she rubbed her hands together and the air around them grew warm. Taking up the comb again, she ran her fingers through Nea's hair until it was completely dry before she braided it.

Finally, she helped Nea into the new clothes. They were much like her Hartswood uniform: a linen shirt, short tunic, and pants, though this tunic was made from red-dyed wool, and the pants were a looser fit.

Satisfied with her work, Janey left the room, taking Nea's soiled clothes with her.

"Aright, let's go." Garret entered and indicated Nea follow.

The guard gave them a glance as they passed but said nothing. And neither did Garret as he led her through the castle hallways.

As they walked into the throne room, Nea's heart began to race. The walls were lined with more faces than Nea could count. Not only courtiers but also members of the guard and palace staff, the latter shifting uncomfortably at the very back of the room. She drew a shuddering breath that failed to fill her lungs and, as though feeling her apprehension, Garret gave her arm a gentle squeeze. If he meant it to be reassuring, it wasn't. Especially once her eyes met Evard's and she saw the predatory look on his face. Beside him, her face a banner of worry, was Margot.

Garret guided Nea onto the small stage in front of the king where a man stood, bound in iron shackles. Garret let her arm go and took a small step back but stayed close by, presumably to grab her if she tried anything. Like attacking Evard. Not that she would. He was too far away for her reach before both she and Margot were struck down.

Evard rose and lifted his arms. "My good lords and ladies, today, I have gathered you to talk about the importance of reputation. See, reputation is a fickle creature. It can be built or destroyed with a single action, a single word. Before you stands one of my most trusted agents. Until recently, he had never failed me. It was a small misstep, one that could easily be forgiven, but now I find myself doubting him. One tiny miscalculation on his part and my whole view of him has been shattered." There was silence from those gathered. "Now some of you have already seen what our lovely necromancer is capable of, and you may have guessed that I will shortly order her to repurpose Harold here."

Harold? Hadn't Declan mentioned that name?

Nea felt all the eyes in the room fall on her. She straightened her shoulders and kept staring straight ahead.

"That would be a simple enough punishment, but as I said, I want to talk about reputation and Nea has a particularly interesting one. Tell me, Harold, have you heard of Nea of Hartswood?"

"Yes, my lord." Came Harold's reply.

"Tell me, Harold, what have you heard about her?"

"She's dangerous, my lord. She was at Kalhanna during the purge."

Nea swallowed. In the pit of her stomach, she knew where Evard was taking this. She clenched her hands together to try and stop them shaking.

Ash rained down on the smouldering ruin of Kalhanna. Nea walked through the bodies, searching. She found Dhen, his face cleaved in two, and the lump in her throat grew thicker. She gathered a charred saddle cloth from the rubble of the stables and lay it over him.

Then she heard the moan, so mournful it almost didn't sound human. She scrambled to find Francesca laying a short distance away. Her legs were crushed; her right arm was missing. Her head lolled as Nea gently lifted her into her lap.

Nea stroked Francesca's hair and started humming softly. It was a lullaby her father used to sing when she couldn't sleep, but Nea couldn't find the words now, just the tune. As she hummed, she rocked gently and focused on the thin threads that tethered Francesca's soul to her body. They were frail and thinning as each moment drifted by and gave away easily under gentle pressure from Nea's magic. One by one, she severed the threads until Francesca gave one final gasp and was gone. As Nea collapsed over the now lifeless body, her ribs heaved under the pressure of her despair and heavy sobs tore from her throat.

A footstep crunched on the ground nearby and her head snapped up to see three men in green tabards moving through the bodies. They spotted her and sneered. She gently lowered Francesca to the ground then stood slowly as they approached—

"Now Nea is going to show you all exactly what she did to those men at Kalhanna. Is it true, Nea, that you can strip a living soul from a body?" Evard's voice brought her back to the throne room.

Nea looked at her feet and didn't answer.

"It is a different process to driving out a possession, is it not?"

She refused to answer.

The king tutted. "And you are normally so full of words. Never mind. I shall enlighten those present." He turned his attention to the room at large. "Necromancers, as many of you know, possess the ability to send the souls of the dead on their way. They can purge possession and also put a soul back into a dead body and reanimate it. One thing they cannot do is strip a living soul from its own body. But Nea is different, special. Aren't you, Nea?"

She refused to meet his eye.

"Might I remind you what happens if you don't cooperate?"

Nea heard Margot gasp and she winced.

"So now tell me, Nea, will you show the court what you did to those soldiers at Kalhanna? Will you make an example of Harold here so those gathered may know exactly what is in order if they fail me in such a manner that I find even repurposing them repugnant?"

"Nea, don't. Harold deserves to die but not like this. If you do this, there is no turning back." Declan appeared beside her, but she kept her gaze on the king.

"Well? It is not advisable to keep me waiting, as you well know."

Nea drew a slow breath and nodded, just once.

"My lord. Please spare me. I've learned my lesson. It will not happen again. You have my word." Harold pulled against the long chain that held him to the stage.

"Silence!" Evard shouted and the room stilled. "It would be advisable for you to stand back, Commander."

Garret removed the bind-shackles. He held Nea's wrists to support her as her knees wobbled under the strain of her keen returning to her body. He then stepped off the stage and moved a short distance away.

Nea stared at Harold and swallowed. She looked up and met Margot's gaze; her mouth was a tight line and she started to shake her head, but the guard restraining her pressed a knife against her throat.

"Enough stalling," Evard growled.

Nea met his eye. She wondered if she was quick enough to kill both him and the guard holding Margot before either of them had a chance to move. As though sensing her thought, Evard lifted his finger and tilted it in Margot's direction. The guard holding her tensed and Nea switched her attention to Harold.

"I'm so sorry." She shut her eyes and focused on the steady thrum of the source. It prickled along her skin as she turned her focus to the hum of energy that was contained by Harold's body. When she found the threads that held him together, she worked the fingers of her keen into them.

Harold started screaming.

"Nea, stop. Please don't do this." The cold shadow of Declan's hands pressed on her shoulders.

"I can't," she whispered.

Harold yowled in agony, blood running from his eyes, nose, and ears. He lifted his hands and gripped his head, raking his fingers down his cheeks and leaving streaks of blood on his pale skin. His body began to shudder and contort.

"Nea, please." There was a note in Declan's voice that made her pause.

Harold curled in a ball, panting and sobbing.

The air in the room had become oppressive. No one dared to make a sound.

Margot's pained gasp was like thunder in Nea's ears.

"I'm sorry," she said to Declan, or Harold, she wasn't exactly sure.

Harold's back arched as Nea grabbed the edge of his soul again. He twisted and writhed but there was no sound coming from his open mouth. Sweat beaded along Nea's brow and her heart pounded in her ears. This was different to using her powers in self-defence or blind emotion like she had done with the men at Kalhanna. It was *wrong*, and every fibre of her being knew it. She closed her eyes and pulled savagely at the fabric holding Harold together. Once. Twice. On the third yank the threads tore and he collapsed, still and unbreathing.

Nea staggered forward onto her hands and knees. No one made a sound. She lifted the back of her hand to her nose and lowered it again, a smear of blood against her pale skin. Still no one dared even breathe.

Then Evard started clapping.

"Oh, my dear girl, how I underestimated you." He thrust his arms out to the court at large. "See now, my dearly devoted, what could befall you if you displease me?"

Hands closed around Nea's shoulders and she was drawn to her feet. The source was churning widely in the wake of what she had done and for once, she was relieved when the cold burn of the bind-shackles closed over her wrists, cutting off her connection to it. The crowd parted, giving the guards leading her back to her cell a wide berth.

"Don't look at me like that. I had no choice."

"We always have a choice, Nea, and you chose wrong this time." Declan was pacing the cell, doing a very good impression of Garret. "You know that sort of power leads to corruption."

Nea huffed and ran a hand over her hair. "It was worth the risk."

"Oh, really?" He stopped pacing and nodded pointedly to her wrist.

She lowered her arm and looked at the thin grey marks that had risen there, ghosts of Amelia's scratches. She traced one with her finger and Amelia's words rang across her mind. *We're sisters, you and I.* She sighed and rested her head against the wall, closing her eyes. She opened them again almost immediately as the images of the past threatened to drown her.

"I'm sorry you had to see me like that." She looked away from the pity in his green eyes.

They were silent for some time when Nea finally said, "I wish you hadn't died."

Declan stopped pacing to look at her. He opened and closed his mouth, then started pacing again. "It is what it is. I made my choice." He sat beside her. "Though I'm starting to think I chose wrong." He too leant his head against the wall. "Harold was an arse, a highly dangerous arse. And I'm not going to lie; I've imagined some very creative ways to kill him. But no one deserves to die like ... *that.*"

Nea hugged her knees to her chest and rested her chin on them. "No ... you're right about that. You must think I'm a monster now." She looked at her hands. "Oh, Nea, what have you done." She pressed the heels of her palms to her eyes and drew a shaky breath.

"Look at me." He moved to crouch in front of her.

She lowered her hands and he gave her a crooked smile. "You're not a monster. Evard's a monster. Amelia's a monster. The jury is still out on Leon ... but you? The fact that you've nearly chewed a hole through your lip with worry since we got back down here tells me you are not a monster, regardless of your ability to flay someone's soul straight from their body."

Nea gave a weak chuckle. "I might just be very good at hiding it."

"No one is *that* good at hiding their true nature." He reached out, as though to brush a stray curl from her face, but stopped with a heavy sigh and looked at his fingers. "How does that work though? As gruesome as it was to watch, I can't help wondering how you do it. Is it true that normal necromancers can't do that? And if so, what makes you different?"

"Can we save this discussion for later?"

He blinked at her. "Ah, right. It's probably an inappropriate topic of conversation right now." He settled his hands on her knees. It was a strange sensation. She couldn't actually feel the weight of his touch, just a lingering coldness, almost like she had been kneeling in the snow. "Are you going to be okay?"

"I'm fine."

He raised his eyebrows but didn't say anything.

Footsteps came down the hall and they both looked up as a guard opened the door. Nea recognised him as Victor, the head jailor, and the one who had interrupted Leon when he was trying to get her to wash in that disgusting barrel on the first day she had arrived. He gave her what passed for a smile but was really the barest tightening of his lips. He wasn't a man of many words and whilst he hadn't been overly kind to her, he hadn't been cruel either. He stepped out of the way to let Garret into the cell before closing the door.

CHAPTER TWELVE

GARRET

Nea was against the far wall of her cell, her violet eyes shining as she studied him. The stare reminded him of the seer from Little Brook, in that it seemed to go straight through him and read the very fabric of his soul. He drew breath. The way she was sitting, hunched with her chin resting on her knees, made her look so small and vulnerable. And he couldn't help picturing Elenora in her place. But Nora wouldn't be capable of what Nea had done. Would she?

"I, ah ..." He rubbed the back of his neck. "I didn't know necromancers could do that."

Nea opened her mouth but he cut her off.

"I mean, I was aware of the rumours. I read the reports from Kalhanna. I thought, given the brutal nature of the siege, that some of it was just exaggeration. But you ..." He ran his fingers through his hair. "How could you?"

She didn't answer him, just closed her eyes.

"Margot is right; I can't let Evard keep you. Not when you're capable of ... that!" He thrust his arm in the general direction of the throne room. "It's too dangerous. *You're* too dangerous. With you by his side, Evard could ... and he will ..." She was being unusually quiet. "Nea, why aren't you talking?"

"You're doing enough talking for the both of us." She tugged her sleeve over her arm and hugged her knees.

"I'm sorry. It's just … a lot to process." At first he had been appalled. He knew in theory what necromancers were capable of, and seeing her reanimate Sally had been a gruesome eye-opener to the actual reality of it. But this thing with Harold? That was something else entirely. "And on top of it, I have to figure out how to rescue both you and Margot without Evard realising I've had a hand in it."

"I'll make it easier for you." Her voice was soft but it cut through his churning thoughts. "I am not leaving."

She *what?*

"I want you to get Margot out and make sure she is safe. Then, next time I am called to the throne room, I am going to kill Evard. With my bare hands if I need to."

Garret almost laughed but the look on her face was so serious. "Don't be a fool, Nea."

"Don't you get it?" She stood and closed the distance between them, somehow managing to look intimidating despite her height. "It's not just Margot. It's Margot today, but tomorrow it might be Nonna or my father or Emil. Then next week it will be all of Hartswood or Del Harol. You said it yourself—you can't ferret away everyone." Her voice rose steadily until she was almost shouting.

"Nea, the guard—"

"Fuck the guard."

He sucked a breath over his teeth.

"What do you do exactly? Hide away at Braemar, pretending to care about the plight of mages? Then swan back here with your *yes, my lord, no, my lord.* You don't think he suspects a thing?"

Her speech reminded him of Molly.

"He knows, Garret. If Leon hasn't told him the truth, Harold surely would have. You can't keep walking the line between the sides. There is a storm coming, and if you don't choose a harbour, you're going to get drowned in the undertow."

She drew a breath, and he rubbed the back of his neck.

He was about to speak when she said, "Harold's the one who killed Declan. I don't think I told you that before."

The way she said it, delicately, like she didn't want to open the wound, was such a contrast to her recent outburst that he was taken aback for a moment. "I had suspected it was Harold."

She rolled her lip between her teeth and lifted her hand to run it through her hair. The movement caused her sleeve to fall back and he stared at the pale skin of her wrist. Skin that was blemished with dull grey marks that looked almost like corruption.

"Is that what I think it is?"

She snatched her arm to her chest and took a step back. "It's not important right now."

"Is that where Amelia scratched you? May I see it?" He held his hand out, waiting for her to show him.

She chewed her lip and slowly held her arm out. "Yes it's where she scratched me, though I don't know why that makes any difference."

"A warden showed up, here in the capital, with corruption which originated in a wound." He took her arm and rolled it gently to inspect the grey spiderweb-like marks.

"Don't be ridiculous; wardens can't get corruption. And you certainly can't get corruption from a wound. It comes from the abuse of power or playing around with things you shouldn't."

"I wouldn't believe it myself, but it was Margot who told me. She said the corruption originated in a stab wound. And how would you explain the fact that your corruption mimics the path of Amelia's scratches?" He traced the marks with his fingertip.

She tugged her hand back and he let her go.

"Is that why Declan was looking for a cure?" She rubbed her wrist.

"Because people who should be immune to corruption were getting it? Has someone figured out a way to give it to non-mages?"

"It's all just speculation at the moment. But how did you know that Declan was looking for a cure? I don't recall telling you that."

Her eyes flicked to something to her left and the corner of her mouth twitched. "I went through some of the things on his desk and I also took his journal from his room at The Leaping Cow."

It wasn't the whole truth, he was sure. "You took his journal?"

"He appeared to be messing around with magic in some very interesting ways and I was curious." She shrugged. "I also wanted to know what he had that was worth killing for."

Garret rubbed his chin, deliberating how much to tell her. Then he remembered Declan saying she was apparently related to Samson, and he drew the small journal out of the inner pocket of his jacket. "This. It belonged to a necromancer who studied corruption—"

"Samson."

He blinked. "So you have heard of him."

"Of course. He was my great-great … great-great?" She tapped her finger tips together as she counted, then sighed. "My ancestor."

Declan had mentioned necromancers were ardent about bloodlines.

"That diary won't be much help though." As she spoke, her eyes drifted to that same spot to her left.

He slipped the journal back into his jacket and glanced to the spot, letting his keen-sense drift out. He could feel the numb void that was Nea, her connection to the source cut off by the bind-shackles, and something else. A kind of niggling feeling, like there was a snag in the source, a single pebble that was enough to affect the flow of power but not enough to divert it entirely. Strange.

"Why would Evard be interested in Samson's research? Interested enough to kill to get his hands on it?" Nea's question dragged his attention back to her.

"I am not sure." As he said it, her face changed to a look of realisation followed very closely by a look of fear so raw it unsettled him. "What's wrong?"

"I knew it. His curiosity about the Between, the decline into outright madness. He was always cruel and controlling but ..." She chewed her thumbnail. "The cases of corruption. You said they came from wounds?"

"At least one that I am certain of."

Her lip was pressed between her teeth again, her eyes unfocused as they stared at something he couldn't see. It was a look Declan had often worn. Absently, her fingers stroked the marks on her arm. "Who has access to Amelia?"

"Only those at Fort Braemar."

"And she is the only being of her type that you are aware of?"

"Yes."

She tapped her index finger against her chin. "He has to have access to another one."

"Another reanimation?"

She shook her head and frowned. "No. She is a reanimation, though I am not sure she's a true one. But that's not what I mean. I mean another deathborn."

Something in the way she said it made the hairs on his neck prickle. "A deathborn?"

Her attention flicked to the left again. "Yes. Amelia is a deathborn. I would stake my life on it."

"But deathborn are a myth."

A strange look crossed her face and she let out a huff of breath. "No, they are definitely not a myth and Amelia is definitely one." She rubbed her temples. "If Evard doesn't have access to Amelia, then there has to be another deathborn that he has. And if that is the case, if Evard is still messing around with things he shouldn't be, then ... then you need to figure out how to get Margot and I out of here and fast."

Garret shook his head as he headed down the hallway to the main castle entrance. He wanted to trust Nea but she was so hard to get a read on. One minute, he thought he had the measure of her, but the next, she did or said something that completely flipped his view. But then Margot and Emil both thought so highly of her, even knowing the power she possessed, and he trusted their judgement. At least, he trusted Margot's; Emil could be a bit hit and miss.

He slipped his hand into his pocket and his fingers found the bracelet. It had been such a constant over the past two months that he often found himself reaching for it when he needed to centre his thoughts.

"Declan, I could really use your input right now."

"Taken up talking to yourself since we last met, I see." A warm voice sounded behind him and he turned to see Evard's son striding his way.

Leith had taken after his late mother with his sandy hair and friendly features. His eyes, though the same shade of grey as his father's, weren't cold, and the fine creases at the sides of them hinted at his easy sense of humour. Garret often wondered how Leith had come to be so different to Evard, but then he'd spent most of his younger years living with his mother in Osmar.

"Your Highness. I didn't know you were expected back so soon."

"Please, Garret. You've seen me drunk enough to run naked through the Bright Temple. I think that warrants dropping protocol when it is just the two of us." He held out his hand and Garret shook it.

"Thank you for the reminder. I've been trying to wipe that memory from my mind." He grinned as he released Leith's hand.

Leith laughed. "Forgive me." He sobered and glanced down the hallway. "You don't happen to be on your way to see Father, do you?"

Garret shook his head. "I was heading back to the warden barracks."

"Ah. Then perhaps you can confirm a rumour for me. I was going to ask Father directly, but he can be tight-lipped."

"It depends on the rumour. I try to keep out of the loop, as far as palace gossip goes."

"I'm not interested in which of the guards is ploughing which of the maids. I'm curious about one of Father's *guests*."

Garret folded his arms. "I take it you mean the necromancer?"

Leith licked his lip. "I don't need details, just a name."

"Nea of Hartswood."

Leith's fists clenched for a moment. He muttered something under his breath that Garret couldn't quite catch. "Can you—" His attention snapped to something behind Garret.

"There you are, my dear." It was a sweet voice, one that hid a mean demeanour. "And Garret." She purred his name and Garret schooled his features as he turned.

"Lady Catriona, a pleasure as always."

The smile on her red-painted lips did not reach her dark-honey eyes. She lifted her hand and pushed her sheet of sleek black hair over her shoulder, revealing the low-cut neckline of her sapphire-coloured gown. Her tongue touched her lower lip and the cloying fingers of her keen attempted to burrow into the back of Garret's mind. He pulled his walls up, blocking out the touch of power, but he was still left with the lingering sensation that he had eaten something too sweet.

Catriona pouted. "Such a deep and steady mind. I would so love to explore it. I'm sure it holds a plethora of sordid secrets."

"Cat." There was a slight reprimand in Leith's tone.

"You're no fun, Leith." She stroked her fingers along the neckline of her gown.

Garret glanced at Leith. "I really should be getting to the barracks. I have a few things to organise for tomorrow."

"Find me later when you have some time and we'll have a catch up. I promise we won't hit the bottle quite so hard this time." Leith smiled as he slid his arm around Catriona's waist.

Garret nodded and hurried away.

When he entered the barracks, the first thing Garret saw was Emil swinging on a stool. Ryan and Sonia sat with him and the table in front of them was littered with cups and dice. A large ginger cat with a very thin patch of fur on its rump was curled up on the other end of the table. It opened one eye as the three wardens scooped their dice into their cups and sealed the open tops with their hands. They gave them a hearty shake, rattling the dice inside then slammed them on the table and peeked at the results underneath.

The cat yawned and stretched before jumping down to saunter over and wrap itself around Garret's legs. Garret bent and scratched behind its ears, pulling his hand back as it lifted its paw to bat at his fingers.

"Care to join us, Commander?"

Garret looked up at the man who had spoken—Ryan, the tall, thin warden with a head of hair nearly the same shade of ginger as the cat.

"Not right now, thank you."

"He's probably still sore from the last time we thrashed him," Sonia, the oldest of the group, said, the lines around her eyes deepening as she gave him a wide smile.

"Maybe a little." He chuckled. "Is Haley about?"

"Haven't seen her. What about you, Ryan?" Emil grinned and Sonia high-fived him as Ryan's cheeks went rosy.

"Haley was on the Dust Town shift today but she said she was going to visit the temple after she finished." Ryan spoke to his fingers which were gripping the edge of the table.

"Thank you, Ryan." Garret was about to leave when the door flew open and a young woman came bounding in.

"Alright, who is ready to get thra—Commander!" She skidded to a stop a foot before she crashed into Garret. The ends of her chin-length sandy-brown hair flicked forward and obscured her large hazel eyes.

"Speak of the Shadow." Emil chuckled and scooped up the cat, who was rubbing against the leg of his stool.

Haley rocked back and gave Garret a warm smile. "I didn't think you'd be gracing us with your presence this evening."

"Neither did I, but something pressing has come up and I need the four of you to be ready."

"I am always ready." Haley dropped onto the bench next to Ryan and took a peek at his dice. "Ooh bad roll."

Sonia laughed and stood. "That's game, boys. Time to get back to work." She picked up the small pile of coins in the middle of the table. "Just tell us what you need, Commander."

Garret looked at each expectant face in turn. Emil would be down for his plan, and Haley as well. But Sonia and Ryan? Whilst he would trust them with his life, he'd never asked them to risk everything before.

"We're the only ones here?"

Emil nodded. "Willem left a while ago and the others are out on patrol."

Garret mirrored Emil's nod and drew a deep breath. "I'm not going to lie. What I am about to ask of you is high treason. If Evard suspects any of you have a hand in it then I am sure you are well aware of what he will do. So I am asking as your friend, not ordering as your commander, and I don't want you to feel obligated to help. I will not think any less of you if you turn your back on me now."

Sonia's eyes narrowed and she ran her tongue along her teeth. "You're not one for melodramatics, Garret, so just cut to the chase."

"Right. I want to rescue Margot and Nea."

Emil dropped the cat. "About time."

"That's no easy task. We might be able to get to Margot; she's being kept in the tower. But Nea? Evard has her stashed away in that rabbit warren of a dungeon," Sonia said.

"I do have a plan. We're going to rescue Margot first and use the chaos from her disappearance to get Nea out."

"You do realise the second Evard discovers Margot is missing, he'll double down the guard on Nea," Haley stated.

"True. Which is why we need to pick our moment." He turned to Emil. "Are Molly and the others back in the city?"

Emil nodded. "They are at the south side safe house. I can pass the word to them if you would like?"

"No, I'll go see them." He said before switching his attention back to the others. "Evard is planning a dinner tomorrow night. He wants to parade Nea around in front of some nobles who were not present to witness what she did to Harold." He swallowed to clear the sour taste in his mouth at the memory of the way the source had buckled and churned in the wake of what Nea had done. And how even hours after, the air in the throne room still felt ... wrong. Almost like the source there was scarred. "It is likely going to be the best chance we will get. Haley and Sonia, you will focus on Margot. Janey will help you with the servants' passages."

"Ah, Garret, you do realise that I can't understand that sign language she uses?" Sonia said.

He nodded. "But Haley knows enough that you should be able to communicate, and Janey can talk if she absolutely needs to. It's just difficult for her." He fished in his pocket and pulled out a small rose-gold-coloured key. "The key to Margot's bind-shackles."

Sonia held her hand out and he dropped it into her palm. "Where will we take her?"

"The south side safe house, but make sure you are not followed."

"Emil and Ryan—"

"We're in charge of Nea, right? Sure, give the girls the easier target." Emil's tone was playful.

Garret folded his arms. "Emil, you are going to get Nea out. Ryan is going to meet up with Molly and create a diversion in the city. Nea will be much harder as we have to wait for the distraction of Margot's escape. I'll get her to Janey, who will bring her through the passages to the corridor outside the servants' quarters. From there, Emil, you will take her out the old service courtyard. There's a gate in the back wall that isn't used anymore. Once you're through, circle around to Dust Town and from there, head into the south side."

Emil nodded. "Okay, and what about you?"

"I'll be trying to cover your tracks and giving you all the best chance of getting out of this with your heads." He studied each of their faces, letting them process the severity of what they were about to attempt. He had meant it when he said he wouldn't blame any of them if they didn't want to be involved, but Mother's grief he hoped he wasn't going into this alone. "So are you in?"

They all nodded, and Garret felt a moment of relief. He *wasn't* in this alone, but at the same time he was concerned for what this would mean for them all. There really was no going back.

Was this how the mages and wardens at Kalhanna had felt knowing that their objection to Evard's ruling would likely lead to their deaths?

CHAPTER THIRTEEN

MARGOT

Margot pressed her palms against her eyes. There had been a headache building behind them all day and now the pressure was almost unbearable. She was worried about Nea and Molly ... and Garret. The bloody fool was going to get himself killed, or worse, and knowing Evard, he'd make Nea reanimate him while Margot watched. She let out her breath in a huff and slouched in her chair.

The weeks she'd been locked in this room, not knowing what was happening, where everyone was, had seemed more bearable than this waiting around for the next time Evard dragged her out to force Nea to do something appalling. She was glad she hadn't been able to feel the source when Nea was stripping Harold's soul. She'd caught a brief glance of Garret's face and seen several other mages and wardens in the room looking ... sickened. There really was no other word for it. She could imagine how it felt. She'd walked with Declan and Garret through the aftermath of Kalhanna. The power the mages had used there, even days after the purge, had left the source rumpled and prickly, like a tunic shoved in the bottom of a basket for too long.

Poor Nea. The haunted look in her eyes, the way her hands had trembled ... Margot knew she couldn't take much more of Evard's abuse. He didn't even have to lay a finger on her to enact his torture. As long as he could threaten Margot, Nea would willingly destroy every last ounce of her own humanity.

Margot clenched her fists and leapt to her feet, ignoring the niggling pressure behind her eyes. "Bright Mother be damned!" she yelled and slammed her hands on the desk.

"Everything alright in there?" The guard knocked on her door and she let out a growl of frustration.

"Everything is fine!" Just one of the people she cared about most in the world was being made to do horrific things to entertain Evard's ego.

There was a thump and the sound of a body sliding down the wall, then the key rattled in the lock. Margot grabbed the chair she had been sitting in and held it up, the four legs pointing at the door which burst open to reveal a young woman with wide hazel eyes and a beaming smile.

"Haley?"

"Well, don't just stand there gaping. Get your arse out into the hallway."

Margot lowered the chair. "What—"

"No time for questions. Come on now." Haley grabbed her arm and dragged her from the room to where another warden Margot knew was waiting.

Sonia gave her a brisk hug. "You've gotten yourself into a world of trouble, Little Mouse."

"Sonia? What—"

"No time." Haley tugged her down the hallway towards an alcove and Sonia fell into step behind them. As they ducked into the recess, Haley knocked on the frame of the painting hanging there and stepped back as it swung open. She shoved Margot unceremoniously into the newly created doorway, nearly knocking over the maid, who was waiting in the dark corridor.

Janey shook her head angrily at Haley as the painting whooshed shut, shrouding all four women in darkness.

"Janey, do you mind giving us a little light?" Sonia asked, her breath stirring Margot's hair.

A warm yellow mage light flickered to life and bobbed gently above their heads.

"Thank you."

Janey shrugged and then waved them along the corridor and away from the painting.

When they had gone down several very thin, twisting sets of stairs, Janey stopped and lifted her hands, signing to Haley, who held up a pink key. Margot nearly cried with relief when she realised it was the key to her shackles.

As Haley touched the key to each shackle, they fell away, and the source came charging into her body. Her short hair stood on end and her knees buckled. She leant against the wall and wrapped her arms around herself, shivering, though not from cold. As hot tears stung her eyes, she pressed the back of her hand over her mouth. Now was not the time for breaking down but after weeks of nothing but a silent numbness, being able to feel the two wardens and the hot flickering of Janey's fire magic was ... indescribable.

While Margot drew a few calming breaths, Janey disappeared through another hidden door then came back and nodded. She signed "*good luck*" and ushered them out into a dimly lit corridor before the door slid shut and hid her from view.

"Now what?" Margot asked. "You can't just walk me through the front door."

"Don't worry, Little Mouse. We have a plan." There was something about Sonia's grin that made Margot nervous.

Haley moved to a door down the corridor and peeked inside. She gave Sonia a thumbs up, then disappeared into the room. Sonia led Margot after her into what appeared to be the laundry. Haley held up a maid's uniform exactly like the one Janey had been wearing: a calf-length green skirt, linen shirt, and apron.

"Here, put this on," Haley said handing the uniform to Margot before moving to watch the door.

Margot stripped to her underwear. "Okay, so you disguise me as a maid, then what?" She pulled the shirt on.

"Then we walk out the servants' gate while Haley causes a distraction at the main gate." Sonia held out a head-kerchief as Margot tucked her shirt in.

"And you think this will work? Did you run this plan past Garret?"

Haley chuckled. "It's Garret's plan. Now, hurry up and stop fussing. The others need us to get you out so they can use your disappearance as a distraction."

"A distraction for what?"

"So the others can rescue Nea," Sonia said. "Get a move on or I'll carry you through the town over my shoulder half-dressed or not."

Once Margot was finished dressing and her close-cropped golden curls were hidden under the head-kerchief, they moved back out into the hallway. Haley bid them farewell and took off in the direction of the main gates while Sonia led Margot to the west side of the courtyard and the servants' exit.

They waited just inside the door until they heard the sounds of Haley shouting and the pounding of booted feet. Sonia peeked out the door, and Margot saw one of the two guards who watched the small servants' gate go running towards the commotion.

"Wait for my signal." Sonia walked across to the remaining guard. He tensed as she approached.

Margot couldn't hear their conversation but it was clear that the guard was getting agitated. Then Sonia drew her sword and the guard followed suit. Margot winced as metal screeched against metal and she rushed forward. She focused on the bones in the guard's arm and twisted the source, making them bow and snap. The guard dropped his sword with a yowl of pain and hunched over, clutching his broken arm. Margot ran past Sonia and out the gate.

Moments later, Sonia joined her. "We have to get to the south side," she said as they ran away from the palace

Margot glanced towards the spire of the temple. "What about Haley?"

"She'll be fine. She will meet up with us at the safe house."

Margot nodded. "Alright. It's probably best if we stay off the streets. Let's cut through the temple."

Sonia looked sceptical. "I don't think that is a good idea."

"Do you have a better one?"

"Well, no." Sonia huffed. "Okay, temple it is."

The temple grounds were a quiet oasis. A small stream wound like a ribbon through the exotic plants growing in their neatly tended gardens. As the path of the stream twisted, it created several small ponds where colourful fish gathered at the surface, testing even the tiniest pieces of flotsam for food. When Nonna had brought her and Nea here when they were children, Margot had wondered what fate would befall the plants and fish over the depths of winter. But the temple complex was always warm. The priestesses insisted it was the light of the Bright Mother but Margot was certain it was the work of a fire mage.

In the middle of the large landing at the top of stairs that led into the temple stood a statue of the Bright Mother. One hand was held in front of her, fingers twisted up in a way that suggested she was offering something to the faithful. The other hand rested delicately over her left breast, covering her heart. Unlike earlier representations, this one didn't show the Bright Mother's bare breasts. She wore a thin robe that fell over her body in delicate folds. The sculptor had been a true artist, most likely a mage, to have hewn the stone in such a way that made the fabric of the robe and the tumbling waves of the Bright Mother's hair look so soft. Margot almost wanted to touch them to make sure they were actually stone.

Sonia cleared her throat, drawing Margot's attention to the dark-haired priestess who was standing a short distance away, watching them. "Best we keep moving, Little Mouse."

Margot nodded and they started across the garden again.

"Wait," the woman called and jogged over to them. "You're the healer. The one from Dust Town."

Sonia tensed and her hand went for her sword.

As she turned to face the woman, it dawned on Margot where she had seen her before. "Yes. I remember you. Cara, wasn't it?"

"That's right. I went back to check on you but the clinic was burned and they told me you hadn't returned after the guard escorted you away."

Margot nodded. A shout outside of the temple grounds made her flinch and she glanced in its direction.

"We really should keep moving," Sonia said.

The priestess chewed her lip as she stared at them. "Come with me. I can help you."

"No. I can't risk endangering you or anyone else here. If the king were to discover you'd aided me, he would have you killed."

"I understand the risk, but it is what *she* would want." She indicated the statue. "Quickly now, before anyone else comes." She ushered them up the steps and inside.

Cara led them across the main chamber of the temple and through a door behind another statue of the Bright Mother. This one had the traditional exposed breasts just peeking through tumbling waves of hair, and both arms outstretched. At her feet lay offerings of food and flowers and a basket of circular wooden charms engraved with a simple eight-pointed star.

Once through the door, Cara hurried them down the hallway. She stepped into a room that was full of books and comfortable-looking chairs, and moved to the wall. She touched one of the sconces and gave it a gentle pull. A *click* sounded and then the grating of a mechanism as a panel of floor slid away to reveal a staircase. "This is an old escape tunnel from the time of Queen Eugenie. No one has been down there in decades, but it apparently leads to the catacombs under the east side of the upper market." She glanced at the door to the room. "When you reach the fork, take the left path and count seven archways, then enter the door on the right. It leads into the older part of the catacombs that connects to the aqueducts which will lead you straight to the market. I am sure you can find your way from there."

"Thank you," Margot said before she started down the stairs.

Once Sonia joined her, the floor grated back into place and they were cast into complete darkness. Margot pulled a small thread of source and formed a mage light that lit the tunnel in a soft green glow.

"You're sure we can trust that priestess?"

"I didn't sense any malice from her and this gets us off the street at least."

Sonia shook her head. "You spent too much time with Emil when you were growing up. I honestly hope Nea at least has her head screwed on straight."

Margot chewed her thumbnail and shrugged.

Sonia rolled her eyes and turned to the only path available to them. "Well, no use standing around in the dark. Let's see where this tunnel leads us."

They walked for a while, the path seeming to curve and twist around on itself. The mage light bobbing in front of them cast long shadows back the way they had come—inky fingers reaching into the darkness that made Margot's stomach tighten and the hair on her arms prickle.

Finally, they reached the fork and started down the left path as instructed. The air here felt cooler and charged with something other-worldly. It was a similar sensation to Nea's magic. Cold but in a way that was almost comforting, like the chill of an early autumn evening soothing away the heat from the day.

As they passed under the fourth archway, Margot thought she heard voices. Sonia must have heard them too because she lightly touched Margot's elbow and pressed a finger to her lips. They stood still, listening in the dark. The mage light flickered, causing the shadows to tremble. Everything was silent, but as Margot moved to step forward again, the voices started and she felt the creep of magic up her spine. Sonia took hold of her wrist and pulled her down the pathway, away from the voices. The air became thicker as they passed under the fifth archway, and by the time they reached the seventh, it was like walking against a gale.

It took their combined strength to get the door to the catacombs open, and when they did, they tumbled through into the still silence. Sprawled on the cold floor and panting, Margot rolled over and her eyes met the vacant sockets of a grinning skull. She sat up and scuttled backwards.

"What was that back under the archways?" Sonia stood and brushed herself off.

"I am not sure, though I imagine Nea could tell us. It felt like a perverted form of necromancer magic."

"That's what I thought. Those voices—I thought I heard Dhen, but he was killed at Kalhanna."

Margot swallowed to clear the taste in her mouth. "Whatever it was, it's gone now, and I don't want to linger here. We should look for the door to the aqueducts."

"Are you able to make the light bigger?"

Margot nodded and focused on the little ball of light. As it grew, it distorted, as though pulled in different directions. Suddenly it shattered, casting them back into darkness for several heartbeats before the room was drowned in light. Margot shielded her eyes until the light settled to reveal sconces in the walls all lit with the flickering green glow of her mage light.

"Well, that's handy," Sonia said as she looked around.

There were three sarcophagi, one against each wall, between the low shelves that were piled with the bones of the dead. The door they had entered through was the only obvious exit to the chamber.

"Perhaps we took the wrong path, unless that sister was lying about this passage being a way out." Sonia moved to the wall across from them and inspected it.

Margot's attention was drawn to a stone pulpit in the centre of the room. The book that sat open upon it was shrouded in cobwebs and dust. Magic shifted over the tome in intricate swirls the iridescent hue of oil on water. She stepped forward and brushed her hand over the open pages to clear the detritus away, but the pages were brittle with age and crumbled to nothing. She coughed as a plume of dust stirred the air.

"Should we try the hallway again?" Sonia asked.

Margot stared at the door. She didn't know what that was out there under the archways but she really didn't want to experience it again. She glanced down at the destroyed book and noted the gleam of metal under its rotten cover. She brushed the remnants of the book onto the floor, creating another cloud of dust, and inspected the top of the pulpit. An untarnished square of rose-gold was inlaid into the dark wood. It looked like robrillium, but Margot had never heard of robrillium being used for anything other than the manufacture of bind-shackles. She touched her fingers to it and they grew cold as her magic pulled away from the metal. She shook her hand to coax the feeling back as she read the words inscribed on the plaque. "Those who seek salvation will find it only when they silence the one who whispers to the dead."

"Do you think it means the archways?" Sonia asked.

Margot shook her head. "Maybe it's something to do with the sarcophagi ..."

Sonia moved over to the closest one and read the inscription. "Johanna of Port Brenna. Port Brenna, where have I heard that before?"

"Mother's Deep. It was originally a large port city with a college at the centre until it was devasted by a great cataclysm that sunk it beneath the ocean."

Recognition crossed Sonia's features. She moved to the next sarcophagus and read the inscription on it. "Richard of Kalhanna. I know this one; he was a healer but something in his mind snapped and he murdered an entire town. His was one of the first recorded cases of corruption, I think."

"Wait. Johanna has something to do with corruption as well. I remember seeing a reference to her in one of those old journals in Nonna's study at Hartswood." Margot chewed her thumb as she tried to think of the passage. "One of body, one of mind, and one of"—she rushed to the third sarcophagus—"soul." She rubbed her hand over the inscription. "Evette of Red Meadow. Samson's wife."

"Samson? Was Evette a necromancer too?"

"If Richard was a healer and Johanna was a mind mage, then I'd bet Molly's crossbow that Evette was a necromancer."

Sonia smiled. "So, the one who whispers to the dead."

"Exactly."

"And we have to silence her? She is already about as silent as you can get." Sonia looked at the lid of the sarcophagus with trepidation.

Margot took a step forward and her toes brushed the tiles under the sarcophagus. She crouched and dusted them off. One tile had a simple engraving of an eight-pointed star.

Margot pressed it.

Nothing happened.

"Okay, so any other ideas?" Sonia asked.

Margot thought for a moment. "Wait, you're a warden!"

"Well spotted. But I'm a bit concerned that you're only noticing now, given I've known you since you could barely walk."

"No, no. What do wardens do?"

"This one is about to shake some sense into her charge." Sonia crossed her arms.

"You suppress mages. You *silence* their connection to the source."

"She's bones and dust. I'm pretty sure her connection has been silenced already." There was humour in Sonia's voice.

Margot rolled her eyes.

"Alright, we'll try it your way, Little Mouse." Sonia held her hands out and the air in the room turned thick, cutting out the constant thrum of the source until it felt like the beat of a distant drum.

When Margot could no longer feel the source in the room, a heavy grating noise sounded, and a panel of wall slid open, allowing a rush of air in that made the mage lights flicker and dance.

"Well, what do you know?"

"Declan would have loved this place." Margot drew the mage light from the sconces back into a small hovering ball.

She stepped through the doorway into another tunnel and Sonia came after her, only releasing her suppression on Evette's sarcophagus once they were both out of the room. As soon as she did, the wall grated back into place.

"Let's see what kind of salvation is waiting at the end of this tunnel." Sonia started walking and Margot fell in behind her.

CHAPTER FOURTEEN

NEA

Nea had discovered that her cell was quite large: three strides from one side to the other and four from the door to the back wall. The anchor points at various intervals around the walls suggested it was built to house multiple chained prisoners, and she was thankful that they hadn't resorted to chaining her up.

She was pacing now. Judging by the time that had passed since the guard had brought her the last plate of food, it was getting towards late afternoon. Still, having no source of natural light, she really couldn't be sure. She was losing track faster now. The longer she stayed in this cell, the more time seemed to warp. At least she had Declan to keep her company as she paced around the cell, trying to stop her thoughts going too far inward to where the memories were.

She ran her fingers through her hair, grasping it by the roots and sighing as the tension in her scalp lessened for a moment. Hearing the scuff of the guard's boots, she glanced to the bars across the front of her cell. But it wasn't the guard.

Nea backed up until her hips pressed against the rough stone of the wall as she met a pair of dark eyes she had thought she'd never see again.

The warden on the other side of the bars ran his tongue along his teeth as he studied her. "Hello, Nea." His voice sent a scurry of cold down her spine and she drew a deep breath. "Not happy to see another survivor from Kalhanna? There are so few of us I would think that promotes a sense of comradery, wouldn't you?" As he spoke, he pulled a knife from the sheath at his thigh and pressed the tip of the dark metal blade against one gloved finger. She recognised that knife—last time she had seen it, the delicately carved handle had been between his ribs.

"Why are you here?" She fought to keep the fear from her voice. There were few people in the world she truly feared, but Willem was one of them.

His lips curved up at the corners, she wouldn't call it a smile though. "Can't I visit an old *friend*?" The words were accompanied by the grating of the blade along one of the bars.

Nea winced at the sound.

"I had hoped Evard would give us a chance to get reacquainted. It was a shame our business finished so abruptly last time." He looked almost longingly at the knife as he stroked his thumb along the edge of it. "But alas, the king denied my request in favour of his new *pet*. It won't stop me though; I'll get my turn and then I'll show you just what this blade feels like as it rasps against your ribs and robs you of your life."

"If you kill me, Evard will—"

"I am not a fool who can't control himself!" he snarled and his thumb slipped on the blade; the coppery scent of blood filled the air.

"Seems like a fool to me," Declan said as he appeared beside her.

Nea paid him no mind and kept her attention on Willem, giving him a rueful smirk. "Who are you trying to convince?"

He let out an inhuman sound. "You—" He silenced himself as his attention snapped to something she couldn't see. "We'll continue this later." He sheathed the blade again and stormed from view.

"Willem." She heard the guard say followed by Willem's agitated growl in response. Then the guard appeared in front of her cell with Janey in tow.

Janey gave Nea a concerned look as the guard said, "His majesty expects your presence for dinner."

Still rattled from Willem's visit, she just blinked at the guard, who cleared his throat. "Come on, Nea, we shouldn't keep the king waiting."

She shook her head to clear her thoughts and then gave him a nod. "I'm sorry, I—" The heavy sounds of another set of boots striding purposefully down the hall cut her off, and she turned her head to see who was coming. It wasn't Willem returning; it was Leon. He'd visited her several times. Thankfully, he had never had the key but that hadn't stopped him taunting her as Willem had done. In that moment, she wasn't sure which she would prefer.

Declan gave her a worried look.

"Open the door." Leon didn't take his eyes off Nea as he spoke to the guard.

"Sir, the king requires—"

"I am aware of his majesty's order and I'll not lay a single finger on her. Unless she decides to show that rebellious streak of hers. Then I shall gladly pull her into line."

The guard unlocked the door, the look on his face a combination of remorse and nervousness. "Come on, Nea. We need to get you ready for dinner."

Nea thought about planting her feet and refusing to go but she didn't want to give Leon an excuse to touch her. She walked slowly out of the cell and Janey gave her a small smile before leading her into the same room as last time.

The guard took a seat at the desk, but Leon grabbed a chair and followed Janey and Nea into the room with the barrel. Janey frowned and glanced at Nea, who shook her head. Leon might have orders not to harm Nea, but she was certain that didn't extend to the maid.

Janey glared at Leon as he leant his head back against the wall and crossed his arms, a slow smile curling the corners of his mouth.

Nea swallowed and turned away from him as she stripped to her underwear. Janey had been heating the water, but she paused and stared at the grey marks on Nea's arm, a concerned frown twisting the corner of her mouth. Nea shook her head again, and Janey let out a breath as she turned her attention to the water once more. Her fingers swirled above the barrel for a few moments before she gave a short nod and handed Nea the soap, then helped her wash as she had last time. Neither of them looked at Leon but Nea could feel his eyes on her the entire time.

After a while, Janey held up a fresh change of clothes including a slip and drawers, and Nea quickly slid out of her old ones, keeping her back to Leon. Janey's green eyes narrowed, and a scowl crossed her lips as Nea felt Leon step behind her.

"So flawless—it's a shame this little birthmark disrupts it."

She twisted away but not before his finger had pressed savagely into the skin covering her hip. Leon smiled cruelly as Nea crossed her arms over her chest and retreated a few steps. She bit her lip, fighting the urge to lash out; without her magic, she had no hope of overpowering him.

"Don't tell me your fight is gone already?" He took another step towards her. "That would be a terrible a shame."

Janey shifted as though she was going to intervene but Nea mouthed the word *don't* and the maid stayed back, giving Leon a look of absolute loathing.

Oblivious to Janey, Leon took another step forward, and Nea backed away, trying to keep her breathing even and the tremor from her hands. An almost hedonistic smile curled the corners of his mouth and he advanced again, forcing her to retreat until her back pressed against the cold wall.

"When he's done with you"—he glanced at the ceiling to indicate Evard—"I'm going to enjoy destroying this pristine landscape." He ran a finger down her arm. "All this pretty, pale flesh just begging to be defiled." He inhaled deeply as he grabbed hold of her hip. His fingers dug cruelly into the flesh above her birthmark and she couldn't stop her gasp of pain.

A chair scraped against the floor outside the room and he released his grip on her and returned to his seat as though nothing had happened.

Janey put herself between Nea and Leon as she helped her slip into a low-cut gown of deep-purple silk. The fabric hugged her curves and the long sleeves, which came to a point over the back of her hands, hid both the bind-shackles and the corruption marks. Janey then took hold of Nea's hair and twisted it into an elegant coil, which she secured with a silver hair fork that resembled a large moon moth, the wings studded with amethysts.

As Janey stepped back to survey her handiwork, Leon stood and moved to Nea's side. "You are dismissed," he said to Janey, who had bent to gather Nea's clothes but didn't leave the room. "*Leave.*"

Janey glanced at Nea, who nodded. "It's alright, Janey."

Janey didn't look happy, but she left, taking Nea's old clothes with her. As soon as Janey was gone, Leon stepped closer.

"She's expected in the dining hall." That was Victor's voice. Nea glanced up to see the head jailor standing casually in the doorway, his eyes locked on Leon.

Leon's lip curled in frustration and Nea thought she heard a low growl in his throat. "Of course. We were just leaving."

"I always knew he was a snake." Declan appeared behind Leon and stepped through him, causing him to shiver.

"Let's go." Leon reached through Declan's torso and took hold of Nea's arm. He shuddered and released her. "Stop doing that!"

"I didn't do anything." She shared a look with Declan, who chuckled.

"Listen here!" He grabbed her again and yanked her forward, a chill rising through her as her body passed through Declan's form.

"Leon." Victor's tone was pure steel.

Leon glowered at the jailor, his grip tightening on Nea's arm until it felt firm enough to bruise her through the fabric of her sleeve. He dragged her out of the room, his pace clipped so she nearly had to run to keep up.

Before she knew it, he was leading her into the dining hall.

"Nea of Hartswood," the chamberlain announced loudly, and all eyes turned to her.

There were some faces she recognised and others she did not. She caught Garret's eye and noted the twist of his mouth as he glanced at the white-knuckled grip Leon had on her arm. Even in his dark dress uniform, he looked out of place and uncomfortable. He was standing with a tall Osmarian woman in a deep red gown that had pearls embroidered along the neckline and on the delicate cap sleeves. They matched the length of creamy pearls circling her throat. Her mouth twisted in appraisal as her eyes drifted over Nea. Beside her stood—Leith.

Nea's heart started to race and she shifted her weight onto her heels, ready to turn and run. Leon gripped her arm tighter and pulled her forward, leading her across the room to where Evard was talking to a scrawny-looking man with a high hairline.

"My lord." Leon released Nea's arm to bow.

Evard waved him away and his attention shifted to Nea. His cold gaze roved the length of her, and a smile crossed his pale lips. "How lovely you look in that colour, my dear." He turned to the man beside him. "Lord Augustus, this is the necromancer you have been hearing so much about."

The lord took hold of Nea's hand and pressed a wet kiss to the back of it.

A sadistic gleam highlighted Evard's eyes as his attention lifted to something behind her. "And you remember Leith, I am sure."

Nea held her breath as Leith appeared beside her, and she let it out slowly to buy herself a few moments to gather her composure. The corner of Leith's mouth tightened as he studied her, and as she lifted her gaze to meet his eyes, she bit the inside of her cheek. She knew now why Garret's eyes seemed so familiar, particularly in those times he let his guard down. They were the same deep shade of grey as Leith's. She licked her lips and dipped into a curtsey, not sure she trusted herself to speak.

"This is the necromancer then." The woman in the red dress sidled up to Leith, her thin fingers snaking around his arm to cup the crook of his elbow.

"Lady Catriona, may I present Nea of Hartswood," Leith said, not taking his eyes from Nea, as though he expected her to disappear if he looked away.

Catriona—Nea knew that name. Second princess of Osmar and rumoured to have a spiteful temper.

"A pleasure. I have heard *so* much about you." Catriona's voice was high and sweet—the kind of sweet that was usually a façade.

"Now we are all here, shall we take our places?" Evard indicated the long table that was dressed for a feast. He held his arm out to Nea.

She stared at it but didn't move. "Where is Margot?"

"She will not be joining us until the after-dinner activities. Should you decide to prove argumentative, however, I can summon her early. A little before-dinner torture never goes astray." Evard's words were quiet, and those already moving to the table didn't appear to hear them.

He lifted his arm again and Nea glanced around at the guards. Without seeing Margot, she couldn't be certain Evard didn't have her stashed somewhere with a guard ready to slit her throat if Nea did anything rash. Not that she could use her powers, but the gleaming knives set out for dinner had not escaped her notice.

"You know how I dislike waiting." Evard prompted.

Slowly, Nea rested her fingers against the inside of his lower arm and his bony hand closed over them as he led her to the table. He showed her to a seat between Lord Augustus and Leith and then took his own at the head of the table. Garret was sitting across from her between two nearly identical women dressed in silk and fur.

She looked sideways at Leith, whose fingers were twitching on the tabletop. "You look well," he said.

Really? She'd spent two, or was it three, weeks as a prisoner.

"Oh that's right. The pair of you have a *history* don't you?"

Nea stilled as Declan leant over her shoulder.

She had to ignore his question though. She couldn't address him here at the table where she was the only one who could see him.

A servant filled her cup with a deep red wine and she picked it up to take a long sip.

Platters of food were brought out: great gleaming plates of different meats and vegetables and a jug of a thin red gravy. Lord Augustus made polite chatter with the ladies across the table, one of whom was the Lady Eudora, his wife, and the other her sister, Tabitha. Tabitha kept adjusting the neckline of her gown to reveal more of her cleavage and laughing in a high whine that set Nea's teeth on edge.

"I am so glad I was never invited to one of these dinners. Though I have it on good authority that Tabitha can be rather *amiable* after a few cups." Declan grinned from behind the woman. "I believe the good prince wants your attention." He nodded to Leith and Nea turned to him.

Leith was looking at her expectantly, like he was waiting for her to answer a question.

"I'm sorry. I didn't quite catch that."

Catriona leant around Leith and smiled sweetly. "I believe we missed quite the show. Such a shame about poor Harold." Her red-painted lips pulled into a smile which didn't reach her eyes.

Nea paled and lifted her hand to run it through her hair, but lowered it again as she remembered the elegant knot that Janey had created.

"I have heard there is a similar display planned for this evening. I am so looking forward to seeing what exactly it is that makes *you* so special." Catriona took a sip of wine, watching Nea's reaction over the rim of her glass.

Nea schooled her features in a polite smile and said nothing.

"Cat, my darling, perhaps this is not the best topic of conversation whilst we are still eating."

"I can see why Garret hates her." Declan rolled his eyes. "Don't let her get to you. You knew Evard wasn't bringing you up here just to wine and dine and make pleasantries."

It was killing Nea not to be able to talk back to Declan, and judging by his roguish grin, he knew it.

She settled her gaze on Garret, who was glancing out of the corner of his eye right at the spot Declan was standing. She didn't think he could see Declan, but maybe he could feel him. She'd have to ask. If she ever got the chance.

Garret's attention snapped to Tabitha, who had placed fingers on his arm.

She leant towards him, her soft green eyes flicking to Nea as she said, "So you are the one responsible for capturing the necromancer? You were so brave, going after her when you knew what she could have done to you. To think you could have ended up like poor Harold."

Nea locked eyes with Tabitha and forced a blasé smile onto her lips. She lifted her glass and took a deliberate sip, not taking her eyes off the other woman until she blushed and looked away. Even when she had been part of the court as Evard's arcane advisor, she had disliked the scheming and social posturing that went on.

"Your concern is unrequired, my lady. At no point in my dealings with Nea did I feel threatened." Garret turned his attention back to his plate.

"Of course not. Silly of me to worry when you are such an accomplished commander."

Shouts sounded in the hall and all eyes turned to a member of the king's guard, who ran into the room, gripping a wound on his upper arm. Leon strode to meet him and they all heard the exchange.

"The healer—she's gone."

Nea's fingers closed over the knife beside her plate. If Margot was free, she could end it now. All she had to do was reach Evard before the guards grabbed her. She knew where to hit—Margot had shown her once long ago. If she managed to sever the artery, then he'd bleed out before they could get a healer to him. She tensed in her seat, ready to stand. Evard's cold gaze met hers and the look in them turned her blood to ice. She had to move now. But why wasn't she? All she had to do was push her chair back and lunge past—

Evard stood and Nea flew into action. Her chair crashed against the floor and she leapt over it, rushing to Evard. But a hand caught the back of her skirt and she fell short of her goal; instead, the knife imbedded in his shoulder. He gripped it, blood oozing between his fingers as he snarled and slapped her hard enough that her vision blurred. "Get her out of here!" he roared.

She was hauled to her feet, but she twisted and swung her arm, her fist catching her attacker in the side of the jaw. She blinked as she met Leith's startled grey eyes.

He tightened his grip on her and tugged her across the room. "Come on."

She couldn't go back to the cell, but she wasn't sure she could attack Leith either. Her breath was suddenly coming too fast, her ribs pushing against the tight lacings of her gown as she let Leith lead her from the room.

The grey walls and green drapery flashed by as Leith took long, fast strides guiding Nea towards the dungeon. Leith wouldn't let her be locked up again would he? Of course he would. He had proved before Kalhanna that he would choose his father over her. She planted her feet, causing him to stagger to a halt, and his momentum jolted her shoulder in the socket.

"I can't go back there."

Leith's gaze softened as he looked at her. "I can't let you go, Nea. Father—" There was a meaty thud and suddenly Leith dropped to the ground to reveal Janey standing behind him holding a heavy-looking bust of one of Evard's ancestors.

"Janey! Thank the Bright Mother. But you attacked the prince."

Janey dropped the bust and shrugged, then she waved Nea towards an alcove a short distance away.

Nea was almost to the alcove when she heard a voice that froze her in place.

"My, my, you are in a lot of trouble now. An attempt on the king's life and that of his heir. Oh, I do hope I am the one that gets to punish you."

She turned to face Leon as he stepped over Leith's prone form.

"Now, I would tell you not to do anything stupid but—"

"Nea!" Janey's thick voice startled her into action as a ball of flame flew at Leon, who twisted out of the way with a growl.

Nea whirled around and leapt into the alcove, disappearing behind a panel of wall that slammed shut as Janey rushed in after her.

They could hear Leon's shout and the pounding of his fists against the panel, but it didn't budge.

Janey had cast a mage light. It bobbed ahead of her as she ran, leading Nea down the twisting passageways. Nea clutched her skirts and tried to keep up but her throat was tightening, preventing her from drawing breath. The burning in her chest reminded her of the smoke from Kalhanna—

"No, Nea! Don't you dare break down now!" She leant against the wall as she berated herself.

When she lifted her gaze, Janey was staring at her curiously. The curiosity made way for concern, and suddenly Janey reached out and placed a hand on Nea's shoulder before pulling her into a hug. Nea stiffened but there was something about the hug that slowed her breath and chased the memories boiling beneath the surface away.

Janey leant back and searched her eyes, then nodded and started running again. Nea followed.

Finally, Janey slowed her pace at what appeared to be a dead end. She pressed her finger to her lips and lifted a small flap in the wall. After a moment, there was a soft click and she thrust Nea out into the hallway, straight into the arms of Emil.

The door behind her closed and she turned, looking for Janey, but the maid was gone. "Janey can't stay here. Leon saw her attack Leith."

"Nea, it's okay. Janey will get away, but she needs to go help the others first. Come on." He took hold of her hand and she was running again.

Emil pulled her through a door into the servants' quarters then, dodging through the beds, he took her out the other door and into a courtyard that was full of old buckets, tools, and several long drying lines. Emil didn't slow his pace. If anything, he quickened his steps as he crossed the yard.

They'd just reached a small gate in the wall when footsteps sounded behind them.

"Found you!"

Mother's grief, Leon was better than a scent hound. His sword sung as it was drawn from its scabbard and Emil twisted around, pushing Nea behind him and out of the gate as he drew his own.

Nea stood on the other side of the wall, listening to the grunts and sounds of swords clashing. She couldn't just wait out here and let Emil get hurt. She ducked back into the courtyard. Emil was on the ground, a dazed look in his eyes and a thin line of blood oozing from his leg.

Leon towered over him, sword raised.

Without a second thought, Nea leapt onto Leon's back and he snarled, twisting as he tried to grab her and drag her off. But she held on tight with one arm, the fingers of her other tearing the delicate comb from her hair. She chose her mark and drove the comb into the thin patch of skin not protected by his armour. It stuck into the flesh where his shoulder met his neck and he yelled. He dropped his sword and thrashed, managing to get a grip on her side. He tossed her off and she slid along the ground, the cobbles tearing the sleeves of her gown and grazing her skin. Leon was on her in a moment, grabbing her by the hair and pulling her to her feet. He threw her against the wall of the garden and his hands closed around her throat.

Black spots danced across her vision as he squeezed.

"I should have snapped this pretty little neck the first day I met you." He lifted his fist and Nea tried to focus on it through the spots.

At the last second, she tilted her head out of the way and his fingers crunched against the stones where her face had been. She brought her knee up and caught him between the legs. He loosened his grip on her as he doubled over with a grunt and she twisted free. She rushed to Emil, who was propped against the wall of the garden, his hands tight around his leg. Nea examined the wound. It didn't appear deep, but she didn't want to risk having him bleed to death.

"Nea, look out!"

The toe of Leon's boot met her side, and her breath rushed from her lungs in an agonising whoosh. Panting, she scuttled backwards as Leon bore down on her.

"Hey, pretty boy!" a young-looking soldier shouted as he charged into the garden and drew his sword.

"Good, Harvey. You can help me subdue this belligerent bitch."

"I don't think so." Harvey shook his head and steadied his stance.

"I am ordering you—"

Harvey tore his green tabard off and threw it on the ground. "I don't take orders from you."

Friend of yours? Nea mouthed at Emil, who nodded.

"Then you'll die too," Leon growled and scooped up the sword he'd dropped when Nea had attacked him.

As the swords of the two men met, Nea tore a long strip of material from her skirt and looped it around Emil's leg, making sure it was tight enough to stem the flow of blood in the way Margot had shown her. She then helped him to his feet as Leon and Harvey continued to fight. Leon was bigger and stronger, but Harvey was fast—faster than any fighter she'd ever seen. Soon Leon was panting, a steady trickle of blood coming from the wound Nea had given him.

"We should keep moving," Emil said.

Nea tore her eyes away from Harvey and Leon and helped Emil through the gate and down the disused path beyond.

By the time they reached the south side, after dodging through shadowy streets and trying to stay out of sight, Emil was looking very pale. He guided Nea to a door, knocked, then collapsed on the ground beside her. The door was yanked open and Nea's eyes met the wide hazel gaze of a thin man sporting a pointed goatee and a head of thick brown hair.

"Is it Margot?" There was a concerned edge to Molly's voice as she brushed past the man. "Oh, it's you. Well, get inside." She reached out to pull Nea through the door when her gaze dropped to see Emil. "Bright Mother's tits. Help me with him, Jasper." She pushed Nea into the warehouse then grabbed hold of Emil, waiting for the man to help her.

They half carried, half dragged Emil into the room and laid him out on the floor. Jasper sucked a breath through his teeth as he inspected the makeshift tourniquet around the wound. His gaze flicked to Nea's torn skirt and he nodded before rubbing his hands together. Then he undid the binding and inspected the wound. He closed his eyes and though Nea couldn't feel the pull of magic, she'd witnessed Margot perform enough healing to know what was going on as a thin green mist coiled around Emil's leg and the sides of the wound slowly pulled themselves together.

"I don't know if it will be enough. He's lost a lot of blood." Jasper looked at Nea. "I certainly hope you are worth the trouble."

Emil groaned as Jasper slid his arm under him and then he and Molly guided him across the room and onto a pallet bed to rest.

Molly glanced at the door. "What is taking the others so long? Margot should be here by now." Her gaze fell on Nea and though she wore the usual look of dislike, her blue eyes softened slowly as she took in her appearance. "You're covered in blood. Let's find you something else to wear."

"Do you think something happened to Margot?" Nea asked as Molly led her into a small storage space off the main room of the warehouse.

Molly glowered as she turned to face her again. "For your sake, I hope not." She pointed to Nea's satchel, sitting on the desk. "Emil insisted we bring your things. Your clothes, however, are still back at Braemar. But there should be something here."

She opened a trunk and started digging through it.

"Here. These were mine so they should fit you. You're too short for any of Margot's old things." She passed Nea a pair of dark-coloured pants and a linen shirt. "If you get cold you can always use this. It's not like ... Declan needs it now." She handed over a grey cloak. "Let me help with the laces on that gown."

Nea took the cloak and ran her finger over the Loch Bastien seal and kelp crest that was embroidered on it, while Molly loosened the laces on the back of her gown. "Thank you, Molly."

Molly let out a slow breath. "You're welcome."

She turned to leave but stopped when Nea said, "I really am sorry about ... everything."

Molly didn't turn to face her again. She just sniffed and said, "We'll see," before leaving the room.

Nea ran her hand over her hair and placed the clothes on the desk. She slid the gown off and rubbed her hand over her eyes.

"It's a shame. I really did like that colour on you." Declan appeared on a vacant chair and Nea lifted the cloak to cover her chest.

"Declan!" she hissed through her teeth.

"It's not like I haven't seen you in your underwear before." He grinned but it faltered the longer his eyes were on hers. "I wish I could fix this, Nea." He stood and crossed the room. The cool shadow of his thumb breezed slowly over the wrinkle between her brows.

"Do you think the others are alright?"

He moved back to the chair. "They'll be fine. They got you away from Evard—that's the important thing."

Nea studied the door and chewed her lip.

"Nea, I know what you're thinking. You need to stay put until Garret gets back."

There was a commotion in the other room and Nea rushed to the door.

Margot and Sonia had arrived. No one noticed Nea standing in the doorway with Declan's cloak held to her chest. Molly was too busy holding Margot's face and pressing a hungry kiss to her lips, tears sliding down her cheeks. Sonia turned slowly, and an easy smile worked its way across her mouth.

"Little Fox! You could have finished getting dressed!" She crossed the floor and gripped Nea in a tight hug.

"It's good to see you too, Sonia." As she pulled back, Nea noticed

Sonia was covered in dust and cobwebs. "Where have you been?"

"Oh, you know, saving the damsel, navigating the catacombs and all that." She waved her hand in a small circle. "Though the more important question is where have you been? Three years, Little Fox, and you didn't think to write a single letter?"

"I—"

"Nea!" Margot gasped and twisted out of Molly's embrace. She rushed across the room and Sonia just managed to leap out of the way as her thin form thudded into Nea's. "I am so sorry."

They collapsed into a heap in the doorway, Declan's cloak pinned between them. "Margot, you're smothering me."

"I am so sorry he made you do that. You should have let him kill me, you stupid, stupid fool." Margot was sobbing against Nea's neck.

Slowly Nea closed her arms around Margot's back. "It's okay, Margot. I made my choice."

"But he made you—"

"It's *okay*." The threat of tears stung Nea's eyes as she cupped Margot's neck with one hand and pressed a kiss to her forehead. "You're safe. That's all that matters. You don't need to worry about me."

"Yes, I do." Margot sat back and looked Nea hard in the eyes.

"I'm fine." She drew a deep breath. "Really." Realising they were sitting on the floor and that she was still only in her underwear, Nea cleared her throat. "I should go and finish getting dressed and you probably should see to Emil." She glanced towards the bed where Emil was sleeping.

As Margot crossed to check on him, Nea backed into the storeroom and closed the door. She sat in a chair and let her forehead drop into her hands. She couldn't remember the last time she had felt so tired; it was as though she was the exiled mage Julius and she was being crushed under the weight of all her transgressions. She could easily picture the fabled mage sitting on his hanging rock high above the churning grey maw of the ocean.

Feeling Declan's eyes on her, she met his gaze, but he said nothing, seeming to sense her unspoken need for silence.

CHAPTER FIFTEEN

GARRET

"The healer—she's gone."

The moment the soldier spoke, Garret's gaze snapped to Nea. Her fingers twitched towards her knife and he started to push his chair back, ready to grab her. She was too fast. The second Evard stood, her chair hit the floor with an echoing crash and she lunged straight for him. Leith leapt at the same time Garret did, his hand grabbing a bunch of her skirt and pulling her up short so the knife stuck in Evard's shoulder. Evard's fingers closed around the handle and his other hand delivered a backhand blow to the side of Nea's face that sent her staggering, despite the blade sticking out of his shoulder.

"Get her out of here!" he roared, and Leith took hold of Nea's arm, lifting her to her feet. She wasn't done fighting though. She twisted in his grip and her knuckles slammed into his jaw. It wasn't the most skilled punch, but judging by the look on Leith's face, it had been effective enough.

"Come on," Leith said as he dragged her across the room and out of sight.

"Commander, the healer can't have gotten far. Find her and bring her head back to me. I am done being civil with these insolent bitches."

"My lord, perha—"

"Did I not speak plainly enough for you, Commander? I want Margot's head stuck on a pike outside Nea's cell so she can stare at it and know what her impertinence has cost her."

Garret swallowed. Evard was all but frothing at the mouth. His fingers twitched to the scar on his face, smearing it with blood, before lowering again to pull the knife out of his shoulder.

"My lord, you do realise that his hesitation proves what I was telling you about the commander." Leon stepped forward. "Who else could sneak the healer out? And what about Leith? Can you really trust him to deliver the necromancer to her cell? There is a history there, after all."

Evard looked down at the knife, lightly twisting the tip against his finger.

"This is lunacy. I have been with you all afternoon, my lord." Garret scoffed to hide his building concern.

"Of course. You're not working alone, after all." Leon's smile was smug but it was the dark look in his eyes that bothered Garret.

"Leon, go and make sure Nea makes it back to her cell."

As Leon ran to do Evard's bidding, the king turned his cold gaze on Garret.

An air of nervousness had fallen over those gathered. No, not nervousness—anticipation. They could smell his blood in the water. "My lord, you know I—"

"Silence! Of late, you have disappointed me, Commander. I always knew you had a weakness, a soft spot for the downtrodden. But I had hoped, given time, it would harden, that your thirst for brutality would grow. But you fall back on your morals, your honour, time and time again. It is a shortcoming you share with Nea. However, I can control Nea and I can control you. What would happen if I were to bring your darling little Elenora here to the court?"

Garret schooled his features. How did Evard know about Nora? "It is unnecessary. I will find the healer and bring her to you."

Catriona walked over and stood next to Evard. "If you wish, my lord, we can have the truth of the commander's loyalty in but a moment." The sticky fingers of her magic brushed his mind and he slammed his mental walls up.

"Don't worry, my dear. I will give you your chance to defile his mind." Evard gave Catriona a doting smile, the same one he had reserved for Nea, before he turned his attention back to Garret. "I will have every secret from that mind of yours, Commander, and then Kieran will turn you and Nea into my willing puppets. He's not as unique as Nea but he can handle a few simple reanimations."

Kieran? He had been missing since before Kalhanna, but if Evard had him then of course he knew about Elenora and Bridie—Garret had to move fast.

"Seize the commander," Evard barked at the remaining guards in the room.

Garret felt the drag of Catriona's magic as he made a dash for the door. He kept his walls up. If she got inside his mind, there would be no escape. As he reached the door, a guard leapt into his way to block his path. Garret thrust the heal of his palm out, but the man caught his hand before the strike could land. It didn't stop Garret. He pushed against the guard's grip, using his weight to free himself. As the guard made another move to catch him, Garret dodged and grabbed the outstretched arm, twisting it back until he felt the moment the guard's shoulder popped out of its socket. The guard yelled in pain and Garret shoved him out of the way and charged into the hallway.

He didn't stop.

The look on Leon's face had been unsettling. It hovered at the front of his mind as he ran down the twisting corridors towards the dungeon. He had to make sure Nea had actually gotten out and that Leon hadn't—

He skidded to a halt. Leith was sitting propped against the wall, rubbing the back of his head. He groaned and looked up at Garret.

"Where's Nea?" they both said at the same time.

Leith staggered to his feet. "She was right here, then someone hit me over the back of the head."

"Are you going to be alright?" Garret really didn't have time to be fussing over Leith, especially given that Nea was now missing. He hoped Janey had found her before Leon. "I have to get out of here. Your father—"

"I'll be fine. Find Nea. Please, Garret, she doesn't deserve to be kept as one of Father's prized pets."

Garret gave him a clap on the shoulder and stepped around him. "I'll do what I can." He started to move away down the hall but a panel of wall opened to his left. He peered in at the darkness and an amber mage light flickered to life, revealing Janey. She pulled him into the passageway and the door clicked shut behind him.

The warm light bobbed above their heads as Janey passed his sword to him and then rapidly signed. "*I hit Leith. Is he okay? I was expecting you to bring Nea.*"

"It's alright. Leith is fine. We need to get out of here. You're sure Nea escaped?"

She nodded and turned waving for him to follow her.

The sky was starting to colour with the pinks and purples of dusk when they reached the small courtyard that Nea and Emil had escaped through. It was there they found Harvey—a bloodstained rag in his hand as he inspected a gash on his upper right arm. He looked up as they neared and Garret noted the already-purpling bruise around his left eye.

"Harvey—"

"Don't fret, Garret. You should see the other guy." He laughed and winced. "Actually, he ran off before I could land any really good hits. But Nea managed to get a mark on him." He held up a hair comb. It vaguely resembled a moth, studded with amethysts, but one of the delicate wings was crushed and the long tines were stained with blood. "She drove it right into the side of his neck."

"Whose neck?"

"Leon's, and he was crankier than a sackful of hungry cats. I delayed him as long as I could, but he was hell-bent on going after Nea. He punched me in the face and while I was flat on my back, counting stars, he ran off. Hi, Janey." He waved and gave her a beaming smile.

Janey smiled and waved back.

"We need to keep moving. Did you see Nea and Emil?"

"Yeah, Emil didn't look good though. Nea was trying to patch him up when I got here. You didn't mention she was so pr—ouch." Janey had given his good arm a light punch. "What?"

"Did they get away?" Garret asked.

"Yeah, I held Leon off long enough that they could."

"Right." Garret headed for the gate.

They didn't slow their pace until they got to the outskirts of the upper market and sounds of a fight reached them. Garret heard a familiar shout and headed towards it. They rounded a corner to see Haley, her short hair sticking out in all directions, facing off against a pair of men in dark warden leathers. John and Arthur. Both were more loyal to Willem over himself—or rather, John was, and Arthur did everything John did without question.

"Commander, good thing you're here," John said when they saw him.

"Stand down."

John looked shocked. "Sir? She aided the healer. We have orders to arrest anyone implicated in the escape."

"Whose orders?" Garret relaxed his posture and settled his weight on his back foot.

"The king's, sir," Arthur said

"Right, well you'd better arrest us too." He indicated Janey and Harvey behind him.

"Sir?" They twisted towards him, keeping their swords raised.

Beside him, Janey was pulling a thin thread of source. The air felt thick and warm as it pooled in his chest. The other wardens shared a look and Garret knew they could feel it too.

"So, what is it going to be?" He moved his hand towards the hilt of his sword. He didn't really want to fight them, but he knew John, like Willem, was one of the wardens happy about the recent changes to the order. It was likely he'd do Evard's bidding without question.

Arthur took a step back, but John locked eyes with Garret. "Have you gone mad, sir? The king—"

"Should never have been handed command of the order." He recalled what Nea had said. "There's a storm coming, lads, and you need to choose a harbour."

"But the king ..." John shook his head, then straightened his back. "I'm going to have to ask you to stand down, sir. Don't make this harder than it needs to be."

Garret raised an eyebrow as a ball of fire whipped past his shoulder and exploded against the side of the building behind Arthur, causing him to yelp in shock.

"John, I don't want to fight the com—"

"Don't be a coward. Sure, it's four against two, but one of them is injured." He nodded to Harvey. "And the mage can be suppressed easily enough."

While they had been talking, Haley had been slowly edging around. She leapt forward and grabbed Arthur, pressing the blade of her sword against his throat. "I don't really want to spill poor Arthur's blood all over the street, especially after the exciting dance we just shared. But unless you back down, I'm afraid I'm going to have to."

"John—"

"She's bluffing," John said, cutting Arthur off.

"Am I?" There was a wild look in Haley's hazel eyes and she increased the pressure on the blade, drawing a thin line of blood and causing Arthur to start shaking.

"Fine, we yield." John lowered his sword and Haley let go of Arthur. But as soon as Arthur was a safe distance away from her, John lunged, lifting his sword and swinging it in a tight arc towards Garret's chest.

Garret twisted out of the way, forcing Janey safely behind him, but the tip of the blade sliced a neat line through the soft fabric of his dress uniform and he felt the hot sting of metal across his skin. The air grew warm again as Janey formed another floating ball of flame. She was about to cast it when the weight of John's suppression suffocated it.

"Get Janey out of here," Garret barked at Harvey, who had drawn his sword and was holding it in his off hand.

"I can fight."

"Get her out of here, now," Garret ordered as he danced away from another strike and drew his own sword. "Last chance to back away, John."

"Never."

Garret blocked as John attacked.

"Why aren't you fighting back?" he growled as Garret dodged again.

"Because I don't want to kill you. You're a good warden, even if our ideals don't align."

"My ideals are aligned with those of the order. I am not some mage sympathiser. *I* haven't forgotten why the order was originally created. We exist to control mages, to keep them in line."

Garret blocked another series of attacks, catching sight of Haley and Arthur out of the corner of his eye. "We were never created to control. We were to work with mages—"

"Like that abomination of a necromancer? I'll never work with the likes of her. She is an affront that should have been put down along with the corrupted at Kalhanna."

Garret blinked. There hadn't been any signs of corruption at

Kalhanna. He was sure that Evard had just used that as an excuse to silence those most outspoken against him.

While his guard was down, John struck again—another slice below the first across his chest, this one slightly deeper.

"You're getting slow, Commander." John gloated and shifted his weight to start another series of attacks.

Garret had to end this. It wasn't getting him anywhere and if they stalled too long, chances were the king's guard and the rest of the wardens would find them.

He blocked the incoming attack and sidestepped, using John's own momentum against him. He stuck his leg out and caught his foot between John's ankles. The other warden lost his balance and hit the ground, losing his grip on his sword. Garret kicked the sword to Haley and pointed the tip of his blade at John's throat.

"You don't have the stones for it. Willem is right; they never should have made you commander instead of him. He's not afraid of putting mages in their place. Why don't you ask that hot-blooded sister of—"

Garret's boot connected with the side of John's head, silencing him with a meaty thud. He had gone to great lengths to keep his family a secret, but it appeared Evard had known about them all along.

"You're not going to kill him, are you?" Haley had a white-faced Arthur bailed up against the wall.

Garret knew he probably should, that John would if the roles were reversed, but like handing Nea over to Evard, killing another warden just felt wrong. It was something he was going to have to come to terms with. He turned to Arthur. "You can throw your lot in with us if you want, but you've probably guessed just how dangerous that will be."

Arthur glanced at John. "I'll stay with the order. You're not going to knock me out too though, are you?"

"No." Garret indicated Haley release Arthur.

When she did, he leant forward with one hand on his knees and touched the thin cut on his neck with the other. "Thanks." He didn't meet Garret's eye as he moved to check on John. "You best get out of here, Commander, before anyone else comes."

Garret didn't need telling twice. He sheathed his sword and indicated Haley follow him as the sky above them started to turn a darker shade of purple, and the shadows cast by the buildings of the upper market grew thicker.

By the time they had wound their way to the south side, making sure they weren't followed, it was dark. They entered the safe house and Garret was relieved to see everyone had made it safely back.

Margot, Molly, Jasper, and Ryan were sitting at the table. Sonia was propped against the side of the pallet bed on which Emil lay sleeping, and Janey and Harvey were sitting by the fire. Haley skipped over to the table and plonked down next to Ryan, lifting the cup in front of him and giving it a sniff before scrunching her nose.

"Where's—" He cut himself off as Nea came in from one of the side rooms. There was a large purple bruise covering one side of her jaw and he remembered her actions in the throne room. Actions that—he drew a breath as he felt anger stir in his stomach.

She was staring at him, the exhaustion in those bright violet eyes edged with concern. "You're hurt," she said softly, taking a step forward.

His gaze dropped to the front of his dress uniform, which was sticky with drying blood. He chewed the inside of his cheek as his attention flicked to the red bars stitched on his sleeve then back to Nea's concerned face. Everything that had been beneath the surface for months suddenly bubbled up, making his anger grow. It wasn't all Nea's fault, but he kept seeing her lunging for Evard, the knife clutched in her hand and—

"What the fuck were you thinking!" The words were out before he could stop them, and she flinched as though she'd been struck.

"Garret!" Margot stood, but he ignored her, keeping his gaze locked with Nea's.

"Do you know how many lives I put on the line to get you out of that dungeon? It could have been all for nothing because you decided to act on a foolish impulse." He was as angry at himself as he was at her but yelling at her felt better in the moment than chastising himself.

"If Leith hadn't stopped me and I had landed the blow—"

"You would be dead."

"And I told you I was happy to pay that price. You can't save everyone all the time, Garret. You need to let people make decisions for themselves."

The others were watching, shifting slightly in their seats.

"You yourself implied we would need you to sort out this mess with corruption, so forgive me if I got the wrong impression." He threw back at her. Bright Mother's tits, she didn't make any sense to him at times. She was like Declan in all the ways that infuriated him; she seemed smart and calculating but then she was dangerously impulsive and did stupid things that not only endangered herself but those around her.

"I didn't think. I just saw an opening ... I'm sorry."

"That much was obvious. You ca—oh." His ran his hands through his hair. The anger was starting to burn out and her quiet apology cut through the last of it.

Margot cleared her throat. "How about we continue this discussion later and you let me have a look at those wounds."

"They're fine, Margot. Nothing a little salve and time can't fix." He flicked his gaze back to Nea and frowned. "We need to move out as soon as we can."

"Yes, we do, but we'll need a cart for Emil. He lost a lot of blood and I can't replace it with my magic. We'll just have to wait for the blood tonic I made him to take effect." Margot said.

"I can get us a cart." Sonia stood.

"I'll help you." Haley jumped up and joined her fellow warden at the door.

As they exited, Garret turned his attention to Molly. "Do we have any of those hair-dying herbs around?"

"Somewhere, I am sure." She moved to look for them.

"I need you two to head to Fengate and pay The Rowdy Badger a visit. See what the rumour mill is turning up. Particularly in regard to cases of corruption," Garret said to Ryan and Jasper.

"On it." Ryan nodded and they left.

"Okay, Garret, I found the dye. Your options are black or black," Molly said as she returned.

"Good. Help Nea dye her hair. The grey stands out too much."

Nea made a noise as though to protest but Janey stood and shook her head. "Come on, Nea," she said in the slow deliberate voice she used when she had to. Nea sighed and followed Janey and Molly into one of the side rooms.

"So, I guess I'm just going to sit here and look pretty then? It's alright. I am quite good at it." Harvey grinned and leant back in his chair.

"No, you can help Margot pack anything she needs to take to Braemar. We won't return for some time." *If at all.*

"Actually, Garret, I am going to insist that you let me look at those wounds before we start packing." Margot crossed her arms.

"They're fine. I'm fine, Margot, you don't need to fuss."

"Now you are starting to sound like Nea. Take off your jacket and sit your arse down or I will make you." She lifted a hand and a thin wisp of green magic flickered over her fingers.

He complied with a sigh.

"Shirt off as well."

Harvey laughed as he watched Margot ordering Garret around.

Garret glowered at him before he lifted his shirt over his head, wincing as the part stuck to his skin with dried blood pulled away. He then sat, and Margot crouched in front of him, her fingers warm as they inspected the skin around the cuts. Satisfied, she drew a thread of the source to her and the soft warmth of her magic smoothed its way up his spine like he was sinking into a hot bath. The soothing sensation was quickly replaced with a sharp pain as the edges of the two wounds started to pull together and his skin reknit in a pair of pink scars.

They itched, and he rubbed his palm over them. "Happy now?"

"Quite." Margot gave him a satisfied grin then snapped her fingers at Harvey. "Alright, let's get ready to leave."

With a huff, Garret headed into the side room to find his things. His pack was sitting on the table. He dug out a shirt and the stone from Declan and put them both on. Then he slipped into his jacket and studied the red bars on the sleeve as he fastened the buckles.

He'd never actually wanted to be promoted to commander. But the choice had been between himself and Willem, and the retiring commander, Reid, had sworn he'd rather die than see Willem in a position of power. He'd died in the end anyway—murdered by Harold the same way Declan had been—because he'd been too outspoken. Garret should have left the order back then instead of dancing to Evard's tune for so long. Maybe if he had, things would be different, but wishing things were different was a waste of time. Right now, Garret needed to get everyone moving, and then he needed to beat Evard's men to Swinton.

CHAPTER SIXTEEN

NEA

Molly and Janey had done an excellent job on Nea's hair. The stormy grey was now a deep black that made her pale skin look like porcelain. Nea had secured the glossy curls into a braid and was sitting by Emil's bed while he slept. Most of the others were out running errands and getting ready to leave as soon as Garret gave the word. He wanted them to move before first light, but the night was wearing on and that would come before they knew it.

"I'm so sorry, Emil." She took hold of his hand and settled it in her lap. "I caused this. Everything since Kalhanna is my fault. If I had just agreed to Evard's terms. If I'd ..." She sighed and rubbed her eyes with her free hand. "What is it Nonna says about regret? More soul-destroying than any other corruption. I believe her now."

Declan cleared his throat softly and she glanced to where he was sitting on the floor at the foot of the bed. He gave her a crooked smile but said nothing.

"Do you remember the last summer at Hartswood before Margot went to Kalhanna? That was the year Sir Frecklepaws was poisoned. You were so sad when we found him in the grove, I just wanted to fix it to see you smile again ... I'm not very good at fixing things, Emil. I never have been. What does death touch that it doesn't spoil?" Her eyes were itchy and she rubbed them again. "Anyway. I'm sorry about your cat. I never told you that before."

"I've heard the cat story."

Nea's attention shifted to Declan again as he chuckled.

"Emil told me a long time ago. He and Margot used to talk about you a lot. Well, not just you; they were reliving the stories of their youth. It seems the three of you used to get up to quite a bit of mischief."

Nea glanced around to make sure no one was in earshot and said, "Somehow I doubt you were any different in your youth."

"Oh, I would have been the ringleader." He gave her a roguish grin. "I can't believe you reanimated his cat though."

Nea chuckled. "It wasn't really *his* cat. Sir Frecklepaws was the Hartswood barn cat but Emil always had a soft spot for him. He was this huge grey thing with white patches. He was rather pretty for a cat but ornery. He hated being petted and cuddled. Emil would persevere with the scratches and bites, insisting that Sir Frecklepaws was just misunderstood—that he really liked the attention but couldn't let people see that because he had to maintain his rough barn-cat reputation."

"Sounds like someone I know." Declan chuckled.

Nea regarded him a moment and then felt a soft pressure in her hand as Emil squeezed her fingers.

"Nea, what did you do to your hair?" Emil blinked at her, his face ashen but a curious smile on his lips.

"I dyed it. It will be easier to get lost in the crowd this way. How are you feeling?"

"Like I could sleep for a month."

"You *should* be sleeping, Emil. Margot said you need to rest."

He smiled but closed his eyes again. "You know, I had the strangest dream. You were telling Declan about Sir Frecklepaws—" He yawned. "It's a shame you never got to meet him. I think you'd have liked him."

"I'm sure I would have." She gave his hand a gentle squeeze. "Go back to sleep, Emil."

Someone cleared their throat and Nea glanced upwards through her lashes to find Garret standing above her, a concerned frown creasing his brow.

"I'm ... ah. I'm sorry I snapped at you before."

She hadn't been expecting him to say that and it must have been apparent on her face because he added, "I still think attacking Evard under those circumstances was idiotic, but—"

"More lives than my own are at risk. I understand."

He studied her for a moment before running his hand through his hair. "We need to get those shackles off. I've seen you fight and aside from some astounding blind luck, you are kind of hopeless without your magic."

Was that a joke? He seemed to be biting back a grin so maybe it was.

Declan hid his chuckle behind his hand. "He's not wrong."

"Do you have the key? I thought bind-shackles could only be removed with the key that was struck at the same time as the individual pair."

"That is true, and I don't have the key, unfortunately."

"So how do you plan on removing them then?"

"There is another way."

"Really?" That was something she was sure she would have known. Especially given that her father was always tinkering about with robrillium.

He rubbed the scar above his lip. "It's complicated and dangerous." A soft noise that could have been a chuckle escaped him. "Just like everything else about you."

"Smooth," Declan said with a laugh.

"I'm sorry, it's going to hurt ... a lot. Show me your wrists." He crouched and held his hands out.

She hesitated but then held out her wrists, the sleeves of her borrowed shirt falling back to reveal the shackles and the smoky corruption marks. He frowned at the marks before taking hold of her wrists, his large hands encircling them with ease. "That corruption doesn't look any worse."

"I imagine the shackles are keeping it in a kind of stasis."

"That makes sense," he said then frowned again. "What will happen when we remove them and it has access to your magic?"

"That's a good point," Declan said.

She studied the marks and licked her lip. "I'm not sure."

Garret nodded slowly. "Should we remove them then? Or would it be better to wait until we talk to Margot first?"

"I want them gone." Her tone was sharp and she added, softer, "Please."

He studied her for a moment. "Alright, ready?"

"Yes."

His thumbs gently rubbed the thin bands of the shackles over the inside of her wrists and pain sliced through her arms. A small gasp escaped her and she bit down on her lip, trying not to pull her arms out of his grip.

The pain disappeared as he let her go. "I'm sorry. Without the key, this is the only way I know. If you would rather we left them ..."

"No." She wanted them off more than she could describe.

"Okay. Deep breaths." His eyes found hers. "Are you ready?"

She nodded, bracing herself as he closed his fingers around the shackles again.

The pain returned in an instant. A burning feeling ran around her wrists and into her palms. Her toes clenched together, and she closed her eyes as the world seemed to tilt away from her.

The pressure around one wrist lessoned and Garret's fingers lightly took hold of her chin, tilting it downwards. Her head felt heavy and light all at once, and her arms felt like they were submerged to the elbows in scolding water. She drew a ragged breath and opened her eyes, shutting them again as a wave of dizziness dulled her vision and made the room spin.

"Nea, look at me."

She swallowed and forced her eyes open once more, fighting back the nausea.

"I need you to stay with me. We're almost there. Deep breaths remember?"

Nea nodded and drew several long deep breaths. Garret gave her a tight smile as his fingers released her chin and dropped to encircle her wrist again.

Tears stung along the edge of her eyes as the pain increased. She bit her lip, mostly to stop from crying out but also to keep the threatening darkness at bay. Garret's breathing grew heavier and a slight quiver trembled through his fingers and into her skin. Something metal clanged against the floor.

The pain grew to a dull ache and it was replaced by the churning twist of the source as it flooded into her body. It rushed along her veins in hot and cold prickles and Garret caught her shoulders as she fell forward.

He gently pushed her back into the chair, and his hand came under her chin again. "Nea?"

She drew a steadying breath and met his worried gaze. "I'm fine." Angry burns ringed her wrists where the shackles had been. She examined them before turning her attention to the thin marks of corruption that were darkening with each heartbeat.

Garret took hold of the afflicted arm, careful to avoid the burns, and gently rolled it to examine the marks. He looked up at her, his jaw tense. "It's growing."

She pulled her arm away, wincing as his hand brushed over the burns.

"Nea—"

"What do you want me to say? Yes, it's growing. It's feeding off my magic." She didn't mean to snap but the sight of the expanding marks frightened her. "I could try Margot's ointment on it. That seemed to work last time."

"Last—"

"My ointment worked on what?" Margot came in from the other room with Janey hot on her heels and Garret got to his feet. "Nea is that corruption?" Margot's brown eyes were full of worry as she took Nea's arm to examine it.

"It appears to be."

Margot frowned. "Necromancers can't get corruption."

"That's not exactly true." Nea scratched at the marks. It felt like something was crawling under her skin.

"How did you get it?"

Nea opened her mouth but Garret said, "Amelia."

"So, the rumours about her were true."

"It appears so," Garret said to Margot before turning to Nea and asking, "Do you have any more of Margot's ointment?"

"Which ointment? My cure-all?" Margot glanced between them with a frown.

Nea nodded. "It's in my satchel in the other room." She pointed to the storeroom and Janey went and got it.

When Janey returned with the satchel, Nea dug the jar out and handed it to Margot, who opened the lid and gave it a sniff. "When did I give you this? I had to alter this recipe because it was mostly ineffective and gave Tobias those hives, remember?"

Nea's chest tightened when Margot mentioned Tobias. "I've had it a while. I haven't found it ineffective at all; quite the opposite, especially for small scrapes."

Margot looked sceptical but took some of the ointment onto her fingertips and indicated for Nea to hold out her arm. Her fingers were warm as she massaged the ointment over the black marks. Nea bit her lip as they burned and itched. Then, as before, a thin black vapour lifted from her skin, leaving it unblemished.

Margot stared at the smooth pale flesh as she screwed the lid back on the jar and handed it to Nea.

"Fascinating. What do you think she put in that thing?" Declan had come over and was staring at Nea's wrist as though it was a puzzle he needed to solve.

"Well, I've never seen anything like that before. I'll have to make some more of this when we get to Braemar. I wonder what Declan would have made of it." Margot glanced at Garret. "I know he tried a few different tonics based mostly on mage bane, but I don't think he tried treating corruption externally." She rolled her shoulders. "Anyway, let's see to those burns." She placed her fingers gently around Nea's still-burned wrists. The warm ruffle of her magic washed over Nea and the throbbing heat cooled as the burns and other small scrapes from her time in Evard's care faded away.

With Nea's wrists healed, Margot lightly touched Nea's cheek and healed the bruise there before taking hold of her arm and examining it closely for any signs of the corruption reappearing.

"You should get some rest, Nea. You could get an hour or two of sleep before we need to move," Garret said as he placed the bind-shackles on the table.

"I'm fine."

"No one believes you, Nea!" Margot snapped. "Go and get some sleep, or do I have to make you?"

"Okay." She let Margot usher her into the storeroom. Nea might have resisted more but it was comforting to have Margot bossing her around like they were children again.

Margot stood in the doorway while Nea settled herself on the bed. "You don't have to pretend to be fine all the time. No one will blame you for being human."

Nea twisted the hem of her shirt in her fingers and tried not to meet Margot's eye.

"Don't worry. I'm not going to give you the lecture about taking care of yourself." She rolled her eyes. "Again." She crossed the room to sit on the edge of the bed next to Nea and brushed a loose curl from her face. "Lay back."

Nea did as she was told, and Margot's warm fingers pressed lightly against her temples.

"I know you won't let yourself relax, but Garret is right; you need rest."

Margot's magic stirred like a gentle caress of warm fingers rolling down Nea's spine and suddenly her eyes were so heavy it was an effort to keep them open. She stifled a yawn as Margot stood.

"Sleep well, Nea."

The last thing Nea felt as sleep took her was the warm press of Margot's lips on her forehead.

When Nea awoke, the warehouse was silent. She sat slowly and rubbed the sleep from her eyes before she got up and pulled her boots on.

Garret was sitting at the worn table in the main room of the warehouse, a piece of parchment in front of him and a quill in his hand. The candlelight played on his skin, softening his features and setting the highlights in his auburn hair aglow. Judging by the way it was standing in messy waves, he'd been running his hands through it. He tapped the quill against his lower lip, seeming lost in thought, then, as though sensing her eyes on him, looked up. "You're awake. Good."

She crossed the room and dropped into a chair across from him. "How long was I out?"

"A few good hours."

Nea looked around. "The others?"

"They've left already. It's just us for the moment."

"You should have woken me."

He shrugged. "We aren't going with them. There are a few things I need to see to and I'm taking you with me."

Nea pulled Declan's cloak tighter around her shoulders. "Where are we going?"

He chewed the inside of his cheek as he studied her. "Swinton."

"Swinton?"

He nodded.

"Why Swinton? Last I knew, it was a small farming community."

He regarded her for a moment before signing the bottom of his parchment and placing his quill aside.

"Okay. You have business in Swinton that you would rather not disclose the details of, so why bring me along? Why not just send me with the others to Braemar?"

"It is a safeguard of sorts. I didn't want to take you directly to Braemar, given that it is exactly what Evard will expect."

"But you sent the others to Braemar."

"They will be fine. You're the one Evard wants so the longer I can keep you hidden, the better. Also, given that Leon managed to steal you right out from under my nose, I need to rat out his co-conspirators before I take you back there."

Nea crossed her arms over her chest. "Maurice is one."

"Maurice?"

"Yes. He said something about Kalhanna right before Leon ambushed me."

A dark look crossed Garret's features. "He lost a daughter there, but I didn't think—"

"Grief does strange things to people."

He nodded. "That it does." He blotted the ink on his letter then folded it as he stood. "It's almost dawn. We should move while we still have the cover of darkness."

Someone knocked and Nea's attention snapped to the door.

Garret answered it and ushered a young boy wearing a grey cap into the room.

The boy's ice-blue eyes caught Nea and he let out a low whistle. "Milady."

He tightened his one-armed grip on his messenger bird and lifted his cap off his head, sweeping it along the floor as he bowed. The bird gave a flustered trill as it was dipped savagely towards the ground then straightened again with the boy's movements.

Garret cleared his throat and handed the boy the letter.

The boy twisted the bird around and secured the letter to its leg. Then the source stirred as he focused on the bird and whispered the destination. The bird flapped its wings and he moved to the door, opening it and tossing the bird unceremoniously into the predawn. Satisfied it was on its way, he turned to Garret, holding his palm out for payment.

Garret counted the coins into it and added a couple of extra.

"Pleasure doing business with you, as always, sir." He slid the coins into his grey jacket. "Milady." He gave Nea a wink and another bow then backed out the door and skipped into the night.

Garret watched the boy go with a shake of his head then picked up his things and extinguished the candles. He led Nea out onto the street and they turned towards the gentle lapping sounds of the harbour.

CHAPTER SEVENTEEN

GARRET

"Just over the next hill is The Crossroads. We can stop there for another rest if you like." Garret glanced to his left and not finding Nea there, turned around.

She was a short distance behind him, her mouth a tired line and her footsteps slow. The entire day she had been keeping up with the pace he'd set and hadn't complained once. It wasn't that they hadn't stopped to rest; they had, just not as often as they should have. And if he didn't have to worry about Nea, he probably wouldn't stop at all until he got to Swinton.

Evard's words kept playing in his mind. "What would happen if I were to bring your darling little Elenora here to the court?"

He shook his head. After Nea had killed Harold, he had been so sure that there was nothing in the world that could make him do what she had done. But then just the thought of Nora in Evard's hands and he'd be waltzing to Evard's tune without question.

Nea reached him and gave him a curious look. "Why did you stop?"

"You were falling behind again."

"Sorry. I was just lost in thought, I guess."

There was a lot of that going around, but he didn't believe her. She looked dead on her feet and if Margot saw the state she was in, she would probably skin him alive. "We can stop for something to eat and a rest just over that next rise." He indicated the hill ahead, beyond which the clouds were starting to take on hues of orange and pink. "We could probably hire a room at the tavern and get some sleep." He didn't want to hire a room and stop for sleep, but he couldn't ask her to keep walking through the night.

She looked at the hill then a road that forked off just ahead of them. "Wouldn't it be faster to get to Swinton from here if we take the road to Kilton and branch off at Lone Oak?"

He crossed his arms. "It would but there is nowhere to stop for the night unless we head into Kilton itself, and we certainly won't reach it this side of midnight."

She chewed her lip and ran her hand through her hair, dislodging a loose curl from her braid. "We can't stop for the night in someone's barn? There are a few farmsteads between here and Swinton. I am sure someone would accommodate us and failing that, I am not above sleeping in the forest."

"But you ..." He shook his head. Was this the existence she had lived for three years? Camping out in the forest or some accommodating farmer's barn?

"Look, it's clear that you need to be in Swinton yesterday, so if we can shave any time off the journey there we should. If I thought you'd listen, I'd tell you to go ahead without me and that I'd meet you there."

Would she though? No, he wasn't letting her out of his sight. It wasn't that he thought she would run, but last time he had let his guard down, Leon had snatched her away. And if Evard got hold of her again, there was no way he would be able to free her.

"I can't ask you to keep going. If Margot saw the state you're in she would have my head."

"But Margot's not here right now and in case you have failed to notice, I'm a grown woman who can make decisions for herself." As she spoke, her eyes flicked to something to his right, the tiniest hint of exasperation in them.

"Why do you do that?"

She froze. "Do what?"

"Sometimes, you ..." He shook his head and waved his hand through the patch of air beside him. It felt cold, though not too dissimilar to Nea's magic. When he looked back at her, she seemed to be biting back a laugh. "What?"

"Nothing." She crossed her arms. "Sometimes necromancers can see things that aren't there in a ... physical sense."

"Like restless spirits?"

"Yes, among other things," she said then sighed. "But you are changing the subject."

"You're sure you want to head directly to Swinton?"

She nodded. "I'll be fine to keep going and I promise I won't tell Margot you made me walk all night. Unless you would rather go to The Crossroads and have a nap at the tavern. Though I imagine that bustling highway taverns are the last place either of us should be seen right now."

She was right.

"Okay, let's keep moving then." He headed towards the road she had indicated. This time he was mindful to keep his strides short and his pace slower.

Around midnight, the lilac-coloured mage light that had been bobbing merrily along beside them flickered as Nea stumbled. She caught Garret's arm and he halted. They should have stopped hours ago, but Nea had refused each time he'd suggested it. He wasn't going to let her this time. "I can't in good conscious let you keep going. You need to rest." He frowned, suddenly realising how tired he was himself. "We both do."

She had been about to protest but rose her hand to stifle a yawn. "Well, we've reached Lone Oak." She pointed ahead to a massive tree that split the road in two.

"So we have."

"Follow me."

"I'm not sure ..." He started to protest as she left the road, but she turned and fixed him with a look, and he followed her.

As she picked her way through the trees, she seemed to be counting something, though what he wasn't sure. The cool touch of her magic stirred the air and he sent his keen-sense out. The snag in the source, the spirit, was beside Nea as it often was but there was something else—little flickers of heat.

"Breadcrumbs," she said over her shoulder.

"I'm sorry."

"I can feel your keen-sense. I'm counting *breadcrumbs*, like in the tale of the lost orphans." She paused and changed direction.

"Let's hope we don't meet the same fate as them then," he said, peering into the darkness around them.

After a few more turns, they stepped through the trees into a clearing at the centre of which was a small run-down shack.

"How did you know this was here?"

She blushed, and the mage light flickered. "I used to come here ... before." She started walking across the clearing.

"Before Kalhanna?"

She nodded. "It belongs to a friend of mine who would use it when he needed to get away from his responsibilities."

Leith? He didn't ask. Though he did know Leith had a lot of boltholes like this one, or he'd used to. "Are you sure it's safe for us to stay here? Who else knows about it?"

She turned and gave him an exasperated look. "Aside from myself and now you, there are only two others who know about it, and I doubt either of them are going to be telling anyone."

He followed her to the small porch and through the door. Inside, the shack was bare save for a large trunk in the corner that Nea opened. She scrunched her nose at the contents before hauling out a pair of sleeping rolls.

"They smell a bit musty, but they'll be better than sleeping on the floor." She handed one to him and unrolled the other with a firm flick. She then kicked her boots off and settled on it, folding her cloak into a pillow.

Garret set his roll up a short distance away and lay back with a sigh. He listened to Nea's breath slowing and closed his eyes.

"It's your family, isn't it?"

He didn't answer.

"That's why you need to get to Swinton. You're worried Evard will beat us there."

He opened one eye to look at her. "We're supposed to be getting some sleep."

She sighed and rolled over so her back was to him. "I'm sorry helping me has endangered them."

He didn't respond. Helping her *had* endangered them but he knew that even if Nea hadn't come along, he had already been at the point where he could no longer stand by and let Evard's madness continue. She had just been the catalyst.

They walked for most of the next day stopping only to buy some fresh-baked morning rolls from one of the farmsteads they passed. By early afternoon, the trees flanking the road started to thin again and they crested a small hill to look down on a familiar homestead.

He was relieved to find it unscathed. Even more so when a young boy of twelve appeared, ushering a lazy cow along towards the field where several of her companions were grazing. Pierce stopped and looked their way. The light brush of his keen-sense drifted over them and Nea's magic stirred in response.

Pierce waved and called over his shoulder towards the house, from which two women emerged. Garret started down the hill towards them and when he got close, the younger hitched her skirt and jogged to meet him.

She threw her arms around his shoulders, engulfing him in a hug that smelt like honey and apples. After a moment, she pulled away and shoved his chest hard enough to make him stagger back a step.

"That's for making us all worry, you bloody idiot."

He rubbed the centre of his chest. "Bridie—"

"Don't *Bridie* me! Six months, and the first letter I get tells me to take the children and run to some fort in the middle of nowhere. As if I don't have enough to worry about with Nora as it is. And you could've been dead in a ditch somewhere for all I knew—"

Nea cleared her throat.

"And who is this then?"

"She's a ..." Garret glanced at Nea, who was watching the exchange with a curious expression. "... friend."

"A *friend*?" Bridie's eyebrows nearly disappeared into her hairline.

"Bright Mother, no. Not like that. Her name is N—" He stopped himself and looked at Nea, unsure whether or not to reveal her true identity.

Nea shrugged, then her attention snapped to his grandmother as the steady press of the older woman's keen rolled over them.

His grandmother stepped forward and reached out as though she was going to touch Nea but her hand stopped short and hovered in the air between them, palm up. Nea looked at the fingers as though they might bite her, then, very slowly, she touched her palm against the older woman's.

Magic stirred the air for a moment, cold and thick, and then his grandmother nodded. "I thought as much. You're one of Abigail's lot—have to be with eyes like that."

"She's my grandmother," Nea responded, her head tilting as she studied the older woman.

"You'd be Niall's daughter then."

Nea glanced at Bridie and then at Garret. "Yes."

"Nea. That was the name. Your father brought you along when he and Abigail ..." She shook her head and glanced at Garret. "I'd never seen such a wee thing with so much hair. Though I remember it was iron grey like your grandmother's." Her eyes flicked to Nea's darkened hair. "I'm Camille."

A look of recognition crossed Nea's features. "A pleasure to meet you. Nonna often talks about you."

"I bet she does." She smiled. "I haven't seen her in years. Is she well?"

Nea looked sheepish. "Last I saw her she was, but I have been away from Hartswood for some time."

Bridie fixed Garret with a stare. "Hartswood? Did you bring her here to—"

"Uncle Garret!" A silver streak raced from the barn and thudded into his legs, her tiny arms wrapping around them as she looked up at him through a tangle of silver hair.

"Nora, you've grown tall."

She rolled her hazel eyes. "You always say that." Her gaze widened as it fell on Nea. "Who is that?"

He felt Nea's magic stir as she brushed it over Nora, her eyes flicking to meet his, a question on her lips.

"This is Nea. Nea, I'd like you to meet Elenora."

Nea crouched so her face was level with Nora's and held out her hand. "A pleasure to meet you, Elenora."

Nora shook her hand. "Your eyes are really pretty. Like amethysts."

Nea chuckled. "Ah, thank you. You have lovely eyes too."

"You're a mage, aren't you? I just felt your keen. It's very different to Mama and Granmama's."

"Yes, I'm—"

"No! Let me guess. Can I feel you? I would have already, but Mama says it's not polite to do it without asking first." She gave Nea a pointed look and Garret chuckled.

"Nora—" Bridie started.

"It's alright. Sure, Elenora. Go ahead," Nea said.

Nora's keen stirred; it was similar to Nea's in that cool, soothing way, but where Nea's magic was steady and controlled, Nora's was unskilled and skipped about: soothing one moment and stabbing cold the next. Nea rolled her shoulders and Nora's magic stopped.

"You're like me. But different." She reached out and lightly brushed the end of Nea's braid. "And your hair is the wrong colour. It should be like mine, shouldn't it? Mama said all mages like me have grey hair."

"She's right. My hair isn't normally this colour. I just had to change it for a while." She smiled and straightened.

"How about I make us a brew and we finish this conversation in the house?" his grandmother asked.

"Can I show Nea my rocks?" Nora turned her bright gaze on her mother but before Bridie could answer, her attention was back on Nea. "I found this red one by the stream and if you squint, it looks like a mouse. And Pierce gave me this green one with brown stripes that he found near the village. And Uncle Garret—"

"Nora." Bridie reprimanded her with a smile. "I'm sorry, Nea. We don't get many new faces around here."

"It's fine." For once, she looked like she actually meant it. "I'd love to see your rocks, Elenora."

"Great!" Nora reached out and took hold of Nea's hand, dragging her towards the house and chatting incessantly about her rock collection.

"Pierce, come and help me make a pot of tea," his grandmother said as the boy returned from seeing the cow to the field.

Garret was left alone with Bridie; he rubbed the back of his neck and gave her a sheepish smile.

"So, you didn't bring Nea here to convince me to send Nora to Hartswood?"

"No. But she needs to go. If Kieran was still around, I wouldn't be so adamant. But now more than ever, Hartswood is the safest place for her. You can feel her magic, Bridie. It's unstable. She needs to be taught by others like her, others who understand the dangers of what she is." He frowned as he thought about what he had seen Nea do.

Bridie's mouth twisted like it always did when she was thinking. "I know she needs to be with mages like her. You and Nea could take her."

"We can take you *all* as far as Fort Braemar. But travelling with us will be dangerous. It might be for the best if you make your own way. I am sure Nea can put you in touch with someone who can get you to Hartswood."

"Is that what this letter was about?" She pulled a crumpled note out of her pocket. "You expect us to drop everything here and head to Fort Braemar because the king has finally figured out you're not as loyal to him as you claimed to be?"

His jaw tightened. "It runs deeper than that now. Bridie, he has—" He stopped himself. "It's not safe for you here anymore. Any of you."

"It hasn't been safe here for over two years, Garret. The second you took over from Commander Reid, we were no longer safe. What does Evard have now that makes it any worse?"

"Kieran."

Her hand flew to her mouth. "How long have you known?"

"A couple of days."

"But Kieran has been gone for four years. He ... he ..." She swallowed and pressed a hand to her chest. "He wouldn't work for Evard."

"Evard has ways of making people do exactly what he wants. All he has to do is find your weakness."

She shook her head.

"You can shake your head at me all you want but that doesn't change the fact that Evard has Kieran. Whether he is working for him or not remains to be seen, but Evard seemed fairly certain that Kieran was under his control when he threatened to have him reanimate me."

She played with the end of her auburn braid; the movement reminded him of Nea. "The children think their father is dead. I thought that was the only thing that could keep him away. I couldn't imagine he would just abandon them ... abandon me." Her voice was soft.

"I'm sorry."

She shook her head. "Is Evard really using him to reanimate people?"

"I can't be certain, though he wanted to use Nea for the same purpose." He didn't need to mention what else Nea was capable of.

"You took her from Evard. That's why he wants your head, isn't it?"

"She's part of the reason. But he's suspected my loyalties were divided for a while now."

"And what does Declan think of your current predicament?" It must have shown on his face because she added, "What happened? Is Declan okay?"

"He's dead."

Nea had been right; it did get a little easier every time he said it.

"Dead? How?"

Garret glanced at the house. "He was murdered. It's a long story."

"Are you alright?"

"I'm coping." He rubbed the back of his neck.

She suddenly hugged him. "Oh, Garret."

"I'm fine. Really. It is strange not being able to hear his opinion on things, whether I'd like it or not." He gave a short laugh. "But each day it gets a little easier."

She let him go and wiped her eyes. "We should see what the others are up to. Poor Nea has probably had her ears talked off by now, and it will be getting on for dinnertime soon."

After dinner, they sat around the small main room. His grandmother was in her chair by the fire, a small piece of wood in one hand and her carving knife in the other. Curly cream-coloured shavings littered her lap and every so often, she would pause and turn the piece, giving it a calculating stare before starting to carve again. Elenora was laying on her stomach at Camille's feet, her tongue between her teeth as she practiced writing letters on the floor by dipping her finger in a bowl of water.

Pierce sat across from Garret, his brow furrowed as he guided a piece of charcoal across parchment with deft strokes. He kept pausing to glance at the other end of the table where his Mother and Nea sat in quiet conversation. After one such time, he placed the charcoal down and ran his hands through his hair, leaving a smudge of black on his forehead and causing the strawberry blond curls to stand on end. Catching Garret watching him, he shielded his drawing from view.

"Are you going to add that one to the wall? Not much room up there nowadays." He indicated the section of wall covered by drawings. There were sketches of different plants and animals in vivid detail, along with drawings of all members of the family, including one of Declan.

Pierce glanced at his current drawing and shook his head. "I can't get the lines on this one right." He went to crumple it, but Garret reached across and snatched it from him.

"Hey!" Pierce made a grab for it but not before Garret had seen its subject. Pierce had somehow managed to catch the haunted look in her eyes and the thin wisps of curl that refused to stay in her braid in perfect detail.

"You're too hard on yourself; there's nothing wrong with that drawing."

Pierce blushed. "I couldn't get the smile right."

"Because your drawings capture the very essence of the subject, and she doesn't smile very often."

"What's that?" Nea and Bridie were watching them.

"Nothing," Garret said, giving Pierce a smile.

"Are they all your drawings, Pierce?" Nea asked, pointing to the wall.

Pierce nodded. "Granmama says it's my gift, but I want to be a warden like Uncle Garret. I have the keen-sense."

"A warden?"

His grandmother made a noise of derision and Pierce gave her a sheepish look. "Granmama says the wardens have changed and don't stand for what they used to. Doesn't matter though, because I can't suppress the source anyway." He looked at his fingers, rubbing them on his shirt.

Nea took a sip of her tea. "I have a friend who couldn't suppress the source when we were younger either, but now he's one of the best wardens I know."

"Apart from Uncle Garret," Nora piped up and Nea laughed.

Garret hadn't heard Nea genuinely laugh before and found himself biting back a smile at the sound. Then she frowned, and her gaze flicked to the door. Her head tilted as though she were listening to something before she stood and rushed outside.

Garret shared a look with Bridie and grabbed his sword before following after Nea.

"What's going on?" Bridie asked as she joined him outside.

Nea was standing a short distance away, her eyes scanning the moonlit dark.

"Nea?" He took a step towards her but realised he could feel her keen stirring the air. He let his keen-sense drift out. There was that strange snag in the source to Nea's left and then farther out in the dark something was coming, something that felt—wrong. "What is that?"

"Nothing good," Bridie said as she turned back towards the house. "We need to get Gran and the children out of here."

"There's no time," Nea said, and she was right. A pair of dark shapes crested the top of the hill. The night became charged with the static prickle of a storm mage and the warm crackle of fire magic.

The two figures started running down the hill and Nea planted her feet, pulling a thin coil of source. Garret drew his sword.

They were both mages, but they felt wrong; their magic was tainted and twisted. Corrupted. The first mage lifted his hand and an arc of lightning charged towards where Nea stood. Garret acted on instinct, suppressing the source, and the magic slammed into the edge of his field of suppression in a shower of bright sparks before snuffing out. Nea had dodged it though and was standing just beyond the suppression bubble, her eyes intent on the second mage, who dropped to the ground, his hands gripping his head.

The storm mage lunged for Garret, casting another arc of lightning that fanned out and died as it met with the void Garret had created around himself. The mage drew a sword and closed in.

Garret danced backwards as the mage's sword breezed past his gut, then went on the offensive. He drove the other man back with a series of strikes, testing his skill. After a few clumsy blocks, the mage tripped and fell onto his hands. He tried to draw the source to him as he scuttled backwards but Garret suffocated his connection and with a quick lunge, drove his sword through his chest.

The other mage rushed forward and tackled Nea. They hit the ground hard and rolled. Then there was a yell of pain followed by the sound of an open palm hitting skin.

"Fucking bitch bit me!" He pinned her to the ground and drew his hand back to hit her again. Garret moved to help, but he felt her power spike and the mage screamed. He rolled off her and she leapt to her feet, releasing the grip of her magic. The mage rolled over, panting. Blood was running from his ears. Garret crossed to him and rested the tip of his sword against his throat.

"End it please, before the voices come back."

"Voices?" Garret glanced at Nea, who looked just as confused as he felt.

The mage's eyes rolled back in his head and Garret saw the black veins working their way up his cheeks.

"Garret," Nea prompted and he drove his sword forward.

"Drop your sword." It was a voice that froze Garret's blood in his veins, and he turned slowly.

A warden with eyes almost as black as his hair had Nora clamped to his chest, his hand over her mouth. *Willem.* Behind him stood John, holding a struggling Bridie, and several of the king's guard, who had Pierce and his grandmother restrained.

Willem eyed Nea as he spoke to Garret. "One more time. Drop. Your. Sword."

Garret threw the sword down and lifted his hands. He let his keen-sense out, testing the edges of John's suppression around them all.

"Let the children go, Willem." Nea's voice had a cold edge to it and Garret noticed her hands were shaking.

Willem gave a bark of cruel laughter and Nora squeaked as he squeezed her tighter. "Sure, I'll let them go if you trade places with her." He lifted his hand off Nora's mouth and ran the back of his fingers delicately down her cheek.

Bridie struggled against John, managing to break free momentarily. "Get your filthy hands off my daughter."

John grabbed her again, he twisted her arms behind her back and grunted with effort as the field of suppression around them flickered.

Nea stepped forward. "Let her go. You can take me—I won't put up a fight." She lifted her hands and took another slow step closer.

Garret bit the inside of his cheek. He couldn't let them take Nea back, but if he had to choose between her and Nora ... He clenched his fists.

Nea edged forward again. "Think about it. You can take her to Evard and I am sure he'll be delighted. But if you hand him me? Well, he'll be practically euphoric."

One more step and she was past the edge of John's suppression.

"Or I could take the lot of you." Willem's top lip curled.

"Sure, you can try." She grabbed hold of the source and pulled it to her like a fisherman hauling in a net. Willem's head snapped back under the brunt of Nea's attack and he dropped Nora, who rushed to Nea's side. "Go to Garret." Nea gave her a gentle push in his direction.

Willem recovered and suffocated Nea's connection to the source. He leapt for her but she danced backwards and he stumbled under his own momentum.

The field of John's suppression popped and the steady pressure of Camille's keen built in the air. The ground beneath them all began to rumble and crack, scattering the king's guard and knocking John off balance. Bridie planted her feet and bent forward, sending John to the ground. She kicked him and ran to Garret, taking Nora from him and rushing back to join their grandmother and Pierce.

Garret dove for his sword and leapt forward to engage John, who had regained his feet and was bearing down on his family.

"Uncle Garret, don't let that man hurt Nea."

His attention snapped to where Nora was pointing. Nea and Willem were rolling about in the dirt. Willem was using all his focus to suppress Nea's magic and as they scuffled, he landed on top of her. One of his hands pinned both of hers above her head, a set of long scratches standing out on his cheek.

"Go," Bridie said as she thrust her arm out. Her fingers fanned and a group of vines erupted from the ground, tripping John. Garret leapt over him as he fell and raced to help Nea.

"Is this bringing back memories?" Willem mocked as he ran a finger down her cheek and she writhed under his weight, her heels digging into the ground. "Wishing you had your wicked little knife?" He pulled out a blade made from a strange dark metal and twisted it mockingly in front of her face. "Hmm, should I kill you or maybe just mess that pretty face of yours up a bit?"

She froze as he lightly stroked her cheek with the blade of the knife, bringing it to a stop just under her chin.

"Either way, you're going to scream," Willem said.

Garret kicked Willem in the ribs, knocking him off Nea, and she rolled out of the way as he got up and drew his sword to face off against Garret.

"I'm going to enjoy killing you. Then I'm going to have some fun with your sister and Nea before I kill them too." He lunged forward, and Garret dodged, landing a slice on Willem's thigh that made him growl. "Maybe I'll keep you alive long enough that you can hear their screams while I pluck out their eyes."

Garret blocked a strike that was heading for his neck and twisted away. Willem could be cruel, but right now, he sounded completely unhinged—

Nora screamed, and he whirled around. The king's guard had backed his grandmother and the children against the side of the house. A ring of sharp stalagmites erupted between them as his grandmother pushed the children behind her.

"Garret!" Nea's yell snapped him back to the fight and he barely dodged a slice from Willem's sword. He was caught off guard though and the other warden managed to knock him to the ground. Willem levelled the tip of his sword at Garret's throat and stepped onto his sword hand, forcing him to relinquish his hold on his own blade.

Garret swallowed as Willem drew back to strike, but the blow didn't come. Instead, there was a meaty thud and the head of an axe was embedded in Willem's side. He stared at it in shock and then at Nea, who was holding onto the handle, panting. She wrenched the axe out of his side and swung it again, but it whooshed through open air as Willem staggered backwards, blood rushing around his fingers.

"F-fucking whore," he spat and lurched back another step. He didn't make it too far before he fell to his knees.

Nea turned her attention to John, who had forced Bridie to her knees and was holding her by the hair, his sword against her throat. "I suggest you let her go," she said as she tightened her grip on the axe handle.

Garret stepped up beside her. "I'd do what she says, John. Willem's dead. If you leave now, you might find yourself with a shiny new title when you get back."

John's eyes flicked to Willem, who was lying on the ground, his fingers gripping the gaping wound in his side, then to the two dead mages. He tightened his grip on Bridie's hair, making her cry out.

"Mama!" Nora stared wide-eyed at the men in front of her.

"You going to murder their mother in front of them, John?" Nea asked. She was gathering a thin thread of the source, but she was doing it so gently Garret didn't think John could feel it. "Well?"

"I'll do it. I'll kill her." John met Garret's eye.

"I don't think you will. You're not Willem. You're not Evard. You're a scared little boy too afraid to make decisions for himself because then he'll have to deal with the consequences. Garret's wrong. They won't make you commander—you don't have the backbone for it." Nea casually rested the handle of the axe on her shoulder.

John's nostrils flared. He twisted Bridie's hair again and his fingers twitched around the hilt of his sword. That was when Nea let him feel the thread of source she had gathered. His eyes widened and he changed focus, suppressing Nea's keen. It wasn't Nea he should have been focused on though. The moment he took his suppression off Bridie, she lashed out. Vines erupted from the ground around the king's guard, hoisting them into the air and tossing them aside like rag dolls.

Then the vines seized John and squeezed. "I don't have to kill you, but if you don't gather the rest of your men and leave right now, I will." Bridie clenched her fists.

The source flickered and buckled erratically as John's keen attempted to quell it, but he had to choose, breathing or suppression, and breathing won out. "Alright," he wheezed.

"Tell them to stand down." Bridie's vines squeezed him again.

"Stand down," he squeaked, and Bridie loosened her hold slightly. "Do as she says; stand down."

The soldiers who had gotten back to their feet shared a look but sheathed their swords.

Bridie dropped John. "Now get out of here before I change my mind." She held her hand out for the axe and Nea handed it to her as John and the other men backed away. She strode to Willem, who was barely breathing, and spat on him, then lifted the axe. "This is for touching my daughter, you vile prick." She brought the axe down on his neck. "And this is for me." She kicked him and drew her leg back to do it again.

Garret cleared his throat. "Ah, Bridie."

"The fucker deserved more than that. I should have cut his balls off first." She turned her gaze to Nea, who was staring at the bodies of the mages rubbing her arm, and asked, "They were corrupted, weren't they?"

Garret nodded. "You should go and check on Nora and Pierce. Nea and I can take care of this." He gestured to the bodies.

When Bridie had disappeared into the house, he walked to Nea's side. She hadn't moved. She was just standing there, staring at the bodies, her eyes far away and her mouth a tight line. It was a look she'd worn before—one he had seen on soldiers who couldn't escape the battles and the things they had seen, the things they had done.

"Nea?" He gently placed his hand on her shoulder.

She leapt away from him and her magic pressed down, taking hold of his core.

"Easy now, it's just me." He lifted his hands, making no attempt to suppress her keen. "It's Garret."

Her magic immediately stopped, and she relaxed. "Sorry, you startled me." Her gaze flicked back towards the dead mages and she touched her arm again.

"Are you ...?"

Her head snapped up and her eyes met his. "I'm fine." She rolled her sleeve back to show him her arm. Her skin glowed slightly in the moonlight—smooth, pale, and free of the marks of corruption.

"Thank you for stepping in with Willem." He didn't doubt that he would be the dead one if she hadn't.

She bit her lip and looked at Willem's body. The discarded axe was lying next to it. "He was at Kalhanna."

Garret knew Willem had been stationed at Kalhanna before the purge, but he had been told that he wasn't present during the attack.

"Those not fit for the fight, the elderly and children ... they were hiding in the library—they trusted him and he ..." Her voice was thick and she swallowed.

"Were there really corrupted at Kalhanna?" He kept his voice soft, not expecting her to answer. She seemed to avoid the topic of Kalhanna. He understood why; he'd seen the aftermath of the purge. It had been a brutal skirmish.

"Evard, doesn't like being told *no* ... Kalhanna was personal for him. The rumour of corruption was just a convenient excuse for the purge. One he thought the public would accept."

Garret had assumed as much.

She walked over to Willem's body and picked something up off the ground. When she turned back to him, she had the dark-bladed knife in her hand and was staring at it. "I thought Willem had died there. I sunk this knife into his ribs when he ..." She shook her head. "But then he disappeared, and I just assumed he'd crawled into some dark corner to bleed out. I should have made sure he was dead."

"We don't need to talk about this if you—"

"It's fine." She looked towards the house as Bridie emerged, carrying two steaming cups of tea.

"Gran insisted you both sit and drink this. It packs a punch so be warned."

Garret sniffed the contents of his mug; the sweet scent of honey barely masked the bitterness of the restorative herbs and the smoky bite of whiskey. "Oh, it's *that* sort of tea."

Nea dropped the knife and took a tentative sip of the tea. She made a face, though he wasn't sure whether it was the bittersweet taste of the tea or the burn of the whiskey that caused it. "That's an interesting brew. How are Nora and Pierce?" She blew her tea but didn't take another sip.

"Shaken. Pierce has a split brow and an impressive black eye but otherwise he's unscathed. They're packing their things." Her gaze flicked to Willem, and she gave a small shudder.

"Are you alright, Bridie?" Nea reached out as though to touch her arm but then her fingers curled back and she dropped her hand to her side.

"Better now that bastard is dead." She hugged herself. "We should have left when I received your letter. As soon as this is taken care of, we'll go." She indicated the bodies.

"We'll take care of that. You just focus on getting on your way." Garret downed the last of his tea.

"I know it's not my place to say this, but Elenora needs to go to Hartswood." Nea kept her eyes on her tea as she spoke.

Bridie looked back towards the house and sighed. "I know. I shouldn't have kept her here so long, but I couldn't bear the thought of her being so far away."

Nea gave her a soft smile. "I understand. You want what is best for her but at the same time you just want to be selfish and never let her out of your sight. It's one of the hardest decisions to make."

Bridie gave her a sly look. "You have children?"

"I'm just very good at empathising. You can't help others with grief if you can't put yourself in their shoes." She took a large sip of her tea and screwed her nose up. "And you don't have to leave her. I am sure Nonna would love to see Camille, and you and Pierce would be welcomed there as well. Or you could go to Del Harol— it's only a few hours ride from Hartswood, so you'd be close."

Bridie studied her before turning her gaze to the bodies. "What are you going to do about them?"

"I'll make sure they've all crossed over and then we'll bury them." Nea finished her tea in one gulp. "I'm hoping Camille's magic can help us with the graves."

"I'll go get her." Bridie took their empty mugs and headed towards the house.

Once she was out of sight, Garret turned to Nea. She had picked the knife up again and was staring at the bodies, but her eyes had that glassy look that suggested her mind was miles away. The ripple in the source that accompanied her was fluttering about near the dead mages and her attention snapped to it. She frowned and gave a decisive shake of her head then shifted her gaze to Garret and held the knife out to him hilt first.

He stared at it and she gave it a tiny shake.

"It belonged to Tobias."

Garret had heard that name before, one of the mages from Kalhanna.

"You should—" he started, but she shook her head.

"Take it please. I can't bear to bury it with Willem or leave it to the elements." There was a hitch in her voice and something flashed in her eyes that he couldn't quite place.

Slowly he took the knife from her and she let out a long sigh.

"Thank you," she whispered and then turned back to the bodies. "We should get to work."

As the coolness of her magic grew in the air, Garret studied the knife. Moonlight glinted off the dark metal of the blade and he traced one of the roses carved into the hilt with his index finger. He shook his head and wondered what Declan would make of everything that had occurred since his death. Wherever he was, he was most likely having a good laugh at Garret's expense.

CHAPTER EIGHTEEN

Nea

By midday the next day, they were well beyond Swinton and Garret was showing no signs of stopping. He had been silent for most of the morning, his jaw set tight and his eyes unreadable. It reminded Nea of those first days after Little Brook. She sighed and glanced over her shoulder to check on Camille, who was riding a knock-kneed old pony with the fluffiest ears Nea had ever seen. Beside the pony walked Bridie, and Pierce, who every so often stopped to rub the back of his legs.

Nea ran a hand through her hair and turned back to look at Garret, who had drifted ahead. For the last hour, he had been carrying Nora, and now she was dozing with her head resting on his shoulder, her arms hanging limply by her sides. There was no point in walking until they all dropped from exhaustion; with a resigned huff, Nea hefted Nora's pack higher on her shoulder and increased her pace to catch up with Garret again.

"I know you're worried about us being followed, but we need to stop. The children and Camille need a proper rest. They need ti—"

"It's—" Garret started. Nora mumbled sleepily against his shoulder and burrowed in closer, making him lower his voice. "It's not safe. We can't stop until I am certain we are not being followed."

Nea increased her pace and stepped in front of him, forcing him to stop walking. "I understand that you just want to keep them safe, but they need time to rest, to process what happened last night. We all do."

He huffed out a breath and Nea saw just how tired he was. It wasn't only the events of last night. He looked soul weary. She imagined he had gotten about as much sleep as she had since Little Brook, which wasn't all that much.

"I can't risk it. Last night was too close. I can't ..." His arms tensed and Nora grumbled.

Nea ran her hand through her hair again then placed her fingers delicately on his arm. "I know." Of course she knew what was really bothering him. He felt responsible for what had happened to Declan and last night had brought all those feelings back to the surface. Seeing his family in very real danger, having Nora threatened like that? He wanted nothing more than to keep them safe, as though that would make up for the guilt he felt about Declan's death. But running everyone ragged was not the answer. "Believe me, Garret. I know what you are feeling but they can't keep going and you can't either. If you run yourself to exhaustion because of an imagined pursuit, then you won't be able to protect them when the danger really does arrive."

He looked down at her fingers with a frown and then shifted Nora's weight. "Alright, we'll look for somewhere to rest."

With a nod, she stepped out of his way and they started moving again.

After another hour, they stopped in a small clearing well away from the side of the road. Pierce rolled onto the grass with a heavy sigh and pulled his boots off, while Bridie helped Camille down before digging in one of the packs strapped to the old pony. She took out a loaf of bread, some dried apple slices, and a small pot of honey.

Nea settled on the grass beside Camille and rubbed the back of her legs as Nora went bounding past.

"Oh, to have the boundless energy of youth again." Camille chuckled, then her expression became more serious as she met Nea's gaze. "Thank you for last night."

"It wasn't just me. Everyone played their part."

"I mean for offering yourself in exchange for Nora."

Nea looked at her hands folded in her lap. "Oh ... but your thanks are not necessary; it was the right thing to do."

Camille patted her knee. "There's a lot of your grandmother in you."

Bridie came over and handed each of them some of the dried apple and a slice of bread layered with honey. "It's not much but it will put something in your stomachs at least."

After they finished eating, Bridie, Camille, and Pierce curled up for a nap. Garret hadn't let himself rest. He just kept pacing the perimeter of the clearing, his keen-sense stirring the air every so often. The sixth time he came around to pass by Nea, she groaned and leapt to her feet, blocking his path. "Sit and have something to eat. I'll keep watch for a while."

"He won't listen to you. When Garret sets his mind to something, he can be frustratingly stubborn." Declan appeared beside her.

Garret's gaze flicked to the spot Declan was standing. "I don't need to rest."

"Yes, you do. You'll be no good to them if you fall asleep on your feet."

He frowned. "If—"

"I spent three years in hiding. I think I am capable of keeping us safe for a few hours while you get some rest."

He ran his hand through his hair, making the auburn waves stand up slightly.

"If it makes you feel better, wait until I've set some wards and you can test them out."

Declan whistled. "You say that like setting wards is as simple as snapping your fingers. You do realise that wards require a specific understanding of an extremely complicated branch of magic, one that most mages will never truly understand. Or at least, that was the spiel my mentors always gave me."

Garret was just staring at her as though trying to figure out whether it was worth his while to keep arguing or not.

"Humour me at least?" Nea asked.

"Fine. Show me these wards." There was a challenge in his tone and he crossed his arms. He didn't believe she could actually do it.

She settled herself on the grass and Nora came skipping over to sit next to her. Nea closed her eyes and focused on the feeling of her keen before pushing it out. First she encountered the coolness of Nora's necromancy, then the flickering static of Declan and the numbness of Garret. She guided her awareness farther out past the steady rumble of Camille's earth keen and the dense green of Bridie's, which was more like the scent of a lush forest than an actual physical sensation. Then she focused on the Between, drawing the barrier close but not allowing it to open.

She picked four anchor points and secured the source to them by picturing it as ribbon and tying a set of neat sailor's knots. As the wards activated, a seamless bubble of invisible magic formed over the clearing. Nea gave it a few tentative prods to make sure it was secure before bringing her keen back into herself. A dull ache settled behind her temples and she rubbed them in small circles, taking a moment to catch her breath. Wards were not overly complicated once you understood them, but they were taxing.

Garret's keen-sense brushed past her as he tested the wards. Each push against the bubble sent a spike of cold down her spine and she shifted her hips. "If anything crosses my barrier, I will know. You should rest. You too, Nora," she added as she glanced at the girl sitting beside her.

Nora had her eyes shut and her tongue was poking out between her teeth as her immature magic stirred the air in icy spikes. "How do you do that?"

"Lots of practice."

"Can we practice right now? Mama never let me because she said I needed to learn from someone like me and—"

"Now is not the time, Nora," Garret said as he settled against a tree trunk not far from where they sat.

"Please." She pouted.

"There's one thing you can practice right now." Garret met Nea's eye and shook his head but she continued, "It doesn't use magic, but it is very, very important." She made her tone sound serious as she said it.

Nora leant forward and whispered, "What is it?"

"You need to sit very still and close your eyes." Nea closed her own eyes and wriggled her hips to adjust her posture. "Then you breathe in very slowly and then out again just as slow. On each outward breath, focus on pushing your keen-sense—"

"But I know how to do that already. Uncle Garret taught me that ages ago."

Nea opened one eye to regard her. "So you have full mastery of your keen-sense then? Using it as natural as breathing? You can successfully identify the keen of any mage you encounter? You've felt the edge of the Between and learned the difference between healthy walls and thinning or damaged ones? You've navigated the gateway through—"

"Okay! Okay, I get it."

Nea opened her other eye and gave Nora a shrewd smile.

"No, I haven't done all those things." The girl folded her arms and Garret chuckled. "Keen-sense isn't exciting though. I want to do something exciting."

"You can't do anything *exciting* until you've got solid control of your keen-sense. As a necromancer, you need to be able to identify the nature of a spirit in the space of a single heartbeat. And that requires you to practice using your keen-sense until it becomes as easy as breathing."

Nora frowned.

"Nea is right." Garret scratched the stubble along his jaw.

"But can't I practice that later? I want to use my magic. Do something awesome, make lightning, like Declan."

Declan laughed.

"Nora, you can't make lightning. You're a necromancer—we're not like elemental mages."

"Ugh!" She flopped back on the grass. "Then what good are we?"

"In the beginning, when the first mages—"

"I know the story of the Bright Mother."

The jaded tone of her voice nearly made Nea laugh. "That's good, but this isn't that story. When the first mages appeared, they were classified into two groups: the elementals and the arcane. Those mages we now know as necromancers, healers, and mind mages all belonged to the group known as the arcane. Their magic was problematic for many reasons. It was useful, but could very easily be turned to dark purposes."

Declan and Garret were both watching her speak with curious expressions, but Nora's mouth twisted like she had eaten something sour.

"But can't any mage use their magic to hurt people? Fire mages can burn people and water mages can drown them. Mama was going to strangle that bad man last night. Why are the arcane any different?"

Nea had asked Nonna the same question when she was learning to use her magic, and in turn, Bran had asked her. "That is a good question and one that many scholars have spent their entire lives pondering. But let's focus on necromancers and why they can be dangerous. What do you think necromancers do? Aside from burying the dead and helping their souls move on."

"We can talk to ghosts. I guess if you didn't like someone you could ask your ghost friends to haunt them."

"Just so we're clear, I am not haunting anyone for you," Declan quipped.

Nea hid her smirk behind her hand. "It doesn't exactly work that way. But what else?"

"We can make bad spirits stop hurting people, put them back where they belong. None of that seems all that bad though."

"Because it's not really. But we can also—"

Garret cleared his throat and cut her off with a look.

"We can also bring people back to life. But I am not supposed to know about that." Nora gave Garret a look worthy of Bridie. "I guess that could be bad, if the wrong person was brought back to life."

"It's *always* bad. No matter who the person is, how good they were in life, or how much we loved them and miss them. None of that matters. We must *never* bring someone back from the dead. It is wrong and it can cause irreparable damage to not only the soul of the person but the Between itself."

"What's the Between like?"

Nea leant back on her hands and considered her answer. "Strange and beautiful, but very dangerous. There are things that dwell there that want to get out and things that want to eat you."

"Eat me?" Nora squeaked.

"Don't scare the poor child."

She ignored Declan and continued, "Not everything that lives there wants to eat you or is dangerous. And that is why developing your keen-sense is so important. When you eventually go to the Between, you will need to be able to tell if the spirits you encounter are good spirits or bad ones."

Nora was quiet for a while and Nea felt a small smile tugging the corner of her mouth as the girl's keen-sense brushed her before retracting again. Garret had closed his eyes and seemed to be dozing but his shoulders still looked tense and his foot kept flicking every so often. Nea wasn't sure she'd ever met someone so stubborn, but at least he wasn't pacing any more.

"What is that?" Nora gasped.

Nea followed the path of Nora's keen-sense and felt it fluttering around Declan, who shifted uncomfortably. Feeling Garret's eyes on her, she chewed her lip before answering. "That is a spirit."

"Do they all feel like that?"

"No, that one is different."

"Why can't I see it? Aren't we supposed to be able to see them? When the miller's wife died, I saw her walking down the street."

Nea glanced at Declan, who shrugged. "As I said, he's different. We can talk about that later. Right now, you need to keep practicing." Her tone was final enough that Nora asked no more questions.

Nea knew she should tell Garret about Declan, but she didn't know how to. Just coming out and saying, 'By the way, your closest friend has somehow jammed himself between worlds and now is my own personal haunting,' didn't seem right. Maybe she should ask Declan's opinion on the situation.

"I'm bored now." Nora flopped back on the grass, her silver hair fanning out in a shining halo around her. "Can't we practice just a tiny bit of magic?"

"I can teach you how to make a mage light."

Nora's brows pinched together, and her keen gave an icy flutter, then a flickering orb of purple light appeared above her. The light was very unstable, dimming and flaring before disappearing completely again. "I can already make lights."

Nea ran her finger along her lip. "I see." She lay next to Nora on the grass. "Give me your hand; you need to feel my keen."

Nora placed her hand in Nea's. Her skin was cool, which was not uncommon for a necromancer. Nea focused on bringing a mage light into existence, then another and another until the air above them was full of tiny lights, all differing shades of purple, floating and flickering like fireflies.

Nora let out a delighted gasp. "There are so many." She lifted the hand not holding Nea's and waved it through the air, scattering the lights. "Can I do that?"

Nea extinguished the lights and pushed a little of her keen through her hand and into Nora's. Just enough to help stabilise her own immature magic and give her an extra boost.

Nora burst into a fit of giggles. "That feels really weird." She let go of Nea and flicked her hand as though trying to dispel the feeling. "Wow." Her fingertips were glowing softly. She sat up and wiggled them. "I feel like I could—"

"Not so fast." Nea took hold of Nora's hand again as she felt her pushing the magic out, reaching for the Between. The massive hedge of roses that Nea always envisioned as the barrier between worlds appeared. Grey blooms were dotted among the pink, almost overtaking them in some patches. Nea sat as the thorn-studded branches reached towards her and Elenora. She lifted her hand and they stopped with a loud groan. Then the whole hedge shuddered in response to her silent order and disappeared from view again.

Nora was blinking at the open patch of air where the hedge had just been. "Where did that hedge come from?"

Nea glanced at Garret. He was looking at her curiously but only necromancers could see the barrier. "That's the barrier that separates our world from the Between. It appears differently to each necromancer."

"I saw a hedge of pale pink and grey roses. Is that what it looks like for you?"

Nea rolled her lip between her teeth. "Yes. Because you saw the barrier through the filter of my magic. If you were to approach it on your own, it may appear different. Nonna sees a hedge of blackberries and my friend Hazel, a wall of moss-covered stones. But forget about the barrier. Right now, we are focusing only on creating mage lights."

"But—"

"We'll get to the barrier. First you need to learn how to focus. Your magic is erratic and that makes it extremely dangerous, not just for you but those around you as well." Nea gave her fingers a squeeze. "Now lay back and close your eyes."

"But how will I know I've created a light?"

"Nora!"

"Okay." She laid back on the grass and closed her eyes.

Nea let out a breath as she did the same. "Do you remember what it felt like when I was creating the lights?"

"I think so."

"Well, try to copy that and I'll help you keep your keen stable." Almost immediately Nora tried to force the source to do her bidding. The harder she pushed, the harder it pushed back until the air suddenly grew frigid and icy spikes prickled up Nea's spine. She heard Garret shifting and his keen-sense brushed her lightly. "Focus, Nora. Don't use so much force. The source is our ally, not our slave. We don't order it around; we work with it."

Nora's fingers tightened their grip on Nea's hand and the magic in the clearing calmed down.

"That's better. Feel that gentle ebb and flow? You want to use that. It's like the inward and outward breath, the rhythm of the song."

"Well, now, would you look at that." Declan's voice sounded and Nea opened her eyes.

The air was filled with dozens of little lights, but instead of the steady purple of necromancer magic, they were every colour of the spectrum.

"Am I doing it? Oh, wow!" Nora opened her eyes and sat up. The moment her focus broke the lights disappeared, but she didn't seem to care. She leapt to her feet and vaulted into Garret's lap. "Uncle Garret, did you see that? Did you see the rainbow lights? Not even Mama can make them rainbow."

"I saw." He looked over the top of her head at Nea and gave her a tiny nod before turning his attention back to Nora. "I think it's time you got some more rest though. We'll need to start walking again soon if we are going to reach Hillside before full dark."

"More walking?" Nora rolled off Garret's lap and flopped dramatically on the grass, her arms over her face.

Garret gave her a doting smile and pounced on her, tickling her sides. She let out a squeal and wriggled out of his grasp, then darted away across the clearing, daring him to chase her.

Declan grinned as he watched them play. "I think that girl is his only true weakness. Tell me, was it your magic or hers that made those lights?"

Nea didn't answer him but she opened her palm and brought a ball of light into existence. It shimmered purple for a moment, then slowly changed to pink, then red, orange, green, and blue. "I just gave her a little boost, but she created the lights. The funny thing about mage light is, it doesn't actually have a colour. When we summon it, it draws along the path of least resistance and gets tainted by our magic. That's why healers have green and storm mages have blue and so on. The reality is, with just a little effort and a different focus, we could have any colour we wanted." She closed her hand and the light extinguished.

"I never thought of it that way."

She shrugged. "We all come from the same source. I think our modern view of magic has made what we are actually capable of much more limited."

He frowned. "Once again you make me deeply regret that I didn't meet you years ago."

CHAPTER NINETEEN

MARGOT

Early morning sunlight bathed the bed. Margot yawned and arched her back, dislodging the arm that was draped over her stomach. Beside her, Molly grumbled sleepily and rolled over, taking the blankets with her. Margot sat up and grabbed hold of the blanket before giving it a good tug and exposing Molly's bare shoulder to the sunlight. Molly rolled back and glared at her, the movement further exposing her torso, including the curve of her breast and one perfect rose-coloured nipple.

Margot bit back a grin. "I missed waking up with you."

"I missed you too." She propped herself up on her elbows as Margot leant forward and caught her lips in a kiss.

Margot smiled against Molly's mouth before pulling back and brushing her sleep-tangled hair behind her ear. The buttery waves shifted to deep gold as the sunlight moved over them.

Molly frowned as her gaze flicked to the close-cut tight curls that covered Margot's head.

"It'll grow back."

"I know. It's just a stark reminder of—"

"Hey, we've been over this. I'm okay. Really." She looped her arms around Molly's shoulders and drew her into an awkward hug, the blanket catching between their bodies. "I'm more worried about ..." She stopped herself. Molly didn't like to talk about Nea. Margot could understand why but it still hurt that they didn't get along.

"I'm sure she'll be fine as soon as she gets rid of Garret and disappears back into the woodwork."

"Molly, that's not fair." Margot sat back. "I know you still blame her for what happened but it's not her fault."

Molly rolled her eyes and sighed. "She owes you more answers than anyone but you just up and forgave her for disappearing."

"No. Not knowing where she was, what she was going through ... that hurt and she will have to make up for that, but I also know she wouldn't have stayed away without a reason."

Molly placed a hand on Margot's knee. "Okay. I'll admit, whilst I'm still not going to trust her, stabbing Evard took backbone and I can admire her for that. Honestly, I wouldn't hesitate either, given the chance."

"And that bloodthirsty impulsiveness is one of the reasons I love you." Margot chuckled and dropped a kiss on her forehead.

"You know what would make *me* love *you* more?"

Margot folded her arms and waited.

"Another hour of sleep." Molly grinned.

Margot gave her a gentle shove that tipped her onto to her back, then she threw her leg over her hips and straddled them. "Is that so? I can think of better things we could be doing instead of having a sleep-in." She lightly captured Molly's lower lip between her teeth before turning the bite into a kiss that elicited a small moan from her throat.

"Better than a sleep-in?" Molly tilted her lips away as Margot went to kiss her again.

"Oh, so much better." Margot laughed and pressed a row of small kisses down the side of Molly's neck and across her collarbone as one hand traced a teasing path over each breast and down her stomach, making her muscles tense.

"I'm starting to see your point." Molly's hips lifted, and her head tilted back as Margot's hand dipped beneath the blanket between them.

A heavy knocking startled them apart.

"You in there, Little Mouse?"

"What is Sonia doing up at this hour?" Molly groaned.

"It is well after dawn." Margot laughed. "Just a minute, Sonia," she called towards the door and got up to quickly throw on her clothes.

Sonia was leaning on the doorframe and she grinned when Margot opened the door. "You're decent. Wonderful, I wasn't expecting that. Good morning, Molly," she called over Margot's shoulder. Molly rolled her eyes and pulled the blankets up higher. "Last night, you mentioned that you would like me to come with you to see Amelia, as a safety precaution. I have time now if ... it isn't too early for you." She didn't even try to contain her suggestive smile and Margot rolled her eyes.

"Now is quite fine. I can grab some breakfast after we see her. Did you want to come, Molly?" she asked over her shoulder.

Molly yawned and waved her away. "No, I'm supposed to be meeting with Emil and Harvey to work on some of the extra defences. I'll catch up with you later."

The south wing was quiet and dark. A line of dull rune marks blocked off the hallway and Margot let her magic out to investigate them. The distinct signature of High Mage Niall's magic clung to the markings, but there was something else, twisted and cloying like knee-deep swamp water.

Uneasiness crept up the back of her neck and she snapped her head up to meet a pair of silver-blue eyes watching her from a face that was paler than even Nea's. The tone of the girl's skin made her lips appear an almost sultry shade of dark pink as they parted into a languid smile that showed a set of bright white teeth.

"Hello, Margot." Her voice was soft and alluring. "Or should I call you Little Mouse?" She looked over Margot's shoulder at Sonia. "You wardens are always coming to protect your mages from little old me. I am disappointed Garret's not here. We have quite a rapport, he and I." She ran her tongue along her lip. "Not to mention he is so very easy on the eyes. Must be that princely jawline."

"Are you quite done?" Margot crossed her arms. She could feel the barbs of Amelia's magic testing her mind, looking for the chink in her armour.

Amelia pouted. "Your lovely *sister* was so much easier to woo and I'm not even her *type*. Had Garret not intervened, she would have been my willing puppet." The sinister smile returned. "No matter. She'll be mine eventually. When she stops fighting her true nature and embraces the darkness. She is more like me than any of you realise."

"Nea's corruption is gone."

Amelia gave an indulgent laugh. "Oh, I'm not talking about corruption. She and I are hewn from the same piece of cloth. Why don't you ask her father all about it? Ask him what he thought when he realised what his precious little girl would one day become. Whether he regretted not drowning her when he'd had the chance."

"Why would he drown her?"

"You should ask him. I am sure you'll find his answers very enlightening." Her head tilted, and she traced her fingers lightly along her collarbone, circling a small birthmark that looked very similar to the one on Nea's hip. "It's a shame Declan didn't think to speak with him before running off to chase a *dead* end." She smiled sweetly.

"Declan was studying corruption. Why would he need to speak to Niall?"

Amelia bit her lower lip. "I'm sure you'll figure it out." She turned and winked at Margot before taking a step away.

"Wait—"

"No, I am *quite* done now." She waved over her shoulder and disappeared into the gloom.

"Well, now, she's a piece of work. You okay, Little Mouse? You look a bit green." Sonia stepped forward and placed a hand on her shoulder. "Garret warned me about her. She likes to play mind games and tries to ensnare people. She nearly succeeded with Nea."

"I can't believe Nea would be that foolish." Margot rubbed her arms.

"You felt her magic, right? Even on this side of those binding marks." Sonia pointed at the row of runes that divided the hall. "She's more powerful than anything I've felt before. Even Nea doesn't come close." She started to guide Margot out of the hallway. "And you saw Nea. She's a shadow of her former self. A ghost wearing a friendly face, as Nonna would put it. I imagine there is a lot going on in her mind that Amelia could latch onto and exploit."

Margot frowned. "What happened to her, Sonia?"

She glanced back towards the darkness where Amelia had disappeared. "I don't know. But Kalhanna changed everything for *everyone,* not just those directly involved. Nea seems convinced she was the catalyst, and so far, I haven't seen anyone go out of their way to correct her."

Margot chewed her thumbnail and her frown deepened.

"Don't feel guilty about that, Little Mouse. Nea hasn't exactly come out and told us what happened. She disappeared for three years, leaving the rest of us with an abundance of questions. And as yet, she hasn't been forthcoming with many of the answers."

Margot bit the inside of her cheek and turned her back on Amelia's hallway. She couldn't be worrying about Nea right now. The corruption was more important. "I should go and check Declan's notes."

They parted ways at the entry hall, Sonia going off to find Lord Alric and Margot heading to the kitchen to grab a quick bit of breakfast before heading to Declan's room.

She paused in the doorway and drew a breath. The room was lit by a slice of slanting sunlight in which a cloud of dust motes shifted and twirled. Stepping across the threshold, she moved to the desk and examined the piles of books and notes. It was hard to tell where to start; Declan had definitely thrived in his own version of organised chaos. She picked up a thin book from the top of one of the piles and ran her finger delicately along the spine before opening it and scanning one of the entries. It was talking about Johanna of Port Brenna:

The subject shows a morbid fascination for chaos and decay. The strange marks that have appeared on her hands and forearms are like no rash I have seen. I would think they were some form of necrotic affliction but the skin is smooth and whole and shows no signs of atrophy. It is as Samson reported with the case of Richard of Kalhanna; the marks appear more like a tattoo or stain than a physical affliction. It is the mental disease, however, that is most disturbing. With Richard, it was the desire to harm, to destroy and corrupt others. In Johanna I am seeing a distinct desire for perverting of the mind, subverting others, and drawing them close with games and fantasies. She promises solutions to the impossible and once her target has been drawn close enough, she lashes out, claiming them by seeding the corrupting disease within them. I have lost three assistant researchers to her games in the past two months.

The description of Johanna bore a remarkable resemblance to Amelia. Margot placed the book aside and picked up another that appeared to be by the same author, Yolanda, before dropping into the chair next to the desk and opening the book at random:

Samson brought Evette with him today. The bind-shackles may prevent the spread of the corruption, but it is clear that her separation from the source is taking its toll on her. I remember reading the works of Bromly and his insistence on comparing mages and the source to plants and sunlight. At the time, I thought his approach was primitive and borderline idiotic, but seeing the effects of long-term disconnection from the source, I find I am starting to agree with him. Evette has become withdrawn and neurotic. She talks in circles about strange shadows and the Between, and is displaying a compulsion to pick and bite at her nails and the skin of her hands. I have resorted to sedating her but it is a temporary measure and I wonder if it would be kinder to administer an overdose and let her die calmly in her sleep.

Margot flipped through to another entry:

Samson has taken to wearing one bind-shackle around his afflicted wrist. He insists that it is slowing the spread of his corruption, but I am not so certain. Though he has yet to show the propensity for violence that the other afflicted possess, he complains about the crawling feeling under his skin and voices in his mind. The night before last, I found him in his study, pacing and raving about deathborn and the Shadow Man, and I can't help but wonder if the focus on mythical abominations stems from his inability to save Evette.

Margot stared at the word *deathborn*. There was a steady black line beneath it much newer than the rest of the ink on the page. She stood and placed the book aside to look at some of the other papers on the desk.

The drawings and patient notes had all made sense to Declan, she was sure. But without having him here to discuss his findings, it was going to be hard to piece everything together. His mind had worked in a way vastly different to her own, though not all that different to Nea's. They both internalised so much and seemed to make unfathomable leaps based on very small bits of information. Almost like they had the cipher to the puzzle all along and grew impatient waiting for everyone else to catch up. No, not impatient. Excited.

Like they wanted everyone else to be as passionate about their discoveries as they were.

As Margot thought back over what Yolanda had written, she realised that the two books had mentioned all three of the mages in those sarcophagi under the capital. She sorted through the other items on the desk and found a third journal, also by Yolanda. It was buried under a pile of other books at the back and as Margot drew it out, the pile shifted and toppled off the desk. She balanced the book on the corner of the desk as she bent to pick up the others.

A loose page had fallen with them. She turned it over to reveal Declan's elegant handwriting. Three names were listed: *Johanna – mind mage, Richard – healer, Evette – necromancer*

The names surrounded a single word, written in capital letters and underlined: *DEATHBORN?*

She placed the page on the desk and stared blankly at the wall. Deathborn were a myth, weren't they? It would seem Declan didn't think so.

She wished she could talk to him about everything, ask him why he believed deathborn were so important—why he thought they might be more than a myth.

There was one other person who might be able to tell her about deathborn, however, and that meant a trip to Hartswood.

CHAPTER TWENTY

GARRET

They had decided to skirt around the town of Hillside, opting instead to keep mostly to the forest. Nea was surprisingly apt at navigating the forest trails and he often felt her using her keen-sense to follow paths that were invisible to the naked eye. *Breadcrumbs*, she had called them.

Now though they were making their way down the main road towards Dunhold. Bridie had insisted they stop for supplies and spend the night in a proper bed as there had been no signs of pursuit and the children needed a good rest. Garret would rather they stayed in the forest but when Bridie set her mind on something, she usually got her way.

"… beat the Shadow Man at his own game." Nea's voice drifted forward as she told Nora a story about the creation of the Between.

"So, he's still trapped there?"

"As far as anyone can tell. He certainly hasn't been seen in this realm since."

"Is he real? Mama says a lot of the old stories are just myths, they never really happened or that the truth has been lost over time, but Uncle Declan believed they were real stories about real people."

Garret's chest tightened at the mention of Declan and he cleared his throat.

"Well, what do you believe?" Nea asked.

"I want them to be real, but Mama is usually right about things." Garret could hear the frown in Nora's voice.

"A lot of people would argue that the old stories are mostly allegory commenting on morality and the hubris of man." Nea's tone was dry. "But I think they're wrong. I believe all stories start with a grain of truth. They serve as warnings but also as beacons of hope."

"What's hubris?"

Nea let out an indulgent chuckle, and the corner of Garret's mouth twitched in response before he turned his attention back to the road ahead.

His smile faded and he stopped walking. Something wasn't right. Was that smoke he could smell? He let his keen-sense wash forward and swallowed. The source felt twisted and scarred, much like it had in the aftermath of Kalhanna or in the throne room after Nea had executed Harold.

"Garret, what's wrong?" Nea stopped next to him, her own keen-sense drifting out in a cool wave. "Oh no." She pressed a hand to her mouth.

"What's that?" Nora's keen-sense was flickering along beside Nea's. "It feels so—"

"Go back to your mother, Nora." Garret tried to keep his tone level.

"But—"

"Now!" She flinched as he snapped.

"Come on." Nea placed her arm across the back of Nora's shoulders and guided her to where Bridie and the others had stopped.

Garret drew his sword and continued down the road. The closer to the town he got, the thicker the air seemed to get; once more bringing up the memory of Kalhanna. The ruined college had held an eerie stillness, the source twisted and scarred. And then the rows of bodies, all shrouded in whatever fabric could be found, laid out at the foot of the great stairs. Margot had broken down then, falling to her knees on the bloodstained ground. Declan had wondered who had prepared the college dead so carefully, but had left the king's guard to rot. Had it been Nea, as Margot had suggested at the time? It would have taken her hours, maybe days without help.

He glanced sideways at her as she caught up to him. Her hands were clenched white-knuckle tight and her mouth was a thin line.

"Are you alright? You can wait here if—"

"I'm fine."

Of course she was.

They crested a small hill and the town came into view. The road below them was littered with dark shapes, bodies slumped and sprawled where they had been struck down as they fled. But they weren't just townsfolk. Some locals had obviously put up a fight as several soldiers wearing the green and gold of the king lay among them. Nea's hand was pressed to her mouth. Her breathing had increased and he could hear the air heaving into her chest. He knew what she was reliving: broken bodies, bloodstained earth, the smell of death and fear ... *Kalhanna.*

"You can stay here if you prefer."

She jumped as he spoke. "I'm fine." Her breath hitched and she swallowed. "I'm alright, really." She started down the slope to where the bodies were the most condensed. She stopped next to the corpse of a young woman with flaxen hair and knelt, closing the woman's vacant eyes with a gentle touch. She smoothed the woman's hair back behind her ear then reached for the creamy-coloured handkerchief that was clutched in her hand. Lifting it, she folded it neatly and ran her thumb along the red embroidered flowers at its edges.

Garret suddenly felt he was intruding on something very

private—bearing witness to a side of Nea that she rarely let others see. He'd noticed it in her interactions with Nora, and the ease with which Nea let her guard down around the girl. In those moments, she resembled the Nea who Margot and Emil often told stories of, the one he found hard to equate with the person she was now.

He drew a breath and studied the scattered bodies. What had happened here?

Noticing one of the soldiers laying nearby, he approached the body and rolled him over. There seemed to be no marks on him but dried blood clung to the skin of his cheeks as though it had run from his ears and mouth. Garret stood and looked back at Nea.

Harold had bled from the ears when Nea had used her magic on him but Garret had also seen healers lash out with similar results. Margot had once explained that it was as simple as turning a person's internal organs against them.

Drawing a breath, he rubbed his finger along his lip and turned his attention back to the town. It looked as though Evard had attacked the town, but why? Perhaps they had been harbouring a fugitive, but would he have condoned the attack on the villagers? Yes, without a doubt. Evard would not care about the massacre; given his recent state of mind, he may even have ordered it. Garret's jaw tightened as he pressed his back teeth together. That was when he spotted a woman with ash-grey hair laying over by one of the buildings.

He strode over to examine her. There were no marks on her and her breathing was shallow but steady. Her short hair was standing in dishevelled spikes, littered with dirt and straw. He'd met her once before at Margot's clinic: Hazel.

He started to turn and call out to Nea when her magic spiked savagely, and she doubled over, gasping for air. He left Hazel and started towards Nea when he felt the magic—a twisted version of Margot's warm healing keen. It's owner, a short stocky man with a heavily scarred face, stepped out from behind one of the buildings, a gloating smile firmly on his features.

"I do prefer to play with my prey a bit first. But when the prey is just as dangerous as myself, well, I'm happy enough to take the easy road." He approached Nea, the knife in his hand glinting in the sunlight.

Garret rushed forward, drawing his sword.

"I will kill her. Oh, He won't be happy about that, but accidents do happen. And knowing how fragile the human body is, it is extremely easy to do. I don't even need this." He waved the knife as he clenched his other fist and Nea screamed.

Garret wasn't close enough to suppress him.

"Now." He crouched beside Nea, who glared at him. "This is a delightful surprise. You're not the one I was sent to retrieve but if I deliver you, Evard will forgive me I am sure. After all, what use is a lockpick when you have the key."

Garret edged forward a step. If he could just get close enough to suppress the mage ...

"Or perhaps we could join forces, you and I, and forget about Evard. Claim the power for ourselves." The mage took hold of Nea's arm. "You've had a taste of it haven't you? You can't tell me that you didn't just want to let it take control and unshackle every ounce of your *potential*." His voice was soft and he stroked the inside of Nea's wrist as he spoke.

Nea's arm shook as she pulled it out of his grasp. "I'll never give in," she rasped.

The man chuckled and took a step back as Nea grunted in pain. "You do realise you are an appalling liar."

Another step, just a little closer.

Throwing caution to the wind, Garret lunged forward, clamping down his suppression on the mage. The man snarled and drove the dagger towards Nea but Garret met his chest with a firm kick that sent him staggering backwards as his breath came out in a tight wheeze.

"You fight dirty for a warden." He coughed. "I like that." He sucked air heavily over his lips and squared his shoulders. "Let's see how long you can keep that suppression up when—"

The air grew ice cold and the man's eyes bulged.

"Two can play that game," Nea ground out through her teeth. There was a small trickle of blood beneath her nose and her eyes were glassy with unshed tears. "Tell me why I shouldn't just rip your pathetic soul from your body." She stepped past Garret, who lost his grip on his suppression in his shock.

"Oh, oh, oh. So this is what your rage feels like?" The mage gasped and dropped to his knees, but the smile stayed firmly on his face. "It's intoxicating, isn't it?" He gasped again as Nea tightened her grip.

"What does Evard think he can gain by killing innocents? He can't just cover this one up like he did Kalhanna." There was something about Nea's voice, a tone that was not her own but distinctly *otherworldly.*

The mage glanced at the carnage around him. "You don't like my handiwork? The guards didn't care for it much either, but *He* doesn't care about the method. He just cares about the result." His body started to shake. "Go on, give in to it. Death doesn't matter to me."

"Nea, stop," Garret said and she gave him a wild-eyed glance.

"He did this! Murdered them all in cold blood." Her voice broke and a tear rolled along her lower lashes.

Her grip on her magic wavered and he kept his voice level. "I know. And he'll pay for it, but not at your expense. Not like Harold," he whispered the last few words and slowly let his suppression dampen her magic. She didn't resist.

As Nea's magic released him, the mage staggered to his feet, still well within Garret's field of suppression. Nea scooped up the knife the mage had dropped and leapt forward. Her weight, though slight, was enough to knock the still disorientated man off his feet again. With her knees against his arms, she lifted the knife and brought it down hard. The man's legs jerked beneath her as she rolled off him. Covering her mouth, she staggered to her feet and raced away out of sight.

The body of the mage twitched; the knife was driven so deep into his right eye socket that none of the blade was visible. Garret cleared his throat and prodded the body with the toe of his boot. He rubbed the back of his neck and stared in the direction Nea had run. He knew he should follow her but he also wanted to allow her a moment of dignity.

A groan behind him made him turn. Hazel was getting gingerly to her feet; she pressed her hand to her forehead and squinted in his direction. "Warden Commander?" She stumbled over, her gaze dropping to the twitching body of the mage. "Nice work."

"I didn't do it."

Hazel looked around, confused. "Then who?"

"Nea." Her name was out before he could stop it.

"Nea? As in, the necromancer who has been missing since Kalhanna? About *this* tall, dark grey hair, weird violet eyes, Nea?"

He nodded and looked back at the dead mage.

"Any idea who that is? He was a healer, but I don't remember him," Hazel said.

Garret shook his head and glanced at the building Nea had disappeared behind.

"That's weird." Hazel's voice drew his attention again. She was crouched beside the dead mage, her fingers holding the hair away to reveal the smudge of a birthmark behind his ear. It was a deep shade of purple and the outline was an almost defined flower shape.

"It's just a birthmark." *Amelia has one just like it.* He spotted Nea coming back, her face paler than normal.

"I think I've seen a similar one—Nea?" Hazel stood as Nea got closer. "It really is you."

Nea stopped in her tracks. "Hazel."

"Nea?!" A white-haired flash came barrelling from the side and Garret's hand tensed on the hilt of his sword.

The flash turned out to be a boy of about fifteen. He grabbed Nea and crushed her in a hug that all but lifted her off her feet. "It is you, right?" He asked as he took a step back.

Like most boys his age, he was all arms and legs that he was only just starting to grow into. Most boys didn't have an unruly patch of snow-white hair though.

Nea smoothed her clothes down and gave the boy an exasperated smile. "Who else would it be?"

"Oh, I don't know. It's a wonder I remember what you look like since you just up and abandoned us all." He gave her a look that was all cheek, then added, "I don't remember your hair being *that* dark though."

She touched the end of her braid and a frown crossed her lips as the boy noticed Garret for the first time.

"Who's the serious-looking warden?"

Nea glanced over her shoulder and met Garret's eyes. "That's Garret. Garret, this is Bran."

Garret held his hand out and Bran shook it.

"A pleasure. I think I've heard Sonia mention you before. You're the commander of the capital garrison, aren't you?"

Garret rubbed the back of his neck. "I was."

"Nea, did you see this?" Hazel pointed to the birthmark, drawing Nea's attention to it.

Nea rolled her lip between her teeth and glanced to the right where Garret could feel the spirit. Bran could feel something too because he squinted at the patch of empty air before waving his hand through it.

"It's just a birthmark Hazel." She rubbed her hand over the back of her hip.

"Don't yo—"

"It's nothing!" Nea snapped and started stalking away towards the bodies. "We need to see to the dead."

Bran gave a soft whistle and jogged after her.

"A bit touchy these days then," Hazel muttered as she followed them.

Slowly, over the course of the day, Nea had calmed back to her usual self, or the version of it that Garret was used to. She refused to talk about the mage though, stating it wasn't as important as honouring the dead. Hazel had let the matter drop, however Garret did notice her and Nea having a whispered conversation that ended in Hazel stalking away with her hands in the air.

While they had made use of his grandmother's earth magic to dig the graves, it was still late afternoon before everything was ready for the rite to be performed.

Nea walked Bran through the process of the rite, her keen stirring as she held her hands out in the direction of the neat rows of bodies. Bran's swelled to join it. Garret knew Nea's keen was different, but feeling it alongside Bran's he realised just how different. Necromancy always felt cold, but Nea's wasn't just cold, it was deep and enigmatic, shifting as though it held a myriad of secrets.

As Nea and Bran finished the rite, Nea let her hands drop to her sides looking more tired than Garret had ever seen her. The tears that had been threatening all day glistened as they rolled silently down her cheeks. She dashed them away with a sniff and let Nora drag her to the edge of the campfire where she had gathered a little collection of rocks.

"She's different," Bran said as he joined Garret.

"So people keep saying."

"Yeah, you didn't know her before did you? She used to be a lot more fun, less ... sad." He frowned. "The old Nea is probably still in there somewhere."

Garret rubbed his scar and led Bran over to join the others at the fire. Bridie passed them both a cup of tea.

"Nora said you and Nea are taking her to Hartswood," Hazel said from her seat beside Nea.

"We were taking her as far as Fort Braemar. Perhaps you could take her for us," Garret said.

Hazel shook her head. "We're on our way to Loch Bastien."

"Why?" Nea asked.

"Nonna is chasing some books that the college has had on loan. I don't know why she couldn't just send a request for their return by bird. Though maybe she *knew* we'd run into you." Hazel sipped her tea.

"I thought she sent us because of that box of Warren's." Bran piped up.

"Why would she think that something of Warren's was at Loch Bastien or that Sophia didn't just have it burned with the rest of his things?" As Nea mentioned Sophia's name, the tone of her voice became strangely bitter.

"Maybe she doesn't know it was his. Nonna seems to think he hid it in the repository before going all ... you know." Hazel circled her finger around beside her ear. "Chances are, Sophia isn't even aware it is there."

"Who's Warren?" Garret asked.

"Sophia's father," Hazel replied. "She doesn't like people to know about him, given that he went crazy and became a hermit before he died."

"Warren's not dead; he's still living in that bolthole in the mountains north of Fengate." Nea traced the rim of her cup. "And he's not crazy. He's … different. But Sophia doesn't associate with different. It could ruin her carefully cultivated reputation."

There was that bitterness again.

"Do you know what's in the box?" Nea asked.

Hazel shrugged. "You know what Nonna's like. It's probably just some old jewellery box."

"And the books?" Nea glanced at the empty space where Garret could feel her spirit friend.

"Just a few old books written by Vanasha. Apparently they have been at Loch Bastien since the time of High Mage Phineas, and Nonna thinks it *high time* they were returned to Hartswood."

Nea shifted in her seat. "What if I went to retrieve the box and the books?"

Hazel stared at her for a few moments before collapsing into a fit of laughter. "Oh, I am sure Sophia would welcome you with open arms. She's likely to burn the books just to spite you."

Nea rolled her eyes and an expression settled on her features that reminded Garret of Margot. "I'm serious, Hazel. You and Bran take Garret's family to Hartswood, freeing Garret up to get back to Fort Braemar, and I'll go on to Loch Bastien."

"You're not going to Loch Bastien without me." Garret crossed his arms over his chest.

Hazel looked from Nea to Garret and then back again. "If you want to go on a scavenger hunt to Loch Bastien in our place, I'm not going to stop you."

Garret studied Nea. There was more to this then she was letting on, but he didn't think she was willing to discuss it in front of the others. Even if they were alone, she might not open up.

He rubbed the back of his neck and looked at the fire. "It probably wouldn't hurt to go to Loch Bastien and see if Aveline kept any of Declan's old notes on corruption. Margot may find them helpful.

That is, of course, if you don't mind escorting my niece to Hartswood in our stead, Hazel."

"We can certainly do that," Bran said. "That is if Hazel is alright with it."

"If it means I get to avoid Sophia then I have no problem with it at all," Hazel said before finishing her tea.

Later, when everyone else had turned in for the night, Nea sat by the fire studying the flames as she folded and unfolded the handkerchief she had taken from the young woman's body. Garret sat across from her. Every so often he'd cast a glance her way as he moved the short blade of his carving knife over a piece of wood that had been intended for the fire.

Nea's fingers brushed her wrist. It was still free of the corruption marks; he had asked her about it when no one else was in earshot. But something was bothering her.

"Are you alright?" He knew what the answer would be but he asked anyway.

"I'm ..." She let out a sound that could have been a laugh. "Not really. Today was hard."

Garret examined the fox that was taking shape between his fingers.

"There was girl at Kalhanna. Millicent. She was so bright and happy, and my friend Tobias had always been a little sweet on her. If he wasn't in the library or his laboratory, then you could guarantee he would be down in the kitchens with Milly." She sniffed and her fingers tightened on the handkerchief. "She kept her hair under a kerchief that looked a lot like this. Cream with red flowers. I asked her about it one time and she said her sister made her a new one every year for her birthday." She fell silent and stared at the flames.

"You don't have to talk about it if you don't want to."

She gave him a sad smile. "Their stories should be told." Looking at the handkerchief again, she smoothed it out on her knee before refolding it. "Milly's birthday was the day after the purge but she didn't survive to open the package from her sister. I opened it for her after the attack and made sure she was wearing it before I wrapped the body. Her old one was ruined." Nea's voice grew thick and she swallowed. "I'd told her to stay in the kitchens, but she wanted to help with the children. *Willem.*" Her fists clenched and tears glittered along her lashes, reflecting the flames of the fire as she glanced to the spot the spirit was hovering.

"He slit her throat." The source quivered as her keen spiked for a moment. Garret had felt the source respond to her emotions before, as though her connection was much deeper than that of any other mage.

"Milly was keen-less. She wasn't a threat; she just didn't want him to hurt the children and he cut her down in front of them. I couldn't stop him. I tried but ..." A small shudder rolled over her. "He's dead now. That's all that matters."

"I'm sorry." The words sounded hollow but Garret didn't know what else to say.

Her attention shifted to him as though she had forgotten he was there. "It's alright. I should probably try and get some sleep." She stood and brushed her hands on her thighs. "Good night, Garret."

"Good night." He watched her head to the small barn where Bridie and the others were sleeping, then turned his attention back to the flames. The spirit didn't follow her. He could still feel its strange, flickering snag beside where she had been sitting.

"Today was hard." He echoed what Nea had said earlier and studied his carving. Gently, he ran the blade of the knife over the wood, coaxing out the details and letting his mind wander. They were supposed to be heading to Fort Braemar; instead they were now going the opposite direction.

Before Declan's death, Garret wouldn't have allowed himself to become side-tracked in such a way. He knew the path and he stuck to it. 'She's different,' Bran had said about Nea. Garret was different now too, and he wasn't sure he wanted to return to the way he'd been before.

CHAPTER TWENTY-ONE

MARGOT

Margot removed a pair of pants and a shawl from her open bag and replaced them with a tidy bundle of Declan's corruption notes. She then turned her attention to Molly, who was watching her pack from her perch on the bed.

"So just to clarify, we're going to Hartswood because Amelia told you to? Amelia, the psychotic dead girl who likes to play mind games and corrupt people." She smoothed out the sheets beneath her.

Margot let out a huff. "Amelia didn't tell me to go to Hartswood. I decided it was the best course of action, given the bent of Declan's research." She watched a bird flutter past the window and tapped her chin. "Honestly, I should have thought of it sooner. Nea isn't the only necromancer who could shed some light on corruption."

"If they are all like Nea, then you'd probably have more luck getting answers from a stone."

Margot fought the urge to roll her eyes. "Nea would have been more than happy to help Declan with his research if she'd ..." She bit down on the words.

Molly didn't respond but the smug grin on her face was enough.

"It doesn't matter. I am sure Nonna will be happy to answer a few questions, or at least point me in the right direction." She hoped so anyway. Nonna could be infuriatingly cryptic at times. *You'll never learn if I just tell you all the answers,* seemed to be one of her favourite sayings.

"Are you about finished packing? Sonia will likely leave without us at this rate." Molly ducked as Margot threw the shirt she had been debating putting in the bag at her.

"I'm trying to make room for Declan's research. I haven't even started to scratch the surface. Given his chaotic method of *documentation* it could be quite some time before I make any headway." She sat on the edge of the bed. "I need to think like him, but I've never been good at that kind of abstract intellectualism."

Molly moved and slid her arms around Margot's shoulders from behind, her wrists crossing over her chest as she pressed a kiss to the soft skin just below her ear. "You are just as smart as Declan was. I know you'll figure it out." Her breath tickled the back of Margot's neck.

"I just—" Her words were cut short as Molly bit down lightly on her earlobe. She pulled away but Molly's arms stayed locked around her chest, keeping her from escaping too far. "I know what you are doing, Mol, and it won't work."

"Oh, really? Well I think it's already working. In fact—OOF!" Molly let out a laugh as Margot pressed her body back, knocking them both into a tangle on the bed.

A short while later, they were crossing the courtyard of the fort with Sonia in tow when a tall white horse came trotting through the gate. His master pulled him up short and slid down. He pushed his windswept sandy hair back and gave Margot a warm smile.

"Leith? What in the Mother's name are you doing here?"

"That is a long story. Is Garret about?" He stepped out of the way as a small group of knights rode into the yard and stood off to the side, as though awaiting orders.

Margot eyed the knights, noting that they didn't wear the green and gold of Evard's guard, nor any other distinguishing heraldry for that matter. "No, Garret isn't here. I haven't seen him since we parted ways in the capital."

Leith frowned. "Did he say where he was heading?"

Margot glanced at Molly and Sonia, who both shrugged, then she shook her head. "He didn't. Though he did expect to be back here as soon as he was able, which could be any day now."

"That is not ideal but if he's on his way here then—" He glanced up as a girl came running from the stables with a message bird tucked tightly under her arm.

"Thank the bright I caught you before you left." She handed a roll of parchment to Margot.

"Thank you."

The girl bobbed into a half-curtsey and then rushed away again as Margot unrolled the message to reveal Garret's precise handwriting. She quickly skimmed the contents, a knot tightening in her stomach the farther down the parchment she read. "Speak of the Shadow. It's news from Garret; there's been an attack on Dunhold."

"Dunhold? What was he doing there?" Molly asked.

"He didn't say. But ..." She looked back at Leith, who shifted uncomfortably.

"My father was responsible for the attack, wasn't he?" There was a defeated note to his voice. "Any survivors?"

"Garret didn't mention any. You knew your father was going to attack Dunhold? Why would he?"

Leith shook his head. "I didn't, but Dunhold is not the first town he's had his men assault. I had thought it was just Fengate." He rubbed a hand over his face.

"Is that why you're here? Is it on his orders?" She shifted her weight onto her heel as she studied him.

"What? No. Margot, I know I've done some idiotic … some unforgivable things under my father's *guidance*"—he all but spat the word out—"but I can't sit back and deceive myself any longer. He's made it clear that I am as expendable as any of his other subjects."

Margot drew a deep breath as she studied him, then she nodded. "We should speak with Alric."

Thomas came out of the stable and Leith handed him the reins of his horse before turning back to Margot. "Yes, let's go see Alric."

"Would you like me to saddle the horses while you see to that?" Sonia asked.

"No, I think you should get Harvey and the others and meet us in the dining hall." Margot looked back at the letter, then at the men who had come with Leith before hurrying inside.

A room of stunned faces stared at her as she relayed the news about Dunhold. Garret hadn't spared many details about what they'd discovered at the village. The sharp strokes of his handwriting stood out strongly, as though his anger had travelled right through the nib of his pen. The thing that unsettled Margot most was the fact that Garret believed the healer they'd encountered was responsible for the bulk of the killing.

"A whole town." Alric leant heavily on the table. "What is Evard thinking?"

"He's not. I'm not even sure it's still my father inside that twisted head of his." Leith drummed his fingers on the mantle as he stared into the flames of the hearth.

"You haven't exactly told me why you're here and not licking your father's boots like a good little prince." Alric crossed his arms over his chest and levelled a calculating gaze at Leith.

"Alric!" Lady Vera stood from her seat at the end of the table. "Please accept my apologies for my husband's rudeness. This news has been most distressing."

"It's alright, my lady." Leith scratched the edge of his eyebrow and then settled his steel-grey gaze on Alric. "In all fairness, that was probably politer than I deserve."

They all looked at him, waiting, and he cleared his throat.

"I should have done something before now, but I didn't realise how far his madness had gone. Dunhold is not the first town to feel his wrath. He also ordered Fengate to be searched and any mage or warden found living outside the colleges to be rounded up. Those who objected were to be *repurposed*." He ran a hand through his hair. "I should have listened to Nea before ... well, I should have known after what happened at ..." He let out a despondent huff.

"Kalhanna," Emil offered.

"Yes, thank you, Emil."

The annoyance in Leith's tone didn't seem to bother Emil, as he added, "You're not the only one who didn't listen to her, you know?"

"No, I wasn't, but she deserved better."

"What-ifs and should-haves won't help us now," Molly said.

"Molly is right." Alric settled in an empty chair. "You are, of course, welcome to stay here. Though, if your father learns of your whereabouts, I imagine that will put this household and all in it in some degree of danger."

"Then we need a plan," Emil said. "We need to think like Garret. If he were here, his first focus would be strengthening our defences in case of any future attacks on the fort."

Haley jumped from her perch next to Janey. "Then he'd start trying to round up possible allies. We should try and get in touch with the wardens we know are against the order joining Evard. If the bastard is openly attacking mages without just cause, then the time for hand-sitting is through."

Janey made a few quick signs, and, for the benefit of those who couldn't understand her sign language, Harvey said, "We should get in touch with the mages too. And surely there are men who are more loyal to you than your father who we can call on," he added in Leith's direction.

Leith nodded. "I have already contacted those I know I can trust." His gaze fell on Margot. "You were leaving earlier?"

"I was. I need to pay Hartswood a visit. However, I can delay the journey if you need me."

"I'd like a word in private before you go—that is all."

Margot nursed a cup of spiced apple tea while she waited for Leith to join her in the library. She had one of Declan's journals balanced on her lap and was trying to make sense of his notes. "I wish you were here now," she whispered as she brushed her fingers over his elegant handwriting and swallowed the lump in her throat.

"I'm not interrupting, I hope." Leith came into the room and took up the chair opposite her. He looked drained, like the weight of the whole world had suddenly landed on his shoulders and he didn't know exactly how to bear it.

She closed the journal and placed it aside. "You're not interrupting. You wanted to see me?"

"I did." He rubbed a hand over his face and then looked at the floor. "How are you really? After what my father did ..." He glanced at her hair. "I'm sorry. If I had been there. If I had known ..."

"I'm alright." Margot took a sip of her tea and watched him over the rim of her cup. "It's not entirely my welfare you're concerned about though, is it?"

He let out a small laugh. "I'm as transparent as always then?"

The corner of her mouth quirked into a brief smile. "She's tough; she always has been."

"True, but is she *alright*? She looked ... defeated. I don't think I've ever seen her that way ..." He stood and walked to the window.

"She says she's fine."

"And you believe her?" He half-turned to look at her.

"Of course I don't. She's not fine. She's barely coping, but what can you do? She's as stubborn as Nonna and has an almost unhealthy tendency to put the welfare of others before herself. Kalhanna didn't change any of those qualities; it just seems to have amplified them."

"Were you there?"

"No. I'd been called away to Loch Bastien to fill in for their head healer. Nea had disappeared by the time I got back."

Leith stared silently out the window.

"You know none of us are to blame for what happened."

His shoulders shifted as he rubbed a hand over his face and let out a long breath, his back still to her. "I thought Francesca was manipulating her, turning her against my father. I should have known better. Nea's never been one to let people tell her what to think." He turned and leant against the windowsill. "I should have believed her when she said my father's fascination with the Between was getting dangerous. That he was messing around with things he had no business to."

"What do you mean? What was Evard *messing around* with?" She rested her elbows on her knees and cradled her cup between her palms, warming them.

He crossed his arms. "I'm not entirely certain, but Nea seemed to think he was trying to manipulate the source." He shook his head. "Of course, I thought she was being paranoid. My father doesn't have a magical bone in his body—there's no way he could manipulate the source."

"Nea has never been one for paranoia or delusions." A chill pooled in her stomach. "Do you remember what she said your father was trying to do?" She swallowed past the lump rising in her throat. Leith's revelation about his father toying with the source was ringing a distant bell in the back of her mind. A story Nonna had told long ago, but the details had disappeared with time and only the feeling of unease was left.

"No. I was so angry at her. No, not at *her*—at the whole situation. I had her in one ear and Father in the other. He kept reminding me she was just a dalliance—that I had to grow up and accept my duties as his heir. It was easier to push her away than it was to go against him." He sighed. "No matter. All that is in the past. The important thing now is that my father's madness doesn't continue."

Margot swirled the remaining liquid in her cup, then swallowed it. As soon as Nea and Garret got back, she was sitting Nea down and not letting her leave her sight again until they'd had a long talk.

Margot had questions, and Nea was going to answer them.

CHAPTER TWENTY-TWO

NEA

The closer they got to Loch Bastien, the tighter the knot in Nea's stomach became. As they crested a hill and looked down on the massive body of water of the lake, she stopped. Her feet felt rooted to the ground as she watched the gusty breeze rippling the surface of the water so it reflected the sunlight in greenish-silver flickers. It was a beautiful sight: the choppy surface of the lake studded with the dark shapes of water birds feeding and splashing in the shallows. Then, farther out, the impressive grey stone tower that sat on the island in the middle of the lake. Nea licked her lips as she stared at the imposing structure.

"Something got you spooked?" Declan appeared beside her and looked down at the lake with a wistful expression.

Nea shook her head. "I'm—"

"Fine? Yes. Of course you are." He chuckled at the expression on her face.

Ahead of them, Garret paused mid-stride and turned, giving Nea a curious look.

With a resigned huff, she caught up to him. "Just taking in the view."

He gave her a look that had become familiar. She knew it meant: *I don't believe you but I'm not going to question you.* Margot had a similar one.

"We can stop for a quick rest at the pier," he said, indicating the little collection of buildings at the edge of the lake. The closest was the boat master's shack, sitting on the middle of a large pier to which a range of boats were tethered.

"I'm fine. We're so close to the college now that it seems silly to stop."

He nodded. "It's not just fatigue, is it? There's something at Loch Bastien that you don't want to face."

"I'm sorry?"

"Just a few observations. The look on your face every time someone says *Loch Bastien* ... Yes, that look. The way you've been dragging your feet since we broke camp this morning." He crossed his arms.

Nea rubbed her forehead and cast a glance at the tower.

"Nea, if there is something I should know before we reach the college ..."

"It's nothing really ..." She chewed her lip. "I'm just ... being childish." The last two words were muttered.

Garret toyed with the scar above his lip as he studied her.

"It's nothing." She gave him the best smile she could muster.

"That look is borderline maniacal. You might want to tone it down a little if you want to convince him."

She glared at Declan, and when Garret's attention flicked to the spot he was standing, she cleared her throat. "It's the High Mage. She's—" She bit down hard on her lip and winced. "She and I have a history, and we don't exactly see eye to eye. But it's nothing worse than a personal dislike of each other."

Garret looked like he wanted to say more but shook his head and started down the slope.

Nea fell into step beside him then halfway down, stopped again. She shielded her eyes as she squinted. On the rocks around the base of the tower there appeared to be a colony of dark grey seals lounging and basking in the sun while others rolled and frolicked in the water. "Are those dark shapes seals?"

"Yes, there are several colonies of them around the lake." Garret looked out at the seals. "They were Declan's favourites. He named half of them when we were younger."

"Eleven. I named eleven before I ran out of scholars to name them after. It all started with this particularly fat one with long whiskers that reminded me of a portrait of Bromly. You know that distinct moustache his portraits always sport." Declan wiggled his fingers above his top lip, mimicking the infamous moustache.

Nea couldn't help but smile, then suddenly, she was laughing.

Garret was staring at her like she had lost her mind, but a smile slowly formed on his lips.

"I'm sorry. I was just picturing a whole bunch of seals named after history's greatest scholars." Her laughter died down to a weak chuckle.

"How did you know you he named them after scholars?"

"I, ah ... just assumed, given what I've learned of him from everyone."

"Smooth save. I doubt he bought it though," Declan said.

Garret studied her. "Back in the capital, you told Emil you thought you'd have liked Declan; I think he'd have liked you too." He ran his hand through his hair. "You know, you remind me of him in a lot of ways."

"I do?"

He made a noise that could have been a laugh. "You have a similar way of approaching problems. Declan could be infuriating at times; he was impulsive and reckless but ridiculously smart, and he loved having a good mystery to solve."

Nea looked at her feet.

"He was also fiercely loyal and ..." He frowned and pulled the diary out of his pocket. "To think he died for this."

"Can I see that?" She held her hand out.

He passed her the diary and she opened it, absently walking down the slope as she flipped through it.

"I thought as much when you first showed me. This is the last journal Samson was working on before he died." She paused and read an entry. "Here you can see these first entries are mostly sane, albeit a little eccentric, but then ... well, you can clearly track the progression of his *affliction*." She snapped the journal shut as she got to the blank pages at the end and handed it back to him.

"The progression of his affliction? Was Samson corrupted?"

She glanced at the tower again, though she could feel both Garret and Declan's eyes on her, waiting for the answer. "Yes."

"But he was a necromancer, and you said it's rare—"

"I know. There have been two *reported* cases of necromancers getting corruption. Two, in the entire recorded history of the disease."

"If Samson was one, who was the other?" Garret asked.

"His wife, Evette."

"Samson and his wife both had corruption?"

She nodded. "Evette had it first, then Samson got himself infected in order to understand corruption better in the hope of curing it. Unfortunately—"

"Wait. Margot said that corruption isn't a contagious disease. How could Samson get infected?"

Nea rubbed her arm and bit the inside of her cheek.

"Of course! It was never stated where he got the corruption from, but Johanna was so much like Amelia, it had to be her, right? But why and how? It had to be Johanna. Or Richard?" Declan clapped his hands together.

Nea lifted a finger to quiet him without taking her eyes off Garret. "That detail is uncertain. But should we really be standing in the middle of the road discussing this right now?" She tilted her head towards the pier where a short, weathered man with a patch of wispy grey hair had emerged.

He started towards them and lifted his hand in greeting as he called out, "That you, Garret?"

Garret's attention snapped to the man, and he crossed the distance to him in several long strides. "Vincent, it's good to see you." He shook the man's hand and waved Nea over.

When she reached them, Vincent gave her a once-over and held out his hand.

Nea glanced at Garret, unsure if she should introduce herself. They hadn't exactly discussed whether she should be using a fake name to go with the fake hair.

"It's alright. Vincent is an old friend."

"Come on, lassie, I don't bite." Vincent grinned.

"I prefer Nea." She shook his hand.

He let out a bark of laughter. "Nea it is then. Come on. I imagine Bess will want to feed you before we cross the lake." He gave Garret a look. "It's cockles and onion."

Garret shook his head with a grin. "It's always cockles and onion."

Nea gave him a curious glance before they walked the rest of the way to the pier.

As they stepped onto the decking, a small neat woman with her white hair secured back in a bun came out of the shack, wiping her hands on her apron. She gave Garret an appraising look and scowled. "I've seen the cat throw up prettier things than you. When was the last time you had decent meal? Don't bother making excuses; the barrel is over there. Wash off that road dirt and sit yourself down."

Nea bit back a smile. Whoever this woman was, she reminded her of Gerda.

"And who is this then? She looks worse than you." The woman's attention landed on Nea.

Vincent laughed. "This here is Nea. Nea, this darling ray of sunshine is my wife, Bess."

"Nea? Well that's a pretty name." Bess blinked and then realisation dawned on her features. "You're Abigail's granddaughter."

"Ah, yes."

"Well then, I didn't recognise you with all that dark hair. Mind you, last time I saw you, you barely reached your grandmother's hip and were missing both your front teeth."

Nea blinked. "We've met?"

"I was visiting my sister in Little Brook, and Abigail had you and that tall blonde girl who was all arms and legs with her."

"Margot."

"That's her name. The pair of you were practically joined at the hip. Prime mischief makers, if I remember correctly." She smiled warmly and Nea blushed. "Well, go on and get cleaned up. I've got soup and bread, and you're not setting foot onto the boat until you've eaten."

Nea joined Garret at the barrel of water. She rolled her sleeves back and washed her hands and wrists before splashing some onto her face. As Garret passed her a towel, his gaze flicked to her wrist, scanning it for any signs of the corruption.

"Well, come on and eat." Bess had returned with two bowls of fragrant soup. She placed them on the small table outside the shack and then settled cutlery and a large bread roll next to each.

"The sister she referred to has to be Gerda. I can't walk past The Leaping Cow without being accosted by a bowl of soup." Nea picked up her roll and broke it in two. The fluffy inside was still slightly warm at its centre.

"It's definitely easier to just accept it." Garret dipped his spoon into his soup.

"Well now, this is cosy."

Nea flinched and nearly dropped her roll as Declan appeared.

Garret watched her over his spoon, his eyes flicking to the spot Declan was standing.

"Is that cockles and onion?" Declan asked.

Nea carefully focused her attention on her own soup. She was surprised Garret hadn't asked more questions about Declan—not that he knew it was Declan she could see.

"How's the soup?" Bess had returned.

"Ah, lovely, thank you," Nea replied.

"Of course, I doubt they feed you properly at those colleges. I'm just glad Declan's not with you today. There's not enough soup in the world to fill that boy up."

Nea had been about to dip another piece of bread into her bowl but paused and watched Garret, who had taken a deep breath and placed his spoon aside.

He ran his hand through his hair and looked up at Vincent, who had come over from preparing the boat. "Declan's dead."

Nea caught the look of regret that crossed Declan's face as he heard Garret's flat tone. Bess's hand went to her chest and a soft gasp escaped her. Vincent just stared at Garret as though he couldn't believe what he had heard.

"I had thought the college would have let you know," Garret said softly.

"As if Sophia would deign to pass on a message to a non-mage," Bess scoffed.

Heat rolled across the back of Nea's neck at the mention of Sophia. She shifted in her seat and forced herself to pick up her spoon again.

When they were done, Vincent ushered them to the boat where a thickset teenager was unfurling the sail. He blushed and fumbled the rope when Nea said hello.

"If you're done gawking, Fergus, I suggest you give us a little assistance," Vincent said as he took up position at the tiller.

The boy jumped, causing the boat to rock gently, and a ticklish coil of magic stirred the hair on the back of Nea's neck as a slight breeze filled the sail.

With Fergus's help, it didn't take them long to cross the lake. About halfway across, Nea felt the pull of the college wards. She rolled her shoulders to dispel the shiver that ran through her.

Vincent guided the boat alongside a small jetty and Garret jumped out offering his hand to Nea to help her. He shifted his weight, half-lifting her onto the jetty beside him; the boat wobbled and started to drift. Nea gripped his hand tighter and pushed herself across the widening gap. Her momentum caused her to bump against his chest and he took a step back, lightly touching her side to steady her. He released his grip on her and turned to give Vincent and Fergus a wave as they pushed the boat away from the jetty to head home.

They turned to walk up the small slope to the tower and a mage in a grey tunic emerged through the massive gate. She was tall and thin, with silver-shot black hair and as she neared, Nea realised she was older than she looked at first glance.

The woman smiled warmly when she saw Garret, but the smile was replaced with wariness when her attention shifted to Nea. She tilted her chin, and Nea felt the wild prickle of the other woman's keen rush down her spine. It wasn't an unpleasant sensation, but it left a throbbing in her knees that made her shift her feet. The woman's thin brows lifted in an expression that reminded Nea of Declan as her vivid green eyes took in the artificial colour of Nea's hair.

Only once she was finished her inspection of Nea did she speak. "It's good to see you, Garret. But who is this rather curious mage you have brought with you?"

"Nea of Hartswood," Garret answered.

The mage nodded, though her expression was unreadable. "Welcome to Loch Bastien, Nea. I am Aveline, second to High Mage Sophia."

Nea tried to keep her face neutral at the mention of the High Mage.

"This way." Aveline started to lead them up the steps.

"Aveline, wait."

She paused as Garret spoke.

"I'm sorry about Declan."

A tremor ran through the other woman's slender form before she turned back to face them, a sheen in her green eyes that hadn't been there before.

"Thank you." Aveline's lips formed a tight line. "How are you coping?"

Garret looked at Nea and let out a sigh. "Better than I thought. Though I haven't had much time to sit and dwell."

"Maybe that's for the best." She started up the steps again.

Nea stopped, her throat going dry as the others drifted away from her.

On the landing at the top of the stairs, another woman was waiting. Her strawberry blonde hair, secured in a severe braided style, caught the afternoon light with hues of pinkish copper. Her blue eyes were bright despite the icy regard they were giving Nea.

Sophia cleared her throat. "Don't dawdle, Nea."

With a sigh, Nea put one foot in front of the other until she reached the landing beside Garret and Aveline. "Sophia," she said by way of greeting.

"You could have at least tidied yourself up." Sophia brushed an invisible piece of lint from the front of her tunic. "Is it really too much trouble to put on a clean shirt and brush your hair? Speaking of which, the black is an interesting choice."

"The dead don't care how I look."

Sophia's eyes narrowed. "Well, I do. You are at my college and you will compose yourself with decorum."

"Sophia." Aveline's tone was soft and her eyes flicked towards Garret.

Sophia's nostrils flared slightly as she drew a breath. "Why are you still standing there, warden? Your kind belong in the barracks, out of sight until needed. Surely you are not so dense that you have forgotten where that is."

Garret was obviously biting the inside of his cheek and Nea touched his arm. He didn't take his eyes off Sophia but his posture softened a fraction.

"Perhaps you *have* forgotten then. Aveline, please show the warden to the barracks."

"Of course. Come on, Garret."

She started to walk away but Garret remained rooted to the spot, watching Nea.

"I'm fine. I'll find you later." She levelled her eyes back to Sophia.

"You, follow me. I'll have a maid show you to a guest room and find you something more appropriate to wear." Sophia turned on her heel and marched away.

Nea glanced back at the lake. It was a long swim to the other shore. Sophia let out an impatient huff when she reached the end of the hallway. With a small smirk, Nea shifted the weight of her satchel and started after the other woman. "Coming."

Sophia snapped her fingers at the first maid they passed. The girl dropped into a curtsey almost worthy of royalty and smoothed the front of her immaculate uniform.

After Sophia had barked a series of orders, the maid jumped to do her bidding and led Nea to the guest rooms. She stood in the doorway while Nea moved to the desk under the window and placed her bag down.

"I'll fetch that change of clothes for you now unless there is anything else you require?"

Nea looked down at her dusty clothes and suddenly could feel every ache and pain from the last few weeks catch up to her. "A hot bath would be wonderful."

"Of course. If you just follow me, I will take you to the bathing chambers." She smiled and turned on her heel, leading Nea out of the room.

They moved down a winding staircase and came out in a long corridor. The air was warm and moist, and Nea pulled at the collar of her shirt.

"This area of the tower sits over a network of natural hot springs. You will find a collection of private bathrooms, a sauna along that wall that opens out onto a path that will lead you straight to the beach, and there is the main hot spring there at the end of the hall." She pointed to each in turn.

Nea could hear splashing and giggling coming from the room at the end of the hall and the murmurs of conversation from the sauna. She looked at the maid, who was waiting expectantly. "Ah, I would prefer a private bath."

The maid nodded. "This way." She ushered Nea into a bathing chamber and closed the door before moving to the valve on the wall near the large sunken bath. She turned the wheel and a small sluice opened, allowing steaming water to run into the tub. Once it was full, Nea stripped and handed her clothes to the maid, who nodded again and slipped from the room.

Nea examined the collection of strange potions and soaps and selected one that smelled like a combination of rose and lilac. She poured a measure carefully into the water and then swished it around with her hand forming a small swell of bubbles. She placed the bottle back on the shelf before stepping into the tub.

A sigh escaped her as the water washed over her, the warmth chasing away aches, along with the dust and grime from the road. She dipped her head under and ran her fingers through her hair, letting the mass of it twist and twirl weightlessly before she resurfaced. Resting her head back against the lip of the tub she closed her eyes, she couldn't remember the last time she'd had a proper bath.

Too soon the maid returned with a pile of clean clothes and held out a towel, prompting Nea to climb out of the water. "I can help you with your hair if you like."

"It's fine. I'd like to leave it loose for a while to dry," she said as she ruffled her hair with the towel.

"The High Mage prefers all members of the college to maintain an immaculate level of personal presentation." The maid said it as though reciting a line from memory.

"Good thing I'm just a temporary guest then." Nea pulled her clothes on and then ran a wide-tooth comb through her hair to work out the snarls. "All done."

The maid eyed the wavy curls that were tumbling down to the small of Nea's back, the ends leaving a slightly damp patch at the bottom of her borrowed grey tunic, but said nothing as she led her to the dining hall.

Several long tables with matching benches filled the space. Nea walked over to the table where Sophia and Aveline were sitting.

Aveline gave her a smile but Sophia's blue gaze levelled on her loose hair with distaste. "As you are well aware, I expect a certain level of *refinement—*"

"I had a bath and am wearing clean clothes as requested," Nea cut her off and Sophia's eyes narrowed.

"Immaturity is not a good look on you, Nea."

"I'll take that under advisement," she said as Garret joined them.

"You seem to have forgotten your place, warden. Your kind sit over there." Sophia indicated a table at the far side of the room.

Declan appeared at Nea's side. "Sophia has always been a bitch, but becoming High Mage permanently wedged that stick up her arse."

Nea couldn't contain her laugh. Sophia and Aveline looked at her but Garret's eyes flicked to Declan.

"I, ah, need to excuse myself." She ran a hand through her hair and walked as quickly as possible across the room and out the door.

She ducked into a secluded alcove. Declan followed her and leant back against the wall, his eyes doing a slow sweep down the length of her.

"Interesting. I've never seen anyone ruffle Sophia's feathers by simply existing before. I came close, of course, especially after that incident in the library, but the pair of you must have quite a history."

Nea bit the inside of her cheek as she regarded him. "She's my mother."

For once, Declan was speechless. After a long pause, he blinked and said, "Wow. I actually do not know how to respond to that information ... Really?"

"In the most basic sense of the word. She may have given birth to me but that's where the maternal instincts stopped."

A shadow crossed Declan's features. "Speaking of mothers, have you talked to Aveline about me?"

Nea shook her head. "Garret did briefly."

"How did she seem?"

"She puts on a brave face, but she lost a child, Declan. That breaks something inside that can never really be mended."

Declan looked down at his hands. "After she lost my father, I promised myself I wouldn't leave her alone and then I went and got myself killed." He ran a hand through his hair. "And for what? Some stupid journal that I couldn't crack before Harold turned up."

"It's not your fault."

He frowned. "I should have waited, taken backup. I knew Harold was sniffing around. I should have been more careful." He raked his fingers through his hair again. "He spiked my meal with mage bane that night and I couldn't use my magic to fight back. I should have been smarter, faster—"

"Declan, stop beating yourself up about it. Yes, you could have done things differently, but the end result might have been worse."

"It was all for nothing! I left them alone because I had to chase after another thread trying to solve a puzzle that has no answers. Then you reappeared and you're ..." He had started pacing the small alcove. "And If I had just waited, took more time at Fort Braemar ... you would have come along with all those answers."

"But I don't have all the answers."

A pair of young mages passed the alcove and gave Nea an odd look.

"You look at corruption the same way Samson did. You ask different questions, form different insights. You knew the journal was worthless the second you laid eyes on it."

Nea let out a breath. "Of course I did because I've read it before. Nonna made me read it when I was younger. But, Declan, you couldn't have known it was worthless ... and it's not. It might not hold the answers that would lead to a cure but it does provide insight into aspects of corruption that only the afflicted are privy to."

He reached for her arm then lowered his hand with a frown. "What did it feel like?"

She pulled her arm to her chest and rubbed it. "Unnatural, like ants crawling beneath my skin and something stirring at the back of my mind—thoughts that niggled and nudged but stayed just out of reach. The harder I fought, the worse it got, and then there were the promises of incredible power if I just gave in, if I let it take over."

"Did you feel the urge for violence? Most afflicted—"

"No. It wanted me to go into the Between, to bring the walls down from the inside. And I can still feel it. It's distant but it's still there, a stain on my soul, waiting for the right moment to resurface, for me to pull enough power to give it an opening."

"But the marks are gone? Aren't they?" Declan made a grab for her arm, but his fingers passed right through it, leaving a chill on her skin. "The possibility of being corrupted without the physical symptoms changes things. You said it was like a stain on your soul."

She opened her mouth to speak but he just kept going.

"So is it a soul disease? I was only considering the physical and mental symptoms but if it goes much deeper than that ... If it's an affliction of the soul then there'd be no simple cure ... only death. But then there's no way to know if even that would work. And, well, you'd be dead. The whole thing is pointless—"

"Declan! Would you just shut up and listen to me?" She huffed and rubbed her temples.

"Nea." They both turned to Garret, who was at the opening to the alcove, his gaze flicking from Nea to the spot Declan was standing. His mouth was pulled into a tight line. "I need some answers. Some *real* answers."

"How long have you been standing there?" She twisted the hem of her shirt in her fingers.

"Long enough."

The silence stretched between them as Garret crossed his arms, waiting for her to speak. But her words were stuck in her throat and she bit the inside of her cheek.

"It's Declan," he finally said.

At the same time, she said, "I should have told you."

She looked at her feet. "I didn't think you'd believe me and, well ... then I didn't know how to tell you."

"This might not be the best place for this conversation." Declan nodded to a passing group of mages who had slowed their pace.

"Right. Is there someplace else we can go to discuss this, away from prying ears?"

Garret glanced at the mages and they hurried away. "I could ask Aveline for the key to Declan's room." His jaw was tighter than she'd seen it in a while. "I wanted to check it for anything that might help Margot with the cure."

"It's as good a place as any."

He led her back towards the dining hall and as they reached the door, a group of mages and wardens came out, laughing and talking amongst themselves. Most nodded in greeting to Garret and gave Nea a curious glance.

One warden, a brunette with soft blue eyes, paused. "Garret, we didn't expect to see you back here." Her smile shifted into a frown. "I heard about Declan ... I'm sorry."

Garret opened his mouth to respond but Sophia and Aveline came through the door and stopped when they saw them.

"Come on, Grace, we better go." Another warden eyed Sophia and she grabbed Grace's arm, dragging her away.

"There you both are." Aveline addressed Nea and Garret with a smile. "I'm sorry to say, Nea, you've missed dinner, but you might be able to find something in the kitchens if you're hungry."

Sophia was looking down her nose at Nea, an unreadable expression on her face. "I expect you to compose yourself with decorum while you are at my college. We are not at Del Harol. You cannot hide behind your father here." She then pushed past Garret and sauntered off down the hall.

"Is it possible to get the key to Declan's room?" Garret asked Aveline once Sophia was gone.

Aveline frowned. "Why would you need to disturb his things?"

Nea understood her desire to leave Declan's belongings untouched. It was a common reaction to losing a loved one, especially when the death was sudden and unexpected. "We wouldn't ask if it wasn't important, Aveline, and we promise not to disturb as much as possible."

"It's about his research?" Her lips formed a tight line as she shifted her gaze from Nea to Garret.

Garret nodded. "So, you understand just how important it is."

With a reserved sigh, Aveline pulled a key out of her pocket and handed it to Garret.

"Thank you."

"You're welcome." She let her hand drop and then walked away.

Garret was silent as he led Nea up the stairs and towards the senior mage quarters.

"He's angry. Do you think he's angry? I mean, it's hard to tell sometimes but you did lie to him," Declan said.

She hadn't lied to Garret, exactly. She'd omitted the truth—not that that was any better, and she wouldn't be surprised if he was furious with her. After all, he'd trusted her enough to share the secret about his family and how had she repaid him? By not telling him the friend who he thought was dead and gone was, well, dead but definitely not gone.

Garret stopped in front of a door and slipped the key into the lock. He turned it until it clicked, then jiggled the handle and paused to rest his palm on the wood of the door. Nea felt the numbness of his suppression and Declan chuckled.

"He hasn't forgotten the wards. I'm not surprised after last time." Garret then opened the door and gestured for her to enter.

The room was mostly neat. Several books were stacked by the bed and a cloak had been tossed haphazardly over the chair by the desk. The desk itself housed a few small piles of clutter but overall it was much tidier than Declan's desk at Braemar.

Feeling Garret's eyes on her, she turned to face him.

"How long has he been hanging around? Since Little Brook? Did you even bother to try and send him?"

"Since Little Brook, yes, and yes I tried to send him. But he won't go."

"And here I thought you were starting to enjoy my company." Declan gave her a mock look of hurt and Nea pressed her lips together.

"Is he one of the restless?"

She shook her head. "No, he's ..." She glanced at Declan where he was sitting on the edge of the bed. "I'm not sure what he is. He performed some sort of experimental magic to try and leave a message for you and instead managed to jam himself between worlds. Or at least that's the most basic explanation."

Garret rubbed his forehead and made a noise that was somewhere between a huff and a laugh. "Bloody idiot."

"I prefer creative genius."

"Look, Garret, I know I should have told you about Declan, about everything."

"So start now." He crossed his arms and leant against the wall. "Declan is dead but can't move on. What else? What about your corruption, the flower-shaped birthmarks, your relationship with Sophia?"

Nea licked her lips. "The corruption is ... I don't know. It's gone but it's not. The physical symptoms are absent but I can still feel it at the very back of my mind ... waiting."

He straightened. "Do I need to get a pair of bind-shackles?"

"No." She started to shake her head. "Not yet. But there's something else. Something worse than the corruption and not telling you about Declan." Her hands were shaking, and she clenched them into fists. "Sophia." She let out a breath and moved to the desk where there was a small basket of smooth beach rocks with neat holes through the middle. She picked one up and rubbed the centre hole with her thumb. They looked like seer stones but they didn't *feel* right.

She could feel his eyes on her, waiting for her to continue.

"Sophia is my mother."

Her back was still to him, but she could picture the look on his face; the raised eyebrows, the finger tracing a line along the skin just below his lower lip as though trying to coax the right words to the surface.

"I wasn't aware Sophia had any children."

"Well, that would be because there are only a handful of people who know. Aveline and my father being the only ones outside of Hartswood."

"But she despises you."

Nea let out a bitter laugh and turned to face him. "It's easier to hate me than to hate herself. Sophia is all about appearances and prestige—we can't let the world know we're the mother of an abomination."

"Abomination?" His eyes narrowed. "Because of your necromancy?"

"No, the necromancy is not palatable but being the mother of a necromancer is definitely preferable to being the mother of a—" She sucked in a harsh breath.

Could she trust him with the truth? She hadn't even told Margot. But Garret was different. He would respond to the news practically, not emotionally. Still the thought of sharing one of her deepest secrets with him sent a quiver through her stomach.

She flicked her attention to Declan whose smile wavered as he took in the expression on her face. Then, with a self-resigned nod, she met Garret's steady grey gaze once more and said, "A deathborn."

CHAPTER TWENTY-THREE

GARRET

The word rang in the stillness of the room before settling in the pit of Garret's stomach. The longer the silence stretched between them, the more tortured the look on her face became. Her knuckles grew whiter as she squeezed the holed stone against her palm so tight she was sure to have a perfect imprint. He didn't know what to say. The revelation about Declan had been confusing enough, but this. What was he *supposed* to say?

"I ... that's a lot to take in. So deathborn *are* real?"

She gave the bed an exasperated look and, knowing now that the spirit she saw was Declan, he could imagine what was being said.

"Yes."

"And what exactly is a deathborn? I know the mythology behind them but myths and reality are often vastly different."

She dropped her gaze and rolled her lip between her teeth. "For the most part there is a grain of truth in the mythology. Deathborn are mages that are stillborn and suddenly revive. There hasn't been much study into the phenomenon because it's extremely rare and seems to be only tied to arcane bloodlines rather than elemental. But those mages who are deathborn often possess a perverted form of their base magic. In my case, because I'm a necromancer, it is the ability to kill by separating the soul or life force from a body." She glanced at Declan again and added with a shake of her head, "It's definitely not a necromancer thing; it's a Nea thing."

"These stillborn babies, are they reanimated?" Garret couldn't imagine someone doing something so gruesome, and judging by the look that crossed Nea's features, neither could she.

"Most certainly not. No necromancer would ever do such a thing." She looked at the stone she still held, turning it around in her fingers as she continued, "A reanimation is, generally, suspended in a kind of stasis state. They don't age, wounds can't be healed, and the soul is trapped until the necromancer that reanimated it breaks the seal anchoring it to the body or the body itself is destroyed."

Garret rubbed his hands over his face and sighed. "So how does a stillborn suddenly revive if not reanimated?"

"No one seems to know the why or how of it. There has been a lot of speculation about where souls come from—how they end up in the body. And that is just when dealing with normal healthy births. A deathborn very well might not be the original soul that was intended for that body. It could be an advanced form of possession. More likely though, it is some kind of delay in the originally designated soul anchoring to the body."

Garret shook his head. He knew she was trying to explain it in basic terms for his benefit, but he felt even more confused. "Okay, let's not worry about how deathborn happen. You said you thought Amelia was one and that you believed there must have been another."

"Yes." She looked at Declan again and shook her head. "I don't know. Can we discuss this later?" She tilted her head towards Garret. "I understand that, but I think *this* is more important right now." She shook her head again and ran a hand through her hair.

As annoyed as he was that Nea had withheld information, Garret felt a smile building as he watched the exchange. Declan could be, well, exhausting when he had latched onto a theory. He cleared his throat, drawing her attention back his way. "What makes you certain there is another if they are as rare as you say?"

She looked sheepish. "One legend says that they often happen in threes. But it is highly likely the legend of three comes from the fact that there are three arcane bloodlines. However the healer at Dunhold was one and—"

"And you didn't think it was pertinent to tell me? How did you know?" He shook his head. "The birthmarks."

Her teeth worried her lip again. "Yes, one account says that deathborn are marked by shadow. I wasn't sure that I believed that either until I met Amelia and saw her mark. But not just that— something in me recognised her for what she was. At first, I thought it was just my keen-sense picking up on the fact that she was dead. But it was more than that, a twisted sort of kinship like—"

"You were sisters?" He remembered what Amelia had said to Nea about them being the same, being sisters. "Can you corrupt others the way she can?"

"No. I suspect that ability comes from the fact that she is dead. She is connected to the Between in a way no living thing can be. That's pure speculation though." She scowled at the bed. "Of course I haven't tried ... I would never." A rare smile suddenly replaced the scowl. "No, not even for science."

Garret felt an odd tightness in his chest. Sometime over the last few weeks, an easy comradery had built between Declan and Nea. It was this realisation that brought the reality of Declan's death crashing back down and he was suddenly aware of just how much he had been bottling up inside. Declan had been a brother to him, and watching Nea interact with his ghost opened the wound that was barely sealed. The lump that had risen in his throat the day they discovered Declan's body shifted, and he swallowed as he pushed off the wall he'd been leaning against. The movement drew Nea's attention and she levelled that soul-searing violet gaze on him, making him feel suddenly exposed.

He scratched the stubble along his jawline and glanced at the door. "I need a minute." Her gaze never left him as he exited the room.

He paced down the hallway and rubbed his hands over his face. "You're going to do this now?" he chided himself.

Maybe it was being back here at Loch Bastien. Maybe it was the knowledge that for weeks he had thought Declan was really gone, only to find out that Nea had been keeping the truth from him. Just when he was starting to trust her, too. How many more secrets did she have?

He rolled his shoulders. Nea was an easy scapegoat but it wasn't all her fault. This mess with corruption and deathborn ... He shook his head.

Deathborn were real and Nea was one. And somehow they were linked to corruption and Nea had admitted her corruption wasn't gone. He clenched and unclenched his fists then raked his hands through his hair. He wished Emil or Harvey were around. He needed a good sparring session to clear his head and centre himself again. He needed—

Nea's corruption *wasn't* gone.

He spun on his heel and marched back to Declan's room. Nea was sitting on the chair near the desk, a book in one hand, the fingers of the other rubbing her lower lip as she focused on the open pages. A curl had dropped across her face and she lifted her hand to brush it back, her attention shifting from the book to Garret.

"I'm sorry about that." He glanced at the window where he could feel the snag in the source that he now knew was Declan. "It's been a long day."

She seemed to bite back a smile as she closed the book. "It's been a long month."

It certainly had. He glanced at her wrist but the skin was hidden beneath the sleeve of her shirt. "You said your corruption isn't gone."

She shifted in her seat and curled her hand against her chest, the other coming up to shield her wrist. "It's ... no." She let out a long breath and sat forward slightly. "The corruption isn't gone. But I think ... I think I can learn how to control it."

"Control it? Is that even possible? Every corrupted I have ever seen is—"

"A rabid maniac. I know. The corrupted are violent and not in control of their own minds, though they can have moments of clarity if their connection to the source is cut off. But Samson had considerable control of himself when he was corrupted and it took Evette's symptoms a long time to exhibit. My best guess would be that it affects necromancers differently. Perhaps it is our natural relationship with the Between or the fact that we are trained to recognise and drive out possession. Not that corruption is a true form of possession, mind you." She drew a breath. "That's why I wanted to come here when I learned Hazel was to collect Vanasha's writings."

"Vanasha?" Garret leant against the desk and crossed his arms.

"She was an Osmarian necromancer who spent much of her life studying possession and the Between. Some of her later writings apparently covered something which exhibited a lot like corruption. And that was well before the time of Samson."

"Wouldn't one of the other college libraries have copies of her work?" Mages could be obsessive about their archives and libraries. Garret found it odd that the only copies of this particular mage's works were at Loch Bastien.

She shook her head. "There was one book at Kalhanna but it was one of her early studies into changeling mythology and rudimentary possession by restless souls." Her gaze switched to Declan. "No, deathborn are not changelings. Changelings are pure myth." She rolled her eyes and huffed. "It's not a pot and kettle situation. Changelings are most likely just an original explanation for the deathborn phenomenon." She turned her gaze back to Garret. "Sorry, Garret."

He rubbed his finger along his top lip to hide his smirk. "It's alright. I know how he can get."

She gave him a half-smile. "Anyway, I thought that one book was all that remained of Vanasha's work. Between Queen Eugenie's heresy decree and the sinking of Port Brenna, the rest have been lost."

"So you had no idea there was a collection here? Wait, if she was a necromancer, why doesn't Hartswood have copies of her work?"

She frowned. "When I asked Nonna that question she told me they had gone missing. Loch Bastien is one of the last places I would expect them to be. However, it does make sense, thinking about it. Phineas was High Mage here during Eugenie's reign and rumour has it that he had several collections of 'heretical' work sequestered away in the repository rather than burning them as ordered." She scowled. "Even with the request from Nonna, Sophia isn't going to let me anywhere near the repository."

"No, but Aveline might."

"I doubt she will. Aside from the surely delightful things Sophia has told her about me, I am a complete unknown to her."

"Which is why I am going to ask her."

"I doubt that will improve our chances all that much."

"Aveline has a hard time saying no to me—something which used to drive Declan mad when we were younger."

Nea's mouth twisted curiously.

He added, "She took over care of Bridie and I after our mother died. I don't really remember her, our mother. Bridie does, but to me she is just a mass of red hair and the scent of warm apples. She lost our father and just ..." He shook his head.

"Lost the will to live?" Her tone suggested she'd seen it happen more than she would like.

"Selfish, Aveline called it."

"It is. Love is perhaps the most selfish thing in the world." She sucked her lower lip between her teeth as she studied him.

"What aren't you saying?"

"Nothing, I was just—" She scowled at Declan. "I was not doing the mouth thing."

Garret felt a smile building. "That little twist and bite that you do when you're thinking? You were definitely doing it."

"Bright Mother, damn the pair of you." She crossed her arms. "I was just curious about your father, but we have more important things to do than swap genealogies."

Garret glanced out the window at the blue-black night. "Anyway, if I ask Aveline, then she is more likely to agree. But it's getting late and this is something that probably could wait until morning."

She nodded.

"Come on. I'll show you back to the guest rooms."

After delivering Nea to her room, Garret found himself in the library. The dark space with its rows of silent shelves had always been a sanctuary when he and Declan were younger. He wandered through the room until he came to a pair of chairs under the window and then he sat and rested his head in his hands. Nea's revelations were bouncing around inside his mind, each one more distressing than the last.

The next morning when Garret entered the dining hall, the first thing he noticed was Nea and her mother standing by the head table. Sophia was leaning forward, her hands pressing on the tabletop, and her entire body tense. Nea had her arms crossed and was rocking back on one foot, the tail of her braid flicking as she shifted her weight.

"Respect is not an entitlement; it has to be earned."

"I am High Mage—"

"Then maybe you should act like it instead of picking petty fights."

The barb in Nea's tone ran through Sophia's form in a fluid jolt. "How dare you." She glanced around and seeing not only Garret but several others who had just arrived, she grabbed hold of Nea's arm and dragged her from the room.

Garret almost followed them but a hand on his elbow drew his attention.

"It's better not to get involved in some battles," Aveline said. "Did you find what you needed in Declan's room?"

"Not exactly."

Aveline indicated a nearby table and he followed her to it as a maid set down two bowls of steaming porridge.

"Can I get you anything else, Aveline?" she asked.

"Not right now, thank you."

The maid nodded before giving Garret a coy smile and moving away with a roll of her hips.

Aveline fixed him with a curious look as she blew on a spoonful of porridge, but she said nothing.

Garret gave the door Sophia had dragged Nea through a quick look then focused on his bowl. The steam rising from it was a fragrant mix of warm oats and spiced honey.

"She's rather pretty," Aveline said.

He glanced to where the maid was chatting with a group of wardens. "Declan would have thought so, but honestly, all a girl had to do was smile at him and he was smitten."

Aveline laughed. "I can't tell if you're being deliberately obtuse."

He shrugged. "Sure, she's nice to look at. Bright-eyed and fair haired, Hortensia would have considered her a muse worthy of immortalising in pigment I am sure. But I know plenty of women whose outsides do not reflect their insides."

"A speech worthy of Declan." She smiled warmly. "But, I'm not talking about the maid."

Oh, he was well aware who she was implying. He wasn't going to bite though. Aveline appeared to realise this as she turned her attention back to her breakfast.

They ate in silence until Garret said, "I need to get access to the repository."

Aveline set her spoon aside, her eyes narrowing. "The repository. Why would you ... of course. Nea needs to get into the repository and the Bright Mother will return before Sophia would allow that."

"I have a request from Abigail of Hartswood but I thought it safer to ask you rather than Sophia." He pushed the letter from Abigail across the table.

She picked it up, her mouth forming a thin line as she scanned its contents. "I'd like to help you, Garret, but we have no writings of this Vanasha in the repository and I've never seen this jewellery box she mentions."

"Can we check anyway? Abigail seems to think they are here, and you know I wouldn't ask if it wasn't important."

She glanced over her shoulder, then said quietly, "It's more than curing corruption now, isn't it?"

Garret looked around; no one appeared to be listening in but still he leant forward and spoke softly. "Someone is deliberately giving people corruption. Not just mages. There have been cases of wardens and non-mages contracting it as well. And mages have been going missing."

"I've heard the rumours but I thought it was a few mages living outside the colleges."

"For now, yes, because those mages are easier targets. But there's something big coming and I don't think mages will be able to lock themselves away inside their colleges and just wait it out."

"What's the alternative though? Kalhanna lays in ruin; Merston has been in lockdown for almost a year."

He opened his mouth to respond but she lifted a hand. "I had a good hand in your upbringing, Garret. I know that if you are tied up in this then it is serious. But you must know that not everyone will be so easy to convince without solid evidence. And frankly, Nea's reputation ..." She shook her head.

"Nea—"

"I'm not finished. I don't know what she did at Kalhanna and I don't need to know. You trust her or at least you respect her, but she is an easy target for slander, given her past. And whoever your enemies are they can use that against you. Just bear that in mind."

He bit the inside of his cheek.

"Meet me outside the repository in an hour." She picked up her empty bowl and left.

Garret leant against the wall, as far from the long arms of the sentry golem as he could get. It was a massive construct of stone and mage light. Rune marks glimmered across its chest in shifting patterns of rusty orange and purple that made his eyes water, and its every movement was accompanied by the sound of stone grating on stone. The sentry had always fascinated Declan. So much so that when he and Garret were younger, they had snuck down here so he could perform one of his experiments. An experiment which left Declan with four cracked ribs and a broken arm, and Garret with a busted lip.

He ran his finger over the scar as he watched Nea studying the golem. She looked tiny in front of the construct as her head tilted back to take in its full height and her keen pooled in the air.

The golem leant forward in response to Nea's keen and Garret tensed. But it merely puffed out a hot breath that smelled of sulphur and dead wood, then inhaled with such force that the curls that had worked free of Nea's braid lifted.

"This one is different." She turned her back on the golem and her violet eyes sparkled, the same way Declan's had right before the golem pinned him to the opposite wall.

"Different?"

"To the ones I've encountered before." She settled her attention on the spot next to Garret where he could feel Declan. "I wasn't planning on *poking* it, but thank you for the heads up."

The golem turned its head and stared at the spot Declan was standing; it gave a gravelly growl of warning before its attention shifted back to Nea and it lifted one of its plate-sized hands. Nea gingerly rested her palm against the golem's and Garret felt her magic stir again.

"Different." Its voice rattled through Garret's skull and he winced. "Like *her*."

"Like who?" Nea asked, but the golem shook its head.

"Ah, I hope you haven't been waiting long." Aveline came down the stairs with clipped steps. "Sophia is on the war path. That's nothing unusual, but you've managed to really ruffle her feathers." Her green gaze dropped to take in Nea's hand resting on the golem's and one inky brow lifted slightly.

Nea withdrew her hand. "It's fascinating. Was this one constructed in the typical way?"

"As far as I know."

"Curious. Do you know the name of the necromancer who

performed the attachment?"

"Not off the top of my head." Aveline gave Garret a look.

"The more you get to know her, the more you realise her mind works a lot like Declan's."

"Bright Mother help us." Aveline chuckled before she squared off in front of the golem and lifted her hand. "Senior Mage Aveline, escorting Warden Commander Garret and Nea of Hartswood, requesting admission to the repository."

"Clearance code."

"Seven, nine, two, four."

"Voice recognised; clearance granted. Your visit has been recorded for security purposes." The golem then stepped aside and allowed them to pass.

As they walked by, Garret kept as far from the construct's arms as possible before ducking through the door and nearly bumping into Nea, who had stopped to take in the room before them.

"How does this fit down here?" she whispered.

"Don't tell me you've never been in a repository before." Aveline headed into a small room to the left of the main door.

Nea followed her. "At Del Harol, the repository goes back into the mountain, and Kalhanna's was sunk into the bedrock below the fort, but this? It must extend under the lake, surely."

"It comes close." Aveline signed a ledger on the podium in the room and indicated Nea and Garret follow suit. "Now where do you think these books will be, or the jewellery box?" she asked as she led them back into the main part of the repository.

"The books will most likely be in High Mage Phineas's private archive. The box ..." Nea's keen stirred the air and she turned her head to the left. "That way." She didn't wait for a response but instead took off, darting between shelves. Garret followed close behind her until she came to a stop in front of a bench with a large item covered by a red cloth sitting on it.

She reached out and snatched the cloth away to reveal an oval-shaped black mirror in an ornate frame. A spirit-glass. At one time they were used by necromancers to communicate across long distances. Due to their dangerous nature, the use had fallen out of fashion and they were rare now. This one sported a jagged crack running diagonally across the fathomless glass and as Nea lifted her finger to trace it, the air grew cold with her keen. He shared a look with Aveline, who shrugged. "This spirit-glass has been broken for as long as I can remember," she whispered.

"You clever old bastard," Nea said as she placed her palm flat on the glass. Threads of lilac magic danced around her fingertips and the surface beneath them flickered then shattered with a resounding crack. Nea stood statue still as shards of black glass filled the air. They hovered around her for several heartbeats, an aura of sharp edges and purple magic, before they liquified and merged back together, forming a large sphere. Nea lifted a finger and touched the floating orb. It shimmered purple for a second, then collapsed into the ornate frame, the surface of the mirror smooth once more.

Aveline sucked a breath over her teeth. "You repaired it?"

Nea nodded. "Now, if I just ..." She pushed her hand into the glass and it disappeared. Moments later she pulled it out, holding a small wooden box with several padlocked chains of pinkish gold wrapped around it.

"So that's Warren's box? Do you have any idea what's in it or where the keys to the locks might be?" Garret asked as she slipped the box into her satchel before replacing the red cloth over the mirror.

"No idea, but I imagine Nonna does. Now, Phineas's archive?" She turned her attention to Aveline.

"This way." Aveline led them back through the repository to a large cell that was blocked off by metal bars.

Magic radiated off the bars in sharp spikes that grew hotter the closer Garret got to them. He could just make out the rune marks that were engraved into each of the bars and that ringed the small panel on the wall beside the door.

Aveline moved to the panel and placed her palm on it. Her magic zinged down Garret's spine and left the hairs on his arms standing on end before the rune marks on the bars lit up and the door whined open.

The door was barely out of the way before Nea was rushing to run her fingers along the spines of the books on one of the shelves inside the cell. She muttered under her breath and pulled a book out, opening it carefully and scanning a few pages before returning it with a frown.

She did that several more times before she looked up, hugging one of the books to her chest. "This is ..." she whispered.

Aveline chuckled beside Garret. "I didn't think there was a person in the world who revered old books as much as Declan."

"Could you imagine if he was here now?" Garret shot a look at the snag in the source behind Nea's shoulder.

Aveline shook her head.

Nea had sat herself down on the floor in front of one of the shelves, a pile of books stacked haphazardly beside her.

"Can I help?" Garret asked as he crouched next to her.

She looked up from the book she had open on her lap. "I don't know exactly what I am looking for, but if you want to take that shelf over there and see if there is anything by Vanasha on it?"

Garret moved to the shelf and ran his hand along the spines, reading the titles. He was halfway along when a very familiar stirring of magic coiled around his fingers. He glanced at Nea but she was nose-deep in a book and her keen was a self-contained cool thrum. His hand dipped into his pocket and closed on the bracelet; it mirrored Nea's magic in a steady beat. Turning his attention back to the shelf, he touched the book again and felt the cold prickle run down his arm. Shaking his hand to disperse the sensation, he pulled the book off the shelf—it was just a copy of Capernibald's *Bestiary*. He investigated the gap where the book had been but there was nothing there.

Garret focused on the book in his hand and smothered the pull of magic clinging to it. The book vibrated and burst into flames. He dropped it and stepped back, drawing the attention of Aveline. Nea gave a small squeak of alarm, her eyes fixed on the burning text. As quickly as the flames had erupted, they extinguished and Aveline gingerly picked the book up.

"What did you just do?" Nea asked as she joined them.

"I'm not exactly sure. That copy of Capernibald's *Bestiary* had some sort of magic attached to it, so I just suppressed it and then ..."

"This isn't Capernibald's *Bestiary*. And why would that be down here anyway? It's never been a restricted text." Aveline handed the book to Nea.

"Clever." Nea was looking at the shelf in front of her with interest. "Can you suppress the entire shelf?"

"I guess." He focused on the shelves in front of them and carefully suppressed the source. Two other books burst into flame but they extinguished quickly and none of the other books were harmed.

Aveline pulled one of the books from the shelf. "*Reanimation, Transmutation, and the Science of Death.*" She passed it to Nea.

Garret grabbed the other. "*The Deathborn Phenomenon.*" He also passed it to Nea, who examined the title of the first book.

"*The Thrones of Eternity.*" She blinked and looked to the spot Declan was standing. "I didn't think they actually existed. But if—"

Footsteps marching through the repository cut her off and her attention snapped to the door to the cell. Garret felt it too—the sticky pull of a finder. Nea shoved the books into her satchel. The stitching along the sides bulged to almost breaking point and the flap refused to close properly. They exited the cell to come face to face with Leon, who was flanked by Sophia and a finder whose magic was laced with the wrongness of corruption.

Garret positioned himself in front of Nea and Aveline. As the chill of Nea's magic slid up his spine, he glanced back at her and minutely shook his head. Behind Leon were at least half a dozen wardens.

CHAPTER TWENTY-FOUR
MARGOT

Margot rolled her shoulders, trying to shift the tightness that had settled there. The forest that led to Hartswood had always set her teeth on edge. It was full of invisible eyes and darting shadows, not to mention phantom touches and disembodied sounds. Even having grown up at the estate, Margot had never become comfortable with the thinness of the barrier here. Nea had once told her that it was the protection wards around Hartswood that allowed the ancestors to walk freely in the forest and waylay travellers who had no business at the estate. Couldn't the necromancers just use a sentry golem like normal mages?

Just ahead of her, Sonia had stopped and dismounted in front of a massive standing stone that had spirals carved into it. Leaning back against the monolith, her arms crossed over her chest, was a woman who looked remarkably like Nea—except her eyes were a vivid emerald green. She pushed off the stone and her form shifted into that of a tall man with a granite-grey goatee and amethyst-coloured eyes. His mouth twisted into a crooked smile and his body changed again until a tiny old woman with hair like clouds and deep blue eyes stood before them.

Molly stepped up beside Margot and whispered, "You know if this goes south, my crossbow doesn't work on ghosts."

"It won't *go south*. These are the ancestors of Hartswood. They are just investigating us."

The ghost of the old woman laughed. "Investigating indeed. It has been some time since we felt you in our wood, Margot." Her blue eyes swept over Molly. "And you, girl. Step forward so we can get a good look at you."

Margot gave Molly a gentle shove forward, and she served her a look of betrayal in return as the old woman lifted her hands and touched her cheeks. Molly shivered.

"You have fire, girl. I like that." The old woman patted Molly's cheeks, then let her go before pointing to Sonia. "You may proceed."

Sonia nodded and drew the blade of her knife along her palm. She pressed the blood that welled there against the stone and then offered the knife to Margot, hilt first. Margot copied her actions before handing the knife to Molly, who stared at it.

"You want me to offer my blood to some random ghosts in the middle of a haunted wood? Ah, no offense," she said as she eyed the ghost.

The old woman shrugged.

"It's just so the guardians know to leave you alone. I promise nothing bad will happen, Mol." Margot gave the knife a little wobble.

Molly frowned at the knife but took it and added her blood to the smear on the stone. The blood shifted, following the path of the spirals before seeping into the ground. Vines bearing glowing white flowers erupted around the monolith. Margot and Sonia each picked a flower and ate it.

Sonia's face screwed up. "Ugh, you'd think they could make them taste better." She wiggled her fingers as the cut along her palm shone green then closed.

"Come on, Mol. Your turn."

Molly gave Margot a dubious look but then plucked a flower and shoved it in her mouth. "Bright Mother's tits, you weren't wrong about the taste." She chewed it fast then swallowed. "I am starting to see why Nea is the way she is. Performing blood sacrifices and eating glowing flowers in a forest full of ghosts—that's a great way to raise a child."

"I was raised here too."

"I stand by my judgement." She gave Margot a playful shove and they remounted their horses.

"I probably should mention there's no escape. You're truly one of us now." Margot laughed as Molly rolled her eyes, then nudged her horse's sides and guided it after Sonia.

Once they were past the stone, the ghost disappeared along with the vines and their glowing flowers. The forest was quieter now. And whilst it wasn't more welcoming, the trees that had been seeming to reach for them before stood back, flanking the twisting path like silent sentinels.

After a while the trees thinned and gave way to a wide field studded with a rainbow of wild flowers that bobbed and swayed in the slight breeze. As the horses were guided towards the stone wall, above which the roof of Hartswood manor could be seen, they pricked their ears forward and increased their pace.

On the other side of the gate the meadow gave way to neat gardens, and the group dismounted. Herbs and vegetables spilled over the edges of their beds onto the wide raked pathways, and the air was full of the aroma of different flowers. Margot ran her fingers through a large silver-green lavender, sending the scent and a litany of bees into the air. She drew a deep breath and closed her eyes. It had been so long since she had been here, but she imagined she could open them and see young Nea and Emil dodging through the garden beds as they played, with Angus calling after them to mind the tomatoes.

"I was not expecting this," Molly said beside her. "It's so ... wholesome."

Sonia laughed and the sound of a bucket hitting the ground drew all their attention to a lithe man with an apron over his blue Hartswood tunic. His dark hair had more grey through it than Margot remembered but his mischievous smile had not changed one bit.

"Bright Mother preserve me, would you look what the cat dragged in." He wiped his hands on his apron and crossed the garden to greet them. His arms enveloped Margot in a crushing hug.

"It's good to see you, Angus," Margot said when she could draw breath again.

"And who is this?" He turned his attention to Molly.

"This is Molly."

"A pleasure." Angus took hold of Molly's hand and pressed a kiss to the back of it.

Behind them, Sonia cleared her throat.

"Sonia? Stars above, Lass, is it time for our annual conjugal visit already?"

"Mother's tits, Angus, you're incorrigible." Sonia's tone suggested annoyance but she was smiling as she stepped between Margot and Molly and wrapped her arms around Angus's neck. "I missed you, you old fool."

"Hey now, who are you calling—"

She cut him off with a kiss.

"Sonia's married?" Molly whispered to Margot, who laughed.

"If you could call it that. More like they share a bed until one of them annoys the other, and then they have a cooling off period before the cycle starts all over again."

"You know, that doesn't sound so bad." Molly laughed as Margot gave her shoulder a playful slap.

"Margot! You don't happen to have that son of mine with you?"

Margot turned at the sound of a booming voice.

Lord Godfrey was striding towards them. He had the same long dark hair as Emil, though two streaks of white erupted from his temples. Like his son, he preferred to wear it back in a neat tail. The lines around his bright blue eyes were deeper than Margot remembered, but otherwise he was the same. Even the hug he swept her into smelt the same: blade oil, leather, and just a hint of clove.

"Emil is back at Fort Braemar. He sends his regards though and this." She pulled a slightly crumpled piece of parchment out of her bag and handed it to Godfrey.

He slid the letter into his pocket and turned his attention to Molly. "You must be Molly."

"You've heard of me?"

"Emil has spoken of you in his letters. A pleasure you meet you." He held his hand out and Molly shook it.

"Likewise."

"If you'll excuse me, I have business with Sonia before Angus whisks her away for a *reunion*. If you are looking for Nonna, she was out in the grove with the children." Godfrey gave Margot a pat on the shoulder then stepped up beside Sonia.

Marot and Molly saw their horses to the stable then found their way to the back of the manor. The plants here were more of the ornamental variety than those found in the front garden, though Margot recognised a few medicinal flowers among the daisies and buttercups. She led Molly across to the tumbling hedge of blood-red roses and slipped through the gate into the small field where several brown cows were grazing.

The grove lay behind another hedge and as they stepped through the gate, Margot noted the small pile of shoes. She slipped her own off and then dug her bare toes into the soft cool grass. A surge of magic raced up her spine, then it settled into a tingling that made the hairs on her arms stand on end. Beside her, Molly let out a startled yelp.

Molly rubbed her arms and a short laugh escaped her. "Margot, your hair."

Margot lifted her hand and lightly touched the statically charged short curls to smooth them down again.

"Is that magic I can feel?" There was concern in Molly's tone. "Is this what having keen-sense feels like?"

Margot shook her head. "It is magic, but this is nothing like keen-sense. The ground here is saturated with the magic of all the Hartswood mages who have been interred here. It is what allows the ancestors to serve as sentinels in the forest. Not to mention the barrier between worlds is thinner here."

They wandered through the grove to the large hawthorn that grew at its centre, where they found Nonna. She sat at the base of the tree, her eyes closed. Her iron-grey plait rested over her shoulder—the hawthorn-entwined antlers of the Hartswood stag, embroidered on her blue tunic, peeked out from behind it. Beside her sat a girl of about nine with tight stone-grey ringlets, her fingers busy weaving a crown from the pile of flowers in front of her.

Margot was about to speak when a small boy came darting around the tree with a fistful of yellow dandelions. The sight of him stopped her heart for several beats. His hair was a wild tangle of curls, the deep grey of clouds heavy with rain. He skidded to a stop and stared at Margot with eyes that were the same steady grey as—

"Is there something Garret hasn't told us?" Molly whispered as she grabbed Margot's elbow.

Margot swallowed and shook her head. The boy's eyes did look remarkably like Garret's, but that wasn't who she'd been thinking of.

Nonna cleared her throat, causing both Margot and Molly to jump. "Figured it out yet?" She opened her dark violet eyes.

"It's not possible."

"You're a healer. Do I really need to tell you how these things work? Kenna, you can take Henry back to the manor. You two, sit."

Margot did as instructed though she watched the boy, Henry, as he followed after Kenna until they were out of sight. "Does Leith know?"

"I imagine not. I didn't even know until Emma brought him here."

"Wait, Leith? As in, son of Evard, next-in-line-for-the-throne Leith?" Molly looked from Nonna to Margot. "You're shitting me. Wait, the boy is a necromancer. Who's the—son of a bitch. What kind of monster abandons her own child?"

Nonna hid her look of impatience well, but Margot knew the signs: the slight rise in her right brow and the way one corner of her mouth pulled tighter than the other. "Are you quite done?" she asked Molly.

"Sorry, it's just … wow."

"I imagine Nea thought it was the safest course of action. If Evard knew his grandson was a necromancer, he'd see him not as a child but a tool to use as he saw fit." Margot frowned. "Better to have him raised by a family of a necromancer bloodline and then have him sent to Hartswood when his keen fully emerged. I can't believe she didn't tell me."

"Emma said that she was the only one aware of Henry, and Nea refused to tell her who the father was. I knew the moment I saw the boy though."

"If Leith is the father, can someone please explain to me why the boy has Garret's eyes?"

"Garret?" Nonna tilted her head.

"He's a warden. He was stationed at Loch Bastien before being promoted to commander of the capital garrison."

"Of course, Camille's grandson. I've only met him a handful of times and he was such a wee thing. Camille thought they were going to lose him. It had not been an easy pregnancy and Keely, his mother, never really recovered." Nonna shook her head. "She was almost as skilled as Angus with her nature magic. It's a terrible shame." She got a faraway look in her eye and Margot shifted as a chill ran up her spine. "I imagine that Garret, like Leith, has his father's eyes and that would be why you see the familial resemblance in Henry," Nonna said, not looking at either of them.

"I don't follow," Molly said.

At the same time as Margot said, "Are you suggesting—does Garret know who his father is?"

"What would it benefit him if he did?" Nonna looked between them. "Besides, this isn't why you are here." She leant on her hands and waited.

"I want to know about deathborn."

The corner of Nonna's mouth quirked. "Finally tell you, did she?" At Margot's look of confusion, she added, "Perhaps not. What would you like to know?"

Margot shared a look with Molly. "Are they real?"

"Very much so."

"How does it work. Are they reanimated?"

Molly sucked a breath over her teeth at the look that crossed Nonna's face. It was one Margot hadn't seen since the time Nea had reanimated Emil's cat and it made her feel very much like a child again.

"You grew up with necromancers. You know that no one would ever dream of doing such a thing. You are approaching your problem in the wrong way, asking the wrong questions because you don't actually know what your true problem is."

"Then why don't you save us both some time and tell me what you think my problem actually is? What is it you think I should know?" Margot flopped back on the grass.

Nonna chuckled and patted her knee. "You haven't changed. The question is not *are deathborn real* or *how do they occur*. The question is how and why are they related to corruption and how can you use that knowledge to construct a cure. *You* can't." Nonna stood and turned her attention to Molly. "Can you cook?"

"A bit."

"Then come along. You can help me get a start on dinner. Margot needs to sit in the grove a while to work on her perspective." She started to walk away.

Molly stood and hovered over Margot. "What should I do?"

"Go with her. I'll catch you up soon." She closed her eyes and listened to Molly's footsteps disappearing towards the manor.

As she lay there, the grove came to life. Small birds flittered about in the branches of the trees, chasing insects and singing to each other. The ground beneath her constantly throbbed like a slowly beating heart and after a while her own heart slowed to match it. She could feel her magic pooling behind her navel as it shifted in response to the magic of the grove.

When she opened her eyes, the sky above was dotted with stars and lying beside her, with her storm-grey hair fanned out like a halo in the grass around her, was Nea. No, not Nea. Her eyes were not emerald green. This woman had near identical features to Nea, though her chin was perhaps a bit sharper, her lips a little narrower, and the iron-grey brows above those jewel-toned eyes were thinner.

She smiled. "In my day, the night sky was referred to as the cloak of the Shadow and the stars represented the souls of the departed. It was a lovely story. But things were different then. The Between was stable and life and death were much more simple." There was an odd lilt to her voice that made her sound almost Osmarian.

"Who—"

"Does that really matter? I have a story for you." She stood and indicated Margot do the same.

The grove looked different; there were fewer trees and those that were there were much younger. The hawthorn was still there, a small fire glowing warmly beside it around which several people were sitting. There was a tall man with silver hair and a thick scar that ran down his cheek and across the corner of his mouth. A young woman with tight ash-grey ringlets sat on the ground near the man, her fingers idly braiding the grass. Across from her the old woman from the forest was sitting on a log, a large grey and white cat nestled on her lap. As Margot neared them, the cat leapt down and after a stretch and yawn, trotted over to wind himself around her legs.

"Sir Frecklepaws?"

The cat meowed in response and flicked his tail.

The older woman shifted over and patted the spot next to her, indicating Margot sit down.

"How—"

"Not important right now. Sit, listen, learn." She tapped her knee and the cat leapt up onto it as Margot sat beside her and the Nea lookalike took up her place on the other side of the fire.

"Once, long ago, when the Bright Mother roamed the world, there was a woman who wanted nothing more than to bear children. But life is cruel, and her womb was so barren that no seed would set therein. The village healer tried all she could to help the woman but to no avail. One night, when her despair became so great that it set upon her chest like a great stone, she climbed from her bed and disappeared into the forest." As the Nea lookalike spoke, images played across the flames.

"There in the quiet dark, she sat and wept.

"Then a man made of shadow and starlight came to her. He cupped her cheeks and wiped her tears. And he was the most lovely thing she had ever seen.

"'Why do you cry?' he asked.

"And though she knew better than to tell a stranger her woes, she found the words tumbling from her lips until all her secrets had been spent.

"'I can give you the thing you seek, but it comes at a cost,' the man said.

"'Name it and it is yours.'

"'Your firstborn.'

"'No.'

"The man shrugged and stood but as he turned away, the woman called out.

"'Wait. Can you guarantee my firstborn won't also be my last?'

"The man nodded. 'I will take only your firstborn. All children you bear thereafter will be yours.'

"'So be it.'

"At the woman's words, the man snapped his fingers. 'Done. Go, lay with your husband and when the time comes, I will return to collect my due.'

"The woman went home and soon found herself thick with child. Then, as the day of birthing drew near, she began to panic. She had promised this child to the stranger in the forest, but over the months it had grown, she'd developed a great love for it and found she couldn't bear the thought of parting with it. So she went to the temple of the Bright Mother and told the goddess of the bargain she had struck. And as her tears fell, the Bright Mother came to her and promised to do what she could to stop the stranger from taking the child.

"When the woman's first labour pain came, so did the man. She begged him not to take the child, offering him all her worldly possessions in exchange. But he refused.

"The babe was born still and unbreathing. The Bright Mother had kept her promise, for the man would not lay claim to the dead child. He left, but not before taking away the gift he'd granted to the woman.

"Once he was gone, the Bright Mother returned and touched the child, bringing it back to life. In the wake of her touch, a small flower-shaped mark marred the skin on the back of the child's hand.

"'The Shadow does not like to be thwarted. If he learns of this child, he will take it. And he will take the next and the next after that. Never will your line be safe.'

"The child grew and the woman made him wear gloves to cover the mark of the Mother. She warned him to stay out of the forest and never to talk to strangers. But one day when he was playing with the other children from the village, they found themselves in the woods, as children often do. And the boy had removed his gloves, as he often did when he was out of his mother's sight. Soon the playing children came upon an old beggar and seeing the mark on the back of the boy's hand, the beggar knew it was the prize he had been thwarted. He threw off his rags and seized the boy by the arm only to let him go again. But in the wake of the man's touch, the flesh of the boy's wrist was left blackened.

"'Tell your mother I will have my due one way or another. She may keep you, but no future generation will be safe. I will take as I so please, and I will not be so easily tricked again.'

"The boy ran home, the black mark on his arm burning as though he had thrust it into a patch of nettles. Seeing the mark on the boy's skin, the woman took him to the temple of the Bright Mother and begged again for her help.

"But the Mother appeared and shook her head. 'I warned you what would happen. Your line now bears the mark of shadow and I cannot intervene again.'

"Since that day, the descendants of the woman who are born of death will eventually be claimed by the shadow."

As the Nea lookalike finished her story, Margot rubbed her eyes. "The boy was the first deathborn?"

"So it is believed, though other versions of the story say that the woman laid with the Shadow and the boy was struck from his seed. In the end, it is always the same; the woman tricks the Shadow and then, realising the treachery, he curses her entire bloodline."

"Was she a mage?"

"Her descendants certainly are, given that deathborn only occur in arcane bloodlines."

"And the black marks on the boy's arm, the mark of shadow, could that be corruption? So deathborn and corruption are linked?"

The Nea lookalike smiled. "Now you are getting to the crux of it."

The flower-shaped mark of the Mother, she had seen that mark before ... "Amelia is a deathborn!" Margot leapt to her feet, Amelia's words ringing in her ears: *She is more like me than any of you realise.* "And so is Nea."

Hard, damp pressed against Margot's back and she felt heavy, like her mind had woken before her body. She opened her eyes and the sky above was a lovely shade of cerulean, studded with the fluffy shapes of clouds. Sitting up slowly, she stared at the ancient branches of the hawthorn before getting to her feet and staggering a few steps while her limbs caught up with her mind. Then she ran, pausing only to collect her shoes and pull them on. The cows lifted their heads as she rushed past them and vaulted over the gate into the garden where Molly and the children were playing a game with a scuffed leather ball.

Molly called after her, but she waved over her shoulder and kept running until she skidded through the door into the kitchen and found Nonna stirring a large pot.

"How was story time?" Nonna tasted the contents of the pot then threw in a handful of herbs.

"Nea's a deathborn."

Nonna wiped her hands on her apron.

"She is, isn't she?"

The older woman poured two cups of tea from the pot on the bench and passed one across to Margot. "What Nea is, is not as important as what she could become. You should be more concerned with figuring out how to defeat corruption. That, after all, is why you came here. Is it not?" She took a sip of her tea.

"It's all interlinked though."

"If you dig deep enough, everything in the world is linked in some fashion or another. Would you like to hear another story?"

"No, I would rather just have the facts." She took a sip of her tea—rosehip and chamomile with just a hint of peppermint.

Nonna laughed. "You never did allow yourself much time to stop and smell the flowers. Perhaps Hartswood is not the right place for you to find the answers."

"Necromancers have the most experience with death though."

"But you are not seeking answers about death. You are seeking answers about corruption, and finding very few. You mentioned that thing from Fort Braemar ..."

"Amelia."

"That is what it calls itself. Perhaps you should go speak to the person who has the most experience with it."

"Niall?"

"I am sure you'll find lots of insight at Del Harol. And while you're there, you can deliver this for me." She lifted a basket from below the bench. It was full of little folded packets and jars. "Just hand it over to Ivan when you get there, and he will make sure they go where they are meant to."

"So, you have no answers for me?"

"I have answers, just not the ones you are seeking." She smiled over the rim of her cup. "But I am not going to chase you off to Del Harol tonight. Put that basket away and then wash up. You can knead the dough for me; it's normally Kenna's job but I think you can handle it."

Most of Del Harol had been carved out of the mountain. It was an impressive sight with a massive waterfall tumbling down one side and sheer rock the other. The wide ring wall that sectioned the college from the forest was covered in a variety of climbing plants that all mingled together to make a patchwork of greens, dotted with the occasional burst of colour from wild flowers.

They were greeted just inside the gate by a tall man whose blond hair had been shaved around the sides and back, leaving a mop of curls that sat askew on his crown.

He gave Margot a warm smile and as she dismounted, scooped her up into a tight hug. "Little Mouse!"

Molly chuckled behind her. "Don't tell me. A relative of Sonia's?"

"No, something much worse," Margot said once she could draw breath. "Molly, this is my brother, Ivan."

Ivan whistled as he ran his eyes over Molly and Margot elbowed him in the ribs.

"Hey, now." He rubbed the spot she had hit. "Older and much more charming brother she means." He held out a hand to Molly.

"Ivan. Yes, I've heard of you." Molly took the offered hand to shake it but Ivan twisted his fingers and brought the back of her hand to his lips which pulled into an off-kilter smile.

"Delighted to make your acquaintance," he purred.

"You didn't mention he was as big a flirt as Declan," Molly said to Margot as she snatched her hand back.

"Sure, Ivan is charming, but he's got none of Declan's class. What have you done to your hair, Firebug?" Sonia stepped past Margot and clapped Ivan on the back. "Looks like you gave up halfway through giving it a trim."

"It's the latest trend in Osmar." He gave Sonia an indignant look that dissolved into a bright smile.

"Here." Margot handed Nonna's basket to Ivan. "Nonna said you'd know what to do with this."

"Oh, so you came on an errand, not just to visit your favourite brother."

Margot rolled her eyes and bit back the urge to remind him that he was her only brother. "No, actually I came to see Niall."

"You can find him in the usual place." Ivan hefted the basket and turned his attention to Molly. "And *you* can find me in the east hall once I've delivered these." He gave her an impish grin.

"Ah, thank you, but no."

Margot chuckled and slid her arm around Molly's waist. "I'd give up while you're ahead, Ivan."

"Oh, I see. Well you always did have impeccable taste." He gave her a grin and turned on his heel. "And Margot, come find me when you're finished with Niall. It won't be a proper visit until I've crushed you at a few rounds of liar's dice," he called over his shoulder, then started whistling as he sauntered away.

Sonia took the reins of their three horses. "Why don't you both head in and see Niall? I'll take care of the horses."

They found Niall in his study, though it was more like a personal library and stretched over three rooms connected by open archways. Various books, plants, and antiquities took up every available bit of space and in the middle of it all, sitting on an exquisitely carved daybed, was Niall. He rubbed his neatly trimmed goatee as he studied the book open on his lap, then, as though sensing their presence, he looked up. The lines around his deep purple eyes crinkled as he gave Margot a warm smile.

"I thought you might be along." He stood and smoothed his hair back. He had the same thick curling waves as Nea, though his were a deep brown shot through with streaks of silver and white. "And you've brought a friend."

"This is Molly. Molly, this is Niall, High Mage of Del Harol and Nea's father."

Molly let out a low appreciative whistle. "You're not exactly what I was expecting."

Niall gave an indulgent laugh. "Come in and sit. I'll make some tea." He moved to the tray of tea things that he kept in the cabinet beside his desk.

Once they were comfortable and the tea had been made, Niall asked, "So to what do I owe the pleasure of this visit?"

"I wish to discuss Amelia."

Niall had been about to take a sip of his tea but hesitated. "I will tell you what I told Emil. Amelia is dangerous and should be left alone."

"Please, Niall, it's important. Someone is infecting people with corruption and my friend was trying to work on a cure. But he died before he could complete it and now I just have his notes to go off and—"

"Okay, slow down."

The gentle pull of Niall's mind magic soothed over her frayed emotions. It wasn't cloying like mind magic could often be, but subtle and suggestive—the deft touch of a skilled hand.

"Did you bring your friend's notes?"

She dug into her bag. "Here. They're a bit hard to follow." She passed a small pile to him, then pulled out her own journal. "I've been trying to collate everything so it makes more sense." She placed her journal on top of the pile.

"So, you're looking for a cure—I wouldn't touch that, my dear, especially if you prefer your fingers attached to your hand."

Molly froze, her fingers just inches from a large purple flower with white spots. The plant seemed to be leaning towards her and quivering.

"I also need to know how a warden or non-mage can become infected. It seems the more I search, the farther from the answers I get. I just ... is that Mother's balm?" She indicated a potted plant in the corner that had crimson five-pointed leaves.

"Hmm?" Niall studied the plant as though he'd forgotten it was there. "Indeed."

"How did you get it to grow in here? As far as plants go, they are very finicky to propagate. Aren't they?" She walked over to get a closer look at the plant.

"It's rare in the wild and does prefer to grow in sheltered grottos near water. Wild specimens can still be found along the spine and in places like Fengate and Loch Bastien. But with a little coaxing, it will grow quite happily in a pot, as you can see."

"Why is it rare?" Molly asked.

Niall shrugged. "Like mage bane, it had a period where it was purposefully eradicated. Unlike mage bane, it was not deemed useful enough to cultivate."

"But what does it—"

The room starting shuddering.

"Mother's tits what's going on?" Molly exclaimed.

There was a loud crash, followed by splashing and then the sounds of raised voices. They all shared a look then barrelled out of the room and turned in the direction of the commotion.

CHAPTER TWENTY-FIVE

NEA

"I'd listen to Garret if I were you. If you both come quietly, then no harm will befall anyone else." Leon's gaze fell to Aveline, and Nea stepped up next to Garret to block her from view. "Should you choose to put up a fight, well, I guess we'll see a repeat of Kalhanna." He seemed to purr the last words and Nea forced herself to repress the shudder that rose in response. "So, what will it be?"

Declan walked through the group of wardens behind Leon and they all shivered then glanced around, looking for the source of their discomfort.

"I'm waiting." Leon folded his arms behind his back and took a step forward. Then Declan stepped through him and he couldn't contain his shiver. He snarled and lunged for Nea, but Garret's fist collected his jaw and he staggered to the side.

The finder scrambled away behind a row of shelves as ice froze the air in Nea's lungs. It puffed out in a cloud and she glared at Sophia, who was pulling on the source, her eyes focused on Garret and Leon as they grappled.

As Sophia let her power go, a bolt of ice flew through the air and skimmed Garret's shoulder before shattering against the wall.

Ice charged the air again. Nea glanced at the wardens, who were rousing themselves to the fight and darted towards her mother, pulling savagely at the source as she did so. As expected, the wardens moved almost as one to suppress her and she staggered under the weight of their power. Her mother let out a savage growl as her own magic was cut off along with Nea's, the recoil of power snapping her head back.

She knocked Nea her off her feet and pinned her to the ground. Her knees trapped Nea's arms against her sides as her long fingernails raked down Nea's cheek, leaving an angry path of stinging skin in their wake "I will not see my college destroyed because of you." She grabbed a thick chunk of Nea's hair and slammed her head back against the floor, causing Nea to bite her tongue.

Tasting blood, Nea thrashed and bucked, trying to throw Sophia off, but her mother just pressed down harder, her weight crushing Nea's chest and making it impossible to draw a proper breath. Magic prickled up Nea's spine then a crackle of lightning filled the air, blinding them all.

Nea used the distraction to pull her own power. She grabbed hold of the edge of Sophia's soul and gave it a savage yank. The colour drained from Sophia's face and a trickle of blood began to run from her nose as she let Nea go and staggered to her feet.

Nea rolled away from her mother and then dove behind a shelf, only to come face to face with the finder.

The other mage's brown eyes were wide with fear and there was an inky fan of corruption marks that spread from under the collar of her shirt up the side of her neck. She rocked back on her heels and tried to scurry away from Nea then stumbled and threw her arms up. "Please. *It* doesn't want me to harm you."

Nea was distracted by Garret, who rolled behind the shelf and landed next to her. When she looked back again, the finder was gone.

Garret pressed a finger to his lips as Leon started banging against shelves.

"You can't hide from me, Nea. I will find you and you will be disciplined for your impertinence." His footsteps were drawing closer. "I wonder how pretty the skin of your back will look after the lash has taken a few bites. Then I'll cut that delicate little birthmark from your hip. I might even let Garret watch—show him what a real man does when he's given the gift of authority." He stamped his feet as he came around the end of the shelf flanked by a pair of wardens. Nea lunged for him, her keen coiled tightly beneath her skin.

The wardens were quick to block her magic, but not before she managed to dig it into the seams that held Leon together. He yowled and dropped to the floor, his hands coming up to cover his ears.

Garret grabbed her wrist and dragged her away from Leon, leading her straight towards the group of wardens who had rounded the other end of the shelves. He stopped, looking for an exit, but they were penned in by shelves either side. Nea threw her weight against one of the shelves, it rocked, the little boxes and jars it contained tinkling against each other. As she pushed against it again, Garret helped her, and the shelf tipped. Its contents rained down on the floor. They leapt through the gap, but a hand closed on the back of Nea's shirt and yanked her hard against an armour-covered chest.

"Enough games," Leon growled in her ear as he pressed a knife to her throat. "I have so much planned for us that it would be a shame to slit your pretty little throat prematurely." He traced the blade lightly against her skin as he inhaled the scent of her hair.

She tried to pull her power, but the wardens were keeping a tight hold on her magic.

"Here." Leon thrust her towards a pair of wardens. One took hold of her, pulling her arms behind her back.

Garret had been restrained by another pair of wardens; one did not look happy with the task he had been given but it was clear he wasn't going to stand against Leon.

Sophia cleared her throat and stepped up beside Leon, smoothing her dishevelled hair.

"Where's the other mage?" Leon asked.

"I'll find her," Sophia said, snapping her fingers at one of the remaining wardens. "You, come with me."

"Several of these wardens were quite close with Garret, especially Grace." Declan pointed to a female warden standing to the side, looking sickened by the proceedings. Nea recognised her from the dining hall. "You might be able to sway them."

"Now." Leon stole her attention away from Declan as he stepped in front of her. The warden holding her tensed his grip and reinforced his suppression.

Leon ran his finger around the curve of her jaw. "I'm starting to think you enjoy the touch of a firm hand." When Nea refused to meet his eye, he grabbed hold of her chin and forced her to do so. "I am going to enjoy breaking you. Many believe it can't be done but I do so love a challenge." He let her go and stepped up to Garret. "And you? The king is going to make an example of you in front of the court, but not before he lets Catriona break your mind apart." Leon looked between them. "What? Nothing to say? You don't want to know what the king has offered me for your heads?"

"I'm sure you're going to tell us anyway," Garret said, and one of the wardens holding him could barely contain his smirk.

Leon ignored him. "He's promised me command of the wardens."

Nea let out a bark of bitter laughter. "Of course. I can imagine how the wardens will react when command of the order is handed to the scared little boy with no keen-sense."

She knew the slap was coming and braced for it, but it still sent a scattering of stars across her vision.

"The wardens belong to the king. They will do as he says or face the consequences."

Declan stepped between them and as Leon reached for her again his hand passed right through Declan's chest. He pulled back and barked at the closest warden, "I ordered you to suppress her powers."

"We are, sir."

Several of the wardens shared a look and Garret caught Nea's eye, mouthing: *Declan?* She gave a tiny nod.

Catching the exchange, Leon growled and lifted his hand as though he was about to strike her again.

"Jumping at shadows are you, Leon?" Garret said with a half-smile.

One of the wardens holding him hid a smirk behind his hand and faked a cough.

"Seems like overkill to me, four wardens suppressing one mage, but what would I know?" Garret's features settled into an easy smile.

One of Leon's fists clenched, and he drew his knife, pressing it against Nea's cheek. "One more word and I will destroy her pretty little face."

A crash sounded at the other side of the repository. Leon flinched, his blade nicked Nea's skin and she bit down on her hiss of pain.

Leon snapped his fingers at Grace. "You, go and see what that is about. And, you, get a pair of shackles on her." He pointed at one of the wardens closest to Nea.

The warden was only young and jumped at Leon's orders, fumbling the shackles. "May I?" He indicated her wrists.

"Don't ask her permission. Just snap them on her and be done with it."

Nea met the young warden's eye and smiled as she slowly lifted her hands and held them out.

"I'm sorry about this." He reached for her wrists, the shackle shaking.

"So am I." Nea grabbed the shackle and twisted it around, snapping it closed on his wrist before giving him a shove towards Leon. The warden still holding her tightened his grip again, but she dropped down and then brought her skull up under his chin so hard his teeth clacked together and her vision dulled momentarily.

A grunt sounded behind her followed by the thump of a body hitting the floor. Someone grabbed her arm. She lifted her fist to lash out, but Garret caught her hand.

He twisted around, putting himself between her and Leon's men. "Don't fight; run." He pushed her along towards the exit.

"We can't leave Aveline."

"We have to."

They rounded a corner and nearly ran into the back of two wardens who were watching Aveline and Sophia square off against each other. There was a wide stain of blood on the sleeve of Aveline's shirt and Sophia's hair was in disarray, the ends slightly smouldering.

The wardens turned to face them. The one that Declan had identified as Grace gave the other a shove, knocking him into Sophia. "Hurry." Grace grabbed hold of Aveline's arm and dragged her away towards the exit. Garret gave Nea a push after them.

As they neared the entryway, Nea remembered the golem. Aveline and Grace ran under its massive arm and Nea ducked, turning around too quick for Garret to catch her.

"What are you doing?"

"Go with Aveline. I'll be fine." She reached the golem and slammed her hand against it, letting her keen wash out. The world felt flipped for a moment and the colour drained from everything around her. She could feel the soft pulse of the soul that was housed in the body of rock and gave it a gentle touch. It shifted in response to her and formed into the figure of a hunched man with wide-set eyes and a very thick, very white beard, but not a single hair on his head. *Help*—she tried to say—but the word got stuck in her throat as the world tilted again and she was thrust back into her body. Disorientated, she glanced at the warden who was suppressing her, then at Leon and the others as they emerged from the repository.

"Help," she called out and the golem turned to regard her, the movement causing Leon and the wardens to jump out of the way.

"It won't listen to you. It is beholden only to the head mage of this college. Seize her!" Sophia called, and the golem regarded her with a slight tilt of its massive head.

It lifted a hand and Garret grabbed Nea, pulling her against his chest and turning his back to shield her as rock grated on rock and the golem's hand swiped forward.

The blow didn't come, however, and Nea peeked over Garret's arm. Leon was sliding down the wall, two wardens pinned beside him.

"You listen to me!" Sophia waved her finger at the golem. It swung at her but she dodged out of the way. Momentum caused the creature to slam its hand against the wall behind where she had been standing.

Confused, it rocked back a step and Nea saw a fissure opened in the wall behind it. She could feel strange magic that way, magic calling her. She twisted out of Garret's grasp. "The wall," she said to the golem.

The golem punched the wall again, opening a hole big enough to for Nea to fit through.

"This way." She didn't stop to see if Garret was coming. They had no hope of getting out if they tried to make a run for the main doors, but the magic that called to her promised freedom.

"Nea, that's the wrong way!" Garret yelled, as she slipped through the gap and into the wide passage beyond.

She ran forward, following the invisible thread of magic until she came to a large chamber at the opposite side of which was a massive archway carved against the wall. Barely flickering rune marks bordered its edges. Her heart pounded excitedly in her chest and she whirled to face Garret, who was followed closely by Grace and Aveline.

"By the stars," Aveline said as she stepped up beside Nea, who had turned back to face the archway.

"What is that? It feels ..." Grace took a step towards it, her hand raised, but Aveline caught her arm.

"A portal! All those years I was sitting above a portal and had no idea." Declan walked right up to the archway and touched it.

Nea moved forward and placed her palm beside Declan's. The ribbon of rune marks shone brighter in response to her magic.

"No, Nea. I know that look. There is a reason portal magic was banned. It's as likely to kill us as Leon." Garret crossed his arms.

"I thought all the portals were destroyed," Grace said, her soft blue eyes widening.

Footsteps echoed back the way they had come and Nea turned her attention to Garret. "We don't have much choice."

His jaw tightened, the muscle just in front of his ear twitching. "It's too dangerous."

"Well. Torture and certain death at the hands of a maniac versus *possible* amputation or death by dismemberment by an unstable relic of a bygone era." Declan held his hands out and mimed weighing the two options. "Personally, I'd take my chances with the relic." He patted the stones between the arch. "I mean, they worked fine some of the time, right?"

"Normally I would try to avoid ancient and unstable magic, but in this instance, I think it's our only chance of getting out of Loch Bastien in one piece." Aveline glanced back towards the passage.

"Aveline, you and Grace can't come with us. It's too dangerous." Garret looked at both of them in turn.

"And we can't stay here. Not when we have openly stood against both Sophia and an agent of the king. For once in your life, Garret, just be a little more like Declan." Aveline turned to Nea. "What do we do?"

Nea shrugged. "Stand back."

Garret looked like he was about to protest further but Grace placed her hand on his arm and drew him back to stand with her and Aveline.

Nea put her palms on the stone wall and sent her keen into it. She knew where there was another of these archways. It didn't have as much residual magic as this one, but she hoped it would respond and that they wouldn't be crushed to a bloody paste against the stone wall at the other end. At least that would be a quicker way to go than Evard would grant them.

The stones vibrated under her hands and a seam of light rushed out just as Leon and the others charged into the room.

"Go!" Sweat beaded along her brow and her arms grew heavy under the strain of keeping the portal open.

"You don't need to tell me twice." Aveline darted through the opening, followed closely by Grace.

"Come on, Garret! I can't keep this up much longer." A burning itch stirred along her right wrist. *Yes. Embrace the—* She slammed her mental walls up against the compulsion that tugged at the back of her mind. "Please, Garret." Her voice broke over the request.

Concern chased the stoic expression off his face momentarily and he stepped through the archway. Nea dove in after him, the portal snapping shut and snipping off several inches at the end of her braid.

It was strange inside the portal. She felt stretched and compressed, almost like she was watching herself from outside her own body. Then came the pull of the door at the other end and she was rocketing towards it.

Please open, please open, please open ...

Cool air kissed her skin seconds before she landed with a splash in a tangle of limbs that were not all her own.

She let out a sigh of relief. They had landed in the reflection pool at Del Harol. Grace and Aveline were standing beside her, looking very green and panting like they had run the whole way from Loch Bastien.

She glanced at Garret beneath her, who was propped up on his hands to keep his head above the shallow water. The look on his face was unreadable. Nea cleared her throat and untangled herself from him, the mosaic tiles beneath the water glittering as she moved. She stood and backed up, checking each of her limbs. Finding no damage, she turned her attention to her fingers, counting them to make sure they were all still there. Feeling Garret's stare, she slowly looked up and met his gaze. It seemed a shade darker than usual.

"Are you alright?" The words were all but grated through his teeth.

Declan appeared beside him. "I wouldn't answer that. He won't yell at you while you're injured. Just feign a mortal wound while he calms down."

She ignored Declan. "I think so. Everything still seems attached."

"Good." He nodded to himself, then drew a breath. "A fucking portal, Nea!"

"Garret!" Aveline gasped, but he ignored her.

"What were you thinking? Oh, wait, let me guess—you weren't. Because you never do when it really matters."

"I was saving our lives." The last time she had seen him this angry was when she had stabbed Evard. But that was different—she had been in the wrong then. This time, she wasn't going to concede.

"You do realise that it is ridiculously lucky that we are all in one piece?"

"But we *are* all in one piece. So, there is no reason to get yourself worked up over what could have happened. Just be thankful that it was still there because we wouldn't have made it out of Loch Bastien if it hadn't been."

"You—I—fuck!" He turned away from her, clenching his fists and taking several steps across the pool.

Grace looked like she was going to intervene but Aveline shook her head.

"Is this just about the portal?" Nea asked, even though she was already fairly sure she knew the answer.

"Yes. It's about the portal. What else would it be about?" He spun to face her again. "I keep thinking maybe you'll stop being so impulsive, you'll learn your lesson and start thinking rationally, but you don't. You just get an idea in your head and charge on with it. It's reckless and infuriating and it's what got Declan killed!"

"It wasn't *my* impulsiveness that got Declan killed," she said, trying to keep the spite out of her tone.

"No, it wasn't. It was Declan's" He closed the distance between them again.

"And you're mad because you couldn't save him. I've told you before, Garret, you can't save everyone."

"No, I'm mad because I should have seen this coming. Nothing goes right with you around. You waltz on through everyone's lives, seemingly oblivious to the wreckage in your wake."

"You—"

"Not only that." He cut her off. "How many lies have you told because you thought you were protecting those around you? How many secrets do you still hold buried deep? I really want to trust you, Nea, but you make it practically impossible." He raked his hands through his hair and let out a huff of breath.

"You think I don't know that being around me is dangerous? I stayed away to keep everyone safe and I would still be out of all your lives if you had just left well enough alone." Blind rage prickled up her spine. "Maybe if you'd actually been at Kalhanna you wouldn't have spent so much time licking Evard's boots. Nora's life wouldn't be in danger and Declan wouldn't be dead." She pressed her hand to her mouth.

Garret just stared at her.

She dropped her gaze to her feet, drawing a series of fast breaths to try and quell the tension that was enclosing her heart. There was a voice whispering at the back of her mind, smooth and seductive, urging her to bury the knife deeper and give it a good twist. She shook her head. She had to get out of there, but her feet wouldn't move.

Someone cleared their throat and suddenly she was aware of their audience—not just Aveline and Grace, but her father flanked by Margot and Molly. She crossed to the side of the pool, dark spots invading the edges of her vision. Someone was speaking but the words were muffled.

She was too angry to focus, but the anger wasn't her own. She pushed it down and ran.

The last thing she heard as she whipped around a corner was Margot asking, "Have you quite finished your tantrum?"

Images of Kalhanna snapped at Nea's heels: bloodstained earth, the bodies in the library, Willem's sneer ...

She nearly barrelled into a group of young mages and muttered a quick apology as she darted away again. Her pace didn't slow until she found herself in the conservatory, the smell of wet loam and exotic flowers bringing her back to her body in a way nothing else could. She collapsed onto a bench and pulled her satchel off. The outside was completely saturated, but the inside had been protected by the enchanted lining and was still bone dry. She wished she could say as much for her clothes which were clinging to her skin, cold and damp.

"I did warn you," Declan said. "If it makes you feel any better, as far as Garret meltdowns go, that one was fairly mild, all things considered ... Are you alright?" The concern in his tone shook Nea and her head snapped up to find him crouching in front of her, his hands inches from her knees.

"I'm—no. I'm not alright." She rolled her sleeve back; a palm-sized circle of black webbing marked the inside of her wrist.

Declan sucked a breath through his teeth and gingerly touched the mark. The shadow of his fingers was cool against her skin, almost soothing.

"What you said to Garret back there ...?"

"I didn't want to say it, but I couldn't stop the words, couldn't calm the rage that was rising." She rested her face in her hands and drew a long breath, thankful that the bubbling anger had receded.

"Nea?"

She looked up.

Molly was standing just behind Declan, her eyes wide as they took in the inky stain on her skin. "Should I get Margot?"

Nea shook her head. "There's nothing she can do right now." She pulled her sleeve down.

Molly sat on the bench across from her. "Most people can't give it back to Garret like that. Generally they just stay silent and wait for him to get it all out of his system. I don't know if I'm impressed or just plain shocked."

"Why are you here?"

"I'm not sure really. Margot was busy with Garret and you looked like you could use ... I don't know. Not a friend, but you know."

"I admit, I never thought you'd be the one to come find me. But I do appreciate the gesture."

Molly made a sound that could have been a short laugh. "So, big day?"

"You could say that. I don't blame Garret. I am well aware of my shortcomings and things have been very tense the last few weeks. It was bound to reach breaking point sooner or later."

They sat in silence for a while until Molly said, "Just so you know, I agree with most of what Garret said. His delivery was shit but we've all been on the receiving end of his temper at one time or another." She smiled to herself and shook her head. "Declan once told me that it was a rite of passage, that Garret only yells like that at people he cares about. So welcome to the inner circle, I guess."

"It's true. He'll calm down eventually and things will be back to normal." Declan sat on the lip of a planter box. "It might take a bit longer in this case though."

She ignored Declan. "Are you feeling okay, Molly?"

"Why? Oh, I'm being nice to you." She laughed. "Never thought I'd see the day either. But I figured if you're going to be sticking around then we need to be on at least amicable terms. For Margot's sake, if nothing else."

"Thank you."

"It doesn't mean we're going to start braiding each other's hair and all that nonsense."

Nea chuckled. "Of course not. But I meant thank you for being there for Margot."

Silence built between them again and Molly shifted in her seat. "It's probably almost time for dinner."

"Don't let me keep you."

Molly left with a nod and Nea stared around at the various foliage until her gaze fell on a small plant with red leaves. She remembered the leaf from Declan's journal and moved over to inspect the plant. It looked a lot like mage bane but the leaves were the wrong colour. And mage bane had a tall spike of blue flowers, where this plant was covered in delicate little star-shaped white blooms. Mother's balm— it was one of her father's favourite plants. She lifted a finger and touched one of the leaves.

The mark on her arm started to itch and she examined it. The edges were changing, shrinking in on themselves as though trying to move away from the plant. Nea plucked the leaf and scrunched it up in her hand, releasing an acrid-smelling oil which she smeared over the black mark.

The pain nearly knocked her off her feet and she rushed to a nearby fountain to wash the plant residue from her arm. The water cooled her skin and the mark seemed smaller, paler than before. She wiggled her fingers and watched as it started to darken again. *Could it be that simple?* She glanced at Declan, who was staring at the corruption mark. Realisation slowly crossed his features and his green gaze snapped to hers.

"That is ... I had tried a tonic made of Mother's balm and mage bane, but the results were, well, not the best. One patient went blind for two days and the other couldn't keep the tonic down. And it didn't cure either of them. I never tried it in ointment form though."

"Mother's balm and mage bane?" Nea ran her fingers through the plant. "That's it. No, it can't be."

"What are you thinking?" There was no masking the eagerness in Declan's voice.

"How did that bloody rhyme go? Two of gold, no that's not right. Starlight, sunlight ... nope." She shook her head.

"Talk to me, Nea." Declan grabbed her elbow and a jolt of cold rushed up her arm.

"It starts with three." She looked around until her eyes fell on a draping vine with star-shaped pale green flowers, the edges of which were trimmed in black. "Three from the daughter of shadow and vice." She spun and pointed to a soft green herb with heart-shaped leaves and white lace-like flowers. "Four from the one who is always nice."

"Oh, I know this." Declan snapped his fingers. "Two from the one the mages hate."

"And a gift from the Mother to mend your fate." They finished together.

"That's it, right?" She met Declan's eye and he shrugged.

"Sure, if you want to poison your patient. If I remember correctly, night's kiss, lovelace, and mage bane go together to make an elixir of living death."

"No. Living death requires equal measures of Osmarian night flower and lovelace. And you don't put Mother's balm in it at all." She bit her lower lip. "Where did you learn that rhyme?"

"Yolanda had recorded it as nonsense that Evette was repeating before her death. They couldn't figure it out, and I didn't think about the possibility of it being a recipe. Where did you learn it?"

"Samson's journal."

"And how did you know it was a recipe?"

"I had a feeling it might be. My friend Tobias used to make up rhymes or songs to remember tonic and ointment recipes and it reminded me of him. I had no idea what it was a recipe for though, and like you, I thought a poison, but what if the inclusion of Mother's balm turns poison to cure?" She rubbed the black mark on her wrist. "My knowledge of healing herbs is limited and most of it revolves around making the end of life more merciful. I need to talk to Margot." She gathered her things and headed out of the conservatory, Declan hurrying along beside her. She didn't know where Margot was staying but her father's study was a good place to start looking so she went there first.

Her father was sitting on the edge of his desk and Aveline was on the daybed. Her attention snapped to Nea as she entered.

"I should give you two a moment," she said as she rose from her seat.

Niall waited until she was gone then slid from his perch. "What sort of mess have you gotten yourself into this time, my girl?" He smiled warmly and crossed the space to pull Nea into a hug.

The moment his arms closed around her shoulders, she was a child again. She melted against his chest burying her tears in his shirt as the thickness in her throat stole her words.

"You're safe." His voice rumbled against her ear and his breath stirred her hair.

"I'm sorry ... so sorry ..."

He rubbed small circles on her back that matched the soothing press of his magic as it rolled across her mind. He didn't burrow into her thoughts but the magic smoothed over the rough edges of her anger and grief, and for the first time in three years she was—calm.

She pulled away and swiped at the itchy tears that clung to her cheeks. "I don't know why I am crying." She gulped air into her starved lungs.

Niall chuckled and gave her arm a gentle squeeze.

After a few more slow deep breaths, she said, "I'm sorry I didn't write to tell you I was safe."

"I have my ways of keeping track of you. Now, I think there is something you need to show me." He held his hand out, his violet gaze flicking to her wrist.

She rolled her shirt sleeve back and gingerly laid her arm against his open palm. His breath hissed over his teeth and he prodded the blemished flesh with his fingertips. "How did this happen?"

Nea chewed her lip. "I had a run in with Amelia. But it was fine until Loch Bastien."

"It's a good thing Margot's working on a cure then isn't it?" He released his grip on her. "It seems we have lots to discuss but I think right now you would benefit from a hearty meal and a good rest."

"Do you know where Margot went?"

"The dining hall." He ushered her towards the door. "You can kill two birds with one stone."

❧

The Del Harol dining hall was deafening in comparison to Loch Bastien. There was no separation of wardens and mages; they shared the space equally, talking and laughing with unbridled ease. As she entered, those closest to the door looked up.

"Nea!" A tall man with a mop of blond curls sitting precariously on top of his head came bounding up to her. "What have you done to your hair?" He engulfed her in a hug then drew back abruptly. "Why are your clothes damp?"

"I took a dip in the reflection pool earlier."

"Do I want to know?"

She shook her head. "It's a long story."

"Here, let me help you." He ran his hands through the air and her clothes started to steam, then they were completely dry in less than a minute.

"Thanks, Ivan. Do you know where Margot is?"

He mocked a wounded expression. "I don't see you in a year and a half, and all you have to think about is Margot. By the way, thanks for helping me with that merchant in Osmar."

Some of the others close by stared at her curiously. Several gave her a small smile or wave.

"Margot is over there." He indicated a table on the other side of the room where Margot and Molly were sitting with Grace.

"Ivan!" A mage from a nearby table waved him over as Nea wound her way towards the long table covered in pots and platters of food, and she heard him ask, "Is that really Niall's daughter? The necromancer?"

After loading up a plate, she moved through the tables to join Margot and the others. As she slipped into the empty seat beside Grace, she caught Margot's eye and asked, "Where's Garret?"

"Sulking, most likely," Molly replied. "Or attacking some poor unsuspecting hunk of wood with an axe."

Declan chuckled.

"Are you alright, Nea?" Margot's gaze flicked to her wrist.

"Yes, though I do need to talk to you after dinner." She turned her attention to Grace. "I'm Nea, but you probably knew that already. Sorry we didn't get a chance for introductions earlier."

"Grace, though I am guessing you knew that as well."

"About what happened at Loch Bastien—I am sorry you got caught up in this mess."

"Don't worry about it. I would have followed Garret regardless. He told us to be careful who we trust, that there was a schism developing in the order and we'd likely have to choose sides. Then that pretentious prick showed up and well ..."

"Leon has that effect on people," Molly said as she stole a sliver of roast meat from Margot's plate, earning her a light-hearted scowl and a jab in the side.

"Speaking of Garret, should someone go and check on him?" Grace pushed her empty plate aside. "Travelling through that portal was not a pleasant experience."

"I'd leave him be a while longer. He's not a *pleasant experience* when he's in this particular mood." Molly grinned.

Margot kicked Nea under the table and she jumped. "What?"

"How about we have that talk *now*?" Margot tilted her head towards the door.

Nea glanced at her plate. "But I'm not finished my dinner."

"Bring it with you." Margot stood. "I'll meet you back at Niall's study in a little while, Mol." She dropped a soft kiss on Molly's cheek then beckoned Nea to follow her from the room.

With a sigh, Nea grabbed the roll from her plate and tore it open. She layered some of the meat and roast vegetables on it then pressed it back together and followed Margot from the room.

"Show me your arm," Margot said once they were behind the closed door of Niall's study.

Nea took a bite of her roll then held her wrist out and let Margot inspect the black mark.

A pale green mage light flickered to life and hovered over Nea's skin as Margot traced the mark with her finger. "It feels different on you. Still ... wrong. But not as—"

"Hungry," Nea said through a mouthful of food.

"Hungry," Margot agreed, scrunching her nose at Nea as she took another large bite of her roll. "When did this happen?" Nea opened her mouth and Margot added, "Swallow first."

"I think when I activated the portal, but I did use a fair amount of magic during the fight with Leon. And things were fairly hectic, so I didn't stop to check for corruption every five minutes."

"Why are you being so blasé about this? It's *corruption*, Nea."

Nea shoved the last bite of her roll into her mouth to buy herself time. "I can't do anything about it. I've been dealing with the feeling of it in the back of my mind since we escaped the capital."

"But the ointment—"

"Cured the physical signs well enough. I'm starting to think ..." She ran her hand over her hair. "There's something I need to tell you. A few things really."

"I know that you're a deathborn." Margot settled herself on Niall's daybed. "And I know about Henry."

"You know about Henry?" Nea swallowed.

"Who's Henry?"

She ignored Declan as he appeared next to Margot.

"I met him at Hartswood. Is he why you left?"

Nea shook her head. "He's part of it. I didn't realise I was pregnant until after Kalhanna. I was scared of what Evard would do if he found out, so I ran. Emma found me after one of her visions and I made her take him back to Little Brook."

"And you didn't think Leith should know."

"I knew there was a history there but I was not expecting a child." Declan was inspecting the cabinet next to the window that was full of small potted plants and strange stones.

"I had to choose what was safest for Henry, and that meant that Leith couldn't know and that I had to stay away. Far away."

Margot let out a huff of breath but nodded. "I understand."

"About the deathborn thing—these might be helpful." Nea dug the books from Loch Bastien out of her satchel and handed them to Margot. "And I think I might know a recipe for a corruption cure. Night's kiss, lovelace, mage bane, and Mother's balm. I don't know if it *is* a cure, but Samson thought it was important and apparently so did Evette."

Margot read the titles of the books and rubbed her chin. "So let me catch up here. Corruption might be more than a physical disease. It is somehow linked to deathborn and the Between, and we have a possible recipe for a cure that sounds an awful lot like a poison."

"Yes, that's the gist of it. And it is highly likely that corruption can only be truly destroyed by going into the Between and pulling it out by the roots." She brushed the crumbs from her shirt. "Oh, and Leon has a finder who is very likely tracking Garret and I as we speak."

"A finder? You managed to evade Marcus. Surely this finder is no different."

She shook her head. "I didn't even know she was tracking us until Leon turned up at Loch Bastien. She was corrupted and that may have affected her keen. Perhaps Father still has some of those travelling wards he was experimenting with a while ago. We might be able to alter them to block the finder." She started towards the door, ducking around Molly, who was just entering the room. "I'll see you in the morning."

"I guess I'll see you in the morning then." Margot's voice followed Nea down the hall as she hurried off in search of her father. A quiver rolled through her stomach at the thought of Leon catching up with her again.

CHAPTER TWENTY-SIX

GARRET

Morning sunlight slanted through the window and hit the mosaics under the surface of the reflection pool, sending rainbows scattering over the silent stones of the portal archway. Garret studied the bracelet wound around his fingers. He really should have given it back to Nea, but he'd grown fond of the cool throb of its presence.

Footsteps sounded behind him and he glanced towards the doorway as Grace entered.

"Margot said I'd probably find you here." She sat on the floor next to him. "Do you want to talk about yesterday?" She eyed the portal at the other end of the pool.

"No." He slipped the bracelet into his pocket.

Grace followed the movement with her eyes before looking back at him with a question on her lips.

"It's Nea's. I had a finder enchant it so I could track her down." He ran his hand through his hair.

They sat for a while, Grace shifting her weight every now and then.

"Why did you get yourself tangled up in our mess?"

She blinked. "You told us yourself that we would have to choose a side and I damned well wasn't going to stick around and follow orders from some power-mad pretty boy." She leant back on her hands and frowned. "I doubt Leon will wait too long to make his next move, not with that obsession he has with Nea. He has a finder, you know, and she's probably already locked onto the pair of you."

Shit. He'd forgotten about the finder. "I need to find ..." He felt the familiar cool touch of Nea's keen before the sound of her footsteps reached him.

Grace tilted her head and glanced towards the door. "I should probably give you two some space." She got up and left, giving Nea a nod as she passed.

Once Grace was gone, Nea said, "Can you give us a minute, Declan?"

The sensation that was Declan disappeared as Nea stopped in front of him and held out a steaming bowl of porridge and a spoon.

"What's this?"

"You weren't at breakfast and I figured you might be hungry since you missed dinner last night as well."

His stomach growled as he took the bowl from her and inhaled the fragrant steam. "Thank you."

"You're welcome. I also got you this; it should help with the finder, until we leave the college at least. As long as you have it on while you're inside the Del Harol wards, you'll be invisible to her." She held out a length of braided leather with a small rose-gold disc set into it. "May I?" She held up her wrist to show him the matching one tied around it.

He balanced the bowl and spoon in one hand and held his arm out.

Her fingers were cool as they brushed against his skin. Once she had secured the braid around his wrist, she covered the metal disc with her hand and let her magic wash over it. His warden keen stirred in response to the magic, but instead of rising to suppress it, the two keens seemed to bend and merge.

When Nea pulled her hand back, a shiver rushed down his spine as the enchantment settled over him.

"You get used to the feeling eventually." She sat next to him and played with her braid. He couldn't help but notice the ends were slightly ragged.

"So, this will really block the finder?" he asked.

"Yes. It's an enchantment of my father's. It works by scrambling the magical signature of a person or object. It's similar, I guess, to the way I used the Between to confuse Marcus."

They sat in silence for a while, though it was not quite the same easy silence that had often fallen between them during their flight from the capital to Loch Bastien. Nea shifted her weight, unbraiding and re-braiding her hair.

As he finally set the empty bowl aside, she said, "I owe you an apology."

"No, you don't."

She stared at him. Something in the very depths of her violet gaze seemed to see right through him.

"I actually do and you're going to pull your head out of your arse and accept it."

A laugh escaped him. "You sound just like Declan."

"I guess he's rubbing off on me. You know it would be so much easier if you could see him." She sighed. "I'm sorry. I am sure you've probably thought that yourself."

He shrugged. "I can feel him. It would be nice to be able to see him, talk to him, but it is what it is."

"You can talk to him. You just can't hear him respond ... Maybe that's not such a bad thing." She gave a half-hearted smile and pushed a loose curl behind her ear. "Anyway ... I'm sorry that sometimes I act without thinking, and I am sorry you upended your entire life because of me."

He rubbed the back of his neck. "It was unfair of me to pin the blame for that solely on you. I made a choice, a few of them actually, and I need to accept the repercussions of those choices." He shook his head. "I think we both know that what was said yesterday needed to be said ... on both accounts."

She nodded. "There's something you should see." She pulled back her sleeve to show him the large circle of black webbing that marked her wrist.

He lifted his hand to touch the mark but at the last moment pulled back. "Did that happen when you activated the portal?"

"I think so. It took nearly everything I had to hold it open long enough for us all to get through."

He clenched his back teeth and swallowed the bitter anger that stirred in his throat. "Nea—"

"I'd do it again in a heartbeat. If Leon ..." She stopped herself.

"I know." He wasn't exactly sure what Leon had done to her whilst she was Evard's prisoner, and part of him didn't really want to know. He hated cowards like Willem and Leon who used the threat of physical violence as a weapon.

She looked at her fingers as they twisted the hem of her shirt.

The movement summoned a small smile. Declan had never been able to sit still either. "It doesn't mean I am happy about it. It was a huge risk, but I understand that our options were limited and we don't always have the luxury of time to plan. And, as Margot so *delicately* reminded me, we all arrived here in one peace."

"Did I just hear my name?" Margot came through the doorway, her arms laden with books. "I'm not interrupting anything, am I?"

"Not exactly," Nea said.

"Good because I want to get started on this cure and I need you both."

Garret stood and took some of the books from her. "Cure? Nea seemed to think that going into the Between was the only way to really cure it."

"I'm inclined to agree with her given that the Between is where it seems to originate. However we may be able to weaken its hold on a mage enough that Nea can sever the link entirely." She met Nea's eye as she stood.

Nea nodded. "It's plausible to assume. However, I wonder if a warden would have better luck with the severing part."

Garret felt the air stir as Declan appeared. Nea's attention snapped to the spot Declan was standing, as did Margot's, the look on her face curious. Had Nea not told Margot about Declan yet?

"What do you mean a warden might have better luck?" Garret asked, drawing both their attention.

Nea shrugged. "Corruption is magical in origin and we know that when the host mage has their magic suppressed, the corruption grows dormant. I am wondering if maybe a warden could use their suppression to isolate and unknit the corruption of the host mage's keen."

They both looked at Garret.

"I am not sure ... maybe. I've never tried anything like that before." He indicated her marked arm. "May I?"

She held it out and he took hold of her wrist before gently rolling her sleeve back to inspect the mark.

"You both might want to sit down, just in case," Margot said as she took up a seat on one of the benches near the windows.

Nea lowered herself back to the floor beside the pool and Garret copied her. He took her wrist in his hand again and pressed his fingers lightly to the mark, letting his keen-sense burrow into it, getting a feel for it.

At first all he could feel was that wrongness that all corrupted mages had, then the cool throb of Nea's keen broke through as it stirred in response to his investigation. The two were tangled together so tightly that it was nearly impossible to tell where Nea's magic stopped and the corruption began.

He pushed deeper, drawing a breath and closing his eyes as he focused on separating the feeling of corruption from the feeling of Nea's keen and following the cool thread to its source. The sunlight shone red through his eyelids as Nea's magic turned from that steady coolness to stabbing ice that prickled up his spine and fanned across his chest. Then there was a bright flash of purple light and he was thrown onto his back.

When he sat up again, a massive hedge of pink roses spanned in front of him. The blooms directly before him were tarnished grey and as he studied them, the grey streaks spread out in all directions, jumping from bloom to bloom. He lifted a finger and touched the closest rose. It's smoke-coloured petals quivered and then with a great groan, the branches of the hedge rolled back on themselves to create a wide opening. Through the opening he could still see Nea sitting beside the reflection pool, her head tilted as she regarded him with avid curiosity, a rare smile slowly curling across her lips. He noted her hair was back to its natural storm-grey and took a step towards her.

As he passed the hedge, his stomach gave a flop and a shiver rushed over his skin. The reflection room at Del Harol appeared before him but it was very different to the room he had been sitting in only moments before. The pool stretched out in front of Nea as a fathomless depth, mosaic tiles floating in fractured rafts on the surface of the water. Across the dark expanse of the pool, the arch of the portal was a vine-shrouded ruin leeching rainbow streams of magic onto the surface of the water where they formed into brightly coloured fish.

"Figured it out yet?" Nea asked, her voice slightly higher than usual.

He glanced around at the windows that had been replaced with mirrors, surrounded by flowering vines. The glass reflected not the room but different lands, from a rich red desert right through to a dense green jungle.

"Is this ... are we in the Between?"

"In a sense. What did you do?"

"Yes, Garret, what did you do?"

Nea leapt to her feet and stepped closer to Garret as a familiar figure stepped from one of the shadowed corners. That infuriatingly smug smile was firmly in place on his lips as he ran a hand through his black hair, making it stand on end. There was something not quite right about the shine in his forest-green eyes.

"I ... how?" Garret looked at Nea, who shrugged.

"Your guess is as good as mine. Just so you know, we are not physically here but that doesn't mean that no ill can befall us." She eyed Declan as he approached.

"Of course, but that's the trick with things here, right?" Declan stared at his reflection in the water. "Ill will only befall you if you allow it in."

Nea took another step closer to Garret.

"We're not so easily tricked." There was that odd high tone again.

Declan's smile was a little too wide as he regarded Nea. "*You* can't be so easily tricked. You are as much a part of this realm as I am."

Nea turned her gaze to Garret. "Don't trust that thing; he wears a familiar face so he can erode your defences."

Nea's warning to Nora about the things that dwelt in the Between stirred in the back of Garret's mind and he shifted his weight onto the balls of his feet, ready to race back to the hedge. He glanced out of the corner of his eye, searching for it, but it was much farther away than he expected. Had he really walked that far?

"You do realise he's a lot smarter than you think? He already knows *you* are not who you are pretending to be," Declan said.

"Don't be foolish—" Nea stopped as Garret took a step backwards. "It really is me, Garret. Trust me." She held out her hand, but Garret took another step back.

"Garret, get away from them!" Margot came bounding through the door. "We have to get out of here. Hurry."

He shook his head. "I'm not going with any of you."

Margot's mouth twisted into a malicious smile. "Then I'll just take what I want." She lunged for him and he reached for his sword, but it wasn't there.

"Uncle Garret!" Nora appeared, dragging his sword. She threw it as hard as she could.

It clattered to the ground several feet away and he dove for it, rolling into a fighting stance as the thing wearing Margot's face attacked. Her fingers lengthened into long knife-like claws and her smile widened into a great maw of pointed teeth.

As she lunged, Garret parried and her claws grated down the steel of the blade, sending a shower of sparks into the air. She hissed and attacked again but he ducked under her defence and brought the blade through the centre of her abdomen. Black ichor flowed over the steel.

"Don't touch that!" Nora yelled.

Garret rolled out of the way as the body of the thing that had been Margot collapsed to the ground. Declan was clapping slowly where he still stood beside Nea. Both turned their attention to Nora as she ran to Garret's side.

"You're not supposed to be here." She pushed her hands against his hip. "Quickly, you need to escape."

Nea tutted and took a step towards them. "Now, you look like the type that enjoys a game," she said in a voice that was too sweet to ever pass as Nea's.

Nora put herself in front of Garret. "No, I won't play with you. You look like Nea, but you're not her. She'd never try to hurt Uncle Garret; she's his friend."

"I don't want to hurt him."

"I'd give up while you're ahead—you have no power here," Declan said to Nea.

She smiled cruelly and made a lunge for Nora but she was knocked back as another Nea appeared in front her.

The two Neas fell to the ground and rolled towards the pool of dark water as they wrestled.

"Go home, Nora. Now!" one yelled, as the other grabbed hold of her hair and dragged her closer to the water.

"You have to help her. If she touches that water, bad things will happen." Nora tugged on Garret's arm.

"Go home," he said as he lifted his sword and took a step forward.

Declan was leaning on the wall, his mouth twisted in mild curiosity as he watched the two Neas gain their feet again and square off against one another.

"Can you tell the difference? Choose wisely; it would be a terrible shame to lop off the wrong head." He snapped his fingers, and everything went dark.

When the light returned, the two Neas were standing in front of Garret, panting. He looked between them. His keen-sense had been going haywire since he arrived, and he couldn't get a good read on either of them.

"Trust your instincts, Garret. This realm can't warp what is intrinsically yours," the Nea on the right said.

Garret swallowed. The Nea on the left folded her arms, the ghost of a smile threatening the corners of her mouth. He pointed to the Nea on the right, who was smoothing the hem of her tunic. "That's the real Nea."

"You're absolutely sure?" the Nea on the left said, her violet gaze going straight through him.

He nodded.

The false Nea snarled and snatched hold of the real Nea, dragging her towards the water again. Garret leapt into action. He grabbed Nea's arm and yanked her from the other's grasp, then pulled her against his chest as he swung the sword and severed the false Nea's head. It rolled into the water which boiled to life as the coloured fish all turned blood red and devoured it.

Declan was clapping again. "Two down. You've done well for one who is not a natural of this realm. I'm afraid, though, you'll have to relinquish your prize. You see, she belongs to me and I will have what is mine, one way or another."

He stepped off the wall and his features shifted. Eyes that once were green were now a shade of purple so dark they looked almost black. His hair lengthened into sleek storm-grey waves that just brushed the shoulders of the starlight-studded midnight-blue cloak he was wearing.

Garret tightened his grip on Nea.

"You may have been efficient against those lesser beings, but you can't hope to beat me in my own realm." He took another step forward.

Nea's fingers wrapped around Garret's wrist and the cold pull of her keen washed over him as the world tilted and he was thrust back into his body. Sunlight and the thin notes of birdsong drifted through the large windows as cold stone pressed against his back, and then a face appeared at the edge of his vision. One that had whiskey-coloured eyes and a worried frown.

"Slowly does it," Margot said as she helped him to sit.

He glanced around and spotted Nea sitting beside him, her lip firmly between her teeth as she regarded him.

"Who or what was that?"

"If I had to hazard a guess, I would say the Shadow Man. I've never actually met him before, but I've heard his stories and read enough about him." Were her hands shaking? "He felt different to what I always imagined though." Her lip trembled and she rubbed her finger along it, her gaze not quite meeting his.

Garret nodded. "Are you alright? Is Nora?"

"Nora is fine. I had Declan check on her, though I am not completely sure it actually was her. Not all things that dwell there are malicious. It may have been a helpful spirit wearing a familiar face."

Margot's eyebrows rose slightly but she didn't ask.

"You didn't answer my first question."

She met his gaze then and he noted a look in her eyes he had never seen before. Something about the Shadow Man had bothered her more than she was willing to let on. "I've been better. I don't know how you managed to do that, but I nearly didn't find you in time."

"Do what?"

She shared a look with Margot. "You ... you channelled my keen."

"What?! That's impossible," he exclaimed.

Nea hugged herself and repressed a shiver. "Apparently not impossible."

"Did you at least manage to isolate the corruption?" Margot passed him a steaming cup of tea.

Garret shook his head and took a small sip, twisting his face at the acrid taste.

"Drink it all," Margot said. Then she tapped her chin and added, "Maybe, given more time—"

"No." Nea stood and paced towards the windows. "I don't think it will be possible." She rolled her shoulders. "Or even if it is possible, it's not worth the risk." There was a note in her voice that caused Margot to leap to her feet.

"Nea?" She lightly touched Nea's shoulder but Nea shrugged her hand away. "Talk to me."

Garret placed the tea aside and stood. "How bad is it?"

She met his eye as she rolled back her sleeve. "I think we might need those bind-shackles now."

Margot gasped. Nea's entire forearm, from the inside of her elbow to the base of her palm, was covered in black marks like a delicate lace glove. As they watched, the mark spread across her palm and immediately Garret focused on suppressing her magic. A look of relief washed over her features and she drew a deep breath as the mark stopped growing.

"You can't suppress her magic forever. I'll go see if Godfrey is back from Hartswood. If not, I'll find his second or Sonia. Anyone who can get us a pair of shackles." Margot started for the door.

"Wait. Your ointment is in my room."

"Nea, half your arm is covered. There's not enough ointment there to help that." She glanced at Garret and frowned. "I'll be as quick as I can."

Garret nodded then sat once more with his tea, trying to concentrate on keeping a seamless bubble of suppression around Nea. She walked over and settled next to him, rubbing her arm and staring at the water of the pool.

"Can you loosen your suppression for a moment?"

He glanced sideways at her. "Are you sure that's wise?"

"No, I'm not. But, please? There's something I want to try."

He took a long sip of his tea and slowly lowered the field of suppression around her, ready to snap it back in place should the need arise.

Almost immediately, her keen spiked like a wild beast testing its bounds. She clenched her fists and bit down on her lip, her shoulders shaking.

Slowly, her keen calmed to its normal comforting chill and she sighed in relief, looking at her arm which was now covered in black web-like marks from the tips of her fingers to her elbow. She cradled the arm against her chest and closed her eyes.

"You can control it?"

"I can endure it. Though, that's not really the same thing."

He finished the tea with one gulp and grimaced. "I'm sorry, Nea."

"It's not your fault. It was my idea and we had no way of actually knowing what would happen." She tilted her head as Declan hovered over them. "Yes, I am sure ... It's too risky now." She got to her feet and paced away. "You *can* see this, right ...? I am not being defeatist." She opened her mouth to respond again but Margot came in with High Mage Niall and Sonia in tow.

Niall crossed to Nea and engulfed her in a hug. "You never do things in half measures, do you? Show me."

Nea stepped back and held her arm out.

Niall's eyebrows nearly disappeared into his hairline and he grabbed hold of Nea's arm, rolling it slowly as he inspected the blackened skin.

Sonia made a noise in her throat. "How are you not frothing at the mouth and trying to tear our eyes out? I've never seen a case so bad in someone who still had full control of all faculties."

"Indeed," Niall said with barely concealed curiosity. It was a look that reminded Garret of Declan.

Nea glanced at Garret before responding. "It seems to affect necromancers differently to other mages. Did you bring a pair of shackles?" She directed the question at Sonia.

Sonia held out a pair of thin rose-gold bands. "You're sure about this?"

"I don't have a choice. Garret can't follow me around waiting to suppress my magic if it gets out of my control."

Sonia nodded. "Okay." She slipped the first shackle around Nea's affected wrist. The parts of the mark that touched the shackle paled slightly and Nea bit her lip.

After a moment, the patches of paler marks seemed to grow until the entire mark was no longer black but a deep grey.

"Fascinating." Niall leant over Sonia's shoulder. "You know Samson reportedly wore a single shackle and managed his affliction reasonably well for some time. I wonder why it affects necromancers differently to other mages." He rolled his lip between his teeth.

So that was where Nea got it from.

"What do you want to do?" Sonia held up the second shackle.

"Let's try just one for now," Nea said.

Sonia turned to Garret and handed him the remaining shackle and the key. "It's probably best if you hold onto these."

"Very good." Niall clapped his hands together. "A word, Nea, if you don't mind." He touched his daughter lightly on the shoulder and led her from the room.

Garret shared a look with Margot, who jumped into action, gathering up her books. "Right, well, this cure isn't going to find itself. If anyone needs me, I'll be in Niall's study."

Garret studied his fingers as the other's left. The soft whisper of Nea's keen was still brushing over them as though clinging to his skin. He gave the hand a small shake then flexed his fingers to disperse the sensation before following Margot.

CHAPTER TWENTY-SEVEN

MARGOT

Margot rubbed her eyes and stifled a yawn. Nea had long gone to bed, surprising Margot when she didn't put up even the semblance of a fight after it was suggested. Molly lay sprawled on Niall's daybed, the open book in her hand tilting closer to the floor each time she stirred and shifted position. Margot stood and took the book from her, then gently shook her awake.

"Time for bed, Mol. I'll be along shortly."

Molly mumbled in sleepy agreeance then took herself off to bed. Margot then turned to Garret, who sat behind the large desk. The book he had been studying was forgotten as he twisted a strange stone on a piece of leather between his fingers.

"You can't shoo me off to bed that easily." He looked up as she neared the desk.

"I wasn't going to try. Tea?"

He sat back in the chair. "After the day we've had, I'm not sure tea will cut it."

She gave him a tired smile. "How about a Declan special?"

"Sure. I haven't passed out and misplaced my boots in a while."

Margot rolled her eyes and moved to the cabinet beside the desk. "Niall keeps tea-making supplies here so he doesn't have to leave what he's working on to go the kitchens."

"Sounds like he and Declan would have gotten along well."

"That's an understatement." She opened a door to reveal a teapot and an urn of water. She poured a measure of water into the pot then added apple, cinnamon, and ginger before she hung it by the fire in the hearth. "Nea told me about Declan."

"She did?"

She nodded. "But who is this Nora that she mentioned?"

He stared at the stone in his hand. "My niece."

"You have a niece?"

"Yes. She's a necromancer."

Margot retrieved the pot just as it started to boil then poured two cups of tea, adding a splash of whiskey to each before she handed one to Garret. "So, you have a niece and she's a necromancer."

"I would have told you before, but I was trying to keep her safe from Evard. Not that it mattered. He knew about her the whole time anyway." He blew the tea then took a tentative sip. "He has her father, Kieran."

"Kieran? But he's been missing since before Kalhanna ... Oh. Evard's always had something of an obsession with necromancers, even before ... everything." She looked at the liquid in her cup. "Where is Nora now?"

"On her way to Hartswood."

"That's good. She'll be safe there."

They sat in silence, sipping their tea for a while.

"You know, Nea doesn't blame you for what happened today. None of us could have known that the corruption would spread that fast." She placed her empty cup aside. "We'll find a cure. Maybe Nea is wrong about needing to go into the Between."

Garret pulled a small battered book out of his jacket pocket and passed it to her. "I doubt it will help, but this is the journal that Declan was looking for when Harold killed him." His voice hitched on the word *killed.*

Margot took the journal and flipped through it while Garret poured them both another cup of tea. "Why are these pages at the end blank?"

Garret shrugged. "Nea seemed to think that Samson died before he could fill them. Most of these entries were apparently written at the end of his life when he was suffering from corruption."

Margot frowned and fingered one of the blank pages. There was something about it, a kind of stirring at the edge of her keen-sense. "Have you *felt* these pages? Has Nea? I doubt this is something she would overlook."

"What do you mean?"

She passed him the book and he placed his palm on the page then looked at her.

"See what I mean? There is something there. I don't think it is just Samson's residual magic. I think those pages might be enchanted." Wow, she'd just sounded a hell of a lot like Nea.

The numbness of Garret's suppression closed in on her as he focused on the blank page in front of him. Nothing happened though, and he passed the journal back to her. Maybe there was a clue in one of the other entries. She flipped through it absently until a sentence stood out: *Corruption is becoming something of a Morgestia puzzle.* *Morgestia* was underlined.

She tapped her chin. "Morgestia. Where have I heard that before?"

"Ruler of an ancient kingdom, had a spiteful temper, and enjoyed torturing her people with seemingly unsolvable puzzles." Garret stared into his cup. "Her story was one of Declan's favourites."

Of course it was. Nothing had made Declan happier than a puzzle with no apparent solution. "I could really use his input right now."

The look that crossed Garret's face sent a pang through her chest. Declan's death had hit him harder than he was letting on. And of course it had; Declan had been a brother to him. If the same thing happened to Nea, Margot wasn't sure she'd be able to function. It had been hard in the three years since Kalhanna, the not knowing, but there was always that hope that she was okay. And now the corruption—her eyes suddenly felt hot and she took a long sip of her tea. "Bright Mother, damn her."

Garret regarded her over the lip of his cup.

"I mean ..."

"You'll figure it out, Margot. You might not have Declan's love of puzzles, but you're one of the smartest people I know. If there's a cure to be found, you will find it." He placed his cup aside and played with the leather amulet around his wrist. "I should touch base with Leith and the others at Braemar."

"If you leave Del Harol, that won't shield you from the finder. Its magic is tied to the wards around the college."

He nodded. "I know. But the finder and Leon were both at Loch Bastien. It will take them a while to reach the fort once they realise that is where I am going, and even then I am counting on Leon's obsession with Nea to offer me some small protection. As long as *she* stays here, she'll be safe."

"This is Nea we are talking about. I am certain you've figured out by now that keeping her out of trouble is the same as trying to keep Declan out of trouble. Honestly, I'm almost glad we never had to deal with the both of them together." She laughed. "Could you imagine it?"

He smiled and shook his head. "I am sure you can handle her for a few days though. After all, you've had more practice than me." He slid the mate to Nea's bind-shackle and the key across the table. "I'll leave in the morning and be back before you know it."

She stared at the shackle and the key then gingerly touched them. They made her fingers itch as though her magic was pulling away from the enchanted metal. "Garret, I don't like this. What if you're wrong about Leon?"

He downed the last of his tea and stood. "I'll be fine, Margot. I promise."

She watched him go with a frown, then pressed Samson's journal against her chest as she whispered to the now silent room, "That's an empty promise these days, Garret, and you know it."

None of them were fine and they wouldn't be, not until they had cure for corruption and Evard was dead in the ground ... Maybe not even then.

Mealtimes were always loud at Del Harol, but her brother was probably the loudest. He was telling Aveline about an altercation he'd had with a merchant when he was last in Osmar. Some misunderstanding about a turkey and a box of goose-fruit.

Nea walked over, hiding her yawn behind her gloved wrist and nearly spilling the cup of tea she was carrying. She paused when she reached the table, glancing at where Aveline and Ivan sat with Grace and Niall, then at the two empty seats across the table from where Margot and Molly were sitting.

"Garret not up yet?" She moved to one of the empty chairs. "That's not like him."

Molly glanced at Margot then at Nea, who tilted her head slightly in silent question.

"He didn't tell you?" Molly asked.

"Tell me what? I haven't seen any of you since I left Father's study last night."

Margot pushed her eggs around her plate. "He's gone to check on things at Fort Braemar."

Nea's hand knocked her cup as she stood, sploshing the peppermint-scented liquid across the tabletop. "What about the finder? The second he leaves the boundary she'll be able to lead Leon straight to him."

"I offered to go with him, but he turned me down. I imagine he didn't tell you because *you* wouldn't take no for an answer." Molly ended her sentence by taking a large bite of her heavily buttered bread. "That, and you're a magnet for trouble," she said through the mouthful.

"When did he leave?" Nea looked like she was going to make a run for the door.

"Nea, sit down and eat something. He wanted you to stay here as you are most likely Leon's main target. And, the reason he left without telling you is because I told him to ... Don't look at me like that," Margot added as Nea closed her gloved fingers on the tabletop. They had all agreed that covering Nea's corruption with the glove was the safest course of action. "Nea, he'll be fine. Besides, I have a job for you."

"You do?"

Margot nodded. "Come to your father's study after breakfast and I'll show you."

When they entered Niall's study, Margot directed Nea to the desk. The pile of books Garret had been working his way through was still there. She pulled out the journal he had given her last night and handed it to Nea.

"Have you had a good look at the blank pages?"

Nea's attention was suddenly taken by something near the window; a strange niggle in the source that Nea had explained was Declan. She tilted her head then turned back to Margot. "Not really."

"Does your keen-sense still work with that shackle on?"

"Barely. It almost feels like everyone is a warden, like I'm feeling your magic through water or over a long distance." She removed the gloves and worked the fingers of her afflicted hand. "Why are you curious about the pages?"

"I think Samson may have been trying to hide something. The residual magic clinging to the journal is almost too strong to simply be the lingering impression of Samson's keen." She couldn't keep the eagerness from tone.

One of Nea's eyebrows lifted then a smile spread across her lips. "You realise you just sounded just like me."

Margot laughed.

"But what makes you think there is something hidden here? I've never—" Her attention snapped to the window again. "Maybe. Well I was about to ask that but you interrupted." Her look of annoyance was ruined by her smile.

Margot crossed her arms. "The pages *feel* like they may be enchanted but I am not sure what type of enchantment it might be. I think this is a clue." She took the journal back and flipped to the entry that mentioned Morgestia.

Nea drew a breath and scanned the entry, frowning. "A Morgestia puzzle? I just assumed he was talking about the impossibility of finding a cure, but it certainly could have been a clue or a code. Is there anything else that stands out as strange?" She frowned at Declan. "I don't—seal bride?" She snapped her fingers. "Why would that be relevant?"

"You know better than anyone, my dear, that legends always bear some relevance." They both turned as Niall spoke, a book balanced open on his palm as he entered the room. "Seal bride? Let's see. 'Ten thousand miles and the waters between us have washed me from your heart.'"

"I used to tell Declan this story all the time." Aveline came out from behind Niall and moved to the daybed. "'But I will not give up on you for as long as the stars turn in the endless expanse of night. I shall pluck the eye from the shore widow and carve a token of second sight to follow your path from this world to the next.'"

"A seer stone! What if you need a seer stone to read the pages?" Nea jumped up. "Do you have any, Father?"

Niall shook his head. "Unfortunately, no. I did have a genuine one a long time ago, but Sophia took it with her when she left."

"Declan had an entire basket of them on his desk at Loch Bastien. I'm not sure they were real though; they didn't feel quite right." Nea glanced surreptitiously at the window. "My guess would be he was trying to manufacture them for whatever reason."

Margot remembered the stone Garret had, the way the light seemed to bend oddly around its surface and the shifting feeling that clung to it. She glanced at the spot Declan was standing, wishing she could see him, then at Nea. "I think Garret has one."

"Why do you need a seer stone?" Niall sat on the edge of his desk and flipped a few pages through his book, casting a sideways glance at Aveline as she lounged on the daybed, her fingers playing idly with the tassels on the woven blanket hanging over the arm.

Margot took the journal and handed it to Niall. "These blank pages at the end—we think they might be under some kind of enchantment."

Niall placed his book aside and flipped through the pages, mumbling to himself, then he snapped it shut and handed it back to her. "You may be right."

"We may be right? You have nothing else to add? No kernels of wisdom? No, 'Well done, you figured out the thing I have been waiting for you to figure for a week'?" Nea folded her arms.

"You're hardly children anymore. I doubt you need me to pat you on the back and say well done. How's that corruption going?" He pinned Nea with a look.

She rubbed her arm. "Fine. Kind of like I have a nest of angry hornets in the back of my head, but it's nothing I can't endure."

"Hector used to say that." When Margot and Nea looked at her, Aveline added, "Declan's father. He's the reason Declan started looking for a cure in the first place." She studied her hands as she folded them in her lap. "He used to say, 'Don't fret, Avie, I can endure it.' And he did. For a while. Then one night I woke to Garret's worried face and I knew Hector had lost his battle. I think that's when Declan decided he would find the cure or ... die trying." Her voice wavered.

Nea moved to Aveline's side. "I am sure Molly or Grace can help Margot here." She started to pull her gloves back on. "How about you and I take a walk. I think we will both benefit from it." There was something about the way she said it that allowed the old Nea to shine through just for a moment.

Aveline glanced at Niall, who nodded. "I personally would like to look at more of Declan's notes; that boy had a brilliant mind, if not a little cluttered."

Niall investigated the pile of books on the desk, pulling one out and taking it to the recently vacated daybed. Margot stared at the door Nea and Aveline had just exited through. She understood why Garret had gone to Braemar but he could have decided to leave *after* they had figured out they needed his seer stone. To think it had been right there last night. She could have read those concealed pages then and there and already been working on the cure.

CHAPTER TWENTY-EIGHT

GARRET

When Garret guided his borrowed horse through the main gate at Fort Braemar, Harry came out of the stable, wiping his hands on a grimy piece of cloth before tucking it into the belt of his leather apron. He took hold of the mare's reins as Garret dismounted and called over his shoulder to Thomas, who came running, a litter of brindle puppies bounding after him.

"She'll need to be walked to cool down," Harry said as he handed the reins to Thomas. He turned to Garret and asked, "Where's the horse from? I can see that she's returned."

"Del Harol. Do you know where I might find the Prince or Emil?"

"The Prince is away on business with Alric but Emil should be in the south field."

Garret nodded his thanks then headed off to find Emil.

As he drew near the field, he could hear the grunts and cheers of a sparring match and rolled his shoulders. He hadn't had much chance to spar since they had left the fort. It wasn't like he could have asked Nea to go up against him; she'd hardly last five minutes. She wasn't exactly built for martial combat. She was resourceful though, and used whatever she had on hand, including her own teeth if need be. Not to mention she was tenacious, and brave, and—he paused mid-stride and shook his head.

"Garret?" a voice called out and Haley came jogging over, her chin-length hair bouncing. "It is you!" She skidded to a stop in front of him. "Are you on your own?" She leant around him as though looking for someone.

"Nea's at Del Harol."

"I wasn't just referring to Nea." She grinned impishly and elbowed him in the ribs before heading back to the sparring men.

As Garret and Haley neared the scuffed ground that marked the outside of the makeshift boxing ring, Emil collided with Harvey. They traded a flurry of blows almost too fast to follow. Emil's shoulder dipped and Garret had been on the receiving end of the next move often enough to know what was coming. Harvey fell for the feint and Emil flipped him. He hit the ground with a satisfying thump and grunted as Emil stood over him.

"Do you yield?"

"Never!" Harvey moved quick as a snake and grabbed hold of Emil's legs, yanking them to knock him off balance.

Emil crashed to the ground beside Harvey and let out an "oof" of breath.

Garret moved over and offered them both a hand up.

"Two against one, hey, Garret?" Harvey grinned, slightly breathless.

"You both look like you could use a rest."

"Is Nea with you?" Emil rolled his wrist a few times before taking the water skin Haley offered him.

Garret shook his head and, at Emil's look of alarm, said, "She's fine. She's at Del Harol."

"Del Harol? How in the world did you two get there so fast?"

Remembering the portal, Garret suppressed a shudder. "I'd rather not talk about that. How's that leg?"

Emil shrugged. "It's fine. Plus, I've got a nice new scar out of it." He took a drink from the water skin. "You think Maurice has that meal ready yet?" he asked Harvey.

"Maurice is still here?" Garret couldn't believe he'd forgotten to warn Alric about Maurice and his allegiance to Evard.

"Of course, he's—hey where are you going?" Harvey called after him as Garret took off towards the fort kitchens.

Maurice was sitting with his feet up on a barrel when Garret entered the room. He looked up and uncertainty touched his features before a sneer chased it away. He took a swig of the flask he was holding and then ran his tongue along his teeth. "Welcome back, Commander. Anything I can get you?"

Garret leant against the large table in the centre of the room. "I thought you might have run."

"Run? Why would I do that?" He replaced the lid on his flask, his fingers shaking slightly.

Garret rolled his lip between his teeth the way Nea did when she was calculating her options. "Oh? So, you didn't betray your lord's trust, drug his entire household, and kidnap one of his guests?"

Maurice's nostrils flared. "I'm not the one who betrayed my *king*." He stood. "After what that doe-eyed little whore did at Kalhanna, I hope Leon gave her what she deserved."

The muscles along Garret's jaw tightened.

"Got nothing to say to that?"

"You realise Evard is responsible for what happened at Kalhanna? He gave the order to purge the college—"

"The *king* did what was necessary for the greater good. My poor Clara would still be alive, and that grey-haired bitch would be in the ground where she belonged, if your order had done their job right in the first place." His speech was slurred, and he swayed slightly. "Tell me I'm wrong." He took a step towards Garret.

Garret crossed his arms. "You're wrong."

Maurice let out a noise like an angry cat and threw himself at Garret, who stepped out of the way and with one fluid movement, grabbed him by the back of the neck. He pinned him forward over the edge of the table, pressing his cheek to the scarred wood. Maurice twisted and Garret wasn't fast enough to block the elbow that slammed into his ribs. He grunted and pushed Maurice's face harder against the table.

Maurice struggled and kicked out, the heel of his boot smashing into Garret's shin. He gritted his teeth but his grip on Maurice slipped. Sensing his opening, Maurice kicked again and as Garret shifted to avoid the strike, he lost his grip entirely. Maurice scrambled away and put the table between them. "I'm going to enjoy watching you hang. The Prince might have everyone scrambling about preparing defences, but it won't help. He's out of time. *You're* out of time."

Garret edged around the table. "It's not too late, Maurice. Evard won't care about you. You're just a pawn like the rest of us—easily disposed of once you've outlived your usefulness."

"You're wrong." Maurice grabbed a long knife and held it out.

"You do realise that Evard considers his own son disposable? You think the cook from some forgotten fort in the mountains is going to fare any better?"

"The Prince is a mage-fucking fool," Maurice growled.

"Recreational activities aside, he is still Evard's heir. His flesh and blood." As he spoke, Garret had been edging closer to Maurice, not taking his eyes off the knife as it quivered in Maurice's hand.

The moment the table wasn't between them anymore, Garret charged forward. The knife flashed through the air and hissed a shallow line along the back of Garret's arm as he grabbed Maurice around the throat and used his momentum to pin the cook against the wall.

Maurice kicked, trying to knock Garret's feet out from under him as he swung the knife again. Garret blocked the strike, smashing Maurice's hand against the brickwork and forcing him to drop the blade. He increased the pressure on Maurice's throat until the other man's hand came up, trying to pull the arm pinning him away.

"Yield and I'll let you breathe again."

Maurice snarled and started to slump. He wasn't as tall as Garret and his toes were frantically trying to find purchase on the ground. He made a gargled sound and Garret released the pressure on his neck marginally.

"I yield." He gasped again.

Garret kicked the knife away. "I'm going to release my grip. I suggest you don't try anything stupid."

Slowly, Garret released him and took a step back. Maurice brought his hand up and rubbed his neck, wincing as he cleared his throat.

Maurice's fist thudded into Garret's jaw and he staggered backwards. Maurice followed him, trying to gain the upper hand. As Garret's back met the table, Maurice pushed his weight against him, his hands coming around Garret's throat.

Garret gripped Maurice's hands as he attempted to bring his knee up between their bodies and kick the other man away.

"Alright, old chap, off you get." Harvey's voice sounded, and Maurice was hauled away from Garret by the back of his belt. "Now I know Garret makes a good punching bag, but there's a time and place for that sort of thing." He gave Maurice a shove towards Emil, who was standing just inside the door, before offering Garret a hand up. "Alright there, Garret?"

Garret rubbed the dull ache in the back of his head where it had hit the table and examined the blood that was staining his sleeve from the shallow cut. "I'm good."

"Care to enlighten us as to the reason for this little wrestling match?" As Harvey spoke, Maurice squirmed in Emil's grasp, but the fight seemed to be going out of him. Garret still wouldn't trust him as far as he could throw him.

"I would certainly like to know why you and my cook were having a brawl in the kitchen." Alric stepped into the room, followed by Leith.

"He helped Leon drug everyone and smuggle Nea out."

Alric's eyebrows lifted. "Is that true, Maurice?"

"Of course not. The commander's gone mad. Most likely his mind has been addled by that bitch in the south wing."

Alric met Garret's eye and he shook his head in response before turning his attention to Leith, and saying, "It's likely Maurice has been sending intel back to Evard the entire time you've been here."

"Maurice?" Alric drew a long breath.

The cook's lip curled as he met Garret's gaze. "That grey-haired whore deserved everything she got. I'm just sorry Leon was the one who got to have all the fun."

Leith made a noise in his throat and his fist flew into Maurice's jaw, knocking his head back against Emil's shoulder.

Maurice's spat then probed his tongue along his now split lip. "Touched a nerve did I, *Your Highness*? I bet she's a real—"

Maurice flinched as Leith lifted his fist again but Garret put himself between them and pressed a hand against the centre of Leith's chest. "Easy now."

"Get him out of here," Alric said to Emil then he turned his attention to Garret. "Welcome back, Commander. I apologise for this unpleasantness. If I had known—"

Garret lifted a hand to stop him. "The fault is mine. I should have sent word about Maurice when Nea told me."

Alric nodded. "It would have been appreciated, but I shouldn't have been so blind to the signs."

Leith rubbed the knuckles of the fist he'd used to hit Maurice. "We probably should get Colin and his men settled, then call a meeting," he said.

"Right you are, Your Highness," Alric said before turning to Garret again. "You might want to get cleaned up and have that arm looked at. I'll have Charles summon Janey and draw you a bath." He started to follow Leith. "When you're ready, we'll convene in the dining hall."

Garret eased himself into the hot bath. He was careful to keep his freshly bandaged arm out of the water, lest he undo Janey's handiwork. The cut was mostly superficial and would heal well enough given time, but one end had required several stitches. He rested his head against the lip of the tub and closed his eyes as the water soothed the aches that his scuffle with Maurice had surfaced.

A knock at the door made him sit forward with a frustrated sigh.

"I don't care if you're naked, Garret. I'm coming in," Leith said as the door opened, and he stepped into the room.

Leith normally appeared put together, his hair neat and his chin clean-shaven. But right then, he looked almost as rough as Garret with a week's worth of stubble and his blond waves in disarray. Garret hadn't noticed earlier, but there was a seriousness to his features that hadn't been there before. Almost like he had aged a decade over the last few weeks.

"Mother's tits, you look like you haven't slept in a month," Leith said as he took up a perch on a bench at the side of the room.

"I could say the same for you." Garret rested his head back against the lip of the tub again. "Margot mentioned you were here, but she didn't go into many of the details. Just something about a disagreement with your father."

Leith let out a bark of laughter. "I would say disagreement is the polite way to put it." He drummed his fingers on his knee. "He decided I was asking too many questions and had my *darling* wife use her power to *subjugate* me."

"If he made Catriona use her powers, then how—"

Leith pulled a small medallion out of his shirt. It was the same rose gold of bind-shackles, its edges notched and worn as though it had had many owners before Leith. "Nea gave this to me the last time ... before she disappeared. She said it would protect me. I didn't really believe her. But I kept it anyway because it reminded me of her. It did work though, in the end." He licked his lip. "Is she here?"

"No, she's safe though. What exactly did you do to rile Evard up enough that he thought turning you into a thrall was a good idea?"

"I questioned his sanity," Leith replied dryly. "I spent so much time away, I hadn't realised how bad things were getting here. Or maybe I always knew; I just didn't want to believe it."

Something had definitely changed in the last few weeks. It was about time.

"There's no sense dwelling on what should have been. Margot taught me that." Leith's voice was so quiet that Garret glanced sideways at him. He was looking at his fingers, his nail tracing the cuticle at the base of his thumb. "Nea would say mistakes are important because they remind us we are only human. They are both right, but if I had been honest with myself, I could have saved Fengate. Instead, I ran like a filthy dog with his tail between his legs."

Okay, Garret had heard enough of Leith's self-pity spiral. He sat forward, causing the water to slosh in the tub. "Pull your head out of your arse. You made a mistake; you didn't trust your instincts, but you're still breathing, and as long as you can breathe, you can fight."

Leith stared at him, unblinking. "You know, most people don't talk to me the way you do."

"If you would rather I spare your delicate feelings, Your High—"

"No. No, definitely not." He grinned and shook his head. "It's refreshing."

A short sharp knock made them both turn to the door. "Ryan and Jasper are back, and they've brought half a town with them." Emil's voice announced through the wood. "You might want to get out to the courtyard."

Garret stepped out of the tub and wrapped a towel around his waist as Leith made for the door.

"Ah, sorry, Leith. I thought Garret was in there," Emil said.

Leith pointed over his shoulder with his thumb. "We were just catching up. Shall we meet him outside?" He stepped into the hall beside Emil and closed the door.

The courtyard was full of people, mostly keen-less but a few wardens and mages were scattered amongst them. Garret started to make his way to Jasper and Ryan, who were standing to one side talking, when Haley went barrelling past him. She threw herself on Ryan, causing him to stagger back a few steps. Garret hid his chuckle behind his hand as he stepped up beside Jasper, who was shaking his head at the pair of them.

"Oh sure, Hales. I'm fine too, thank you for asking; it's not like we shared a womb or anything." He mocked a scowl and Haley punched his arm lightly.

"I was worried about you too, you big idiot."

Ryan's cheeks burned with colour and he cleared his throat as he turned to Garret. "Garret."

"Alright there, Ryan?"

Ryan nodded. "Better now we've reached the fort. Things are not good west of the capital."

"I've heard some of it, but it would be good to get a first-hand account. Do you know why Evard attacked Fengate?"

"He was looking for something," Jasper responded.

"Looking for something?" Evard had also been looking for something at Dunhold—Nea hadn't revealed what she knew about it and with everything that had happened since, he hadn't exactly had time to ask her.

"Or someone," a voice behind Garret said, cutting off Jasper's reply.

He turned to see a woman with eyes so dark brown they were almost black. Her magic lightly caressed the back of his mind, seductive fingers seeking to override every inhibition. He cleared his throat and shut the magic down with a gentle brush of suppression.

Her full lips pulled into a delicate pout and she coiled a lock of deep chestnut hair around her finger.

"Penny?" Leith said from behind her, and a wide smile crossed her features as she turned to face him.

"Leith, you look as dashing as ever." She kissed each of his cheeks. "Is Nea with you? I need to speak with her urgently."

"You know Nea?" Garret asked.

"She's an old friend." She looked like a cat sizing up its next meal as she turned back to face Garret. "I'm Penny."

"Garret," he said. "You said Evard was looking for someone."

"Indeed, I did." She licked her lip. "He will find his target is not so easily smoked out though."

"Who was he looking for?" Leith asked, and Penny's dark eyes flicked to him.

"He was looking for me."

"Why?" Garret crossed his arms.

"Because I stole something from him, and he needs it back." She held her hand out. There was a whorl of gold staining the centre of her palm. "Now, where can I find Nea?"

Garret shared a look with Leith.

Penny rolled her eyes. "You know this whole macho mind-speak thing you are doing is only going to delay the inevitable. I mean her no harm. *You* should know that better than anyone." She directed the last bit at Leith.

Leith frowned. "She's—"

"Prove you mean her no harm, then I'll tell you where to find her," Garret said, cutting Leith off.

Penny's smile became triumphant. "What would you have of me?"

"What did you steal from Evard?"

Reluctance brushed her features before she schooled her expression again. "Technically, I didn't steal it. Nea did. I'm just holding onto it for her."

Garret crossed his arms.

She held her hand out, the one with the golden mark, and Garret took hold of it. He traced the mark with his index finger, studying the subtle brush of magic that was coming from it—magic that was not Penny's mind magic, or really like anything he had ever felt before, and yet a flicker of familiarity stirred at his core. As he inspected the mark, Penny's keen brushed his mind again, stirring images of Nea to the surface, and he pulled his mental walls up, blocking her out.

"It was worth a try," she said. "This mark is what Evard wants. It's a soul, or a fragment of one. I'm not sure whose, but Nea was adamant that he not get it."

"Why would Father need a soul?"

"Nea didn't say exactly, but she did say it was important, and I trust her judgement." She gave Leith a pointed look. "She has never given *me* a reason to doubt her."

Leith's cheeks coloured and he looked away at where Emil and Harvey were laughing with Jasper.

"Look, I understand that you want to protect her." She took a step towards Garret and the heady scent of roses tickled his nose. "I know there is nothing I can say that will get you to trust me and you're not one to be easily wooed by a pretty face. But maybe I can show you." She reached for him, but he took a step back. "To show you, I will need to touch you."

"Show me what exactly?"

"My true intentions."

He let out a huff. "Fine."

When she shifted forward and reached for his face again, he didn't retreat. Her fingers were cool as they brushed over his cheeks and laced into his hair. Her palms pressed lightly against his temples and his vision blurred as her keen stirred; it wasn't like cloying fingers trying to burrow into his mind, rather like an alluring smoothness across the back of his neck, pulling him out of his own body.

The world faded and a host of emotions not his own overwhelmed him. Then he heard Penny's voice as though it was coming from all around him. He couldn't make out the words but he could feel the sincerity; she honestly didn't mean any harm. Then everything grew silent, the kind of silence that was thick and pressing and made him want to shift his shoulders.

"You can open your eyes."

He hadn't realised he had closed them but when he did open them, they were standing in some kind of repository. The wall across from them bore a mosaic showing the dove and mistletoe of the Kalhanna crest. Voices sounded and then Nea came running around the corner followed by Penny. He glanced sideways at the Penny that stood next to him.

"It's a memory; my memory." She pressed a finger to her lips and pointed to where the two women had stopped in front of the mosaic wall.

Nea's clothes were torn and covered in soot and blood. Her hands trembled as they clenched and unclenched by her sides and there was something about the set of her shoulders, the way she refused to really meet Penny's eyes. She was broken, more broken then he'd ever seen her. He swallowed.

"It's a blank wall, Nea," Penny said.

Nea held up a hand and pressed it to the mosaic, leaving a smear of blood on the white tiles that made the body of the dove. A shadow of her keen stirred the air and the wall grated away from her touch to reveal an alcove, just large enough to house a thin pedestal on which sat a large glass flask. Nea delicately retrieved the flask from the pedestal and brought it out into the light. It contained a twisting orb of golden smoke.

"You know you don't have to do this; I can find someone else." Nea gingerly cradled the base of the flask in her hands as she met Penny's eye for the first time.

Penny looked at the flask and licked her lip but nodded. "I know you wouldn't have asked me if it wasn't important."

The relief that crossed Nea's features brought a lump to Garret's throat. Here she was, with only one ally in the repository under Kalhanna, and judging by the state of her the attack had already happened. Her friends were laying above them, dead. He'd learned enough from Margot to know that few people she trusted had listened to her in the lead-up to the attack. But Penny was there, standing by her without question.

He glanced at the woman beside him as she watched the scene unfolding. She met his gaze before nodding back to the scene where Nea had pulled the stopper from the flask and pressed the mouth of it to Penny's palm. They both dropped to their knees as a web of gold raced up Penny's arm and her eyes began to glow.

Nea muttered something under her breath that he couldn't catch and her keen stirred, then the gold receded to the small spiral it was now.

"Are you alright?" Nea asked a ashen-faced Penny.

Both women were panting but Penny nodded slowly. "That was something else. So many thoughts that weren't my own." She blinked and rubbed her hand over her forehead.

"I'm sorry. I tried to keep it under control, but it was stronger than I was expecting. It's trapped now though and can only be released by my magic." She got to her feet and held out a hand for Penny.

"Where are we going now?"

Nea shook her head. "*We're* not going anywhere. You should go to Osmar; Gendry and Wren will take care of you."

"If you're not coming to Osmar with me where are you going?" Penny placed her hand on Nea's arm, but she shook her off.

"South. That's all you need to know for now."

Penny glanced at the ceiling above them and frowned. "Nea—" She cut herself off and bit her lip as she met Nea's gaze. "Be careful." Her voice broke as she pulled Nea into a hug.

"Okay, we've seen enough," Penny said as the memory faded and they were standing in the courtyard at Fort Braemar once more. She let go of him and took a step back.

Garret rubbed the back of his neck. "You were at Kalhanna during the attack."

She shook her head. "I arrived too late. After we got the soul out of the repository, Nea let me help her shroud the dead, then we parted ways. I went to Osmar as she suggested, and I didn't see her again until just over a year ago when she sought refuge with our friends, Wren and Gendry. She said she was just passing through and needed a safe place to rest for a few days, but I think she was checking on me."

"I am still not sure I trust you, but it appears Nea does. Or at least she did."

"I'd like you to know that, aside from Nea, you are the only person alive I have allowed inside my head. If that helps."

Garret rubbed his finger along his lip, then nodded slowly. "She's at Del Harol."

"Then that is where I am going. Thank you, Garret." She turned to walk away, then stopped and looked back over her shoulder. "One last thing—you might want to strengthen your defences given that Evard has an army on its way here." She sauntered away without another word.

"Well, she's something else," Garret said.

Leith was watching her go with a strange expression on his face. "Penny? She's certainly *different* and perhaps a little unpredictable."

Different and unpredictable sounded like a certain violet-eyed necromancer who kept creeping into Garret's thoughts. He wondered how she was fairing with the corruption, if she and Margot were getting any closer to a cure.

He shook his head. He needed to focus on what was happening here at the fort, and the first order of business was getting the refugees settled and out of the way. Second was to send scouts out to verify what Penny had said about Evard's army. And third, he needed to have a good look at the fort's defences.

He clapped Leith on the shoulder. "Let's go see Alric. It appears we may have a battle to prepare for."

CHAPTER TWENTY-NINE

MARGOT

Margot placed a blanket over Nea as she dozed on the daybed in Niall's study. She hadn't been sleeping well; she said it was just her preoccupation with figuring out the cure, but Margot knew better. She'd watched Nea sleep, the way her eyelids fluttered erratically, the whispered murmurs and twitching. Whether it was memories or nightmares, it was clear that Nea's dreams were not pleasant.

Nea murmured and rolled over, her hand dropped off the side of the daybed and the book clutched in her fingers fell onto the floor. Margot bent and picked it up, a sheet of parchment coming loose and fluttering to the ground. Recognising Garret's handwriting, she picked it up and after a moment's deliberation, scanned the contents. She walked over to Molly and lowered herself to the floor to sit next to her.

"What's that?"

"A letter from Garret."

Molly's eyebrows rose slightly. "What's it say?"

Margot handed the letter to Molly, who read it quickly and sucked a breath through her teeth. "When do you think she was going to tell us?"

Margot folded her arms.

"What? It's important. If Evard takes Braemar then the rest of us can kiss our arses goodbye."

"Garret doesn't seem concerned about that though—or at least he doesn't want Nea to be concerned about it. More, he's worried about the intentions of Penny."

"Do you know her?"

Margot bit the inside of her cheek to stop the nervous chuckle that threatened to rise. "I know her."

Something must have shown on her face because Molly gave her a look and asked, "Just how well do you *know* her?" There was no hint of jealousy—just a curious playfulness that made Margot's cheeks burn.

"Rather well. She's a mind mage and an old friend of Nea's. I can understand Garret's concern. Penny can be a bit ... assertive, for lack of a better word."

Molly chuckled and touched her lips lightly to Margot's cheek. "As entertaining as watching Nea sleep is, I promised Sonia and Grace we'd run through a few drills." She got to her feet and picked her crossbow up from beside the desk. "I don't want to get rusty if Evard's going to be breathing down our necks." She hefted the bow and checked the sights. "If you need us, we'll be in the east field."

The sound of the door snapping shut caused Nea to stir. She sat up and looked at Margot as she covered her mouth to hide her yawn.

"This is not like you, Nea—falling asleep in the middle of the day. Are you sure you're alright?"

"I'm just tired. Most likely because my body is constantly fighting the corruption." She rubbed a hand down her dishevelled braid.

"I thought the bind-shackle had made the corruption dormant again."

"As dormant as it gets." Her gaze dropped to the letter in Margot's hand. "So, you are aware that Penny is on her way here then?"

"Yes, and that Evard has plans to attack Braemar." She held the letter out.

Nea took it, her fingers lightly brushing over the text before she folded it and tucked it inside the cover of the book she had been reading: Vanasha's *The Deathborn Phenonium.*

They didn't talk much after that but the silence that fell between them wasn't awkward. It was companionable, much like it had always been. Nea thumbed carefully through the pages of her book, making small notes or pausing to discuss something with Declan's ghost. It was strange to think Declan was there with them, and hearing only Nea's side of the conversation could be incredibly confusing at times, but it still brought a bittersweet smile to Margot's lips knowing he was not completely gone.

As the light steaming through the windows started to dim, Niall came in to check on them. "Look who I found." He indicated the willowy brunette who followed him into the room. Her dark chestnut hair shone even in the dim light and the look in her in deep brown eyes was one that suggested she could give you anything you desired. All you had to do was ask.

"Penny." Nea stood slowly.

"You're a hard girl to find these days." Penny's smile changed into one of warmth as she stepped around Niall and pulled Nea into a hug. No sooner had she released Nea, then it was Margot's turn to be swept into an embrace that smelt of roses at the height of summer. "It is good to see the pair of you together again. Niall, do you still keep tea-making supplies in here? I could *kill* for a cup."

You could never be exactly sure that Penny was joking.

"Same place as always. I'll let the three of you get reacquainted," he said and stepped out again.

Penny busied herself making the tea. The scent of jasmine soon filled the room and Nea made a face.

"I haven't forgotten," Penny said as she measured peppermint leaves into the third cup before covering them with hot water.

"Not that it isn't good to see you, but why are you here, Penny? I thought you had no intentions to leave Osmar," Nea said as she sat delicately on the daybed once more.

"I never said I had no intentions to leave. I was on my way to visit my family when Evard made things personal." A bitterness touched the corners of her mouth and she hid it with a sip from her cup.

"Your family—"

"Are safe. But I am sure you've heard about what happened at Fengate."

Nea nodded.

"Wait, how did you get tangled up with Evard?" Margot was sure she was missing something.

Penny looked over the lip of her cup at Nea. "You haven't told her?"

Nea removed her glove and showed Penny the corruption marks. "I've been a bit preoccupied."

Penny sat forward, spilling a few drops of her tea. "Is that corrupt—"

"What haven't you told me?" Margot cut her off.

Nea bit her lip and looked at Declan. "Before Kalhanna, Evard was trying to access the source."

"Leith told me that much," Margot said.

Nea frowned at the mention of Leith. "How much did he tell you?"

"Not a great deal, just that you suspected his father was playing around with things he shouldn't and it caused a disagreement between the pair of you."

"That's an understatement, but yes. I found out Evard was trying to manipulate the source, specifically in an attempt to access the Between." Nea took a sip of her tea. "You know he always had a fascination with necromancers. He's not alone in that. Many people who fear death have an at times morbid fascination with it. But Evard's wasn't a harmless fascination—it was an obsession." She traced the rim of her cup with her finger. "I didn't think it was a problem at first but then I found a text he had been studying. It was *old* magic. Magic that if it worked could bring down the barrier between worlds and damn us all. That was the first time I refused to help him but he seemed to accept that and things went back to normal ... or so I thought."

Nea let out a long breath and Margot wasn't sure she was going to continue but then she nodded to herself and glanced at the place Margot could feel Declan. "But then the cases of corruption started to increase and I learned he'd been performing experiments." She rubbed her fingers over her afflicted wrist. "That was when Tobias and Francesca got involved. They were concerned with the rise in corruption and the reports of mages who were going missing. When they came to me I told them everything I knew; what Evard was planning, how I intended to stop him. And for a while I managed to stall his plans. Until he figured out I was deceiving him and he threatened to burn Hartswood to the ground if I didn't comply. But I knew he was still missing a few crucial pieces to the puzzle. If I could just find them before he did then maybe I could sabotage his plans entirely. I wasn't fast enough. Evard realised what I was doing and then ..." Her breath hitched and she sat her cup aside with shaking hands. "Then ..."

Margot moved to crouch in front of her and placed her hands delicately on her knees. "You don't have to keep going."

Nea's eyes snapped to Margot's. They glittered with unshed tears which made them look like finely cut amethysts. They narrowed, darkening as they did so, and her next words were in a tone so cold it rose goose bumps on Margot's arms.

"Then I decided I would end Evard's madness or die trying."

"How did Leith take that?" Penny asked.

"I didn't tell him. We'd already been arguing about Evard. Leith accused me of being irrational, of letting Francesca cloud my judgement. By then it had become clear that no matter what, Leith's loyalties would always fall to his father. So when Evard cornered me I lashed out. I failed and then I ran. I knew Evard was planning an attack on Kalhanna; his earlier attempt to take control of the wardens had failed so he used the only available avenue left to him. There hadn't been a purge since the time of Eugenie but I still knew that was what he intended. My only hope was that I didn't arrive too late." She let out a gasping sob and pressed her face into her hands.

Margot slipped her arms around Nea's shoulders and they both slid to the floor. Nea's body trembled as she buried her face against the side of Margot's neck.

Penny cleared her throat and Margot looked at her over Nea's head. She placed her cup aside and the cloying sensation of her mind magic filled the air. It settled over Nea like a shroud and her sobs slowed to empty hiccups. Then with a last sniffle, Nea pulled back and gave Margot a watery smile.

"Kalhanna is where I came in," Penny said drawing both of their attention. "The problem with Evard's plan was ... is its complexity. Reweaving the fabric of the universe requires a certain number of pieces to be in place, as Nea has already mentioned. And the first of those pieces was a very specific soul stolen at the moment of its birth." She traced the golden mark on her palm with her index finger. "It's a shame that someone got there first and snatched it away from him."

"That's not possible. Is it?" Margot glanced at Nea, who nodded slowly.

"I told you it's *old* magic. Evard is playing around with things that we cannot even fathom—lost magics from before the creation of the colleges. That's why he has a fascination with necromancers and deathborn; and why we are seeing an increase in corruption."

"So that's a soul?" Margot stood and held her hand out and Penny placed hers on top, palm up. Margot traced the spiral with her finger. A gentle throb radiated from the mark, like a heartbeat, beating not quite in time with Penny's. And it contained magic ... strange magic that whispered in the back of her mind. "How did you ...?"

"With great difficulty."

"I thought necromancers were the only ones who could manipulate souls."

Nea settled back on the edge of the daybed. "Stealing is one thing; holding onto is another."

"Meaning?"

"Neither of us stole this soul. It was taken long ago and kept in the repository at Kalhanna. I took the phylactery that housed it and Penny agreed to be its guardian." She gave Penny a small smile. "It was a simple matter of removing the soul from the vessel and securing it to Penny." Now they were discussing the mechanics of the magic, all signs of Nea's breakdown were gone.

Ever since they were children, Nea had been good at hiding her vulnerability. Nonna used to say she was like a duck—all calm and cool on the surface but underneath everything was churning. Margot couldn't remember the last time she'd seen Nea break down like that—she didn't know if she'd ever seen it. Was it the impact of everything that had happened, which honestly would not be a surprise. Or was it a symptom of the corruption? Either way she needed to keep a closer eye on her. She rubbed her hands over her face then massaged her temples. "I can't even begin to make sense of this. So, in the grand scheme of things, where does the corruption come into it?"

"What Evard is attempting to do has been attempted before," Nea replied.

"During the time of Samson?"

"Exactly. I believe someone back then was playing around with magics they shouldn't have been. They loosened the chains binding the Shadow Man to his prison in the Between. Just enough that his influence could once again be felt in this realm, but not enough that he could leave the Between entirely. He uses corruption to enact that influence. That is why it acts like a type of possession and why once a mage gets corruption, they can't be cured. Their souls are stained by his touch." She rubbed the marks on her wrist.

"And deathborn?"

"Deathborn belong to him. Whether they are his descendants, children of a cursed bloodline, or something else entirely, they are intrinsically tied to the Shadow Man and his fate. Which is why they are such important pieces of the puzzle."

Penny stretched, and Margot gave her a curious look. She hadn't reacted at all to the casual talk of deathborn.

"Penny knows what you are. You told her." She failed to keep the barb of hurt from her voice. She couldn't believe Nea had confided something so serious in someone other than herself.

Nea opened her mouth but Penny cut her off. "I picked the information right out of her head the day I met her. Both she and Niall swore me to secrecy." She swept her chestnut hair back over her shoulder and her stomach growled. "Perhaps we could all use a break from this conversation. I'm thinking it's time for dinner."

Margot prodded the small flame under the glass flask and watched the liquid contained within begin to bubble. Talking to Nea had only opened up more questions, but Nea had assured her that curing corruption was still the most important focus for their time. Each mage who was corrupted was one step closer to Evard getting what he wanted. She added a handful of leaves to the flask and the liquid turned a dull pink.

Regardless of Nea's assurance, Margot still couldn't shake the feeling that things were spiralling out of their control. It was like one of those epic stories where ordinary people suddenly found themselves pawns of the gods. It was bigger than just a simple matter of stopping Evard and curing corruption. Could they ever just go back to how they were before? Could the world?

She added several small white flowers to the mixture and turned a small valve which allowed the steam to run through a series of coiled pipes, where it condensed and dripped steadily out into a small vial. She was weighing out a measure of animal fat when a knock disturbed her. After shutting off the valve again, she moved to the door and opened it. Nea was standing there, a haunted look in her violet eyes. She thrust the letter she was holding into Margot's hand.

"Evard is advancing on the fort. They don't stand a chance."

CHAPTER THIRTY

GARRET

Garret let out a long breath as he stared at the faces around him. They'd just received word that Evard's forces were marching for Braemar. It was going to be nearly impossible to hold the fort; maybe they should cut their losses and let Evard take it. But that would mean also giving him Amelia, and that could prove catastrophic.

"We're not just going to give him the fort without a fight, are we?" Emil asked, breaking the tension in the room.

Suddenly everyone was speaking at once, arguing with each other over numbers of fighters and refugees who couldn't fight. It would be a massacre. No, they couldn't just flee with their tails between their legs.

"Enough!" Garret didn't yell but there was enough authority in his voice that everyone suddenly shut up. He turned his attention to Leith. "You're the highest rank here. What do you think?"

Leith's cheeks flared as he blew out a breath. "This is not my area of expertise, Garret."

Yeah, well, it wasn't exactly Garret's either. He was combat-trained but not on this scale. His skills lay in small skirmishes, not open battles.

"Janey has a suggestion," Haley said, drawing Garret's attention to them where they sat side by side.

Janey's hands moved quickly as she signed, and Garret nodded in agreement. "You're right, Janey." He turned to Alric. "We should get Lady Vera and anyone else not fit for the fight out of here tonight. Janey and Haley can escort them to Del Harol. I am sure the college would accept them, and Nea and Margot are already there."

Alric looked at his wife. "Go prepare your maids."

Vera rose, one hand lightly on the swell of her stomach. She pressed a kiss to Alric's cheek then left the room.

"Right, and the refugees?" Leith asked. "The elderly and the children?"

"I'll go get them ready." Haley stood and Janey went with her.

Garret studied the map of the fort on the table in front of him. "If they breech this wall, then we are done for. Leith, have your men positioned along here."

They spent the next few hours laying out plans until Garret was satisfied that they could hold their own for as long as possible.

After helping Haley and Janey sort out the refugees and seeing them off, Garret moved up to his room and sat on the edge of the bed. He took the stone from Declan out of his shirt and rolled it around between his fingers. The magic it gave off was strange and twisting. It whispered across the back of his mind like it held all the secrets of universe. Dropping the stone, he fished out Nea's bracelet and gave it a squeeze. The cool keen clinging to it stirred in response and he drew a slow, steadying breath before nodding.

The odds might be stacked against them, but Nea wouldn't give up without a fight and Garret wasn't going to either.

Now all that was left to do was wait.

No attack came that night.

In the morning, Garret did a round through the courtyard to check on the barricades and general morale of those left at the fort. It was a modest force; nothing compared to Evard's. He caught up with Leith, who was playing a round of liar's dice with Emil, Harvey, and Ryan, but Garret was too on edge to join them himself.

He found Alric in his study, a bottle of liquor on the table in front of him next to a pile of balled-up parchment. Alric met his gaze and lifted the bottle, tilting it in Garret's direction by way of greeting before taking a swig.

"This wait is killing me," he said as he offered the bottle to Garret, who shook his head.

"I'd rather keep my wits."

"Suit yourself." Alric swallowed another mouthful then scowled at the crumpled papers. "How are you with heartfelt declarations?"

Garret took up the chair opposite him. "Heartfelt declarations?"

"I've been trying to write a letter for Vera ... in case we don't make it out of this, but I've never been good at all that emotional blather. I doubt telling her she's the most handsome and sensible woman I have ever met makes for an endearing correspondence." He cleaned the nib of his pen and then pulled out a fresh piece of parchment.

Garret touched the bracelet in his pocket. "I think she would appreciate candour in this situation. You should write as though you expect that Vera will be the only soul to read it."

"Candour?" Alric took a gulp from the bottle.

Garret nodded. "Be honest and be yourself. Tell her all the things you're terrified to tell anyone else. Bare your soul and admit exactly how shattered your world would be if she was no longer in it ... You can't remember what life was your like before she came along and you don't want to imagine it without her. The beat of her heart so perfectly matches yours that if it ever stopped beating it would be the death of you too." He sat back in the chair. "Tell her you're sorry you won't get to meet your child, that you regret you won't be there to support her through the dark times that are coming. Most simply of all tell her you love her. If you don't survive what is to come, no amount of pretty words are going to soften the blow but you can rest easy knowing you told her just how you feel."

Alric gave him an appraising stare that shifted into a wide grin. "Sounds like you are speaking from a place of experience. Is there some fair lass you should be penning a letter for?"

Garret rubbed the scar above his lip. He'd already written his letters last night—one for his family and one for Nea. It wasn't a declaration like Alric was implying but it had surprised him that of all the people he could have written to when he was facing down the prospect of his death, Nea had been the first to spring to mind. He told himself that it was *only* because they had spent so much time in each other's company over the last few weeks, but he knew that was a lie.

Alric cleared his throat and Garret's attention snapped to him. "Would you like a pen and a piece of parchment?"

"No. I've taken care of that already." He patted the pocket where the letters sat.

With a knowing smirk, Alric picked up his pen and a fresh piece of parchment. "Seventh time's the charm."

Once Alric had finished his letter, he followed along with Garret for another round of checking the defences and then they joined Leith and the others.

The waiting was almost unbearable.

By evening, Garret and Emil were sitting on the main wall, watching the field and road for signs of movement. Emil shifted uncomfortably beside him and he immediately understood why; there was a creeping wrongness that stained the night air. It nearly hid the steady rumble of magic that shook the wall as it tested the wards.

Dark shapes were moving across the field towards them, a line of soldiers closing with each passing moment. The wall shook again as the warded stones fought back against the magic that assaulted them. Garret lifted his arm to indicate to the other men farther along to be ready as he let his keen-sense out to check the wards. They were holding strong for now. He turned his attention back to the field as the hulking form of a catapult rolled into view.

"Move!" He gave Emil a shove as a ball of burning peat came hurtling towards the wall. The wards closest succumbed to the assault and the wall shuddered, nearly throwing them from their feet as they raced along it.

With a creaking boom, the stones gave under the magical assault and exploded inward, throwing them from the wall and scattering debris over the courtyard.

Breath wheezed through Garret's chest as he rolled onto his hands and knees. "Emil?"

Emil lifted a hand to indicate he was fine before he climbed to his feet. Garret's attention snapped to the hole in the outer wall as men leapt through the gap. His sword was in his hand in moments and it sang as it met the blade of one the first attackers. He dealt with the soldier quickly as a sickly coil of magic twisted through the air. Locating the mage, Garret charged towards her, slamming his suppression down as soon as he got close enough. A young warden leapt between Garret and the mage. He darted inside Garret's reach and the blade in his hand flashed in the moonlight. Garret danced backwards as the edge of the knife tugged against the armour at his side.

He brought his leg up and kicked the warden squarely in the stomach, knocking him back.

One opponent blurred into the next as the grey light of evening gave way to full night.

Firelight flashed off metal as two fighters met each other; he recognised Alric's considerable size. The man he was fighting was staggering backwards, holding a bleeding wound in his gut. Alric pressed his advantage as hot magic coiled through the air. Garret wasn't fast enough. The magic hit Alric and the mage twisted his hand, snapping Alric's neck.

As Alric's body hit the ground, Garret lunged, killing the mage with a quick clean blow. Charles rushed to Alric's side and a look of sheer hatred clouded his features. He picked up Alric's sword from where it had fallen and, with a blood-curdling roar, charged into a group of soldiers, tearing through them with brutal accuracy.

Jasper emerged from the fort. The massive doors were hanging opened in splinters and the tiles of the entryway were slick with blood. Jasper was holding a bleeding wound in his side; his keen stirred the hairs on the back of Garret's neck and there was a loud crack, then a thud as a solider behind Garret fell to the ground, his neck broken.

"Thanks."

"Don't mention it."

Garret pulled Jasper out of the way as another soldier bore down on them. He met the man's strike with a block that sent a quiver through his arms. Then he pushed, forcing the man back and stepping inside his defences to drive his fist into the man's nose.

"Garret, what are we going to do?" Jasper asked as they stood back to back. "We're losing ground. Alric's dead. Ryan is injured." He clenched his fist, his keen flaring white-hot for a moment. There was a wet gurgle behind Garret. He turned as the soldier fell, a trickle of blood between his rasping lips.

"Amelia?"

"Still secure but I don't know for how long. We always knew we couldn't win this one. How deep is that wound?"

Wound? Garret pressed his fingers to his side and they came away red. He wasn't even aware he had been struck. "It's fine." He cast an eye over the fight. He didn't want to relinquish the fort but Jasper was right; there was no way they were going to win this one.

"We should retreat while we can. Surely it's better that we live long enough to take this fight to Evard another day."

Garret flicked the blood from his sword and gave a resigned sigh. "Sound the retreat."

Jasper nodded and hurried away.

"I've been waiting for this."

Garret turned to face John.

"You can't hide behind the women this time." John jabbed his sword forward and Garret danced backwards. John kept pressing his advantage and Garret deliberately dropped his guard. When John took the opening, Garret spun out of the way and drove the heel of his palm into the centre of John's chest.

John staggered back, stunned. "I should have killed you back at the capital," he wheezed as he charged forward again, forcing Garret back with the fury of his strikes.

Garret blocked each blow, which only served to incense John more. Then the other warden gave him a clear opening. Garret's sword sung through the air before snagging against the slight resistance of John's forearm; the flesh and bone gave way. John's sword clattered to the ground as he dropped to his knees with a scream, gripping the stub where his hand had been.

Garret left John and did a sweep of the courtyard, looking for any of their men. Finding Harvey grappling with a soldier, he slammed his sword hilt into the back of the enemy's head. As his opponent dropped to the ground, Harvey glanced up and gave Garret a wide grin before he winced and lightly touched his hand to his ribs. Garret indicated Harvey follow him and they made a run for it.

✌

Garret and Harvey were hurrying through the undergrowth. A branch snapped loudly and they both drew their swords, whirling to face the sound. It was just Emil and several mages from the refugee group. There were a few with minor injuries, but no one looked too worse for wear.

"Any sign of the others?" Garret asked.

Emil shook his head. "Not yet. Are you both alright?"

"I've been better." Harvey sagged against a tree and winced. "I think I've got a couple of cracked ribs, but I haven't had time to stop and fully assess the damage. So try not to make me laugh." He gave a pained chuckle and pressed his hand to his side.

"I'm fine. A few bruises and scratches," Garret said as Emil's gaze dropped to the stain of blood at his side.

"Alric ..."

"I know. But we can dwell on the fallen later. We need to put as much distance between us and the fort as we can."

After a short while, they came across Harry, who had his arm in a makeshift sling and Thomas, who was carrying a pair of wriggling brindle puppies. "The fool of a lad wouldn't leave the bloody dogs," Harry said as he indicated the satchel slung over Thomas's shoulder which was making a series of whimpering sounds.

"Is that arm broken?" Garret asked.

Harry winced. "I think it's my collarbone, but it'll keep until we get to safety. Have you seen Charles?"

"I'm here." Charles stepped through the trees. He was covered in blood, though not much of it appeared to be his own. Behind him were a small group of men: a mixture of Alric's and Leith's, carrying a makeshift stretcher with a cloth-shrouded body. "Evard will pay for Alric's death, if I have to take the payment from his skin myself."

"Alric is dead?" Harry asked, his gaze moving to the body on the stretcher.

Garret nodded. "He didn't go down without a fight though—took a mage attacking from a distance to actually do it." He was angry that he hadn't been faster. Maybe if he had, Alric would still be alive.

A grim look crossed Harry's face but he nodded.

They all froze as crashing sounded in the trees nearby.

Jasper and Leith emerged with Ryan slung between them; the left sleeve of his shirt had been scorched off. The skin underneath was red and blistered from his wrist all the way to the side of his neck and face.

"We need to find somewhere safe so I can heal Ryan's burns. Everyone else will have to wait." Jasper's voice was strained, and Emil stepped forward to take over supporting Ryan. Jasper lifted Ryan's eyelid and then checked his breathing. "If I don't tend to him soon, I'm afraid we'll lose him."

Garret let out a huff of breath. He studied the grim faces around him. Had any of them realised what future they would face now that Amelia was in the hands of Evard? His only hope was that Evard wouldn't be able to break Niall's cage and set her free. He pushed the fear of what this defeat meant for them—meant for the world—down and focused on what was more important now. Survival. They couldn't stay here; dawn was approaching and they would be easier to find once daylight broke. And if they had any hope of defeating Evard, they needed to evade capture and reach Del Harol. With a resigned nod he opened his mouth to speak but became aware of a strange prickle in the source. It was a sensation he had felt before and he let his keen-sense out. There was another farther away and then another right at the edge of his senses. *Breadcrumbs.* He silently thanked Nea then started along the invisible trail, beckoning for the others to follow.

CHAPTER THIRTY-ONE

NEA

The grass was cool and damp along Nea's spine, the sun warm on the skin of her cheeks. Colours danced across the backs of her eyelids as she breathed slowly in and out again, letting her mind wander from the physical sensations and into the dark shapeless void. The shackle around her wrist prevented her from using her powers, but she could feel the Between just beyond her reach, edging away as she got closer.

She could also feel Declan beside her, his energy frantic as he paced, muttering under his breath in a vain attempt not to disturb her. She opened one eye to regard him and he gave her an apologetic smile.

"Have you thought about what will happen if it can't be cured?"

"It will eventually win, and I'll have to be eliminated."

His mouth formed a tight line. "I'm sorry—"

"Don't start that again. None of this is your fault. It's not really anyone's fault."

Declan flopped onto the grass next to her and ran his hands through his hair. "There is a small part of me that wonders what will happen to me when you die. Will I be stuck here unable to interact with anyone? Will I be able to cross over? Will I just cease to exist? I think that one scares me the most."

"You really think I'd die without making sure you were going to be okay too?" She lifted her grey fingers and wriggled them. The sunlight made the edges glow slightly purple.

"I—"

Pounding footsteps drew their attention as Sonia came running over. "Gloves on, Little Fox. We've got a situation in the main courtyard."

"Garret?" Nea sat and pulled on the gloves. Ever since they had received news of Evard's plans to attack the fort, she had been on edge.

Sonia shook her head. "No, but I thought you'd like to know."

Nea followed Sonia to the main entry of the college where a large group of people were milling around. Margot was checking them over for wounds and Molly was hovering nearby with both Grace and Aveline. Nea made a beeline for her father, who was talking with a warden she recognised from the safe house, and Janey.

As she stopped beside them, she glanced at the group of people before spotting Lady Vera. "Are all these people from Fort Braemar?"

Janey shook her head and the warden beside her, Haley, if Nea remembered correctly, said, "Some are, but a lot of them came from Fengate or farther afield. Garret wanted us to get safely out before the attack. He said High Mage Niall would grant us sanctuary."

"That's enough of that *High Mage* nonsense. Just Niall will suffice and certainly, you are all welcome here. Shall we see about getting everyone settled?"

The warden nodded and let Niall lead her away. Janey looked curiously at Nea, and then, without warning, gave her a quick hug, the same way she had when they were escaping the palace. She pulled back and patted Nea's shoulder, then smiled and wandered off after Niall and Haley.

Several days had passed since the refugees from Fort Braemar had arrived. Nea was trying to pay attention to Margot but she kept glancing out the window. Declan had assured her that Garret, Emil and most of the others were fine despite a few injuries. He'd also passed on the news that Alric was dead but Nea could do nothing with that until the group from Braemar arrived. It would be too hard to explain otherwise.

"Margot! We need all available healers at the gates. The rest from Fort Braemar have been sighted just beyond the wards," said a young healer.

Nea nearly beat Margot to the door. They hurried down the hallway and out into the courtyard. Emil and Charles were carrying a stretcher on which Ryan lay, the skin on the left side of his face and his whole arm covered in fresh pink burn scars.

"Oh, Ryan." Haley ran to the stretcher. He smiled meekly up at her. "What's wrong, Hales? Girls find scars attractive, right?" His voice was thin and tired.

"I'd punch you if you didn't look half-dead already."

Ivan and another mage took the stretcher from Emil and Charles, and moved Ryan into the shade so Margot could check him over.

"Alright, Nea?" Emil asked.

She nodded. "You?"

He shrugged. "A few new scars but I fared better than some of our number."

Harvey came over to them. "I think Emil might have slept through the fight in the stables." He chuckled and winced. "Better go and see Margot about these ribs. Jasper wore himself out on the more serious wounds." Harvey wandered towards Margot.

The next group of people to come through the gate were joined by a litter of puppies, who seemed to be following Thomas like he was their mother. Nea scanned the rest of the faces but aside from Harry, she didn't recognise any of them. A small contingent of soldiers were next, one leading a pony that was pulling a cart on which a blanket-covered lump lay. The soldier's mouth was a grim line and the men who walked either side of him wore the battle-stained uniforms of Alric's personal guard.

There seemed to be a long pause when no one else came through the gate, then Leith appeared with Jasper and Garret.

"Nea, your hair!"

Nea hadn't realised how tight her chest had gotten until Leith spoke, his shock at her darkened hair breaking through the tension.

Emil let out a chuckle.

"Alright, Nea?" Garret's gaze flicked to her gloved wrist.

"Doing better than you, by the look of things."

"Nea." Jasper gave her a nod of greeting then winced as he stepped around Leith to hobble over to Margot and the other healers.

"I had better go and find my father." Emil bid them goodbye and Garret glanced sideways at Leith.

"I'm sorry for everything," Leith said, at the same time as Garret said, "We need to talk."

Nea looked between them.

"You first," they said together then shared a look.

"Is it just me or did things just get really awkward?" Declan appeared beside Nea.

Garret glanced sideways at Leith then rubbed the scar above his lip. "I can wait ... I should check in with the others," he said before jogging away to catch up to Emil.

"Definitely awkward." Declan chuckled.

"Well—" Leith started but Nea cut him off.

"What are you doing here, Leith?" She crossed her arms.

"You know Margot asked me the exact same question when I showed up at Braemar?"

"And what did you tell her?"

"I can't stand by and let my father's madness continue," he said sombrely.

Bitter anger rose in the back of her throat and she pressed her lips together.

"I should have listened to you before Kalhanna."

"Yes, you should have." She turned to go and see if Margot needed help.

"Nea, wait." He caught her arm, his gaze dropped to the glove and a confused frown creased his brow. "Why are you wearing those? You hate the way gloves make your fingers feel."

"No. You are not allowed to come here and pretend that things are still okay between us. Not after you stood back and let your father purge Kalhanna. I trusted you and you abandoned me the one moment I needed you most."

Leith glanced at the people around them. "Perhaps this is a discussion for elsewhere."

"There is no discussion to be had. Not right now." She started to walk away again. The now familiar anger that was not entirely her own flooded her body. She was finding it was the hardest symptom of the corruption to control.

"I'm sorry, Nea."

She waved his apology away and stormed straight past Margot and into the college.

Nea found herself in the conservatory and sat on one of the benches, removing her gloves. The cool stone beneath her soothed her frayed nerves and slowly, her anger drained away. She let out a long breath then opened her eyes.

Declan was sitting across from her, a lazy smile on his lips. "You know, I thought Garret was the only one who treated Leith like a normal person. Mind you, I guess you have more cause for it, given you know each other *intimately.*"

Nea rolled her eyes. "You're lucky you're not corporeal right now, otherwise I would punch that smile off your face."

"You could certainly try." He chuckled. His attention flicked to the door as someone cleared their throat. "I might make myself scarce for a little while." He disappeared, and she turned her attention to Garret as he approached.

He winced as he sat across from her.

"Are you sure you're alright?" she asked.

"I'm fine."

She folded her arms. "You're forgetting I'm the queen of that lie. What's wrong with your side?"

"It's just a scratch."

"Bullshit."

He blinked at her.

"I may have been spending a bit too much time with Molly."

He smiled and shook his head. "I'm fine, really. It is just a scratch."

"Then you won't have any trouble showing me." She leant back on her hands.

With an exasperated sigh, he pulled his shirt up to show her the thin slice on his side.

She sucked a breath through her teeth and slipped off the bench to kneel in front of him. "Did you show this to Margot?"

"Not yet. She's a little busy."

He winced as she touched the skin around the wound. It felt hot and angry, but that that didn't concern her as much as the black marks that radiated out from the edges of the cut. "Have you had a good look at this?"

"I don't need to look at it. I can *feel* it."

She got to her feet and plucked a few leaves from the surrounding plants, muttering as she did so, "Mage bane and Mother's balm. That's what Declan was using before." She crushed them between her fingers, allowing the oils to mingle together. Her corruption marks burned and started to pull away from the skin where the leaves touched, but she ignored it as she returned to him. "Take your shirt off."

"Nea, I don't think rubbing some crushed-up leaves on it is going to help ... Okay, but I've seen that look on Declan's face, usually right before something exploded."

She chewed the inside of her cheek while she waited.

Garret pulled his shirt off and placed it on the bench beside him. He had a bandage around his forearm and a fading bruise over one side of his ribs. She stared at the seer stone hanging around his neck. That could wait though. The more pressing issue was the corruption.

Nea crouched in front of him. "This is going to hurt, but I promise that nothing will explode." She pressed the crushed leaves to his wound, holding her hand over them to keep them in place.

Garret gritted his teeth and the muscles under Nea's hand clenched, but he didn't move away. Instead, he covered her hand with his own and met her gaze as he drew a series of slow, deep breaths.

After a few moments, he relaxed, relief flooding his features, and Nea pulled her hand back to check the skin under the leaves. It was still red and inflamed, but the black marks were gone. She sat on her heels and waited, watching to see if the black marks returned. When they didn't, she let out the breath she had been holding. "How does it feel?"

"Like you pressed a handful of hot coals into it. But the feeling of corruption is gone—or at least, it's not scraping against the back of my skull anymore. Is that what it feels like for you? The constant fight for control?"

She looked away. "I can endure it. I have to." The last three words were said in a whisper.

"Nea ..." He took hold of her chin, making her look at him.

As his grey eyes searched hers, she was acutely aware that her wrists were resting on his knees, using him as an anchor to keep her balance. Her mouth felt suddenly dry and she swallowed before running her tongue along her lip. His thumb traced the path her tongue had taken, and a pleasant knot tightened in her stomach.

"May I?" The request was so soft that if it wasn't for the gentle brush of his breath over her lips, she wouldn't have known he had actually spoken.

She gave a tiny nod, not trusting herself to speak, and shifted her weight onto the balls of her feet, leaning closer ... His breath hitched. The space between their lips closed to a single hair and Nea's eyes slid shut—

"Nea, are you in here? Margot needs y—oh. I hope I wasn't interrupting anything."

Nea rocked back onto her heels, then leapt to her feet as Molly entered the room and stopped short. Her blue eyes flicked from Garret to Nea, and she made an odd sound in the back of her throat.

"On my way." Nea's cheeks were red-hot.

A sly smile flitted across Molly's lips. "She's in your father's study." She turned on her heel and hurried away.

Nea glanced at Garret, who was pulling his shirt back on. She had almost made a grave mistake. If she kissed Garret, that would mean she would have to admit the feelings that had been steadily building over the last few weeks. But she couldn't. If she owned those feelings, then Evard could use them against her. If Molly hadn't interrupted—She bit down on the inside of her cheek.

Garret toyed with the scar above his lip. "Nea—"

"I shouldn't keep Margot waiting," she blurted out. "And you should get that wound looked at and keep an eye on it in case the corruption comes back. We still don't know how it affects wardens, and Declan only found Mother's balm and mage bane to be a temporary fix." She backed towards the door. "I'm glad you made it back mostly in one piece. I know others weren't so lucky."

Garret said something as she stepped through the door, but the words were lost as she raced away.

"You took good care of Garret I hear," Margot said with a smirk as Nea entered the study.

"Whatever Molly insinuated, she got it all wrong. He had corruption from a knife wound in his side. Have you checked all the others just in case?"

Margot paled slightly. "He had corruption?"

"He's fine, for now. I imagine his suppression was keeping it from growing out of control, and I put some mage bane and Mother's balm on it. You'll need to keep an eye on him though."

"*I'll* need to keep an eye on him?"

Nea nodded. "You're the healer."

Margot opened her mouth to respond but then closed it again. "Wait, what did you say you put on it?"

"Mage bane and Mother's balm. I—"

"You left these in the conservatory." They both whirled to face the door where Garret was, holding out Nea's gloves.

"Ah, thanks." Nea took them from him.

"Show me this wound." Margot rolled her sleeves back.

"It's fine," he said, crossing his arms.

"Are you a healer now?" Margot quipped.

Nea busied herself sorting the pile of notes on her father's desk as Garret pulled his shirt up to show Margot the cut.

She tutted under her breath and prodded his skin with her fingers, causing him to let out a hiss of pain.

"It looks a lot like the wound Peter had. You said you applied mage bane and Mother's balm. How exactly?" Her gaze pinned Nea.

"I crushed the leaves and pressed them directly against it. I didn't exactly have the time or facilities to make a salve."

"Show me your hand." She crossed to Nea and held her hand out, waiting.

Nea placed her hand palm up on it, and Margot made a sound in the back of her throat. The corruption marks on the inside of her palm were much paler than the rest, and in isolated patches, they were completely gone.

"Maybe we've been looking at this wrong. What if we distilled the oil from the leaves and tried that neat instead of diluting it and making an ointment?"

"She might be onto something there." Declan appeared beside Nea and she jumped.

"How many times have I asked you not to do that?"

"Thirteen."

"It was a rhetorical question."

"What's Declan's opinion?" Margot asked.

"He thinks it might work."

"Hmm—where do you think you're going?" Margot's attention snapped to Garret, who had one foot out the door. "Shirt off. I want to heal that wound—it looks infected."

"You don't need to worry. It will heal fine on its own," Garret said.

Margot rested her hands on her hips and put on her serious healer face. The one that Nea knew better than to argue with. Garret was obviously familiar with it also because he stepped back into the room and pulled his shirt off without any further argument.

Margot covered the cut with her hand and the edges started to pull together. Satisfied, she stepped back and gasped. Nea walked over to look. The wound was nothing more than a thin pink line of newly healed flesh, but the corruption mark was back and twice as large as before.

"We *need* that cure. Mother's balm and mage bane obviously aren't enough on their own. Perhaps the other plants Samson mentioned—" Nea's eyes fell on the stone hanging around Garret's neck. "May I borrow that for a moment?"

His hand closed over it protectively. "Why?"

"It's a genuine seer stone. It might allow us to read the blank pages of Samson's journal."

Garret lifted it over his head and handed it to her, his fingers brushing her palm briefly and leaving a tingling trail across her skin.

"While Nea does that, let me check that concealment charm has started working again now you're back within the wards." Margot indicated the charm still around Garret's wrist.

Nea moved to her father's desk and pulled out the journal. She lifted the stone to her eye and looked through it at the blank page. Ink crawled in lazy patterns over the paper and she nearly dropped the stone.

"What is it?" Declan leant over her shoulder, the press of his ghostly form a cold shadow against her back.

"There is definitely something here," Nea said.

"A cure?" Margot rushed over.

"I'm not sure. Can you remove this for a moment?" She indicated the shackle.

Margot frowned. "Are you sure that's wise?"

"No, but I think it's necessary ... I think the page needs my magic."

Margot glanced at Garret, who shrugged. "I can suppress her if the need arises."

Margot pulled out the key and unlocked the shackle around Nea's wrist.

Nea shivered as all her keen came back into her body. It was like she had been swimming too long underwater and her lungs were starved of breath. The corruption that had been laying mostly dormant rose up.

She forced it down and pressed her palm onto the blank page, letting a coil of her magic caress the paper. There was no change when she looked through the seer stone again. She glanced at Declan and he opened his mouth but shut it again with a shake of his head.

Garret was tracing the scar above his lip with his index finger. "I could try suppressing it, but that didn't seem to do anything last time."

Nea shook her head and studied the seer stone. Its magic fluttered against her fingertips. *What if…* She put the stone between her palm and the page and let her magic wash forward through the hole in the centre. The corruption stirred, rising up like a hungry dog catching the scent of an easy meal, and Garret's suppression brushed her lightly. It wasn't enough to cut her off from the source, but it was there, ready to snap down at a moment's notice. "Wait. Don't suppress it just yet."

He pulled his power back but didn't look happy about it.

Nea focused on the wrongness of the corruption before pushing it through the stone in the same way she had her magic.

Margot gasped and took a step back.

"Bright Mother's tits!" Declan said beside Nea, as words flooded onto the page.

Nea started to pull her magic back into herself, but the corruption latched onto it, resisting every step of the way. A voice rose deep in her mind. *You can feel it—all the power of the realms at your fingertips.* An agonising itch accompanied the words. It tore up the skin of her arm and sent sharp fingers raking over her the back of her neck. The air grew cold as her magic flared out of her control. *Yes,* the voice hissed. *Claim it. It's your birthright. You were meant to be a god.* She bit her lip and shook her head, trying to block out the voice and reel her magic back in.

The weight of Garret's suppression threatened to drop her to her knees, and then something cold snapped around her wrist, giving her a modicum of control. "Both," she rasped as she held her other wrist up, and Margot closed the second shackle around it.

"Nea, that was too close," Margot reprimanded.

Garret's jaw was set tight, and Nea was sure his teeth were grinding together.

"It worked though." Nea indicated the pages that had been blank but were now covered in complex calculations and notes.

"Was it worth the risk?" Garret's tone was almost as tight as his jaw. "That journal has been nothing but trouble."

"You need to see this." Margot flipped a few pages through the journal. "That recipe is a cure but only a temporary one. It will keep corruption at bay for several months, provided the mage does not attempt to channel too much source. But long-term, it seems to have a similar effect on mages as an overdose of mage bane, so Samson concluded that in all cases, corruption is fatal. Unless ..." Margot swallowed and looked up at them.

"Unless?" Nea's heart was trying desperately to escape her ribs.

"Unless someone goes physically into the Between and finds the root of it."

"Why hide it?" Garret paced to one of windows, his hand dropping to rub his side.

Margot shook her head. "By this stage, Samson's motivations would have been addled by the corruption. Or maybe he hid it because he tells us exactly how to *physically* breach the Between."

"He does?" Nea moved to Margot's side, accidentally bumping her out of the way with her hip. "Wait, why a warden? I would think a necromancer would be ... Bright be damned. That's why he's been trying to corrupt wardens."

"Who?"

"Evard. If he can get a corrupted warden into the Between, then he can bring the walls down and he won't need me at all."

"And how's he going to get said warden into the Between without a necromancer?" Margot asked.

"He has one already; he has Kieran," Garret replied.

Margot looked between them. "But he doesn't need just any necromancer; he needs a deathborn doesn't he? And we have the only deathborn necromancer alive. Don't we?"

"He has at least one deathborn now that he has control of: Amelia," Garret said.

"Yes, but Amelia is not a necromancer," Nea said. "Of course, it doesn't specify a necromancer deathborn, but given the relationship with necromancers and the Between, it makes sense that it has to be a necromancer." She rolled her lip between her teeth. "Then again, Amelia is like nothing I have encountered before, so ..."

Declan snapped his fingers, drawing her attention away from Margot. "Forget Amelia for a moment. Is it possible for a necromancer to take a soul that has crossed over and put it in a willing host?"

"It's not impossible, but it's far easier to pick a soul that is in transit. Why?"

"You're not the only deathborn who has been a necromancer. Could Kieran find one of your ancestors and put them in a body?"

"Maybe, but there are a lot of factors involved. The body would at least need to belong to a mage, though a necromancer would be preferable, and he would have to find a soul that hadn't been interred into the ancestral grove at Hartswood. Or he'd have to somehow breach the Hartswood wards and perform the reanimation or forced possession—depending on the status of the host body—within the grove itself to have access to those souls interred there."

Declan ran his hands through his hair. "So still not impossible."

Margot and Garret shared a look, but Nea ignored them. "No, not impossible, but given that all my ancestors have been interred in the grove, it is highly unlikely tha—"

"Not all of them have though, Nea," Margot said. "Evette was buried under the capital with Richard and Joanna."

"That doesn't mean her soul isn't in the grove." But if Evette was in the grove, Nea had never encountered her before. Nonna had mentioned something once, a long time ago, about certain necromancers who did awful things not being interred at Hartswood.

Garret had been awfully quiet, but he cleared his throat. "How do we get to the Between? I imagine getting there physically is different to the normal way necromancers do it."

Nea and Margot both just stared at him, and Declan laughed. "I knew one of these days I would rub off on him."

"*We?*" Nea asked.

"If it needs to be a warden, then I won't risk anyone else."

"You're not going to like it," Margot said.

"I'm aware of that, but if it's the only way."

Margot nodded. "Alright. You might want to go and get Niall and meet us in the reflection room."

As Garret left, Margot turned her gaze to Nea. "You don't have to do this. To go to the Between, you're going to have to take the shackles off and there's a chance that we'll lose you."

Nea mustered up a reassuring smile. "It has to be me. But even if it didn't, I wouldn't risk anyone else either. I need you to do something for me though. If we don't make it back, can you take Leith to Hartswood and introduce him to Henry? He deserves to know, and Henry deserves at least one parent who won't abandon him."

The corner of Margot's mouth twisted in a stern frown, and her hands settled on her hips. "You don't think Leith *deserves* to hear it from *you?*"

"I—ugh." She crossed her arms. "I hate it when you are right."

"I know." Margot gave her a smug smile which melted into tenderness. "I don't fault you for leaving Henry with Emma. It was the right thing for him at the time." She slid her arm around Nea's shoulders and guided her out of the study. "Come on. We have a lot to get ready."

❧

"He's my heir. I had a right to know." Leith folded his arms as he regarded her.

"I did what I thought was best given—"

"Of course you did because you *always* know better than everyone." He frowned. "I'm sorry. That was unfair. If you had told me, things might—things *would* have been different."

"No they wouldn't have. You chose your father over me." She glanced at the door. They were currently alone, but how far were their raised voices travelling? This wasn't a conversation she wanted the entire college privy too. She lowered her voice and continued. "I'm sorry but I couldn't bear the thought of what Evard would do when he found out about the child."

"So you punished me to spite my father?"

"I didn't do it to punish you. Your father would have used Henry to get to me or worse ... and when he realised Henry was a necromancer, he would have taken him and groomed him into a monster." She kept her voice calm despite the emotion that threatened to smother her.

Leith's face softened. "Henry? Is that his name?"

She nodded.

"It's a good name. Why did you choose it?"

She looked at her reflection in the pool in front of them before answering. "He has two great-grandfathers with that name, one on each side. It seemed appropriate."

He smiled. "What's he like?"

"I don't know really. I handed him over to Emma for safekeeping

400

six months after he was born. But he has your eyes and my hair." She chewed her lip. "He's at Hartswood now. I asked Margot to take you there if things ... if you want to meet him."

"I would like that." He glanced towards the door as Margot entered, followed by Garret, Emil and Niall.

"I had better go and talk to Garret before things get under way here. Emil's a good man, but if Garret leaves him in charge, this resistance is likely to be over before it begins."

"Resistance?"

"You've been a bit busy. You probably didn't notice the field of tents." He started away but then stopped and turned to face her again. "Be safe, Nea," He pressed a kiss to her cheek before heading over to Garret and Emil.

Nea sat at the edge of the pool of reflection and drew a breath before turning her attention to the massive stone arch at the other end. Declan appeared beside her. He said nothing, just sat there, staring out across the water.

Nea rolled Garret's seer stone between her fingers. In the mad rush to get ready, she had forgotten to give it back to him. It was strange the way things had come together. She wasn't sure she believed in divine timing, but it was hard to write the events of the last few months off as mere coincidence.

"Ready, Nea?" Her father held out a vial of golden-green liquid. "You know you don't have to do this. We can find another way, do some more research."

"There's nothing else to research." She held her wrists out and he unlocked the shackles. Immediately, the gnawing compulsion of the corruption rose in the back of her mind.

After uncorking the vial, he poured the contents onto her afflicted arm. Her skin felt like it was on fire and the voice in the back of her mind screamed in protest. As the oil soaked into her skin, the mark faded until it was a very pale silver-grey. The voice still brayed weakly in the back of her skull, a distant echo promising anger and darkness.

She stood and stepped into the pool, her pants becoming soaked to her knees as she walked towards the massive archway.

"Nea, wait." Margot splashed through the water towards her and threw her arms around her shoulders, pulling her into a crushing hug. "Be careful. Both of you," she said, giving Garret the same hug she had given Nea as he joined them.

"Margot—"

"No, don't say it. I'll see you both soon." She swallowed and backed away, her eyes suddenly glassy.

Nea held the seer stone out to Garret. He took it with a small smile of thanks and slipped the thong that held it over his head. His hand slid into his pocket and he drew out her bracelet. The amethyst roses glinted softly as he offered it to her.

She hesitantly lifted her fingers to take it, but at the last minute, she drew them back before lifting her wrist. Garret looped the bracelet around the offered wrist and secured the clasp. "Shall we?" he said, as he eyed the archway.

She nodded and stepped towards the portal. With one last look at those gathered at the other end of the pool, she placed her palm on the edge of the archway. The magic still clinging to this one was more dormant than it had been at Loch Bastien. It was harder to coax it to the surface. But after a short while, the rune marks flared to life, and Garret placed his hand on the other side of the archway with a nod to Nea.

She focused on the Between and the stones in the middle of the arch shimmered, a crack forming in the centre. It was different to how it had been at Loch Bastien; it was like the portal wanted to open for them, like this was exactly what it had been waiting for as it slumbered.

Drawing a deep breath, Nea placed her palm on the crack and it sprung open wider, revealing the twisted landscape of the Between on the other side. There would be no turning back once they stepped through the portal.

She hesitated, and Garret's fingers brushed the back of her hand. At the light touch, she twisted her wrist so her fingertips caressed his. He laced his fingers with hers as he gave them a small reassuring squeeze. Then they stepped through the doorway, and the moment they were clear of the arch, the portal slammed shut behind them.

It was the same sensation as travelling before. Like her body was being stretched and compressed and her soul was neither in her body nor out of it. Their destination was a point of swirling colours that seemed to be constantly moving. One minute it was so close they could almost touch it—the next it was miles away, taunting them.

Suddenly, they were speeding out of control, and the colours slammed into them so hard that they stole Nea's breath and she lost her grip on Garret's hand. She was falling head over tail until she landed on her back, the darkness all around her closing in until it consumed her.

To be continued ...

GLOSSARY

Bind-shackles: Bands of robrillium that prevent a mage from using their keen by blocking their connection to the source. Each pair is struck with its own key. If this key is lost that pair can only be unlocked by a warden's keen.

Deathborn: A mage who appears to be stillborn but reanimates within the hour following its birth. Only found among healers, mind mages and necromancers, and even then, extremely rare.

High Mage: The head of each college of mages. There used to be an arch mage who was the head of all mages, but the position was dissolved long ago.

Keen: The soul essence of an individual or the "flavour" of their magic. Interchangeable with the word magic, however, *keen* generally refers to the feeling of the lifeforce of an individual and how that part of them interacts with the source as a whole. Magic is more so the direct effect they have on the world through channelling the source.

Keen-folk: A general term that covers all types of magic-users, not just mages and wardens, but seers and other gifted also.

Keen-less: Those without any magic.

Keen-sense: The ability to sense magic. Something all keen-folk innately have but also something that certain keen-less can possess, though this is rare.

Keen-touched: Sometimes interchangeable with keen-folk but generally used to refer to those keen-folk who are not mages or wardens. Seers and those gifted with "low-magic" i.e. savants and prodigies who cannot control the source but have uncanny abilities regardless.

Mage: Keen-folk who have complete control of the source in one element e.g. weather (storm mages), fire, earth, water, healing, mind, death and the spirit world (necromancers) etc. There are certain nuances among the generic types of mages, for example: Sophia is a water mage but she is particularly skilled with frost and ice magic. Declan is a storm mage who has an affinity for lightning, something not all weather mages are comfortable with.

Robrillium: An enchanted metal. Though generally only used for items that block magic, like bind-shackles, it can also be programmed for other functions. It ranges in colour from light pinkish gold through to a deep rose gold.

The Barrier: The veil between realms as seen by necromancers. It can appear a range of different ways depending on the individual interacting with it e.g. Nea's barrier is a hedge of pale pink and grey roses and Nonna's is a bramble of blackberries.

The Between: Thespirit realm that the souls of the dead are believed to pass through on their way to the grove of the ancestors.

The Order: The term used to refer to the wardens as a whole. Has a specific hierarchy of splinter cells and commanders.

The Source: The fabric of the universe. It lays like a blanket over the realms and is where where keen-folk get their powers.

Warden: Keen-folk who can suppress the keen or connection to the source in other keen-folk. Theorised to be a type of mage even though they don't channel the source. Originally called ward mages.

ACKNOWLEDGEMENTS

There is a saying that it takes a village to raise a child—a book is not all that different. There are so many people behind the scenes, even when an author chooses to self-publish.

Firstly, I'd like to thank my family for giving me space to get the words down and being patient when I got so caught up on figuring out the next plot hole that we ended up having dinner late.

Next, my friends Blake and Cinna who heard this story in its earliest incarnation and encouraged me not to give up on it. Thank you for all the coffee and cake and listening to my sometimes incoherent ramblings about dastardly plot bunnies.

Then there are those whose services and support are invaluable, and without them this book would never have seen the light of day. The team at Creating Ink, in particular, Lauren and Anna, whose keen eyes and no-nonsense approach helped me whip this manuscript into the shape it is now. Thank you for making this story the best it could be.

The thanks for the beautiful cover go to Julie and Uwe, from Joolz & Jarling, who took my rough ideas and turned them into a truly breathtaking piece of art.

Lastly, *you*, the one reading this. Thank you for taking the time to give my book a chance. I sincerely hope you enjoyed reading *Deathborn* as much as I enjoyed writing it.

About the Author

C. E. Page writes emotionally rich, character driven tales of magic and adventure, primarily in the adult epic fantasy genre. Her stories feature demigods and other divinely assisted misfits who would prefer it if megalomaniac fools would stop trying to destroy the known realms in their search for power.

She lives on the east coast of Australia with her partner Evan, their two children, and one of the world's quirkiest dogs. An avid reader and gamer, she loves devouring a good story in whatever form it takes.

Follow the link below for news about upcoming releases and future projects:

THE DEVIL'S TANGLE

WOVEN FATE #1

A stolen rose, a mad prince, a sister's sacrifice, and the dark curse that binds them.

Music is Dahlia's life. Born with the uncanny ability to play any instrument she picks up, her songs seem to possess the power to transfix, soothe, and even heal their listeners. But in her world of expected propriety and dutiful acceptance of her future as the wife of Lord John Beaumont such a gift has no place. Like the ruined castle at the center of the wildwood it reminds people of the old stories of enchanted beasts, changelings, and immortal bargains. Stories better forgotten. But on the night of solstice those ancient tales come crashing into reality when Dahlia's younger sister, Helena, plucks a rose from the ruined castle's overgrown garden.

For centuries Caspien Greythorn has been a loyal servant of the Master, the fae prince who guards the forgotten castle that was once a bridge a between realms. But when a foolish mortal girl steals from the palace garden and her equally foolish sister begs to be punished for the theft in her sister's place that loyalty is stretched to breaking point. Who is this strange young woman with eyes like burned honey and the exiled prince's gift of song? Is she the soul rumoured to be able to break the Master's curse or is she just a deadly distraction?

What is the price of a single rose? For Dahlia and Caspien, it just might cost them everything.

www.ingramcontent.com/pod-product-compliance
Lightning Source LLC
Chambersburg PA
CBHW032113110726
47902CB00003B/570